Praise for *The New*

"Full of tenderness and looming menace . . . Gripping . . . Weil meticulously imagines people and their histories, and presents them as a product of their places. This is perhaps the hardest thing for a fiction writer of any age, working in any form, to accomplish. . . . Keep writing novellas, Josh Weil, because you write very good ones. You think on it, and we'll watch."
—Anthony Doerr, *The New York Times Book Review*

"Weil's debut is a stark and haunting triptych of novellas set in the rusted-out hills straddling the border between the Virginias. . . . Taken individually, each novella offers its own tragic pleasure, but together, the works create a deeply human landscape that delivers great beauty."
—*Publishers Weekly* (starred review)

"[Weil's] language is exquisite, his sentences glorious. In fact, [he] writes the kinds of sentences you want to go sniff and then slosh around in your mouth for a while before heading into the next paragraph. The kind that make you set the book down and think, the kind that can break your heart with their truthful simplicity. . . . Refreshing and engaging."
—Sherri Flick, *Ploughshares*

"I was captivated and moved by each of these finely made novellas. The quiet, mostly ordinary lives of the characters who populate *The New Valley* shine with a strange and intense luminosity that is at times heartbreaking, at other times triumphant. There is a magic and gentle beauty in this book that makes me remember why I had always wanted to be a writer."
—Tim O'Brien

"Josh Weil's debut book *The New Valley* has a sense of the notable on every page. This is the very rare but clear case of the sky being the limit for a young author."
— Jim Harrison

"In these meticulously crafted narratives about rural life in the Virginia hill country, Josh Weil explores masculine loneliness with classic richness and depth. This is old-fashioned storytelling in the very best sense."
—Helen Schulman, author of *P.S.* and *A Day at the Beach*

"With *The New Valley*, Josh Weil makes a spectacular entry in the art of American storytelling. His rendering of place is as strong as Flannery O'Connor's; his engagement with the moral landscape as sure as Cormac McCarthy's. In their contemplation of the past, Weil's characters —earthy, scrappy, often comic—seek restoration. These three fine novellas remind us with wit and energy that we are all in for repair."

—Maureen Howard

"In these three beautiful novellas, the sky above and the soil below bear witness to stories so elemental and stunningly intricate that they seem carved from hickory.... Writing about plain-mouthed, flawed, of-the-earth characters requires understanding, much compassion, and a kind heart.... [Weil] gives voice to those without, to those entombed on forgotten hillsides, to those orphaned and tending calves and tractors, reminding us that no matter how isolated, how lonely, tender hearts burn everywhere, they burn bright, and they burn on."

—Don Waters, *The Believer*

"[*The New Valley*] renders the mysteriousness of the human experience in delicious detail: every shaft of sunlight, each well-oiled bolt, memories, dreams, and conversations—all hover within delightful reach, products of a ghostly place only resting partly in the imagination."

—*Orion*

"Weil's prose is quiet and assured . . . These stories are real heartbreakers, ringing true with loss and loneliness.... Finely crafted . . . Unforgettable." —Susan Larson, *New Orleans Times-Picayune*

"A restive nobility binds the sorrowful protagonists of Weil's stellar debut collection of novellas, each a tender anthem to a starkly unforgiving Virginia countryside and the misguided determination of its most forsaken residents.... Throughout, Weil limns a rugged emotional landscape every bit as raw and desolate as the land that inspired it, delivering an eloquent portrait of people who defiantly cling to a fierce independence." —Carol Haggas, *Booklist*

"[A] meticulous and imaginative portrayal of characters shaped by rural life." —*Narrative* magazine (Writers to Watch)

"Keenly observed . . . Absolutely and utterly devastating . . . Weil's major talent—and it is major—lies in making the gears and levers of the book operate seamlessly, like the engines and equipment that litter its pages. He writes with little pretense or adornment, content to let the story come to him. . . . *The New Valley* does not feel exploitative or condescending. Every word feels necessary. Weil's keen observational eye brings the smallest details of the lives of these three men to light, and their acuity makes his other analyses gleam with truth. . . . Weil makes the reader aware of [his characters'] humanity, and their emotions and heartbreak give this book a quiet heaviness, like the Blue Ridge Mountains that loom in the background."

—James Scott, *The Rumpus*

"Critics claiming that American short fiction is on life-support should sample the healing elixir of Josh Weil's breakout collection. In this mesmerizing debut, Weil offers up three razor-sharp novellas . . . that ring sincere and rarely hit a false note. . . . These are quiet stories of struggle, survival, heartbreak, and grace. . . . Readers will find glimpses of Bobbie Ann Mason's depictions of the small-town poor mixed with Annie Proulx's evocative landscape language. . . . [Weil's] writing is understated [and] as strong as steel."

—Cody Corliss, *Charleston Gazette-Mail*

"*The New Valley* heralds the introduction of a master storyteller to literature. The depth of sadness his intricately drawn characters experience in this trio of linked novellas is only equaled by the exquisitely described settings."

—Largehearted Boy (Favorite Novel of the Year)

"In langauge that's sure, quick, and almost magical in its ability conjure dimension from flat paper, Josh Weil has created portraits of hard lives that will stand the test of time."

—Tony Buchsbaum, *January magazine* (online)

THE NEW VALLEY

THE NEW VALLEY

Novellas by
JOSH WEIL

Grove Press
New York

A portion of *Ridge Weather* appeared in *Narrative* magazine.
Stillman Wing line drawings by Josh Weil.

Published simultaneously in Canada
Printed in the United States of America

ISBN-13: 978-0-8021-4486-7

Grove Press
an imprint of Grove/Atlantic, Inc.
841 Broadway
New York, NY 10003

Distributed by Publishers Group West

www.groveatlantic.com

10 11 12 13 14   10 9 8 7 6 5 4 3 2 1

For my father,
who loves the land

CONTENTS

RIDGE
WEATHER

It was the hay bales that did it. The men and women who knew Osby least, who nodded at him from passing trucks or said "Hey" while scanning cans of soup in the Mic-or-Mac, they might not have seen the change come over him. But the few who knew him a little better would have noticed Osby's usual quietness grown heavier, that he stuffed his hands in his sweatshirt pocket a little more often. They would have chalked it up to him missing his father, figured it for nothing more than a rebalancing of the weight of a life that suddenly contained one instead of two people. They would have been wrong.

The truth was, it didn't even make sense to Osby. How could rolls of old dead grass scare him so? What was the sense behind it being *that*—the sight of those wasted bales on that wasted government land—that finally dug from him his tears? But it was the bales. And afterwards, he had known only that it was going to get worse.

In those weeks, as the memory of old Cortland Caudill receded to the horizons of peoples' minds, even those passing Osby in the supermarket aisles would have felt the sadness still hanging off him. Though it probably would have seemed pretty normal to them. In a place like Eads County, people sometimes get like Osby did. They're scattered all over the valley, hidden from each other by the old ridges and thick woods, by log walls of age-sunk cabins, new ranch-house brick, by paint-peeling clapboard and trailer home siding so thin the propane bill is twice what it should be, never mind the electricity for the glowing space heaters that struggle in each room.

The First Congregational Church of Harts Run had always looked pretty to Osby. Some early mornings, when he was out on Route 33 before the sun had scaled the ridge, he would round the bend and see the church way up ahead, perched at the top of the hill as if God had put the limestone there as a plinth. Once in a long while—it had happened just a few times in all his thirty-eight years—the sun would rise exactly as Osby came barreling around the corner, and the church would light up right before his eyes. Times like that, he would take a sip of coffee, turn the radio down so it blended with the rumble of the Sierra's engine, and imagine it was his headlights, and not the sun, that pulled the church out of the half-dark. He liked to pretend that if he hadn't come along just then, the church would have stayed dim all day. That, as much as anything else, was why he chose to hold the funeral there.

The day of the service, it was warm for January in the hills. When Osby arrived at the church, about an hour before everyone else, he swung open the truck door and held out a hand, palm up in the air, gazing at the sky, testing the sun like most people would rain. Thirty-eight, thirty-nine, he thought to himself. If it kept up like this, the pastures would stay clear of snow; he'd save on hay. He wondered if the ground up at the family cemetery would have thawed a little if he'd waited a day on the funeral. Not much, he decided. It was always colder on Bowmans Ridge. Even on those fall days, years ago, when he was a kid and they used to go up there for picnics. Earlier that morning, breaking up the frozen topsoil with a pickax, the memory had come to him: his father, shivering as he walked beneath the old apple tree, over dry leaves between the graves, searching for a good patch of sunlight in which to spread the blanket.

Now, Osby switched on the radio and sat in the truck cab, waiting for the DJ to hand over the weather report. Every autumn, as far back as he could remember—five years old? four?— he would climb the apple tree, shimmy out on the twisted limbs, and shake down a fast thumping of fruit. From twenty feet up, he would watch his father wander below, stooping to pick up the few good ones, carrying them back to Osby's mother. She would sit in the sun, soft and edgeless in a thick, lilac sweater, her knees drawn to her chest, gazing over the valley. His father would crouch next to her, peeling an apple with his pocketknife. He would hand her slices. She would reach up and take them from his fingers.

The year before she died, his mother was too weak from the chemotherapy to handle the rough ride up to Bowmans Ridge. So it was just Osby and his father standing by the truck, the breeze between them making noise in the leaves. After a while, his father strode to the tree, yanked an apple off, came

back. Osby listened to him chew and watched the furious movement of his jaw. Halfway through the apple, Cortland snapped
open his pocketknife and cut off a slice. Carefully, Osby took it
from the offered palm. They looked out at the valley. Osby was
twelve.

In the truck cab, the DJ blared on. Glad of the noise, Osby
shook his head, smiled a little. What a strange man his father
had been.

Forty-one degrees and sunny, according to the radio.

Osby grinned. He'd figured out long ago it was about three
degrees cooler up in the hills. He glanced around the empty
parking lot, as if looking for someone who might congratulate
him. There weren't even any tires grinding up the gravel yet.

The church never did get more than half full, but the minister gave as good a sermon as could have been expected. Some
of it was pure bull—how Cortland had stayed by his wife to the
end; how to his last days he had never questioned God's will.
Some of it was half-right—how Osby's father had worked all his
life to make the farm prosperous; he had never meddled in
business that wasn't his; he had single-handedly raised his son
into a fine man. And some of it was dead on—how Cortland
Caudill had loved his cows.

Osby figured he couldn't have done much better. His father had not been a communicative man. He wasn't a bad man,
not even a bad father. He wasn't mean to anyone; he just wasn't
especially nice to anyone, either. Outside, melted snow dripped
off the church eves. It sounded like spring. Osby felt he ought
to miss his father, but he didn't, not really. Neither, he guessed,
did the others in the church. His father hadn't really cared to
make many friends.

Osby looked around at the thirty-odd people, most of them his father's age. They looked peaceful. The minister didn't mention the one thing that would have made everybody uneasy, didn't even acknowledge it with any special condolences to Osby. So there wasn't much to be upset about in the room. Swaths of sunlight streamed through the windows, warm like only strong sun through glass on a winter's afternoon can be. Inside, Osby guessed, it was a comfortable sixty-nine, seventy degrees.

At the end, the minister asked if anyone wanted to say something, and the whole roomful of people looked at Osby. He wished they'd go back to sitting happily in the sunlight. The minister shut the Bible very quietly and smiled right at him. Osby smiled back, but felt just afterwards that it was the wrong thing to do. He glanced at Carl and, sitting at Carl's side, Lynne and their two boys further down the pew. Carl scratched his newly trimmed beard, jowls shaking, and flicked a glance back at Osby. It was a look Osby knew: the worry that came over his friend when Carl realized Osby was going to say something.

Osby wasn't considered the smartest man in Eads County. But then no one, not even Carl, knew him well enough to realize that he wasn't all that far from it either. His problem was that people could hear only what he said, and not what he thought. His words almost always came out saying something other than what he had intended; and, even when he did get them right, they were usually the last thought of a sequence. Without anyone knowing the process he'd taken to get there, what he finally got to rarely made much sense. Over the years, it had worn him down, so now he seldom said very much of anything to anybody.

Slowly, Osby stood up, taking as long about it as he could, letting the pew's groans and creaks fill the silence. He stood there for a moment, looking at his cracked, red hands pressed against the edge of the pew in front of him. He tried to think of what his father would have liked him to say, tried to think of what Cortland Caudill would have said himself, and then, failing at that, Osby just tried to remember something good about his dad. The thing that came to him wasn't one memory, but a series of them: his father trying out names for the new calves while clanking around under the dump truck, or while picking through clothes at the church donations store in Ripplemead, or ruining their hunting by calling out potential calf-christenings—"Woodrow?" "Lloyd?" "Skeeter?"—from his tree stand to Osby's. Years and years of it, from as far back as Osby could remember. He knew there were other things that made his father happy, but he couldn't recall them.

"Well," he finally said, "Dad thought an awful lot of his beef. Once he give a calf its name, that's what he called it. Heifers, cows, bulls, named them all like they was dairy cows. Never knowed anyone else to do that. I don't believe he once named a calf the same, neither. Not in all his years." It wasn't until after he said it that Osby realized just how incredible that was. "We got some cows been calfin' eight, nine years. I guess they'll miss him." He thought his father would have liked to leave it at that, but it seemed wrong, so Osby said, "I guess we all will."

At the muddy jeep trail up to Bowmans Ridge, they slid the casket out of the hearse and lifted it into Osby's pickup. Anyone with a car left it at the side of 247 and piled into the trucks. The wind was blowing up at the Caudill cemetery, and it was colder, like Osby had known it would be. They didn't take long getting Cortland in the ground. Everyone was glad to get back in the trucks and drive, caravan style, into Pembroke for a late lunch at the Buttercup.

By the time they were done and driving back, the day was on its way out and Osby was starting to feel the letdown that hits after an event, just because it's over. His tie crammed in his shirt pocket and lumpy against his chest, he drove behind Carl, a few other trucks and cars following him, rising and dropping over swells.

As they neared Harts Run, the vehicles turned off onto side roads, one by one, leaving dust where the gravel spilled out onto 33. As he passed by Alva's store, the last car behind him pulled over at the pumps. The road, suddenly empty in his rearview mirror, seemed to lengthen behind him. A few miles later, the taillights on Carl's truck glowed and his friend's thick arm jutted out the driver's side window, hand casually open. Osby raised a couple fingers off his steering wheel and watched the mud-freckled Ford turn off onto 288. Nothing in his windshield now but the wide valley and the long black line of asphalt cutting through it. Well, Osby thought, that's that.

Before going home, he decided to check on each of the five small herds they ran. In his head, he corrected himself: the herds I run. He wound along through lingering patches of sunlight and the sudden, cold shadows behind the hills, starting with the herd furthest from home, the field his dad—now he—rented from Sheldon Ballard alongside the government land. The ground was freezing up again, and the truck rocked and bumped over the pasture. Spread out below the hill, the cattle turned toward the engine noise all at once, the way a flock of birds rises in unison at some imperceptible signal. Osby got out and bunched his

thick neck a little further into his collar. It was going cold, fast.
The sunlight was at its deepest orange, just before it went red.
It always looked to Osby like it should be at its warmest then,
and it seemed to him a major flaw, a failing of someone's, somewhere, that the light contained no heat at all. He watched the
cows as the shadows crept out of the swales and covered the
herd. He had just shy of a quarter of his beef pastured in this
field: twenty-eight reddish-brown cows, four of them already
calved. Mostly Angus-Lemosine, some with a little Hereford in
them. No heifers; the heifers were in the two fields closest to the
house so he could keep an eye on them. He and his father bred
all their bulls and they ran them regular. They had a two-year-old
Black Angus in with this bunch. At the fringes of the herd, Osby
spotted a new dropped calf suckling from its mother. She was
a good cow, had given them eight or nine calves—those wide
Lemosine hips—and now he tried to remember what his father
would have called her. The name didn't come to him. He scanned
the rest of the herd, looking for signs of compaction, foot evil,
making sure all the calves were there. A few of the cows were
showing bags beneath their tails and he watched them negotiate
their legs under swollen bellies. One or two looked as if they
might drop their calves anytime, but they were old pros. The
swath of hay he'd rolled out that morning was still catching the
sun at the top of the hill. Everything looked fine. Everything
looked the same.

　　By the time he got home, it was fully dark. The moon hadn't
yet risen. There were no lights on in his house. He drifted past
the driveway, wishing there was one more pasture to check on
or something he had to do in town. Maybe he'd drive over to
Carl's place, just to say hello; it had been years since they'd sat

on Carl's back porch, drinking beer and throwing sticks for his bird dogs. As he rounded the bend, his headlights sucked the Old House's mailbox out of the night. It had collapsed against the giant chestnut stump and the letters his grandmother had carefully painted were half gone; they read *he Ca ills,* now. He braked, his ribs suddenly feeling too small for all the stuff that had to fit in his chest. Slowly, he turned onto the dirt. A few feet up, he stopped. The truck idled under him. Grass and weeds had grown between the tire tracks and last spring's rains had gouged the driveway. Up the hill, beyond the reach of the head- lights, the Old House stood blackly against the stars, a hole in the sky. His home, the newer house he and his dad had lived in, had been built nearly a century ago, but the original family place, the Old House, was twice that age, the walls in its living room still made of logs from the homesteaders' one-room cabin. After his grandmother died, his father used the house for stor- age: bags of fertilizer, car batteries, cattle medicines.

Osby flicked on his brights. The windows that still had glass flared. He hadn't been in there since the day he found his father. He could make out the glinting shape of Cortland's pickup, parked at the top of the driveway. The front door to the house was still open. He'd forgotten to shut it. Or the ambu- lance guys had. Or the cops. They had come, looked things over. There wasn't much guessing to do. Osby asked them not to clean it up, said he wanted to do it himself. It would help him seal the thing shut, he said, put a cap on it. When the neighbors offered to take care of things, he told them he'd already scrubbed and swept and burned what had to be burned. Truth was, he hadn't touched a thing in there. The idea of going back in made his bowels go watery.

The truck sputtered, and he gave it a little gas, shook a cigarette out of a pack of Winstons, and sat, smoking. He knew he
ought to go up there and close that door.

When Osby's mother died, his father hadn't let anyone
help them take the body to the funeral home. They had wrapped
her in the sheets and carried her downstairs, his father holding
her under her arms, Osby clutching her cold ankles. She had
smelled like old cabbage. Her body sagged, heavy as wet sand.
His thin twelve-year-old forearms strained and he struggled to
keep his fingers locked around her legs. Halfway down the stairs,
he dropped her. Her heels thwacked the hard wood step, and
he had thought how much that would hurt if she was alive.
Outside, they hoisted her into the pickup and drove into town.
His father hadn't even let people gather in the house after the
funeral. He had refused the casseroles and cakes they brought.

The next Saturday, Osby had helped him with an excavating job and they had sat in the bulldozer's shovel, out of the cold
wind, passing a thermos of steaming coffee between each other.
"Ain't going to have 'em walking all over our place," Osby's father had said. "Big show." And a week later, in the kitchen, digging shotgun pellets out of a rabbit with the tip of a knife: "When
I go, I don't want no noise about it. Don't want the whole of 'em
traipsing around, tearing up the driveway, snooping around the
Old House. Just dig a hole and dump me in."

When he'd finished the cigarette, Osby rolled down his
window, tossed out the butt, shoved down on the clutch, and
put the truck in first. Behind the Old House, Bowmans Ridge,
solid and black, smothered the bottom edge of the sky. After a
while, his left calf muscle started to shake. He shifted into reverse, backed up onto the road, and drove home.

Quiet smothered the bang of the truck door almost as soon as he shut it behind him. He could hear the night animals moving around, small birds, opossums, squirrels, making crackling noises too big for them in the dry leaves. They went silent as his feet made their noise from the truck to the porch.

Inside, the house had gone cold. Osby clomped into the kitchen, opened the flue on the woodstove, and stirred up the remaining coals, watching them feed on the draft. When they were glowing, he shoved a couple overnight logs on top, waited for them to catch, and then shut the stove up and let it go to work. He scanned the twenty-odd cans lined up on the kitchen counter. He and his father never bothered putting the soup in the pantry. That was for the things they bought on a whim and ended up never looking at again, things like cake mixes or cloves of garlic, things that needed what Osby and his father called "major preparation." Cans of soup, cans of beans, cans of cranberry sauce, jars of pickles; those things were useful; they stayed on the counter where they could be got at.

Osby chose a can of chicken and dumplings, shaking his head a little at all the clam chowders. His father had loved the stuff. Osby couldn't stomach it. Now he was stuck with a dozen cans. He rinsed a saucepan under the faucet, using his thumb to rub away most of the crust left from last night's soup, dumped in tonight's chicken and dumpling, lit the stove burner with a match, and got out the bowls and spoons.

The kitchen opened up right onto the living room, and Osby went in there, turned on the TV, and watched the weather report while he unbuttoned his shirt and tugged it off his arms. Not wanting to put his good shirt on the floor with the rest of his clothes, he held it in one hand while he took off his shoes and pants, and then held those bunched in the other arm, while he listened to the forecast for the next day. There was a slight chance of snow.

"Hope not till afternoon," Osby said aloud to the empty house, feeling foolish immediately afterwards. When he heard the pot spitting soup, he hurried into the kitchen, dumped his clothes on the counter, and emptied the chicken and dumplings into a bowl. For a second, he stood, perplexed, staring at the second bowl. He didn't remember taking out two. He put the extra bowl and spoon away and took his soup into the living room to finish watching the local news. It was still cold in the house—the heat from the woodstove never really reached all the way into the living room—and he turned on the electric space heater, pulled it close to the couch, sat in his underwear and T-shirt and the brown socks that looked strange to him on his feet, slurping the soup while the space heater's warmth started to tingle on his skin.

An hour or so later, during the ads between two sitcoms, he glanced to his side to see if his father had fallen asleep yet. The other end of the ratty brownish-orange couch was, of course, empty. Seeing it, he tried to feel whether he missed the old man. He couldn't tell. He lay down, stretching his legs out all the way along the couch. True, it felt odd to do that. He tried to picture his dad sitting there where his feet were now. It should have been easy; after all, Cortland had sat there nodding off practically every evening since Osby was a kid. But he couldn't picture him. When he looked back at the TV, he thought he saw his father's face looking in at him through the window, not as he looked in life, but as Osby had found him three days ago in the Old House: his lower jaw and half of his right cheek blown off, one eye exploded in its socket.

Osby made himself stay still and stare at the window, where there was nothing but his own reflection, until his heart had gone back to thumping like normal. Then he scraped up the last of the soup, sighed, and carried the bowl to the sink. As he clinked it against the other dishes, he had a sudden urge to wash them all, to wipe down the counters, get the place clean. He filled the sink, watching the steam billow up through the soap bubbles.

Through the window, he could see the occasional pair of headlights drift along Route 33, a couple miles off down the valley. After they were out of sight, he could still follow their progress for a while, watching for the patches of hillsides swept briefly by the faint yellow glow. He wondered if he was going to be lonely now. He didn't see why he should be; his father had never been much for company. He didn't think he *was* lonely.

He scrubbed at a bowl—he hadn't gotten even one dish washed yet—and spent the next couple minutes picking at dried pieces of partially burned rice welded to a pot. When he was done, he decided that he probably was just lonely. Maybe he even missed his dad. That would be normal. But he didn't feel like calling anybody, or driving the half hour into Pembroke to go get a drink and play some pool at Ten Points. He didn't feel like visiting Carl. Even the TV, he realized, was bugging him. He went into the living room and turned it off, leaving soapsuds on the knob. When he came back to the sink, he put his hands in the water. It wasn't warm anymore. He ran some more hot water through the tap, and, listening to it thunder in the sink, watched another pair of headlights wander through the distance. He wondered who it was out there, if it was someone he knew or not.

It didn't really matter.

He stared at the almost clean pot in his hands. The rice he'd scrubbed off—his father had made that rice; his father had eaten half of it.

He wondered how long it would take for him to quit thinking about his father. In some ways, he felt he had already begun. He wondered how long people would remember him, if he were to go out to the Old House tonight and blow his head off. Not long, he thought.

"Yeah," he said out loud. "I guess I'm just lonely."

Osby was out a half hour before dawn, walking quickly through the cold air that still clung to the fields, not even a whisper of wind covering the whisk-whisk of his jeans. The moon was gone but the stars still pinned up the night sky. He'd zipped his work coat tight and pulled his camouflage hat low, but his ears and nose still stung from the cold and his whole slightly mashed-looking face was numb with it. In front of him, the flashlight beam washed the darkness off the grass and shoved it through the gaps between the fence rails. He opened the gate and shut it behind him with a clang. The flashlight caught the cows' eyes like a hundred flecks of Formica in the solid black field. Groans. Some lowing. A spatter of hooves. He swung the beam over each one, checking hides, mouths, hooves, and calves suckling at udders. He didn't see anything wrong. Everything looked okay. He found his way back to the herd, the sky going blue, the cows still black against a less black field, large lumps of life, moving occasionally.

* * *

By the time the sun was over the ridge, Carl Veltre had already been up for three hours. He had milked the Holsteins before Lynne was awake, washed down the milking house while the kids were eating breakfast, and brought the school bus around to the house just as Lynne handed lunch bags to their two boys and sent them down the driveway. For the last forty-odd minutes, he had nursed the aging bus along winding back roads, practically standing on the gas pedal to get it to crawl up the steep hills, and stopping at all the least convenient places—blind corners, the very bottoms of long climbs—to pick up kids as young as five and as old as nineteen, an age bracket that, on mornings like this, Carl understood as the widest range of possibilities for obnoxiousness that the school system would allow.

"Hey, you all," he shouted to the wide oblong mirror that framed pretty much the whole bus. "Whoever threw whatever that was I saw come from somewhere back there—are you smilin' at me?—Whoever that was better not be smilin' an' better not do it again, neither."

He pressed his hand to the windshield in front of him, slowly enlarging the clear spot in the foggy glass. The defroster had been working yesterday, when he didn't need it. Any day now, he figured, the Virginia board of education was going to vote to include colicky one-year-olds and divorced, depressed, middle-aged dope addicts on welfare in the Eads County school system only.

"How 'bout ever'one," he shouted back at the entire bus, "tries one whole minute of sittin' still an' shuttin' up."

His stomach growled. He set the bacon and ham sandwich on his lap and unwrapped the cellophane with one hand, stopping a couple times to shift. He was about to ask his two boys, sitting in the seat behind him, what their mom had made them for breakfast (it was a question he asked every morning in a poorly disguised bid for sympathy) when he saw a man standing in the fresh sunlight at the side of the road, one arm out, like someone flagging down a ride.

"Dad," Luke, his youngest kid, said at his ear.

"I see him."

"Oh, man," Brian groaned. Brian was twelve and embarrassed by everything. It just about killed him that Carl made him sit up front with his brother. Having to put up with his father driving the bus was bad enough, but when, occasionally, Osby Caudill (who was the biggest loser of all his Dad's loser friends) got on to chat, Brian couldn't contain himself: "Can't you just pretend you didn't see him?"

"No," Carl said in a voice that he knew would quiet Brian. "I can't."

Though he wished, especially this morning, that he could.

It wasn't that he didn't like Osby; he liked him fine. They'd been friends since high school, more than twenty years. Maybe that was the problem. All his other friends he'd made in his years after high school, working on construction, or because of Lynne, or through the school where Brian and Luke went. Osby just didn't quite fit in anymore. Maybe, Carl thought, as he brought the bus squealing to a stop in front of Osby's driveway, he never had. He was always a bit of a loner, a sad sack. Lynne called him a mope. She made it clear she'd rather not have him over to dinner. "He just sits there," she'd said. "Antisocial. Comes to visit and just eats. What kind of example is that for the kids?" Oh, he was still a good hunting buddy, but recently—hell, for the past three, four years—it had been more obligation than anything else that kept Carl friends with Osby. These days, Carl always felt a sense of guilt being around him, so that, more and more, he found himself avoiding Osby—and resenting it when he just showed up, like now, as if it were the old days.

Plus, Carl thought, what am I supposed to *say* to him, especially now after all that with his old man?

Osby chuckled quietly to himself, waving his hand a little as the bus slowed, remembering the three or four years after high school when he'd stand at the bottom of the driveway, just like now, and wait for Carl to come up the road in the souped-up silver-gray Dodge D-100 they'd fixed together. He'd gun the motor as Osby got in and they'd roar off, the sun not even up yet, and nothing in between them and the job site but an hour and a half of open road, the tunes blasting from Carl's radio, the fresh coffee and fried apple fritters they'd pick up at the Harts Run store, good fritters Alva Linton made herself, good time to talk. They'd talk of the women in Carl's life, the best buyer for their beef, where they'd try for turkey that weekend, smoking, shouting over the wind whipping in through the open windows, the Penthouse Pet air freshener twirling from the rearview. Those were some of the best times of Osby's life— good money, too, working construction. He was feeling lucky all of a sudden; he could still come down here fifteen years later, wait at the driveway, and hop on with Carl to talk. Even if it was a school bus now.

When Carl stopped and he got on, Osby felt the whole bus go suddenly quiet, thirty pairs of kids' eyes staring at him.

"Hey," he said to Carl, climbing the steps.

"Hey." Carl grinned at him. "You in the first or second grade?"

"I don't know," Osby fired right back, trying not to smile, "Momma just said to get on the bus!"

They both grinned. It was an old routine, same thing every time: built-in comfort. Whatever question Carl asked—"Did you remember your lunch? Has your daddy been whupin' ya?"— Osby always answered, "I don't know. Momma just said to get on the bus!" Some years ago, they had thought that was hilarious. Now they grinned because not to grin would have been admitting something neither one could bring himself to admit, just yet.

"You boys slide 'cross the aisle," Carl said, though his sons were already moving.

Osby squeezed into the seat behind the driver's.

The kid noise started filling the bus up again, moving from back to front.

The sun painted the windshield with glare. Carl leaned forward, as if that would let him see better, and, behind him, Osby leaned forward too, out of habit. They stopped and picked up kids and drove on and stopped and picked up more. Osby didn't say anything, just watched the kids when they got on, nodded at them. They looked surprised when they saw him; they looked at him the way they looked at adults. That still felt odd to him.

The bus rounded the hilltop bend and started down the long drop toward Harts Run, a shuddering beneath the seats as Carl shifted to a lower gear. They passed the old schoolhouse half hidden behind scrub trees grown up in the yard where, long ago, Osby and Carl had played. It was where they'd first met. Five, six years old. Something about a tractor tire, Osby remembered, one of them sitting on it holding to the chains it hung from, calling out for the other to come give him a spin. He didn't remember how they'd gone from that to inseparable. But he remembered the guilt he'd felt later, when his mother died, how he had skipped school to help with the burying, and all during the funeral he kept thinking of what Carl was up to, missing his friend instead of her. He tried to catch a glimpse of the place through the trees—some rusty poles, maybe, some dangling chain busted loose from what it had once held—but there was barely time to make out the brick beneath the knitting of brown vines, the high windows shot through with missing panes, before it was behind them and hidden near the hill.

"You want a bite?" Carl said. He held his greasy sandwich up near his head.

Osby thought there was a hint of annoyance in his voice, but he figured Carl just didn't want to give up part of his breakfast. "No, you go ahead," he said.

That was it for a while. Osby sat looking at Carl's greasy hair and deep-creased neck in front of him. He could smell Carl—it was a familiar smell, kind of sour, but sweet, too, like spoiled milk heated up in a saucepan, and Osby tried to breathe it in without showing that he was. The whole bus smelled like people. It was steamy from them. Sitting there, Osby thought that he could forget for a while the feeling lodged in his guts, impassable, that seemed to grow leaden when he was alone in his house.

When they were off the last of the back roads and gaining speed on 33, Carl said, "What can I do you for, Chief?"

The question threw Osby. He couldn't very well say, Let me sit here with you and smell the kids.

"Somethin' on your mind?" Carl persisted. "Somethin' I can help you with?" And then, reluctantly, as if out of duty, "You holdin' up okay? You know, Dad Caudill an' all."

"Oh, yeah," Osby said, as if they were talking about a sprained ankle. "Sure. You know."

He was conscious of Carl's boys across the aisle, Brian staring moodily out the window, Luke sitting there watching Osby, hard. He didn't mind the boy's stare. It was nice to be looked at, to feel someone's eyes on you once in a while.

"What'd you do with that 'fifty-nine Dodge?" Osby asked, with sudden eagerness, leaning a little over the back of Carl's seat.

"That ol' gray D-100?"

"Yeah. You remember how we fixed her up?"

Carl nodded, stared straight ahead.

"She was a beaut, huh? You still got her?"

"Yeah."

"Back there with others? Up near them woods back there next to that spring box? I'd love to fix her up. What d'you think? How bad off is she, anyway?"

"Pretty bad."

"You think we could fix her up?"

"Oz," Carl said, "you know you could get me in trouble comin' on the bus like this?"

Osby watched the back of Carl's head. His neck was stiff, his shoulders tensed, both hands gripping the steering wheel.

"I mean," Carl continued, "if you've got somethin' to talk about, all right, you know, but if it's just—I mean, I'm not supposed to pick anyone but kids up. You know that, right?" Carl's eyes flicked up to the mirror, but when Osby saw them looking at him, they darted back to the road.

"Yeah," Osby said, quietly. "I just thought I'd say hi."

"Well," Carl's laugh was strained. "You got a telephone, don't you?"

"Yeah," Osby tried to chuckle, too, but he couldn't do it. "Boy," he said. "I'll tell you, I never realized what a big house that is."

"You know what you need?" Carl's voice was suddenly loud, as if he were trying to smother his previous words. "You need to rent that house out." He looked at Osby in the mirror again and this time his eyes stuck. "Yeah. I'm serious. Get you a renter move in with you. Get some dough, fill up the place. Hell, Oz, I know how it is."

"Yeah," Osby said. "I don't think—"

"You get a renter," Carl cut in. "You take out an ad in the *Eagle*, put up a sign or two around town, get you a renter."

"Well, no, I don't—"

"Listen—" Carl said.

"Yeah, I just don't think that's it."

"Listen, the best time of my life was before I got married. Don't go lookin' for a woman," Carl bounced the seriousness in his eyes off the mirror and down to Osby. "You don't need that."

"Oh, I wasn't—"

"You're lucky. You're in a lucky spot. When I went off and worked crew on that job down in Virginia Beach, lived down there for a year, you remember that? You stayed on with your dad. You remember? And I went down to Virginia Beach and me and four other boys from the crew rented a place down there. Four of us! Best time of my life."

Osby watched his friend's face in the mirror. It was beaming. He hadn't seen it like that in a long time.

"You get you a renter," Carl said. "Best time of your life."

The idea crept up, unwanted, on Osby: is that how he looks around his other friends, when he's not around me?

"Yeah," Osby said. "All right."

He sat back in his seat. It seemed to him that if he reached out and tried to put his hand on Carl's head, his arm wouldn't reach even halfway. Osby looked across the aisle at Luke. The boy was still staring at him. They looked at each other, both their faces blank, as if they were separated by clear Plexiglas. Osby had the feeling that if he spoke to Luke the boy wouldn't be able to hear him, and if the boy said something Osby would just see his mouth moving dumbly.

Osby turned in his seat and looked at the bus full of kids behind him. Every one of them has a daddy, he thought. Thirty fathers out there. He thought that maybe, if he had a kid, a child, his child, if he were responsible for a baby, a baby connected to him by his own blood, dependent on him . . . The idea was so strange his mind backed off from it, drifted aimlessly over the faces of the schoolkids. The whole bus full looked back at him. It was as if that Plexiglas wall had extended, curved, encircled him, so that now he was encased in it.

In front of him, Carl was talking about that year he'd lived in Virginia Beach with all those guys.

"Yeah," Osby said, quieting Carl in the middle of a sentence. "That Dodge was a beaut, though, wasn't she?"

By the time Carl dropped Osby off back at his driveway, thick clouds had rolled over the mountains. At home, Osby threw two Pop Tarts in the toaster, and then put two more in while he ate the first ones. He made himself a thermos of instant coffee, shook sugar into it for about three seconds, shook some dried creamer in for two, screwed the lid tight, shook the thermos, and drove in no-radio quiet over to the Geller place on 236.

Tom Geller, who lived an hour away past Coalsburg, was having his mother's forty acres of woodland logged and he'd hired Osby to bulldoze the road up through the pastures to the edge of the woods. He'd just started when his father had died. The muck-yellow Caterpillar was still halfway up the hill, right where he had left it when Tom's mother, Eula, had come huffing up behind him with the news that Osby's father was on the phone. By the time he'd gotten down to her house, Cortland had hung up. He'd never known his father to call him on a job, not once, so he'd driven back home and then over to the Old House, where he found him.

Now, Osby got the truck up the pasture, driving alongside the unfinished, muddy road, and parked it by the bulldozer. The clouds had blanketed the sky by then, and he watched them suck the round sun up out of the last clear strip of blue. The treads were gunked up with mud and grass and cow shit. He wiped dried spatter off the sign on the side—*New Ground Excavating, Caudill & Son, Harts Run, VA, 544–7293*—grabbed the cold metal handle and climbed up, sheeting the water and thin skin of ice off the vinyl seat with his bare hand before sitting down. By a combination of timing, skill, and luck, he managed to get the knob on the dash, the lever to his left, and the pedals at his feet to all work the way they were meant to: the old machine roared to life, blowing the quiet out of the field and halfway up the mountain.

Sometime in the afternoon—he had forgotten his watch and the sky had stayed the same shade of gray all day—he caught

a movement in the corner of his eye. Eula Geller made her way
up the hill toward him, her bright blue windbreaker billowing
in the cold wind, something aluminum glinting in an arm
tucked against her chest. He raised the shovel, brought the lumbering thing to a stop, and walked down the hill toward the old
woman. It was strange seeing someone else after working alone
all day. Just before he reached her, he had the troubling sensa-
tion that he'd have to consciously remember how to speak.

"Looks good," she called to him over the noise of the wind
and the huffing bulldozer in the distance.

"Thanks." He scanned the ripped-up, reddish, muddy gouge
in the hillside. "It looks frozen, but once you tear it up it's just
wet as can be."

The old woman nodded, but he could tell she wasn't really
listening. Her look touched his face all over.

"Here," she said, thrusting the aluminum-covered package at him. "It's blueberry."

The heat of the pie came right through the bottom of the
pan and warmed his hands. "Thank you, Mrs. Geller," he said.
"That's real nice of you."

Her eyes were so full of sympathy, he couldn't look at her.

"You know," she said, "Your grandma used to babysit me
when she was a girl. I ever tell you that?"

"No, ma'am." She had told him at least twice before. And
that, later, she herself had babysat his father.

"Right in that house." She pointed down the hill. "And I
used to babysit your daddy."

He nodded, glanced back up toward the bulldozer, which
was coughing gray smoke at the gray sky. When he looked back,
she was watching his face with that heavy sympathy again.

"Uh-huh," he said, just to fill the quiet.

"Here." She held out a fork.

He took it from her. "I can't eat the whole thing."

She nodded, but it was about something else. "Our daddy," she said, "went the same way."

Her eyes were still on him, but he could tell she was seeing her whole family again. The wind rippled her jacket and she pulled her knit hat further over her ears. Somehow, the motion made her look smaller.

"You help me eat this, okay?" Osby said.

"Terrible," she said. "To do that. Isn't it?"

He held the fork out to her, but she didn't even look at it.

"Shame on them!" She spat the words so vehemently that Osby jerked the fork back.

"Shame on them," she said again, quietly. Then, after a few seconds, "That thing sure makes a racket."

"It's noisy," he said, and took the chance to turn away from her and look up the hill at the bulldozer.

When he turned back, she was already a few yards away, bent against the wind, hurrying downhill to her house.

That evening, Osby brought new salt to the pasture by the government land, hauling the pink mineral block out of the truck bed and into its housing box. The cattle converged on the salt lick, letting off bellows loud as foghorns in the quiet. He checked them over as they crowded each other, looking for signs of pinkeye or wooden tongue, the struggled breathing that might be a first step toward the pus-filled bulge of bone and lumpy jaw. He didn't see anything wrong, no tears draining out of yellowing

eyes, no tongues hanging out of drooling mouths. At the fringe
of the herd, a white-faced Hereford-Lemosine cow had a swollen belly, and he thought—almost hoped—that she might be
compacted. But it was too early to tell.

The only thing he could find to worry about was a cow gone
missing: a young Angus that had gotten hip locked on a calf last
fall. He drove slowly around the perimeter of the pasture, peering out the open window, his eyes straining to clear the thick-
ening dusk out of briar snarls, patches of cedar, the scrub-filled
gully. He hoped he'd find her in trouble.

The longer he drove without seeing the cow, the more excited he got. Maybe she's hip locked again, he thought. Maybe
she's about passed out from it. He pictured himself arriving just
as the cow was about to lose consciousness, scooping the calving chain off the seat, leaping into the truck bed, grabbing the
jack, and flinging the halter over his shoulder. He'd hurtle over
the side of the truck, already running as he hit the ground. Up
ahead, the cow's eyes would roll at him. Maybe the calf was half
out, hips jammed, or turned around with a rear hoof sticking
out. He'd harness her to the trailer hitch, strip off his jacket,
roll up his sleeves, douse his hands in alcohol, and reach
in, shoving his right hand past the calf, stuffing the hoof back
in with his left, straining to get the thing turned around.

Rattling over the lumpy pasture, he hoped this time the
calf would be too jammed, hoped he wouldn't be able to get it
facing the right way. He'd chain the calf's leg to the jack, lock
that jack up against the cow's hips, and start pumping. The calf
would probably smother. But maybe he'd do it fast enough and
it would slide out with a shhlluck, splattering him with blood

and amniotic fluid. He'd kneel down, wipe the placenta off its nose and mouth, the calf's body shaking as it sucked at the air.

Even alone in the truck, his giddiness embarrassed him. He'd helped birth hundreds of calves. It was just part of raising beef. He tried to laugh at himself, but even the puff of air that came out was thin with excitement. No matter how many times he helped a cow give birth, there was always that quick shot of elation at the end, the feeling that somehow, despite his gunked, slick arms and chest, he'd been cleansed. And, more, too: the irrefutable fact that a living thing would not exist if it weren't for him.

The cow bolted in front of the truck. He was so caught up in his thoughts that he almost didn't see her rush out from behind the thicket, and he slammed the brakes on too hard, smacking his forehead against the steering wheel. He sat there for a second, dazed. She crossed through his headlight beams into the bluing dusk again, lumbering back toward the herd. Still pregnant. Just fine. Osby pressed his palm to his forehead. It came away blotted with a small smear of blood. He swung the door open and went around to the back, where, shoving the jack out of the way, he grabbed a milk jug full of water and poured some of the half-iced stuff over his forehead. It felt like it froze the backs of his eyes. He shook his head a few times and stood there, catching his breath.

It was then that he glanced across the fence line to the government land and saw the hay bales. They were stacked in a row, maybe twenty of them, tucked up against the fence at the edge of the woods. Once, they had been large and round, but they'd sat there for almost three years now and had sunk in on themselves, decomposing, just mounds of rotten grass.

Standing there, his thick-fingered hands stuffed in his pockets against the growing cold, Osby stared at the line of forgotten hay bales, remembering how mad his father had been when the government took the land from him. His dad had almost gone to court over it, but had backed down rather than face a slew of strangers staring at him. Osby hadn't wanted to face them, either, but he had thought he and his dad ought to at least retrieve the hay they'd cut and baled off that field over the summer. His father wouldn't let him. "Neither you nor I's settin' one foot on that land again," he'd said. "Them hikers can watch that hay rot." Osby doubted they even noticed.

Now, what had been a smooth field of good grass was mostly scrub: junipers, cedars, broom sedge, briars that were getting worse all the time. The trees along the fence used to be trimmed in a clean line five feet above the ground, as high as the cattle could reach. Now, their branches drooped low across the fences and over the hay bales.

Osby remembered the day his father had cut that field. He had seen him from the road: the tractor moving slowly across the top of the hill, looking small, the man riding it even smaller, the sickle bar mower invisible behind it, but the swath of cut grass showing clear enough. He remembered baling the hay a couple days later, after it had dried. Those bales had been shiny, tightly wrapped swirls, all lined up straight and neat against the fence when he was done, looking as good as if satisfaction itself had been rolled up in them.

Remnants of light lingered on the horizon, buried behind the hill at Osby's back. The bare tops of the trees jutted above the fence line, as hard and cold as metal rods—almost as black, too—against the darkening sky. He pressed his arms tighter to his body. There was no wind at all, but the chill bit through his sweatshirt even without it. His ears were cold. It seemed sad to him that those hay bales were just rotten lumps now—more than sad. A feeling pressed at his chest like a giant hand pushing with a spread palm. A cow, somewhere, lowed a couple times, and then was quiet. It was a little while before Osby realized he was crying. He unpocketed a hand and wiped the wetness from under his eyes, the callused tip of his finger rough on the soft skin there. Some men would have told themselves it was because of the cold. Osby just knew that it wasn't because his father was dead. It wasn't because he missed him. Standing there watching those hay bales that had once been full of what it took to feed a whole herd of cows and had been left to rot, he knew that it wasn't just loneliness, either. It was something bigger, something worse, and it scared him.

A few cows had rounded the hill. They stood perfectly still, looking at him. When he walked back around the truck, the rustling of his boots in the grass was silenced by the loud, seemingly endless splattering of a cow pissing in the dark. He climbed in, started the motor, and sat in the cab smoking the last two cigarettes left in the pack, watching night fall around him. By the time he'd finished, the heat blowing out of the vents was so hot he was sweating. He opened the window, sucked in the clean air, and started back toward the road.

The whole ride home, he couldn't stop thinking about those hay bales. He remembered everything about the day he'd baled them, remembered turning in the tractor's seat to watch the baler behind him, remembered the afternoon steadily packing the sky with clouds, the wind coming out of nowhere, the first drops spotting his dusty hands, the rush he got racing to get the hay up before it stormed. And then he had forgotten, completely, for years; his father had forgotten. By the time he turned into his driveway, he was almost angry about it, angry at his father, angry that the old man had grown that hay—good hay, good seed, *alfalfa* in it—and then sold that land. And left that hay there. And let it rot. And never given it another thought.

He banged out of the truck and stalked to the porch, suddenly wanting to know how much the government had paid his father, how much it had offered for an easement first, an easement that would have meant the Caudills could still graze the land, still cut hay, an easement his father had refused to give. He'd go through his father's desk, find the paperwork. He burst through the living room into the kitchen, and stopped.

The two doors that led from the kitchen to the rest of the house were shut. He hadn't been through them since his father died. He usually used the upstairs bathroom, but he'd been using the one off the living room instead. He'd slept on the couch by the space heater. He hadn't gone upstairs at all.

Outside, a truck rumbled by on 247. Through the kitchen window, Osby watched its headlights sweep the Old House in the distance—a flicker of glinting glass. Then it was gone and there was just darkness out there across the creek bed.

Once, when he was fourteen, his father had entertained a woman guest and sent Osby to his grandmother's for the night. Walking across the field in the dark, it had struck Osby as odd that only the bottom left corner of the Old House was lit up. The rest was as black as if it were abandoned. When he entered, he noticed that the door to the left of the hallway was shut and blocked with boxes, that the stairway in front of him was mounded with trunks, old clothes, a menagerie of dust-collecting things. From the kitchen, he could see the flicker of the black-and-white TV washing the wall in his grandmother's bedroom.

"Grandma?" he'd called.

"Hello?" she called back.

"It's Osby. You in your bedroom?"

After a moment, she appeared in the doorway. "Well, where else would I be?" she said.

Even then, of the eleven rooms in the Old House, all but three had been shut off from use.

Now, standing in his own kitchen of his own house, staring at the two shut doors, Osby saw the way it would be: just like his grandmother, shut up in a dark home, gradually moving in a smaller and smaller space, until, one day, it would be too much effort to go into the kitchen and he'd bring the groceries right into the living room, eat the soup from the cans, wash the dishes in the bathroom sink, until, finally, he would find himself unable to move from the couch, withering in front of the TV, forgotten.

Osby crossed the kitchen and flung open both the doors. Maybe Carl was right. Maybe he needed a housemate. At the very least, he decided, he was getting the hell out of the house that night, away from the TV, and going into town.

Forty-five minutes later, he pulled into the parking lot outside Ten Points, a pickup turning in behind him, the taillights of another flaring as it backed out. It was pretty busy. Osby tried to remember whether it was Thursday or Friday night. He parked. The music from the bar filled in where the engine noise had been. Rockabilly blues. The drumbeat tapped at Osby's wind-shield, and he listened to it, hoping to get some of the bar into him before leaving the truck. He hoped he could just slip in, unnoticed, already moving to the same rhythm as everyone else. He had taken a shower, clipped his toenails, put on a clean shirt and fairly clean jeans. The sneakers he found by the stairwell were old, but at least didn't smell like manure. Now, looking in the rearview mirror, he ran a comb through both of his side-burns, took off his camouflage hat, worked the knots out of his hair. He felt like he had heartburn.

A burst of laughter blew out of the bar, carrying two women with it. Through the open door, Osby could see dark figures milling under unnatural colors. The band was winding up its set. Still holding the door open, the two women stood there, shouting at the people inside. More laughter.

Osby put the comb back in the glove compartment and slipped his hands into his sweatshirt pocket. If he went in, the laughter would die out like someone had shut off a valve. People would nod to him uncomfortably, trying to convey sympathy with forced smiles and a few hesitant slaps on the back, a few quick handshakes. He wished the band could have played one more song, just long enough for him to get in there and hunker down. He switched on the radio again. Bruce Springsteen sang, low and slow, telling the night how he was on fire. Osby lit a cigarette, sucked smoke, and backed the truck up.

The bar seemed to have snagged all the cars off the road. The only vehicle behind Osby was a semi, a clump of small lights surrounding the blast of headlights like fireflies around a porch lamp. As he passed the Buttercup, his stomach dipped. He hadn't eaten since the blueberry pie that afternoon. The clock

radio in the Sierra's dash had it at 9:15. Fridays and Saturdays
the Buttercup was open until 9:30. He turned into the restaurant's parking lot, his tires rumbling over the gravel, and passed
by at a crawl. Half the overhead fluorescents had been shut off.
Hazel, sweeping the floor, looked up and shook her hand and
head at the same time, as if one appendage was saying "Nope,
closed" and the other "Sorry." He waved back, but she was already looking at the floor again. The semi blew by on the road.
It must have been Thursday.

Up ahead, a white sign marked the turnoff for 33. He tried
to think of something to keep him from having to go home. The
Pine Top Restaurant over toward Ripplemead on 42 would be
closed. The Mic-or-Mac would be closed. He could drive back the
other direction, pass right by 247, take 56 into Coalsburg, and eat
at the Mexican restaurant that was open late for the college kids.
He looked at the clock again: 9:17. It would be 10:30 by the time
he got to Coalsburg, midnight by the time he got home. On the
radio, Johnny Cash was singing, "Burns, burns, burns."

C & O Quickmart lit up a chunk of night. He could fill the
truck, at least. He pulled in under the Chevron sign, shut off
Johnny Cash, and got out under the bright greenish glow by the
pumps, tossing the last of his cigarette.

The cold bit at him. He felt a little more alive, a little angry.
What was so great about Ten Points, anyway? Everyone getting
drunk. Everyone laughing. Probably wasn't even funny, whatever it was, probably something stupid.

The gas made a thumping noise as it pulsed through the
hose.

I can go in there, he thought, looking toward C & O, get a
six-pack, get drunk as easy as anyone.

"If I want," he said out loud.

He glanced up from the nozzle, shocked out of his thoughts by his voice, surprised, and a little scared, by the vehemence in it.

Inside the Quickmart, the heat was turned up. The door jangled as he entered and a woman's voice said, "Whew!"

"Hey, Deb."

"I can feel that cold from here," she said.

"Yeah. I'd say it's twenty-two, twenty-three out there."

She laughed, smiling at him over her book. He wasn't sure what she was laughing and smiling about. Osby moved down the aisles toward the refrigerators in back, opened one of the doors, and stood there for a second, trying to decide between Coors and Moosehead.

"It's gonna get down to thirteen tonight," Deb said.

Osby nodded, thinking, In the morning I'd better check and see if the water's frozen. He pulled out a six-pack of Moosehead and looked for something to eat in the snack food aisle. Once, when he glanced up, Deb smiled at him, and he looked down quick, thought, I guess she doesn't like that book too much.

He was wrong; she liked the book fine. She just knew she had another hour and a half of reading time behind the counter and at least an hour after that in her bed, sitting up late reading under the lamplight. The book was *Devil's Embrace*, but Osby, when he came to the counter, didn't notice that. Nor was there any way for him to know that Catherine Coulter was her favorite author (unless, sometime over the past five years, he had thought to ask her about anything more than how her husband was). She was wearing a teal sweatshirt with two pink teddy bears on it and she had matched the colors to her eyeliner and lipstick. She'd been dyeing her hair for sixteen years, and that night it was showing a little purplish. Her eyes were small for her round, pudgy face, but they were bright, so that men often took a second look at her, thinking maybe she was better looking than they had thought. Once, long ago, she had wanted to be a doctor, or at least a nurse. She liked carrots better than almost anything else and had baked herself the best carrot cake in Eads County for her birthday. She had excellent night vision. In high school, her volleyball teammates had called the look she got in her eyes Death by Debbie. Even her husband would have admitted she had a beautiful smile. She was four days older than fifty.

Osby set a box of a dozen assorted doughnuts on the counter next to the Moosehead. He noticed that Deb smiled at him a lot and that she was leaning back on her stool in a way that made him anxious.

"Which is your favorite?" Deb said, as she rang him up.

"Doughnuts?"

"Yeah. I like the chocolate. But then, I like anything chocolate. Who doesn't, right? Which one are you gonna go for first?" She smiled and laughed a little. Osby thought her laugh wasn't quite as nice as her smile, though until then he hadn't realized how nice her smile was. "The cinnamon?" she said. "You probably just pour the whole box into your mouth." She laughed again.

"Well, it's dinner, you know," Osby said, by which he meant he was so hungry that the flavor really didn't matter.

Deb paused just before punching the final buttons. "*That's* dinner?"

Osby tucked his hands in the pocket of his sweatshirt. "Well . . ."

"You better eat somethin' better'n that. We got sandwiches back there. They ain't the *most* freshest, but Janice makes 'em herself in the mornin'." Deb got up off her stool and came around the counter. "We got ham and cheese. Chicken salad. Though that one might be soggy by now. Hot dogs you can just pop in the microwave."

Osby followed her back along an aisle. She seemed awfully energized by something. When she opened the fridge door for him, he chose the first sandwich he put his hand on.

"You just put that in the microwave," she said, "it'll be good and hot."

"It's all right like this."

"It's cold."

He looked at the sandwich, as if its temperature were something to be discovered by close inspection.

"You can't eat cold meatballs," she said.

"It's all right."

This time, Osby thought, her laugh was even more nervous. "Gimme that," she said.

He handed it to her, feeling his whole face heat up.

They stood together by the microwave while the machine hummed, watching the numbers tick down from ninety seconds.

"I'm sorry 'bout your dad," she said. "I heard the funeral was real nice."

He nodded. The numbers said seventy-three.

At fifty-two, Osby said, "How's Greg?"

"I don't see him much, anymore."

He remembered hearing something about them splitting up, and felt the heat rushing to his face again. "Sorry 'bout the divorce," he said.

"Oh, we ain't divorced."

He sighed, wishing there was some way other than talking to say things. It was like he wasn't even meant to be a person. He would have been better off an animal, communicate by raising the hairs on his head or putting off some kind of smell.

"Not yet," she said. "But we're separated, though. We're through."

"Sorry 'bout that." he said.

"Don't be."

When the microwave dinged, they went back to the counter and she rang him up again.

"It must get lonely out there without your dad now."

It was quiet after the noise of the register. Osby held his hands around the warm sandwich. "Carl thinks I oughta get a renter."

"That's a good idea," she said. "It's good livin' with someone. I'm in my sister's place right now, but she's gone with Mike to Germany, you know. He's posted there."

Germany, Osby thought. Just the word seemed like a crazy idea.

"You could put up a sign out on the bulletin board," Deb said. "That's twenty-eight-thirty, with the gas."

He dug his hand in his pocket, pulled out his wallet. "Germany, huh?" he said.

"Yeah. I've got the run of the place for nine more months." She took the cash from him. "Hey, hold on." She ducked behind

the counter and came up again with a sheet of pale green paper
and a black magic marker. "You write out a sign right there, stick
it up on the board outside."

He looked at the paper much as his father had studied the
contract the government man had offered him for an easement
on the land.

"My writing's just chicken scratches, anyhow," he said,
smiling at her, hoping she'd let him off the hook.

Instead, she picked up the pen. "What do you want it to
say?" She looked at him expectantly.

He thought about the kitchen with those two shut doors.
Where else would I be?

"I guess, Room for rent. Route 247. The Caudills." An
image of the half-toppled mailbox came to him. "No," he said.
"Uh, just say, call Osby Caudill, 544–7293." He watched her
finish writing in her round, careful hand. "And," he said, because it seemed the right thing to add, "put down there it's a
good price."

"What is it?"

He shrugged. "You can just say it's cheap."

When she was finished, she handed him the sign, telling
him there were tacks already out there. While she was count-
ing out his change, she said, "I wouldn't take him back for anything."

Osby nodded and took the plastic bag from her.

"I'm a free woman, now," she said. Her laugh was a small
sound accompanied by a shrug.

"Well," Osby said. "Thanks for the sign."

"Uh-huh."

"You have a good night."

"Uh-huh," she said. "You, too."

He heard her settle back on her stool as he walked to the door. He was sure she was staring at him. When he was outside and the door had shut behind him, he glanced back over his shoulder. She was hunched over the counter, reading her book.

Outside C & O, he walked over to the bulletin board and, looking around to see if anyone was watching, slipped the flier behind a piece of paper advertising a 1988 Toyota Tercel for sale. All you could see of his sign was *544–7293 Very Reasonably Priced,* in Deb's neat writing. He zipped up his coat and started to turn toward the truck when something at the bottom of the board caught his eyes. A little Asian girl's face looked out at him with huge, sad eyes, printed on the front of a pamphlet stuck in a paper holder stapled to the board. He slid the pamphlet out, as if it were almost too brittle to touch. In the cab, he put the key in the ignition, but didn't turn it. Instead he sat there for a second, holding the pamphlet in his cold fingers, looking at the little girl's face in the greenish light from over the pumps. *Save the Children,* it said. He mouthed the words, once, silently, then laid the pamphlet on the seat next to him and pulled out on the road.

From the radio on the dash a woman's soft, sad voice sang a cover of a half-remembered song.

All along route 33, the lights of houses pricked the dark like chips of stars fallen from the night sky to the night earth. Osby drove past them, thinking of Germany. When he was little, his mother used to show him a black-and-white photograph of her father, his grandfather, in a long wool coat with tin-looking buttons, smoking a cigarette and grinning at something the

soldiers next to him must have said. A month after that picture
was taken a German hand grenade blew the man to shreds. Now,
watching his headlights chase the blackness in front of them,
Osby tried to remember whether there had been anything in his
grandfather's face that hinted at his death.

From the speakers on the door the woman's soft, sad voice
sang her cover of the half-remembered song. Ahead, the high
beams tore at the dark.

He wondered how his father's face had looked when he
had made that phone call to Eula Geller's house.

Above Harts Run, the church on the limestone hill was
invisible in the darkness under the big hickories. There was only
a small red light up there, flickering. Osby watched it, thinking
of the girl in the pamphlet, starving in a place even further away
than Germany, a place where no one even spoke his language.
His headlights clutched the road. When he was past the church,
something tugged his eyes to his rearview mirror and he saw,
up there where the church should have been, two white lights
splintered by the trees. There, then gone. There, then gone.

In the cab of his truck, the air was all piano and guitar and
the breathing of the woman on the radio waiting for her turn.

In the morning, Osby spent an hour opening doors and airing
out rooms, shoving back curtains, clearing boxes out of the
hallway. By seven, the windows were throwing hard, clear light
over the place. It looked better to Osby, a little less like a stor-
age shed, a little less like the Old House. He was late getting
out to the pastures and he worked fast, running around the front
of the truck to crank the hub locks into four-wheel drive, jump-

ing out to swing open the gates, driving almost straight up each hill, the bale on the back of the truck shedding flecks of hay. When he'd get near the top, he'd lower the spike, drive forward a few feet, let the hay slide off. He'd hop out, jog around behind the truck, cut the twine and give the bale a shove, watching it unravel in a long trail as it rolled down the hill. He'd take a few minutes to look over the cattle as they came for it, trying to stifle excitement whenever he thought he saw a limp or a swollen jaw. But it never turned out to be anything worth getting worked up about. Even the heifers were calving easy.

Half the cows had given birth and it was time to put some weight back on them, bring them in again for the bulls. With putting out the extra bagged feed, it was full into day by the time he got to the last herd. The jeep trail running through the pasture was still churned up from the funeral. Osby shook three bags of shell corn into the feeding trough, scanning the bright, sun-flooded trees along the top of Bowmans Ridge for the glint of a headstone. He didn't see anything. The heifers lumbered toward him, shouldering each other as they crowded around the feed. He watched the calves, standing back in a clump, waiting for their chance to suckle.

He was about to get back in the truck and drive over to the Raines brothers' last logging site—they had left him branches and end chunks to collect: two days worth of chainsawing and splitting, but enough wood to last through winter—when he stopped and ran his eyes back over the herd. A cow was missing. No. The six calves were all there, and the couple heifers who looked ready to drop their young were still bulging, their sacks still swollen beneath their tails. Then, in the distance, Osby caught a glimpse of brown. It was the brown of dead leaves on

a forest floor, lumped way down in a gully at the lowest corner
of the pasture where the fence line came up against a snarl of
bare-branched cedars and blackhaw. Osby stood watching that
brown shape. The stagged yearling, he remembered, the late-
born steer that had been too young to bring to auction that fall.
His dad had planned on selling it with the calves that spring.
Dead? What would have killed it, though? Coyotes or a mountain lion might get a newborn calf, but not a year-old steer.

Suddenly, its legs kicked out, jerked, pawed at the air and
mud. It was on its side, its head flailing, smacking the ground
over and over. He knew then that it wasn't any coyote or mountain lion that had done it, wasn't anything that stag could have
run from or Osby could have shot.

By the time he got to the eroded side of the gully, it was
still again, its eyes rolled upwards to look at him. Quick breaths
blew bubbles in the froth at its mouth. Every few seconds its
ears twitched. A shudder rippled over its face.

Osby crouched down at the edge of the gully, not wanting
to come any closer and start the steer flailing again. A flicker of
excitement licked the inside of his chest. He frowned it off, let
worry cover it. He'd never seen a steer come down with grass
tetany. It was always cows, usually pregnant or just after they'd
dropped their calves. He'd had a bad run of Holstein-Charlay
cows who had died from it over the years. His father always said
it was because they were such big milkers. One year, it was so
bad he and his father had just dug a pit and left it open, filled it
with six cows before spring was over. But that was before they'd
started using the mineral blocks instead of straight salt, and in
a year when the hay didn't have enough seed in it. He hadn't
had a grass tetany problem in years.

He watched the steer's wild, rolling eye looking at him. His father would have just put a bullet in it.

Osby stood up from his crouch and it was as if unbending his knees released a rush of adrenaline from his legs to his chest. Sometimes, you could save them. Occasionally, if you got the Cowdex right into their jugular, then kept hitting them with it under the skin, you could keep them alive. Once, he'd seen the injection hit the blood just right, as if it punched the cow right in the heart, and she'd been up, kicking, wild with sudden life. He told himself to quit getting excited. Almost always, you had to put a bullet in them. It was bad. Tomorrow—hell, that evening —another could be down, and more in the morning. From the sudden cold? Something wrong with the hay? He tried to walk calmly back up the hill, but even the muscles in his legs were thrilled. *This is it, this is it, this is it,* kept going through his mind to the rhythm of his feet.

By the time he reached the truck, his chest was heaving and he banged his breastbone with a fist, trying to knock the air loose in his lungs. He drove too fast out of the pasture toward the house, the truck jolting over the frozen ground. It wasn't until he was through the gate and past the junkyard that he remembered the Cowdex was stored in the Old House with the rest of the medicines.

When he drove up the old driveway, there wasn't anywhere to park but behind his father's Ford. Osby stared at the house, at the half-open front door. So what if his father had walked that path, gone in there, up those stairs? He unlatched the Sierra's door, let gravity swing it open. In front of him, the rusted tailgate on his father's truck was down. He stared at it, then flicked his eyes up to the Ford's rear windshield. It seemed perfectly possible that his father's squashed-looking, wrinkly head might be there above the headrest, close-cropped white hair prickling his scalp like cactus spines. Osby breathed hard out his nose, trying to unpack whatever was filling up his chest. The old man couldn't even walk over, he thought. A quarter mile. Had to drive in comfort. Probably had the radio on. And the heat. All cozy, before he did it.

Osby shoved out the door, headed for the house. Passing by his father's truck, he reached out, on reflex, to shut the tailgate. Instead he punched it, hard. One, quick, metal-rattling punch. The bang jerked his neck, as if it had been someone else's fist slamming metal. He pressed his knuckles into the soft skin at his cheek, trying to smother the jabbing ache. A crow fled a nearby tree, cawing, leaves shaking behind it.

Osby headed for the front door, walking fast, trying not to notice the dead man's boot prints still frozen in the mud. He shoved the door the rest of the way open, walked straight into the dim hallway and right to the steps, staring ahead of him as if his neck had cramped and his eyes had frozen. The medicines were all on the stairs: boxes and jars, cans, bags, drums, bottles piled up to the second floor landing. He shoved through them, knocking stuff a few steps down before it got caught up in other junk, his movements more and more wild as he neared the top, his breathing ragged. His head was down; his eyes locked on the piles on either side of the staircase. He didn't look up to the landing, didn't once check to see if the cops had left the door up there open or closed. Four steps from the top, he found the plastic packets of Cowdex and, on the next step, the needle and catheter coiled at the bottom of a rag-filled box.

No more than five minutes later, he was skidding heavy-booted down the red mud gully, the warmed jar of Cowdex in one hand, the catheter gathered in the other, the halter slung over his shoulder. *This is it, this is it,* the blood in his temples was beating again. This thing can't live without me, he thought, and almost said it to the steer, his eyes locking on its: You can't live without me. As if it had heard his thoughts, the stag heaved its neck up, eyes bulging, the white half of its face ruddy with mud. Its stiff legs started paddling again, smearing the pile of fresh shit that had run down around its hindquarters, their movement eerily disconnected from the rest of its body.

It made Osby feel powerful, seeing the steer's muscles go crazy like that. His hands felt as skilled as a surgeon's as he attached the needle to the catheter, the catheter to the jar of Cowdex. It was as if the adrenaline had cleared his veins, his arteries, his neurons, his marrow, everything that connected one part of him to the other. He was moving fast, but controlled, trying to get it done before the Cowdex got too cold. He wrestled the harness over the steer's ears and muzzle and tied it tight to a nearby fencepost, yanking the head back so the neck was stretched taut, the ribbed throat like knuckles pushing out at the skin from the inside. The steer followed him with its bulging eyes as he came back around and knelt in front of it. He put one hand on the warm neck, took aim, and jammed the nail-sized needle into the jugular. The steer kicked, tried to thrash its head against the rope. Osby didn't even notice. He was already standing, lifting the jar of Cowdex off the ground, focused on raising it just right, not too high, not too fast; if it flowed in too quickly, if too much of it hit the steer's heart, he'd kill it. When the jar was drained, he jerked the needle out, gathered the tubing up, and stood back.

The steer lay there.

Osby watched it breathe steam through a bubble of saliva. Dark blood seeped around the needle hole. He stood perfectly still. The adrenaline that had bolted around in his body a minute ago seemed to have drained out through the catheter along with the Cowdex. Slowly, he wiped his face with the back of his hand. His knuckles smelled like the steer.

His heartbeat felt tired. The sun had risen high enough for its light to reach the corner of the pasture where he stood, and he felt it hit the back of his neck, saw the shadow of his head against the scrubby grass: a dark, squashed-looking bump.

Couldn't even do that, he thought.

The steer breathed more evenly now, almost as if it were sleeping.

"Well," Osby said, and finished the thought silently: we'll try again tomorrow. The steer could eat, crap, piss, do anything but get up. As long as its head wasn't downhill, it wouldn't smother. He'd heard of a cow surviving for weeks like that. He couldn't remember if it had died in the end, or not.

His father would have just put a bullet in it.

Standing there, watching the steer's ribs swell with its breathing, he remembered his father sleeping in a chair at the kitchen table by the woodstove, legs spread, head back, mouth gaping, two partridge lying limply at his elbow, the barrel of his shotgun gleaming in his lap. Of course, it had been the Ruger, not the shotgun, that he'd used.

Osby watched the steer breathe. He'd come back tomorrow, give it an injection under the skin. He'd try it for a week, if he had to. He'd try it for two.

He'll be all right, Osby thought, until he isn't.

That night there was a new moon, and outside the world was unnaturally black. Osby sat on the couch, eyes closed, jeans rolled to his knees, his fat calves blue-skinned in the light from the TV. He'd filled a big pot with hot water and carried it, sloshing, to the living room. Now, feeling his toes wrinkle, he smiled. When he was a small boy, his mother used to sit like that, soaking her feet like that. On the TV, a woman won $250,000 and was going to risk it to try for half a million. He got up and walked to the bathroom, the warmth draining out of his feet in wet, dark stains on the cold floor. In the kitchen, the woodstove had gone out.

A few days later, down in the gully, Osby gave the steer its fourth injection, holding his breath while the medicine drained in, the way, when hunting, he'd still his lungs to steady the rifle. Afterwards, he held a bucket of water and listened to the steer's noisy drinking. A few dry kernels of shell corn were embedded in the mud just out of the steer's reach. A mound of cow shit had piled behind its haunches. Watching the heaving belly, Osby remembered last year when he and his father castrated the bull calves: his father standing behind each one, bending the tail over its back so it couldn't kick, while Osby crouched, the bucket of water steaming, the knife wet with alcohol. Splash the scrotum with

Creolin, slice off the bottom of the sack, reach in, yank the slippery balls down, cut the cords and toss the testicles. But this
one, born late, this nine-hundred-pound-no-longer-calf lying at
his feet, this one had only one testicle in the sack.

"The other hasn't dropped, yet," he'd said to his dad.

His father just nodded: Well, get it out. He'd reached into
the sack, into the groin, almost to the belly, working upward with
his knife and fingers, searching for the nut. The calf had tried
to rear, rolled its eyes, came as close as a calf can to screaming.
He probably could have gotten the nut out, but he'd stopped,
shook his head. "Gonna have to leave him stagged," Osby said,
knowing it wasn't good. His dad wouldn't like having a steer
grow up acting like a bull, but infertile, the meat good only for
hamburger or roast.

The stag wasn't even worth that, anymore.

The vet had said it could have been the sudden cold, the
young grass, old seedless hay, a urinary problem. He'd never seen
grass tetany in a steer. In the end, "Keep up with the Cowdex,"
was all he offered. "Or shoot it."

Now, Osby watched it breathe. All the cows, even the heifers, were calving without a hitch. He hadn't had to help one.
You can't live without me.

Bullshit, he thought. He had no more to do with it than he
did with anything else. He reached out and touched the stag's
flank. It was warm on his cold fingers.

That Sunday, the cows broke through a fence line into the woods
on Bowmans Ridge. Osby walked beneath the trees, hunting
them out, passing between beeches and elms no thicker than

himself, grown over the same years he had, their pale trunks rising around the huge, dark stumps of the chestnuts logged long ago, before he was born, before the blight had rid the woods of every last one. He sat on a stump—black with age, big as his truck hood, solid still—and shut his eyes to listen for the moving of the cows.

He worked the rest of the day at fixing the fence. It was so clear and cold the trees looked sharp and the sounds had edges. Behind him, in the dead grass, a long row of new, dark postholes marked the fence line.

Later, stretching the wire from post to post to post, there was just the clacking of tree branches in the wind and the throaty cawing of crows. He glanced at the sky as he worked. High above, three of the black birds dove furiously at a red-tailed hawk circling in thin sunlight. A tilt of wide wings, a sideward glide; it dodged gracefully, unperturbed.

After a week, the Cowdex injection felt like a formality. Osby came to sit and keep the steer company. A few days ago, he started talking to it, whispering at first, looking around anxiously every now and then. Now he sat on the cold ground, arms wrapped around his knees, telling the steer about the check he wrote to Save the Children the night before. "Two hundred dollars," he said, shaking his head. He told the steer he knew it was a crazy thing to do, that his father was probably hiking down from the cemetery right now, revived by the magnitude of his son's stupidity, that if he wanted to give something away, he could have helped someone in Eads County instead of halfway around the world. It felt good to say it out loud: Helped someone.

"Little Asian babies," he said to the steer. "In China. Korea. Vietnam. Hundreds of thousands of 'em. Starving."

The steer watched him with weak eyes. Absently, Osby picked a kernel of corn out of the grass and put it in the mud by the steer's mouth. Its long tongue lapped it up.

"Two hundred dollars," he said again and let out a burst of breath that was almost a laugh.

The steer blew air and snot out of its nose.

When he was too cold to stay sitting, he got up, said, "So long," and climbed the muddy slope to his truck.

The weather chose to freeze, hard, on the one day he had to be away till late. By the time he got back from the farm auction in Ripplemead, the streams and ponds were frozen solid. He drove straight to the pastures, never mind dinner, hauled the crowbar out of the truck bed, and went to work. In the grainy flare of the Sierra's headlights, shards of ice sprayed like sparks from a welder's torch. Around him, the cattle, little more than movements in the night, stared. By an hour before midnight he had two creeks and one pond to go.

"Wendell," Osby said, half awake, his mind wandering, some days later while lying back against the steer's chest. It was a little warmer that afternoon, down in the gully, shielded from the wind. It was almost comfortable. His arms folded over his chest, Osby watched a small cloud drift across the blue sky. The stag's warm body rose and fell underneath his head. It took a dump: the thick, heavy plops, the rush of piss. For the past three days,

Osby had shoveled away the crap. Even so, the smell was bad on a warm afternoon.

If one of the heifers would have trouble calving, if one of them would just give him a chance to *do* something, he knew he wouldn't come down here with the steer nearly as much. He felt a little guilty about that. After a while, he shut his eyes, enjoying the warmth of the sun on his face and the almost too bright redness of his eyelids.

"Wendell," he said again, realizing, suddenly, that was the kind of name his father would have given a steer.

For two days, off and on, sleet fell like old rain. In the middle of the field next to the government land the wind buffeted the mineral box; its weather vane, giving in to the push of nature, turned the roof to shield the pink block of salt. Clumps of cows stood still under shaking trees, calves pressed close to their sides, out of the wind. Across the fence line, against the woods, the row of abandoned hay bales rotted.

Two weeks after the steer came down with grass tetany, the hydraulics on Osby's dump truck gave out in the middle of a job. He was over in the auto graveyard behind the field that separated the Old House from the one he lived in, hoping to avoid a trip to the Pfersicks' garage all the way across the valley near Narrows, trying to salvage a cylinder off an old front-end loader when he heard a truck approaching up the road. He didn't recognize the small green-and-tan pickup with a dirty white cap that turned up the driveway toward his home. Or the young guy who stepped out: skinny, his flannel shirt flapping around him, his jeans sun-bleached along the front of his legs. A bushy, red beard flamed around his face when the sun hit it. Glasses glinted beneath a green hat. The guy looked around, walked up the front porch steps, and knocked on the door.

Osby stayed where he was.

The guy walked back down the steps, peered around the house, and shouted, "Hello? Hello?" After a second, he walked back around the porch, back up the steps, knocked again, shouted again, and then returned to his truck.

Osby watched him get in, waited for him to shut the driver's door.

Instead, the guy got back out, and walked back to the porch. There was something in his hand. A book, Osby realized. The guy sat down on the front steps of Osby's home, opened his book, and started to read.

After two or three minutes, Osby jumped down from the front-end loader and headed across the shortcut between the houses. When he came around the porch, the guy was already standing.

"Hi," the guy said. "I'm here about the room." He talked twice as fast as Osby was used to. "My name's Tim. I saw the sign about the room? I hope I'm in the right place. Are you Osby Caudill?"

"Yeah."

"I'm Tim," the guy said again as they shook hands. "I hope I'm not bothering you. I mean, I know it's the middle of the day and—"

"No, no," Osby said.

"This is a wonderful place."

Osby looked at the sagging porch, tools scattered over the peeling floorboards, rags, a couple rusting lawn chairs. "Lived here all my life," he said.

"Really? Wow. Born here and everything?"

"Yeah."

"Incredible."

As far as Osby could tell, the guy really thought it was. Osby stared at him, thinking he looked like a kid, thinking: This kid wants to rent a room in my house.

"I'm a grad student over at VTU," Tim was saying, "In agronomy. Getting my master's. I'm working on this project trying to introduce kenaf. It's a kind of crop, kind of like . . . well, anyway, it's a crop, and I'm trying to—"

Osby interrupted him. "You lookin' to rent a room *here*?"

Tim's free hand went to his beard. "Uh," his fingers hovering at his chin, "I saw a sign . . . I . . . Did someone rent it already?"

Osby stuck his hands in the front pocket of his sweatshirt and tried to think of how to answer that. After all, he'd put that sign up. And the kid was so excited he didn't feel right lying to him. "Well," he said after a second, "There's no one usin' the room, now."

Tim nodded. "Do you think I could, uh . . . Would it be all right if I took a look at it? Just to . . . make sure."

How could he say, No, you can't look at it. "Yeah," he said. "Come on."

He clumped up the stairs, Tim talking behind him.

"I bet you're wondering what the heck kenaf is," Tim said. Maybe, in the dim light of the hallway, the kid thought there was a nod somewhere in the way Osby moved up the stairs in front of him. "Hardly any of the farmers around here have even heard of it, but it's revolutionary. I mean it. It's going to revolutionize agriculturally based economies in regions of the country like this one."

At the top of the stairs, Osby turned to the right and headed for the room his dad had slept in all the years Osby had known him.

"Do you grow any crops?" Tim asked. "I saw most of the land around here is in pasture."

"Clendal Veltre down bottom 247's got dairy cows," Osby said. "Your corn, soybeans. I'm just beef, here."

"See, corn and soybeans," Tim said, "if you're growing them as feed for your cows, okay, but as cash crops? You can't make a living at it, right?"

Osby pushed open the door to his dad's room. "That's her," he said.

Tim went as far as the doorway, stood, looking in. Osby backed up a bit, trying to think what he'd say if the kid liked it. He couldn't imagine he would—a college kid, carrying his books around, thinking up new ways of farming and everything. The room was just as his father had left it: muddy work clothes strewn over the floor, lamp made of a deer's leg on the bed stand, old apple crates full of older clothes stacked against the wall next to the dresser, the Nascar pillow on the sagging bed.

Tim didn't let on whether he liked it or not. He just kept talking while he looked at the room. "See," he said. "Kenaf, that's the crop I'm doing my thesis work on, it's from Asia, mainly India—"

"Asia?" Osby said, thinking of the little girl on the pamphlet. "Like Korea?"

"Well, not Korea, I don't think," Tim said. "Sri Lanka. China, a little. Mainly, though, in India."

"Uh-huh," Osby said. It suddenly seemed incredible that a graduate student at the university in Coalsburg, someone who knew what kinds of things grew in countries like India and China, was standing in his house, looking at his father's room thinking of renting it.

"Yeah," Tim went on. "The thing is, we're trying to introduce it into the States. It's not like any crop we grow here, really —well, it looks a little like sugarcane, a little like big, uh . . . you know . . . cannabis—but," he moved on quickly, "it's almost woody, very stiff, large stalks and—this is the thing—you can use it for a whole slew of things from paper to—this is what I'm interested in—as biomass plant material that could provide this entire country with its own renewable, environmentally tenable, domestically produced energy source."

Osby just nodded, but he was paying close attention. Not to what the kid was saying, but to how excited he was about it. Imagine feeling like that, Osby thought. Tim was talking about carbon and the atmosphere and something about the dinosaur age. Osby didn't listen so much as watch. The guy's hands flew everywhere. He could hardly stand still. His eyes looked like they were powered by something completely foreign to Osby, completely different from whatever it was inside him. This kid, he thought to himself, thinks he's going to save the world. It was the kind of thing people usually laughed at around Eads County, but it seemed to Osby like something wondrous. Not that this kid was actually going to do any of this stuff, but that he thought he could. He really believed it. Some kind of pot plant from India replacing coal and oil in the whole of the United States.

It seemed to Osby that he had never even thought of anything close to something that big. Here he was, he thought to himself, putting a check in the mail to help out one little Asian kid, helping a cow give birth to a calf that was going to die in a year anyway, trying to keep a one-balled steer alive. And he couldn't even do that.

"Well, this is great," Tim was saying. "I mean, I guess the clothes and stuff are someone else's, but the room comes furnished like this, right? 'Cause I actually have all my stuff here with me in the truck." Tim laughed, awkwardly. "I've been staying over at Whistler's Meadow."

Osby had never more than nodded to any of the commune people who lived in that strange place out near Narrows on 42; he'd never thought he'd actually speak to one.

Tim must have seen it in his face, because he said, fast, "Just camping on their land. They let me, you know, until I found something. Do you think, I mean, if it's okay, if you don't have anyone else lined up, or anything, do you think I could move in today?"

Right then, Osby didn't see how someone like him could refuse someone like Tim anything.

"I wouldn't touch the clothes," Tim said. "I mean, whoever's they are—if they're yours or anything, the clothes and stuff, we could just move them out when it was convenient, you know?" He laughed again. "Boy am I tired of sleeping on the ground."

"Yeah," Osby said. "All right."

"Great. That's really great. Thank you."

"Sure."

Tim seemed to be waiting for something. Osby was still trying to imagine living with someone other than his father in the house. "Uh," Tim said, "what kind of, you know, rent were you thinking?"

Osby peered in at the room, as if getting a better idea of the dimensions would help him decide on how much rent. All he could think of was those plants of Tim's and India and China and things like that.

"Two hundred," he said, finally, thinking of the little girl on the front of that pamphlet and the check he'd sent in the mail.

It took Osby a while to replace the hydraulic cylinder on the dump truck, and he finished spreading his last load of gravel in fast-approaching dark, the bits of gray stone on the Whorleys' new driveway holding onto the light longer than the fields and yard. When he got home, the house was lit up like he'd never seen it before: upstairs windows glowing; the downstairs ones, too; even the porch light on. The ruts in the driveway seemed to fall in the wrong spots. Osby listened to the weeds scrape the dump truck's belly as if he'd never heard the sound before.

When he climbed out of the truck cab, he went suddenly still. Strange music came from the house, Indian or Arab or maybe even the kind of stuff they played in Korea. He took a few steps back and looked up at the window to his father's bedroom. From in there, a woman's voice sang in a language that seemed like an entirely new way of making sound.

Even the creaking of the trees sounded like a different forest below an unfamiliar ridge. It was almost like watching a movie, except the screen was wrapped all the way around Osby. He looked up at the sky. The stars, still and distant as ever, hadn't changed. In his father's bedroom, a figure crossed the patch of yellow-glowing glass, just a dark shape, any man, any person, in any window of any house. Except his.

The temperature had dropped—he figured it was close to fifteen. A gust of wind stung his face. He would have liked to go inside, make some coffee, bring his thermos with him to the pastures. Instead, he walked quickly to his pickup, as if sneaking through the light thrown from the porch. The kid's truck squatted alongside his, the tailgate and the cap's rear window open. It looked empty. Osby wondered what kinds of things had been moved into his father's room.

It took two hours to break up the ice on the creeks and ponds, to spike the five hay bales, roll them out in each pasture, do a quick roving check of each herd. When he had swung the last gate shut, he leaned against it, his cold hands on the freezing crossbar, and tried to think of what else he could do to keep from going home. Whistler's Meadow, he thought. They had bought Don Demastus's farm a couple years ago and turned it into what they called communal living, a group home. He tried to imagine what that could mean. There had been times when he had driven past the sprawling compound and felt a pull in him, a need so strong it scared him: to be touched—on the shoulder or cheek or anywhere—by some other human's hand. Now, he knew it wouldn't have done any good. Behind him, the truck's taillights reddened his back, painted the shadow of his shape into the reddened grass.

He wondered what the kid was doing back at his house. Probably making dinner. His stomach gurgled. What would a kid like that eat? Probably vegetarian. Leaves and grass. He suddenly knew that his kitchen would smell like Indian food when he got home, however Indian food smelled. He imagined the kid, in slippers and a bathrobe, cooking things on the stove. He saw himself standing in the doorway, feeling as if he had done something rude by not taking off his boots. The kid might offer him dinner. Over plates of strange food without any meat in it, the kid would tell him all about his plans to change the world with trees from India.

Osby shoved off the gate, letting it clang, and drove the forty minutes into town.

At the Buttercup, all but two tables were empty. The few diners greeted Osby when he came in. A nod, a quick hello. Then Gary Huffman returned to cutting up his daughter's meal. Powell and April Avehart went back to the quietness of eating together. Old Mose Hamblin gave his attention again to getting his shaking fork into his mouth. Osby settled onto a stool at the counter, his back to the room, and ordered the $4.95 special. When it came, he hunched over the plate, cutting a chicken liver in half, easing it onto his fork, eating as slowly as he could.

In the kitchen, Vance was yelling. Hazel entered the dining room, forcing a smile onto her face, and Osby wanted to tell her that without her, the old men who came in each night might not ever eat dinner. He wanted to tell her she was indispensable. *Indispensable.* Thinking of the word, he was suddenly sure that if he said something she wouldn't even hear him.

He eased a sliver of fried onion onto a square of green pepper on top of the half of a chicken liver. The onions were fifty cents extra, the green peppers another fifty. He felt like he could spend everything in his wallet, clean out his bank account with a check, and it wouldn't matter.

Forty-five minutes into his meal, the mashed potatoes cold, he realized he had forgotten to give the paralyzed steer the Cowdex. He finished chewing. All the tables were empty now.

Should have put a bullet in him from the start, he thought.

At 8:30, the restaurant closed. By then, Osby had finished three peach cobblers with ice cream and he could tell by the way Hazel slapped the chairs upside down on the tabletops that he was overstaying his welcome. His belly sloshed as he climbed into the Sierra. Under the cab light, he peered inside his wallet: two crinkly dollar bills. His jeans pockets, front and back, held a quarter, three dimes, and a penny. In the restaurant, slowly picking at cold, gooey slabs of peach, he had gone over his life, scavenging for something he could change to make him indispensable to somebody.

So it seemed almost inevitable that he passed the sign for 33 and pulled into the C & O parking lot. He parked by the Dumpster in the back and killed the engine. Quiet filled the air. He listened to a car pull up to the pumps around front. Another picked up speed heading out of town. He had the impression that he was drifting first one way and then the other, but always down, as if he'd driven his truck off a roadside into deep water. He zipped up his camouflage jacket so the metal tab jutted against his chin. Waves of wind rolled over the top of the cab.

At a quarter to ten, he roused himself, stiff with cold, and made his way around to the front of the store. His legs felt unused to walking, his face puffy. The doorbell's high jangle almost took the strength out of his knees. Everything in his chest felt packed in too tight.

"Osby," Deb said as she came out of the restroom, as if him standing there was a big surprise pulled out from behind someone's back. "You just made it. I was 'bout to close up an' go home."

"Oh," he said. "You want me to leave?"

"Leave?" She peered at him. "No, you got five minutes. Go on an' get whatever you came for. I'm not gonna slip out and lock you in."

He could feel her eyes on him, and he was sure she must be able to see his pulse at his throat—it felt like twice the blood was being pumped through there. He headed down one of the aisles, just to move, and, remembering how she made him get a sandwich last time, headed for the refrigerated closets.

"That meatball sub," he said, when he put the sandwich down on the counter. "Janice knows how to make 'em, huh?"

"She makes good ones."

She started ringing him up, and he almost panicked, seeing the whole exchange finished and nothing for him to do but walk back out the door. "Hey, wait," he said. "I guess I better microwave that."

She paused, looked at him queerly. "I don't know if it'll be good hot."

"Yeah," he said. "It was real good."

"The meatballs?"

"Yeah. You was right 'bout that."

"This is chicken salad," she said. "Did you want meatball?"

He stared at the sandwich. "No," he said, sticking his hands in his jacket pockets. "That's all right. This 'un looks good." He raised his eyes as if asking for confirmation.

"Uh-huh," she said. "I go for Janice's chicken salad."

His smile hung on his face longer than he wanted it to.

"That'll be $3.50," she said.

He remembered, then, that he only had two bucks and change. "Okay," he said. He wedged his thick fingers into his pocket, dug out his wallet, opened it, and tried to look surprised. "Oh, no." The words tasted tinny in his mouth. "I don't have but two bucks. I better put that back."

He watched Deb's eyes take in something, realize something. Her look changed from perplexed to pleased, right there in front of him.

"I just rang you up," she said, smiling.

"I know. I'm sorry 'bout that." He reached for the sandwich, but she took it, and put it in a bag.

"Oh, come on." She patted his hand on the counter. "I'll lend you a couple bucks."

He was going to say "No, I already ate, anyways" but it was as if the sudden tension in his hand had shot up his arm into his neck and frozen his jaw.

"Someone put a flyer over your ad," she said, taking a couple bills out of her purse. "But I pinned it up again where somebody'd have a shot at seein' it."

"Thanks."

"Uh-huh."

He handed her his last two dollar bills and she finished up the sale.

"You ever find anyone?" she asked.

"Yeah. He's gonna change the way we farm around here. Make it more like India. That's his thing."

"He already moved in?" She didn't seem to want to give him the bag with the sandwich.

"Probably playin' his Indian music right now."

She laughed, and he smiled, though he hadn't meant to be funny.

"Well," she said when silence had sunk down around them again, "now what're we gonna do?"

For the first time, as if suddenly discovering it, he thought, That's a woman I'm talking to. A woman. With a pretty smile and little teeth, smaller than any he'd ever seen. His own teeth felt like big chunks of wood in his mouth.

"Hey," Deb said, her voice suddenly soft, "you don't know anything about propane, do you?"

"Well . . ."

"I can't get the tank out at my sister's to work right. The gas doesn't seem to want to come through. Can't get any hot water."

"Oh," he said. "You checked the tank to see it's full?"

She nodded and then stood up, very straight, and crossed her arms in front of her. "Hey," she said again. "Would you maybe mind comin' out to take a look at it?" Her voice cracked a little at the end of the sentence and she rushed on. "I could make you dinner while you're out there. If you haven't eaten yet. I suppose you've already had dinner. I forget how late it is because I usually have dinner when I get home after work, which is later than most people, I guess."

Right then, fixing something for someone else seemed like an amazing thing. If he could get her hot water working, Osby thought, he'd go home happy that night.

"No, uh-uh," he dropped his eyes. "I ain't ate, yet."

In the store's bathroom, Deb reapplied blush and eyeliner and powder. Through the door, she could hear him nervously running his jacket zipper up and down. The last time she'd been on a first date was before she was married, almost thirty years ago. She remembered making up her face in the mirror, just like now, only with Greg waiting outside the movie theater bathroom, eating cold popcorn. Back then, she hadn't known how, after twenty years of marriage, the smell of his skin would make her queasy. Now, she watched her fifty-year-old face in the mirror; it looked like a face that had learned.

To stop herself from getting upset, she thought about sex. It seemed she could always get excited about that these days. She had even got a subscription to *Playgirl*. Greg hadn't made love to her for the last three years of their marriage. She hadn't had sex in almost four. A few months ago, she had started getting hot flashes. An old lady, she thought. A dry old lady.

"No, ma'am," she whispered to the mirror.

But in the back of her mind, she wondered if she would need some kind of jelly, now. Maybe her sister had some in the bathroom vanity.

This might be the last time she ever had sex. At her age, the opportunity wasn't bound to come up too often. Maybe, she thought, if I do everything right he'll come back again. Her face hardened and she dug quickly through her purse, looking for her Swiss army knife. Greg had always liked her neat and trim down there. He said all men liked that. She forced her pants over her hips and shoved them down to her calves. She ran the faucet, soaking a handkerchief in warm water. When she was clean, she sat down on the toilet, leaving the water running to cover the sounds of the Swiss army knife scissors, and sat there, resolutely snipping at her tangle of pubic hair.

They drove in tandem on the night road. Osby watched her taillights, thinking about what might be wrong with her propane, with the valve or the connection or the pipe. Maybe something was blocked, or froze up. If he did a good job, he thought, maybe she would ask him to fix the next thing that went wrong, and the thing after that—an electrical problem, or something with her car. He went over everything he knew about the workings of a Chevy Cavalier. He'd find out more, he told himself, ask around, see if Carl had one junked behind his house. Osby pictured himself on a dolly under her car, streaked with grease, rolling out on his back and saying to her, "Try her now." It would start up sweet and she'd bounce in her seat, him standing there, wiping his hands on his overalls, grinning. "I don't know what I'd do without you," she'd say.

By the time he eased the truck into her driveway, he had envisioned reshingling her roof, installing a new toilet (one of those silent-flush kinds), fixing up a secondhand VCR to go right in her living room.

He hardly paid attention to what she said to him as she led him up the steps (one was half-rotted and needed replacing) and into her home (the spring was missing from the storm door and he had to pull it shut behind him). Inside, his eyes scoured the place as she flicked on lights. He stood in the middle of the living room, planning renovations and improvements, while she went into the kitchen and got each of them a beer. He was so juiced up he said thanks twice when she put his can on the coffee table in front of him. Then she reached out and took both his hands in hers, and everything stopped.

He looked at her. She seemed shorter. His hands felt huge in hers, like slabs of meat that had nothing to do with him.

"You must be starved," she said, holding his eyes to hers. "I know I am."

He nodded.

"I'll make somethin' in a sec. You like pasta? It's quick."

The idea of her cooking depressed him. He wished she'd sit down, let him make her dinner.

"I can boil noodles," he said.

She laughed and nudged him toward a big brown easy chair. "You just sit down and enjoy that beer, okay?"

"All right," he said. The chair groaned and the vinyl puffed around his thighs.

They opened their beers.

"I've been in these clothes all day," she said. "I'm gonna go get out of them, real quick. Put on somethin' that doesn't feel worked in, okay? You sit tight."

He watched her recede down the hallway and disappear into a room.

Osby took a long swig of his beer, set the can on the coffee table. In the kitchen, the fridge clicked on. He listened to it hum. Maybe, he thought, he was all wrong about what she was doing. Maybe he was imagining things. He tried to convince himself of it, tried to picture her coming out of her bedroom dressed in comfy slippers, jeans, a thick fuzzy sweater. They could sit down to dinner together, and then he would go around back and figure out what was wrong with her propane. After all, he told himself, she had only held his hands. Lots of people hold other people's hands and it doesn't mean anything. He looked at his. They were balled into fists on the armrests. He spread his fingers and wiped his palms on his jeans, but they still felt hot and sticky, so he got up and padded across the room to the kitchen sink. It wasn't until he was putting the soap back on its dish that he realized the tap water was warm.

He heard a door open and she emerged from the room into the light of the hallway, a pink teddy hardly covering the tops of her thighs. The water drummed at the sink. When she got to the living room, she cocked her hips a little and ran her hands down them, looking at Osby. Her fingers shook. The slight smile gripping her lips just made her look scared. Osby wanted, more than ever, to fix all those things for her, but all he could do was reach to the faucet and shut off the water.

The quiet afterwards was worse.

"Well?" she said, struggling to hold onto her smile, her voice shaky. "Is it okay?"

"Uh-huh," he whispered.

She looked as if she were going to wrap her arms around herself, but instead, her hands came together and she held them in each other. "What's wrong?" she said.

A car's engine moaned faintly way down the road, grew louder, passed by in a rush, and sank into the night again. When it was almost gone, Osby said, "I better look at that propane."

He crossed the room, pulled open the door, and shut it quietly behind him. Outside, it had started to snow. He walked down the steps and over to his truck. When he was safely in the cab, he allowed himself to look at the trailer home. All the lights were on in the windows and through one of them he could still see her standing there. Somewhere in the darkness, a brook gurgled. He drowned its noise with the truck's engine and backed up onto the road, watching the white flakes glow red in his taillights as if pretending to be something other than snow.

* * *

It was falling fast and thick by the time he was back on Route 33 and the truck's headlights showed nothing but flecks of snow surrounded by millions of others. It seemed to him that if he were perfectly still, they would come at his windshield no differently. The only way he could tell that he was moving was by watching the tracks on the road in front. For a long time, he didn't look at anything else. After a while, he had the unnerving feeling that he wasn't following the tracks at all. They were coming at him. He almost lifted his hands off the steering wheel, then. He doubted it would make a difference. The truck would keep following the tracks without him. The gearshift looked ridiculous. The whole idea of pedals seemed silly, the never-ending movement of the wipers pointless.

At home, only the porch light was still on: a faint yellow blur behind a gauze of snow. He climbed the steps, stopping himself from knocking the snow off his boots, not wanting to wake the kid. Inside, it was hot. When Osby crept into the kitchen, he saw the woodstove glowing, the cast iron a fiery red. The kid had packed it too full, could have burned the place down. Osby stood in the dark kitchen. Turning on the light seemed too bold a thing to do in a home no longer his alone. He crept to the sink, opened the cabinet, took out the flashlight, and beat it against his palm until it came on. Slowly, he swept the beam over the room. The dishes were all washed and drying in the rack. The counter had been wiped clean. The row of cans was gone. The table had been cleared of everything but one piece of paper.

Moving went great. Thought I'd clean up a little. Hope you don't mind. Made dinner—there's a plate for you in the oven. Seems like you work late.—Tim

The kid had left the oven on at 150 degrees. The plate was warm to the touch: pork chops, fried cabbage and onion, potatoes. Osby slid it back on the rack and shut the oven door. A sound came from upstairs. Osby flicked off the flashlight. Listened. It must have just been the wind, or a squirrel on the porch roof. He stood in the dark, watching the glowing stove. Outside, the wind was picking up. He listened to it come through the thousand cracks in the house.

In the morning, he thought, the kid will come down here and make me breakfast and go off to school to do his great things.

He unzipped his jacket, wiped his sweating forehead with his sleeve. The light from the porch bled in through the front windows of the living room, and when he went in there he saw the sleeping bag had been folded into a puffy square and placed neatly on one side of the couch. On the floor above Osby's head, the bed creaked. There was a thump. He felt a rush of panic to get out before the kid came down and found him. Trying to quiet his breathing, he knew he couldn't sleep on that couch, in this house. Upstairs, the bed creaked again and he sensed the kid's weight shifting on the mattress as clearly as if he'd been standing by his bedside. In less than a minute, Osby was back on the porch.

He headed around the side of the house, the sleeping bag clutched under one arm, the wind shoving at him. Snow clung to his eyebrows and hair and the snot inside his nose froze jagged and sharp. He couldn't see more than a yard through the whipping snow, but he'd walked this way a thousand times as a kid and he knew the rise and drop of the hill under his feet.

Inside the Old House, he slammed the door shut behind him. The house threw the sound around its rooms. He didn't look up at the second-floor landing, just swung the flashlight to his right, trying not to think of anything as he pushed open the door to the kitchen, flinging the flashlight beam ahead of him, crossing fast toward his grandmother's room, where there was a bed, and quiet, and, if he remembered right, a gas space heater.

Once in there, he felt better. There were two shut doors and a staircase between him and the room where his father had done it. He put the flashlight on a side table, standing it on its end. The ceiling reflected a faint yellow light over the room. Everything was as he remembered it: the bed neatly made—he had sat on it when his grandmother was sick, playing cards with her—the smell of her, the slow rot of old skin; the matches still on the dresser in a small china bowl embossed with pink roses. The matches were dry, but when he found the old space heater in the corner, he couldn't get it to light.

Nothing to do but spread the damp sleeping bag over the quilt. He unlaced his boots and peeled off his socks. The rug was gritty under his bare feet, and he could feel the hairs left from his grandmother's long-dead German shepherd. The sheets, he discovered when he pulled them back, had been chewed nearly to lace. A line of dark mouse turds bordered the pillow, a few scattered on top. He banged it clean against his hand, brushed the sheets off, and got in. The wind gusted. Every few seconds a burst slammed the house and rattled the windows. It knifed through cracks in the walls, whined around the upstairs rooms, and Osby lay there, listening to it. When the flashlight beam on the ceiling began to dim, he reached over and clicked it off. Mice scurried in the walls. He shut his eyes and tried to sleep.

*   *   *

Two, three, four hours later—time didn't seem to matter anymore
—Osby gave up. He lay still, his face freezing, the sour smell of
his grandmother so strong around him that the air seemed made
of it. Lulled by the rhythm of his own breathing, he tried to remember whether his mother had smelled like that toward the end.
He wondered if that scent had hidden under his father's skin as
he had walked across the hill from the new house to the old, if it
had started to leak out as he climbed the stairs to his boyhood
room. When the gunshot blasted through this house, had that
scent burst out of his father like the yellow powder out of the stink
balls Osby used to stomp on when he was a kid? He wondered
if his father had smelled it on himself when he had called Eula
Geller's that day. Osby held his fingers under his nose. He
couldn't tell. He turned his hand over and cupped his freezing
nose in his palm, his breath steaming, and he remembered, suddenly, the heat of his father's breath on his face.

The day they buried Osby's mother, his father went straight
from the funeral to the pastures. He didn't bother to show up
at the potluck, didn't let Osby go, either. On the ride home, Osby
sat in the truck, shoved up against the door, glaring at his father. The man's face was completely still. He looked to Osby like
he was thinking about how to get more weight on the heifers or
whether it was time to separate out the bull calves. If his father
felt Osby's hatred, he didn't show it; he simply stared at the road,
then at the muddy tracks leading to the field behind the Old
House, then at the gate, waiting for Osby to get out and open it.

A pile of clouds hung low over the April green grass. They
had gotten two cuttings of hay that past summer and a line of
bales, three deep and twenty long, was stacked up against the
side of a collapsed barn. His father brought the truck around

and backed up toward the bales. But when he'd skewered one, he didn't raise the spike, didn't drive off. The truck idled. The man stared straight ahead, rigid, his shoulders bunched. One hand was propped up by the steering wheel, the other gripping the cable control that would raise the spiked bale. Osby could see the muscles in his father's fingers clamping up, the blue veins bulging, the knuckles going white. When his father finally lifted his hand off the control, it shook. His whole forearm spasmed and he grasped one hand in the other and squeezed until both were still.

For a minute, maybe more, Osby watched him. Cortland sighed, looked at his son. He tried to smile, but it came out more like a grimace.

"Well," he said.

He reached out and clapped a stiff hand over Osby's shoulder. He pulled his son to him and kissed him on the back of the neck, so hard Osby felt his father's teeth. When he drew away again, the smell of his breath lingered, the spot on the boy's neck still warm from it.

A second later, the heavy bale rose off the ground, the cable groaning, the truck's engine breaking up the quiet.

"Next year," his father said as they jolted through the pasture, "we got to get the hay up faster. This stuff's lost too goddamm much seed."

Now, balled up for warmth between his grandmother's sheets, Osby knew why his father had rushed to get back to the herd. Those cows were the only thing that depended on him, the only part of his life he had any control over.

They weren't enough. Maybe that's what his father discovered three weeks ago, the day he came out here to the Old House and blew his head off. Maybe he just finally knew it wasn't enough. If there wasn't the herd . . .

No. Osby sat up, shoved himself back against the headboard, the cold air sucking the heat from his skin. That wasn't true. He swung his legs out from under the sheets, over the mattress. His father had *him*.

Osby let out all the air in him on one short breath. That was why his father had called Eula Geller's. Why the hell had he been up there on that hill digging at the ground? Why hadn't Eula Geller come faster? Why didn't she tell his dad to stay on the phone? He could have run down to the house. He had *walked*. Walked for two whole minutes. He had spent half a minute scraping mud from his boots outside the door before he finally went in and picked up the phone.

In the wind-wrapped quiet of the Old House, the heels of his hands pressing his temples, Osby heard again the buzz droning through miles of wires between him and the emptiness where his father should have been.

After a time, he dragged his sleeve under his nose and rubbed first one eye, then the other, with his palm. A shiver ran up his spine, shook his neck. He breathed in, long, stretching his lungs until they hurt. Then he rose and in the darkness felt along the frozen floorboards for his socks. They were as cold as the wood under them. He laced up his boots with fingers that felt barely attached to his knuckles, zipped his jacket, flicked on the flashlight.

He moved through the house, the beam finding pieces of linoleum in the dark, an overturned ceramic dog bowl broken in two, the worn wood stairs, until he was on the second-floor landing, facing the closed door to his father's boyhood room.

He stood there, fingers around the cold knob, holding the door shut as if the hinges would swing it open on their own. Above him, the old shagbark hickory scraped at the roof. He pushed the door open and stepped in.

His boot kicked something: metal, small. It rolled and rolled and then hit something else and stopped. The bullets, he remembered, had scattered all over the floor, spilled from the carton. Had his father's arms flung outward? His legs bucked? Osby felt another under his boot. He picked it up and slipped it into his back pocket. Bullets glinted everywhere. He picked up another, and another, slowly making his way into the room, clearing the floor of them.

When his back pockets were full, he stopped gathering and turned the flashlight's dim beam on the rest of the room: a few sun-spared light patches on the wallpaper where photographs once hung, a couple dust-dulled county fair ribbons, an old pair of shoes lying in a corner as if a boy had just kicked them off. Osby picked one up. It was so small it fit in his hand.

His grandparents had left his father's outgrown clothes hanging in the closet when they had moved the family into the new house. They were spread out across the floor now: shirts, pajamas, pants, jackets. There was no mattress left on the bed, so his father had taken the clothes out of the closet and spread them neatly on the floor to soak up the blood. Osby had found him just like his father had planned, his shattered skull emptied out onto a wadded pile of young boy's clothes.

Osby stooped down and touched a small, thin shirt. It was stiff with blood. He carefully lifted it off the floor, carried it to the closet, and hung it on a hanger.

When he was done, the closet was half full and the floor was clear again. The wood boards were still stained where blood had seeped through the clothes, still splattered where the bullet had blown pieces of bone and brain under the wire springs of the empty cot. The flashlight was little more than a faintly glowing bulb now, its beam near to dead by the time it reached the floor, hinting at glints of metal here and there. One of them, Osby knew, was the Ruger. The blast must have kicked the rifle across the room. He made his way carefully to the black mass of the wall, and then knelt down and rubbed his hands along the floor until he touched the cold barrel. When he picked it up it felt too light. It seemed to him a thing that had done what it had ought to be heavy, ought to strain his forearms. But it was just a gun.

The hickory shook against the house. Two gray squares had appeared in the walls where the windows were. Osby was glad his father's room was clean. Standing there, his body loose and calm, he tried to think of what else he had to do. He shifted the rifle to his other hand as he walked out of the room, the sound of his boots on the wood floor disappearing after each step.

Outside, it wasn't snowing anymore, and the sky was one dark slab of gray. The mountains were just dim distant shapes no more or less solid looking than the sky behind them.

At his own house, Osby dropped the Ruger on the kitchen table with a clunk. He didn't care if the kid woke or not. He ran the water hard in the sink, waiting for it to warm up. After half a minute, it was still cold. He felt the iciness of it on his fingers, felt it drain the heat from the blood in his hand. It didn't much matter, anyway, he thought, and tore open a packet of Cowdex.

It had grown lighter in the few minutes he'd been inside, and as he climbed into his truck he could see the clouds rolling overhead, strands of them hanging down like wool pulled off the edges of a blanket. The engine blew a brief pocket in the wind noise. He backed up and drove past the kid's snow-covered pickup, heading for the north field.

He didn't turn on his lights. The night's squall had scraped the pasture free of all but a few inches of snow; the rest was piled deep against fence lines. The truck's tires left long, dark gouges.

When he opened the truck door, a gust nearly tore it out of his hand. The cold cut through his clothes as he angled across the field, the jar of Cowdex in one hand, the rifle in the other. He couldn't hear anything but the roar of the wind and the shrushing of his footsteps through the thin unblown snow left blanketing the land between the drifts.

The stagged steer watched him with one steady eye as he approached but didn't lift its head, didn't even snort. Shivers rippled over its whole body. There was something horrible about the involuntary movement of its muscles under its skin.

Sheltered from the wind, the gully was quiet, eerie. Osby could hear the steer's struggled breathing, the working of his own lungs. He put down the jar of Cowdex, let the catheter drop into the snow, a loose, dead-snake coil. Looking at the steer's wide eye, he felt like a fool for bringing the medicine. A weak, sentimental fool. Anger stiffened his neck: what would his father have thought? The old man would have looked away in disgust. Christ, he would have said, just put a bullet in him.

The light click of the Ruger's bolt made everything after it quieter. Osby dug in his back pocket. In his dirt-grayed fingers, the bullet glinted like something precious, almost delicate. Plenty more, he thought, and slid the bullet into the chamber, locking the bolt.

Dark lumps of shit had smeared down the steer's hindquarters, mounded under its tail, frozen. Except right by the flank, right where it came out: that was still soft. A ring of reddish brown earth encased the steer where its own heat had melted the snow. Osby tried not to look at that—it made his spine feel brittle. As he raised the rifle, the tip of the barrel shook. He wondered how his father had held the gun steady enough, if he'd had to jam the metal under his chin. It seemed almost worse than anything else, that the last touch would be a hard, cold edge jabbed into soft skin.

Well, Osby thought, that's how it is.

He steadied the barrel end against the steer's skull. Its eye never left his face. Osby squeezed the breath from his lungs, hoping that if he could get his shoulders still, his hands might stop shaking. A spattering broke the quiet. The steer pissed for a long time, the yellow arc instantly melting a dark line in the snow. Osby stared at the steam rising off of it. It suddenly seemed incredible to him that a body could make something so warm, that it could have such heat in it. He watched the steer's foggy breath rise from its mouth, and lowered the gun.

He knew then that it was over. If he had just pulled the trigger, he might have driven back home, made breakfast in the quiet kitchen, satisfied with the knowledge that he had done something that could never be undone, that he had left a mark on another being as strong as any that man, or even God, could make. But he had not.

He wished the truck weren't out there in the pasture behind him. It seemed wrong to leave it cluttering up the clean

snow. He hated, too, to leave the job of burying the steer for
someone else. He wondered what would happen to the house,
if it would go the way of the Old House, rooms packed with hay
or bags of fertilizer, car batteries and cattle medicine on the
stairs. He felt bad about the kid; he would have to move again.
Osby looked at the jar of Cowdex and the catheter in the snow,
and then at the steer staring back at him. The liquid would be
so cold by now it would kill it as soon as it hit its heart. That
seemed easiest on everyone.

Osby carefully leaned the rifle against a snow-smothered
rock. He straddled the steer's neck and knelt against it: the solid
meat of it under his legs, the sudden warmth on his frozen jeans.
For a second, he watched the jugular throb. All the time he'd
spent down in the gully with the steer, the way he'd talked to it,
given it a name—he was ashamed of that. He didn't say any
good-byes, just jabbed the needle in. The steer's eye bulged. The
muscle under Osby's leg jerked, once. He raised the bottle high,
wanting the liquid to run in fast, do it quick.

And then Osby was off the ground. The mass of muscle
and meat erupted under him, slamming against his chest, the
moist, hot scent of it so close it was as if he was smelling the
inside of its ribs. His knee twisted painfully under him, his other
leg yanked almost out of the socket. Something cracked against
his chin and his head whipped back, hit ground, his shoulders
smacked against the earth. The dark belly of the thing was over
him, mud, snow, shit-smeared flecks of ice raining down, a spray
of something wet and hot. It swayed, massive, heavy, hooves
tearing the mud around him—and then it was gone.

Osby rose and clawed up the frozen bank, grabbing tufts
of Broomsedge, his boots digging at the mud. The wind blasted

through his ears. Fifty feet away, the steer charged back and forth, skidding in the snow, flailing its head on its bloodied neck. It bolted away up the hill and Osby climbed after it. At the top, he stopped. Hands on his knees, breathing hard, he watched the steer barrel down the other side, still twisting and throwing itself wildly. He stared after it until it was just a small brown shape moving through the vast white field.

Slowly, he straightened up. The wind hit him so hard he had to strain to keep his neck from tilting forward. It blew by him down the hill, blasting sprays of snow before it. Behind him, the trees were in a frenzy. He heard a tree trunk crack, the explosion of snapping branches as it fell, and he turned and faced the pounding wind. It could not move him an inch. Overhead, gray masses of clouds churned, so close to the top of the hill it seemed that if he were to reach up he could rip out a handful and bring it down in his fist.

Up at the top of Bowmans Ridge the very tips of the branches were going pink. Osby cupped his hands to his face and, breathing into them, warmed his cold nose and cheeks, looking for a glint of white up there among the trees. All around him, his cattle were spread out in his pastures, the whole valley full of them moving slowly through the new snow. They had pawed the ground where he'd rolled out the hay the day before and the hills were striped with dark, wet trails. Only way in the distance, alongside his northernmost pasture, was the snow smooth and unbroken. He wondered if any of that hay on the government land was still good. If he scraped off the rotted stuff, he might save 30, 40 percent. That afternoon, he'd drive over and see.

STILLMAN
WING

The Deutz was back there where it had been all the years, and Stillman, who had been there almost as many, was back there looking at it. Dawn. Or should have been. The clouds had thickened overnight and behind the giant metal sheds of Pfersick & Son the back lot looked as black as the field beyond it that looked as black as the trees that abutted the hills, which were blacker. All was still: dark crawlers with their frozen treads, bulldozers motionless as boulders, backhoes with bent necks and sleeping hearts and shovel-mouth jaws pillowed on gravel. And tractors. An antique Case Model DEX in signature flambeau red, last year's twenty-foot-tall New Holland TV140 gleaming like a groomed thoroughbred, Minneapolis-Molines and John Deeres and Steigers and Fords and still, among them all, nothing quite like the Deutz.

It sat there under the halogen beam of Stillman's head lamp. Between them, the string of blue light stretched like an

umbilical cord. Slowly, he moved his head. The beam roamed
the exhaust pipe, a sickle of steering wheel, the block body painted
battleship gray and solid as a panzer tank. The iron wheels had
corroded to hoops of rust-leaf. The metal scoop of seat cupped
dead leaves turned sog. The front grill was dented and gouged.
They'd let it go to hell. It made Stillman's teeth hurt and his eyes
ache just to look at it.

Far off a car engine droned. The only other sound was
Stillman's breath pushing at his ribs. Shutting his eyes, he tried
to bring it back to calm. He settled his weight, anchoring his
heel bones in the memory-foam insoles of his walking shoes,
drawing the bond between his feet and the gravel up through
the calf-grip of his graduated compression socks, into his pel-
vis, along the bones of his back, so that it filled his chest beneath
the ripstop shell of his windbreaker and straightened his skull
on his spine. He pressed the tip of his tongue against the top of
his palate and squeezed his lungs empty: seven short sharp
breaths. For a moment he held himself devoid of air. Then, with
a long sucking noise, he filled up on the cold, fresh stuff of
autumn high in the Blue Hills.

He could feel the Deutz watching him. It looked at him
as if its teeth hurt and its eyes ached, too. *No,* he told it in his
thoughts, *not for me, Charlie.* He was in as good shape as he'd been
in all his seventy-one years. Never needed glasses, never doubted
his ears. True, his hair had gone white, but it was as thick as when
he was a boy, and he still wore it to his shoulders. The sinewy
muscles of those shoulders ran like high-tension wires up his neck
to his jawbone, tight even in sleep. He was part Iroquois and part
German, his face a crag of corners and crevices with eyes as dark
and deep as spring water pooled in caves.

He opened them now, watched the tractor back. Stillman Wing and the Deutz. This mountain-raised, long-working, hard-minded, fear-driven man. This MTZ222 fourteen-horsepower, water-cooled, semidiesel, six-thousand-pound tractor. Both built in 1928. One assembled in a factory in Frankfurt by a hundred German hands, the other made right here in the valley of the Swain, and hands the least of it. Face-to-face: they'd been like that for half a century. Ever since old Pfersick hired Stillman and Stillman had seen it out there, where it was now, looking at him with blood knowledge in its steel.

In the distance, that car was struggling up the hill toward him. Even now, he couldn't help trying to diagnose the engine noise—a clogged carburetor, a leak in the vacuum gasket. That part of his brain stirred from the oily soil smell of this lot where he had worked for fifty years. *Retired,* he thought, and ended the idea in an unmouthable amalgamation of everything from *bullshit* to *my ass.*

Seventy-one, Pfersick's son had said. *Too old,* he'd said.

Half my goddamn age, Stillman thought, *and calls himself my boss. Well, not anymore.*

They'd thrown the retirement party, *forced* retirement party, *firing* party, Friday. Cola he would not drink, and coffin nails he would not stand near, and four eighteen-inch grease pies he could feel clog his veins just looking at them. Kept calling it his last day, the bunch of them. Well, here it was the next day, his birthday, and here he was back. And he'd brought the trailer with him.

He got moving. Lithe as a teenager, he undid the pins, lowered the gate, loped up the ramp and onto the trailer, his jeans whisking and his mind churning over the penalties for auto theft, or if there was something else for heavy machinery, or antiques, or if this was plain larceny, and what the punishment was for that. None so bad as the one Caroline would dish out if she had to get him out of jail, of that he was sure. She was the first reason he'd tell them all—from Pfersick's son to the county judge—to go to hell. If he were gone for a year or two, she'd die on him. She was too much woman, too much pure flesh for one person to take care of. He knew because there was only one person taking care of her now, and that was him. He unlocked the winch, grabbed the hook end, and started back down the trailer in a thunderous unraveling of chain. He had looked it up: only two even close that he could find, a 1932 320 and a 1931 30 hp with rubber tires added, and neither one for sale, though there was a machine a decade younger and not half as rare that was going for upwards of four grand. After the idea of leaving Caroline alone, the only thing that worried him about jail was the food. He kept his guts clean. And had seen what happened to men his age who didn't—watched them clog up and die.

At the bottom of the ramp, he stopped. Somewhere toward the north edge of the lot, the Pfersicks' dog whined. Stillman glanced at the brick ranch house up the hill, at the darkness below it that he knew held that husky, or malamute, or elkhound, or whatever wolfish beast it was. He shifted a little in his sure-grip shoes. The fur sack rattled its chain.

"Hush," he hissed.

It let out a howl. That dog was bark impaired, but it could howl on par with hounds.

Up on the hill a light went on. Stillman snuffed his head lamp. He watched the rectangle of yellow float in the gray. The

bathroom window. The dim shape of a man moving in it. Eric
Pfersick. Do it now, he thought, now while old Pfersick's son
was still in the shower. Before he had even finished the thought,
he had crossed the lot and was eye to eye with the Deutz's grill,
reaching past the drag link to loop the chain around the front
axle and, climbing on the draw bar, knock off that brake, release
that clutch, put her in first. . . . Out in the lifting dark that long-
snouted slabber-jawed son of a bitch had worked itself into full
howl. He felt a shiver crawl his spine.

He had just given the winch a test tug when he heard the
bell. A high, rapid, epileptic fit of ringing. From his crouch,
Stillman looked up at the house. The front door was gone. In its
place sat old Les Pfersick. The light flared around his shrunken
shape, the wheelchair's square back trying to give the frail chest
solidity, the thin-boned arms, that small hickory nut of a head,
that black knob of a hand on that armrest ringing at that bell.

Two years ago, after Les was sideswiped by the stroke,
broken and muted in one blow, his son had taken the bell off
his first ex-wife's bike and rigged it on his father's wheelchair
handle, and now old Les Pfersick sat up there in the doorway
letting loose the nerve-jarring ringing he had taken to so well.
Could have been meant to shut the dog up, or a *Hello, friend*, or
Get the hell off, a summons for the son, or just old Les doing the
best he could to make up for a voice pipe gone soft. There was
no way to tell. Never had been. Even before, it had been damn
near impossible to nail their friendship down. They'd known
each other the whole of their lives, worked together for two-
thirds, and, at the end, Stillman was still unsure of whether
to call him boss or friend, of how to read a proffered cruller,
an invitation to a baby shower, and finally, the ringing of that

damaged man's damn bell. But then, Stillman didn't have a knack for knowing things like that, and didn't have the opportunity to practice. On the chart that tied Stillman's life to others, Les Pfersick could pretty much pick a place. So long as it was far behind the only other two: Stillman's onetime nearly wife, and Caroline.

The dog was going back and forth on its zip line now. The lights had come on in the kitchen windows. Stillman could see the son moving around in there, wrapped in a towel, Mr. Last Day himself paying no heed to his old man's bell. Mr. Time to Retire was an offspring too busy getting breakfast. It pissed Stillman off. And made him thank God—or his almost-ex—one more time for his daughter, and no husband yet to take his Caroline from home, and the fact that she was, still, not dead.

He jogged back to the truck cab, reached in to flip the switch, and got the crank going. The chain slithered along the gravel, yanked taut. For the first time in half a century the Deutz moved. Moans of metal, hoop wheels crumbling stones, the winch struggling with the load, the entire truck trembling with it. Six thousand pounds of iron and steel woke and rolled. Stillman watched it come.

It wasn't until he was back in the truck and pulling out of the lot that he looked to see what kind of trouble he was in. The rearview showed the dark grass and glint of dog chain and, coming down the hill from the Pfersick house, a flurry of cloaked figure with waist sash fluttering behind like a tail. *Look at that fat son of a bitch run,* he thought. Stillman spat gravel and hit road. Right out from under Mr. Past Your Prime's nose. Right out from under Mr. Time to Take It Easy's bathrobe-flapping, soap-scrubbed balls. Adrenaline coursed through his cheeks.

His heart ricocheted like it had come loose. Calm down, he told it, reached to his chest to rub as if the thumping muscle were a too excitable pet.

Back there, in the last few seconds before the trees blocked it out, he could still see the old war machines—a Howitzer, a 613 Earthmover, a glass-nosed B-26—spread out at the top of the distant hill where Pfersick had displayed them for the passersby. Between them and Stillman, just the light in the doorway of the dark brick house and that almost imperceptible glint flickering over and over: the lever on the half-dead man's warning bell.

Then he was around the bend and it was gone. Ahead were the thick miles of trees. For a minute more he drove the asphalt curves, eyes flicking from road to mirror, expecting with each glance to see the Pfersick son's headlights spring into view. Just the trailer hauled behind and the tractor's grill, that bold logo—DEUTZ DIESEL—in the red of his taillights. Normally, he did not like to look up at the mirror, didn't like to tempt misfortune with his eyes absent from the road, but he couldn't keep them off the Deutz. No more than he could keep Caroline's truck reined to a less reckless speed. The speedometer said nearly sixty. His normal limit was forty. On the six-lane highway that slashed across the state, he pushed it to fifty, but only because Caroline had convinced him that anything slower would put him at more risk. *I'm not talking accidents,* she'd said. *I'm talking someone's gonna shoot out your fucking tire. Hell, I'll shoot it out, I get stuck behind you doing forty on 81.*

Now, he brought the needle on the dash down to an even thirty and kept it there, steady as he could. He concentrated on a picture of his heart like that, that steady, that calm. And he

slowly brought the beating down, too. His daughter had left her
Road Hawk driving glasses on the dash. He put them on. The
world in his headlights went anemic, but it was true: he could
see things sharper. He had bought her the night-vision glasses
a couple Christmases ago, hoping they'd help her drunk eyes
enough to get her home safe. She'd hooked on the big black
frames with their big yellow lenses, hunched her massive shoulders, put her hands to her ears, and swiveled her pillar of neck
from side to side. "Hoot," his daughter said.

Near the top of the ridge, in government land, the orange
bar of the Jefferson Forest gate popped into his headlights. It
was open and he turned in, trading prying eyes in oncoming
cars for the deep cover of the pines. Inside the national forest,
the land hugged the high granite slabs and shadowy knobs of
the Urquhart Range. He topped the ridge and headed down the
other side, seat belt on, one hand hovering over the emergency
break, the truck crawling in first, until he emerged from under
the grotto of trees into the gray of first morning.

Below, in the fog, stretched the valley of the Swain. He could
just make the river out, glinting where it oxbowed in pastures and
twisted along the edges of fields. Between it and him lay the
Demastus farm. The national forest road cut down through the
beef pastures with wire fencing on either side, switchbacking
toward Route 42 below. He could see the Demastus home place
and the leaning barns with their caved-in roofs, abandoned since
the Demastuses had switched to the plastic-covered round bales
everyone was using now. All along the high edges of the pastures the old chestnut fences were stapled into the fog: they had
been made by Damastuses no longer living, out of wood logged
by hill families long gone, from a species of tree felled by blight,

extinct now from all the valley. It pained him to think of that, the same way the sight of the hand-hewn split rails, standing after all these years, made of a wood that refused to rot, boards that would remain forever, gave him peace.

He pulled up, double-checked the hand break, punched on the hazards. To get out, he had to jump. It was his daughter's truck, a half-ton Power Ram from the early years of the last decade, and she had jacked it up high on its oversize tires. Plus, the years of her full weight had smashed the driver's seat so flat he'd had to take a cushion off the couch to use as a booster. He had bought her a swivel cushion to go under her—a lazy Susan padded with poly-fleece that the catalog swore made getting in and out a breeze—but she had installed it in her room instead, on the floor in a corner flanked by mirrors; under all her weight it made a whimpering sound when it turned; he had heard it going on nights she brought men home. He didn't like to think on that. He leaped down from the truck cab, thinking of her knees, instead: his could take it, sure, but hers . . . He stamped his mind with a note to install a couple foldaway steps before the week was gone.

Beneath the rumble of the Power Ram's engine he could hear another rumble, deeper. He shook his head, once, as if the sound was stuck in his ears, then, walking around to the truck bed, pulled out a tarp, Caroline's, camouflaged in orange and brown. It leaked an ammonia scent, the thick plastic crackling in his arms.

He had it over the Deutz, and was tying down the last corner, when a gunshot cracked the air. He froze. That was no bird gun. That was meant to take down something big. He listened to the under-earth thunder that followed the shot. It sounded like a stampede on a barn floor. A sudden volley of rifle cracks rolled up the swale toward him, each one biting at the tail of the last, and he was around the trailer, then, fast, yanking open the driver's door . . . A scream. He froze, foot on the runner. The ding ding ding of the truck's warning sound. An animal cry, a bleating moan. He snapped the headlights off. The sound was furious now, a whole valley full of wailing rising up the slope to him, the calls stretched one on top of the other, split by gunfire, gathered again in panic and fear: it was a sound he'd heard hoofed animals make only in the worst of panic and pain. Beneath the crack and boom of the guns came the wild lowing, and beneath that the thunder of hooves on wood. He left the truck door hanging open on its hinge and ran up the rise, pushed past the shaking cedars and into the old chestnut fence, hands on the splintery wood, blood thumping, looking down at the valley below.

They were killing the whole herd. Down there, hidden from the road, where the pasture dipped low, a backhoe showed its teeth above a hole it had disemboweled of soil. The gouge was deep and wide enough it could have fit all four pickups parked at its rim. A sickle of trucks half-surrounding three stock trailers and blasting them with their headlights. Wood-sided and double-wheeled, the trailers were packed with beef cattle. Through the yellow lenses, in the gaps between the boards, Stillman watched the frenzy: slats shaking, bodies slamming, a roiling churn of cattle, slick sheens of blood, the whole mass of meat smashing against each other in a panic to flee the bullet storm. Perched on pickup hoods, standing beside open doors, half a dozen Demastus kin lay down a hellish fire. The trailers spat pieces of their wood slats into the headlights. The last animals left—bleating calves and gut-shot heifers and a big bull with his giant skull swinging from the severed muscles of his neck—charged for the openings left by shot-away slats. The Demastuses poured it on.

Stillman watched until they were all dead. The men moved carefully about in the new quiet, easing a gun down on a truck hood, pressing a door shut, as if the dawn had suddenly become too fragile for hard sounds. Gradually, they tried to fill the void of no cattle noise with their voices. Stillman, watching them, thought how he had always respected the clean, well-grazed pastures of the Demastus farm, liked to see the fields full of spindly-legged new January calves and the brothers out there checking them in the morning. Now, the Demastus men woke their trucks, hitched them to the death-loaded trailers, backed them up against the burial hole. The banging of trailer gates flung open. The groan of the backhoe shoving animal carcasses onto the dirt. It made no sense to Stillman, slaughtering the entire herd, burying all that good meat. Was it some dread disease? Some desperate insurance scam? He had always heard the Demastuses made it good in the business of beef. Well, not anymore.

He rolled the Power Ram over the cattle guard, shaking with the metal ribs, all that animal death lingering in his mind. The rush of the tractor heist was gone. He wanted only to get the Deutz hidden. He crossed the bridge over the Swain, the trailer clattering behind, and left 42 for his homeward road. In the valley fog, he passed riverside trailers half-eaten by sumac, ancestral homes hunkered beneath hundred foot oaks; gates and cattle guards and lone rusted mailboxes, signal arms amputated at the flag; and then, suddenly, in the headlights one bright green and bulbous, plastic deterrent against the baseball bats of teens: number 282. The Wings.

It was a home made of logs. Once, there had been five others like it strung out in half-acre plots along the riverbank. Growing up, he had always thought to take over his daddy's place on
the other side of Narrows, out near Harts Run, and then, when
that was lost to his parents' reckless ways, he had thought all
through his twenties that he would one day buy it back. The
fading curve of that decade met the rising one of the next in a
spinode of years so hopeful with love he had begun saving to
make his move back home. But 1961 reshaped his nearly-wife
into his nearly-ex-wife and bereaved him of all that as suddenly
as 1938 had bereaved him of his parents so long before. Two
dark dates that seemed to him, some days, to be just waiting
for a third. He had bought the log home on the bank of the Swain
three years after 1961, in the panic of his daughter's sudden
arrival. There had been something easeful about the solidity of
whole tree trunks, the dull thud when he knocked his fist against
the walls. The first settler homes had been made of logs. You
could stumble on them still, scattered around the valley in
tangles of briar: chimneys crumbled, doors turned topsoil, but
those near-black ancient chestnut logs still solid as the hills. In
the sixties the Swain valley was still so rural there was no electricity on that road. No neighbors, but a rumor of hill people
who kept to themselves somewhere way up where the water first
spilled off the ridge. *You won't see them,* the real estate agent had
said, as if they were ghosts, as if he was worried that Stillman
might believe in such things enough to back out of the deal.
Stillman had been the first to buy. Maybe that had given the
developer false hope. One log home caught a toss of lightning
and burned to the ground. Two more went unsold, finally disassembled to leave gaping basement holes and parts scattered

in the weeds. The fourth one, right next to Stillman's, was bought and sold every decade until the last when Rog and Arlene Booe moved in and started on improvements like they meant to stay.

Stillman had made his own improvements long before the Booes'. Over the past thirty-five years his home had become as much a reflection of him as was his Caroline, full-grown and still living inside. After the first flood, he raised it eight feet up on posts. The Swain had never risen more than a foot above its banks, but Stillman was not a man to abide slipshod ways. He had covered the entire inside, upstairs and down, in stain-proof carpet, installed a second safety rail on the staircase, a smoke detector in every room, and compact fluorescents that took long seconds to sputter on but were guaranteed to have ten times the life of any regular bulb. The couch in the living room had been replaced by a straw mat that he imagined was in the Japanese style; the TV paired alongside a two-foot plastic waterfall mounted in a fishless fish tank and trickling a soothing sound.

The whole south wall had been redone in triple-paned glass. Originally, it had looked out on a view of the river, but the farmland had grown up in sumac and possum haw, scrawny maples and hornbeam that the deer loved to chew. They would gather so thick in the scrub woods behind his home that in the heat, when Stillman would open the windows to hear the river he could no longer see, the breeze brought such a powerful stench of lice-ridden hides and antler molt that he would have fired at them with a shotgun, if he had allowed guns in the house. Instead, he would open the screens, search out the fire-crackers his daughter stashed for her yearly risk of limbs, put on his welding gloves and mask, and, bent on branding deer minds with whiz-boom panic, fire off bottle rockets into the trees. On the opposite side of the house, across 364, the apple orchard rose on its hill. To the west, a carport with room for his and Caroline's vehicles side by side. To the east, his workshop: big garage door, small windows, cinder-block walls, and all the tools he'd gathered over all his working years.

Before turning in, he shut off his headlights to keep them from stealing in through his daughter's windows—Caroline home (he hoped) and sleeping (he hoped) in her room. The motion sensor smacked him with the flood. He sat in it, the truck idling, looking at the carport. It had been empty when he'd left the house two hours ago at four a.m. when Caroline still wasn't home, as usual. He'd persuaded her to trade that night: her Ram for his Toronado Olds. Now the Oldsmobile was back from wherever she'd taken it. And beside it, squatting in the space allotted for the truck, a brown station wagon. Not the one that had been there earlier in the week, or the one owned by last weekend's fucker, or any of the other fuckers that he could re- member. He didn't use the word out of meanness. *Fucker* was simply a more accurate portrayal of the role than that inapt in- sult to the truth: *lover*. He didn't recognize the fucker's car, but he could paint a picture of whatever man drove it: skinny, shame- filled, and from a town far enough away that she wouldn't have to run into him next week. With Caroline and men it was paint by the numbers. This one had a bumper sticker: *My child is an honor student.* An orange and yellow stuffed animal clung to the rear windshield, paws suctioned to glass, staring back.

He backed up, wrangled the truck around, and eased the trailer to the mouth of the workshop. Jumping down from the seat, he dragged the tarp off, punched the remote. The metal door squealed on its track. Behind him, in the truck's taillights, a wide black hole gaped with inner walls blood red. Winch groaning, he slid the tractor in. When he had planted it inside, he stood back and beheld it: the Deutz. Moribund, cadaverous, a shell of what it once had been. But his now. He got the garage door shut. No one had seen it. No one would. Not even Caroline. He had sworn to himself: *Not even Caroline*. Not from now until it was done. Not until that day when he would bring it out, and drive it into Narrows, some autumn evening of the Festival of the Hills, when town was full up with crowd. He would call them all with its sound, show them how he had brought it back and made it whole, how for every nearly junked part he had cheated death's lot of the Deutz.

A noise. He held his breath. Shouting. From the Booe house. He pressed the button on his watch to make it glow: 6:08. What the hell were they doing up? The Booes were weekend sleepers; on Sundays—like today—their house stayed quiet and dark till noon. But there was Rog Booe shouting something about the minivan, the hospital, all interspersed with Arlene telling him to calm down. He knew married couples were supposed to live longer, but he also knew stress cut your years. From what he'd overheard since they'd moved in, he figured the best the Booes could hope for was a wash.

Their house door smacked open. Stillman crept to the privacy hedge the Booes had planted just that month. Over the too-short sprucelings, he watched Rog race down the front steps, fling open the minivan door, start it up, run around the passenger side, fool with the seat, and get back to the house steps by the time Arlene was on them. She was moving slowly and carefully. Her hands cradled her distended belly. Rog tried to take her waist. She smacked him away. He tried to take her

elbow. The same. He hovered over her until she stopped mid-
way to the truck, and seemed to seize up, and then he started
his shouting all over again. For a moment, he was all movement
—jerking and dancing around her like a fly at a lightbulb—
and she was all not. Then she started again and a minute later
they were backing out the drive. Rog put his construction site
flashers on. They whirled their orange light over the road, the
shriveling orchard leaves, the tops of the tiny spruces, Stillman
watching. Then the flashers sucked their light around the last
of the curve and, in the stillness after, he felt someone looking at him.

Turning to his house, he watched the high window back.
There, in the dark of her bedroom: the shape could have been
hers—those huge sloping shoulders, that heavy sense of sag—
but when he waved to it, it disappeared. He let his arm drop.
The fucker would probably wake her now. *Is that your husband
outside? Your brother?* And she would come to the window. He
waited for a light to bloom—the sudden battering of moths and
his daughter, freshly awake and wearing her girlhood sleepy face
in the yellow lamplight, searching the yard for the sight of him—
waited for the window to slide open, hoping.

From a couple miles away, way off in town, his ears—
sharper than that soon-born's would ever be—caught the sounds
of a nail gun perforating the air. Thwop, thwop, thwop. Distant
and undeniable as the sudden pricks of first stars. They were
putting together the stage. It was morning. In less than a week
the Festival of the Hills would begin. Behind him, he could feel
the fullness of the garage and the Deutz nested inside, asleep,
waiting.

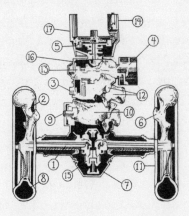

This next morning, this same hour, there is only Stillman and the tractor and the hinge-creak of him shutting the door on the November world outside his workshop. He thuds a heavy canvas thresherman's kit onto a worktable, loosens the ties, working at the knot with his turkey-foot hands, fingers steady as a surgeon's. The canvas roll falls open, spread on the table like an autopsied cadaver's chest. He hunches over it, eyes traveling the long spine of tools: cope chisel, rat-tail file, tinner's snips, punch. Lately, there have been times, moments, just hints of a second, really, when it feels to him as if his vertebrae are collapsing, one on top of the other, becoming crushed. He keeps it to himself. Pliers, nuts, split pin box . . . There is the wrench. Holding it, he lifts his arms high above his head, aligning his skeleton bone by bone, rising onto his toes and reaching as if to grasp the electrical wires strung across the ceiling, as if to push his fingers all the way through to the autumn sky above.

Outside the small window, beyond the cinder-block wall, he can see the last yellow leaves and a blot of grackle smudging the witch-broom branches of a hackberry tree. A fortnight ago the woods beside the Swain roiled with black birds feasting on the purple fruit. Thousands flown in for Thanksgiving as if to replace the leaves, then gone by December, leaving the branches even more bare. Now there is just the one, clacking its beak. Not a beautiful bird, but Stillman admires it—most birds its size die after a dozen years or less, but it is known to hang on long past twenty. So black. Such a black spot. Every time his eyes flick that way he can't see anything else. Well, it will be gone tomorrow. Tomorrow he will remove the sheet metal.

But the Booe child is crying. It cries most mornings. And most nights. A wailing that rips the air: long, ragged rents that never quite close up before they are wrenched open again. Listen to it! He can almost see the red, wracked face. Peering through the window, out over the sprucelets, he sees Rog in his pajamas hurrying toward the minivan, arms around that wailing bundle. The man slides open the cargo door and shoves the thing in like it's going to blow. He gets in with it. Stillman can't imagine why. He has never been around a newborn. He does not like children—harbingers of a time he will not know—and he especially dislikes that Booe one with its sharp blue eyes always trained on him. Over there, the minivan spews its exhaust. Rog rocks inside. In the corner of his eye, Stillman can see the spot where the grackle used to sit. The hackberry's thin, leafless branches wear a New Year's coat of perfectly unmarked snow.

Back at the tractor's side, he removes the hood, side panels, grille. The rain drums at the flat roof. Beneath its ceaseless rhythm time shakes loose of its track. The operator's seat, the generator. It feels good to work with his hands, down on his knees on the newspapers stuck to the floor by dark pools of grease. Sometimes he plays this game: sits on his meditation mat in the living room, eyes closed, challenging himself to remember where the tachometer was in Pfersick's garage, which cabinet held valve clearance tools for Fords, whether the January girl on the calendar above the office desk had dark hair or blonde. And February? And March? He ratchets loose the bolts that held the steering wheel, feeling the weight of them like pulled teeth in the palm of his hand, slipping them into the ziplock bag, scrawling black ink on the masking tape. He has not yet hit anything he can't recall perfectly if he gives it enough effort and time.

But God his knees hurt on damp mornings like this, when spring means frost as much as redbuds and Stillman still has to worry about growing careless and letting the pipes freeze. Damn his finger joints. He works the spoke loose, removes the steering knuckles, pries off his kneecap, digs out his wrist bone, and soaks them all—bell housing to the back of the carburetor—in kerosene. He stuffs rags in the manifolds and mounting holds and degreases them, too.

There goes the Booe child making a fuss again. It has fallen. Arlene is bent over it in the grass, her shorts showing ribs of fat on the backs of her thighs. She is telling it *It's okay* and *Upsie-daisy* and Rog has come out, dressed for work, drinking orange juice. "How far'd he get?" Rog calls. "Two whole steps," Arlene sings back. And the child wailing and screaming in the grass.

Stillman watches it through the veil of mosquito netting that hangs around his head, warding off hot-weather insect disease. It seems to him that for a thing to wail like that, for so little reason, and all the time, it must be full of a pain so bad nature knows it has to put it in early enough that no one can carry the memory into their adult years. He figures it is what comes with growing bone, building muscles, jamming a mind with all new details of the world. He wishes the child was old enough to understand his words. He would sit it down and talk to it, try to glean from it a sense of the inverse he knows must one day come: Would his bone grinding away feel the same? His muscles rotting? Time ripping out bloody hunks of his memory? *Think on that, pup*, he would say. A mosquito hums its anger at his net. He lets it stew. Out there Rog is trying to calm the child by swinging it around his head, flipping it. Death-tempting acrobatics. Stillman tries to calculate the numbers: twenty years from now, he'd be ninety one. In thirty, just over a hundred. In forty he'd be celebrating his century and ten. Forty years? Plenty of kids die younger than that. Carelessness, risk taking, lack of precaution: he could outlive even a thing that young. *Watch yourself, pup*, he thinks, feeling better.

He uses the wire brush to get rid of the last gunk on the chassis, then the putty knife to scrape the metal to a shine, works until there isn't any more he can do without a sandblaster. He will get one tomorrow. In the late summer heat, his sleeveless undershirt clings to his chest like an opaque second skin. He makes his way around the engine, a roll of duct tape in his hand, ripping off strips and pressing them on, covering any crack or crevice with the small silver bandages gleaming beneath the bulb. The sandblaster roars in his hands. If he could, he would stand in front of it and blast his own bone frame this way.

When he shuts the machine off the grackles drop back, returning from their scattered flight. The entire yard outside the windows is alive with them. They have come early this year, still

October and already on their way north, descended upon the valley like some biblical plague. They fill every tree. The branches sag with them. Their clucks and high swelling screeches smother every other sound. The first beams of early morning sunlight come over the thinning trees and hit the horde, revealing, for a moment, the myriad colors of their feathers—as iridescent as spilled oil— that had, until then, appeared simply as black. Below them, on the lawn, the hackberry fruit—bone-colored pits in gnawed red pulp—is scattered like handfuls of rubies amid the fallen leaves. Bent over his Deutz, Stillman works on. They will pass, too.

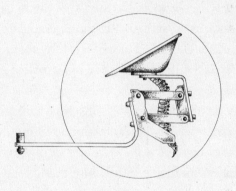

He was in the ascending wing lift of "Rising Crane," arms floating upward to tap the backs of his wrists above his head, when Caroline came home. On the TV screen beside the artificial waterfall the plump-cheeked middle-aged Oriental made his lissome moves. It was a new video—the second he'd bought—and Stillman didn't like it as much as the first. The first had an old Oriental on the cover, Sifu Wu Dong, white haired with a pointy dragon-master beard and eyes that the advertising material divulged had seen a hundred and seventeen years. His hair stuck up like egret feathers and his whole body seemed to hum. The plump Oriental on this new video—he had an American name, but Stillman couldn't stop thinking of him as Chow Young Fat—was half Stillman's age, a third the dragon master's, and didn't do it for Stillman quite the same way. Even so, he mimicked the movements, trying to feel the weight at the end of the string tied to his tailbone, and then the string tied to the top of his head tugging upward. *Shut your eyes*, Young Fat said. *Feel the toxins drain out from your chest, through your shoulders, tingling in your fingers as you raise you hands, slow, slow, like wings, up, up, up* . . . Scooping at the air, Stillman tried to gather between his palms what the instruction manual called chi, and life force, and soul energy, but what he thought of as whatever the hell kept that whitebeard dragon master alive into his hundred and teens.

Still, none of it soothed the muscles of his face, loosened his arms, like the sound of his daughter pulling into the drive. It was just after eight. She'd been gone all night, again.

It had become their routine: him doing his Chi Gong in the living room, sheathed from ankles to neck in midnight blue polypropylene long underwear, his feet kept from the cold by Smartwool socks with no-slip soles, his hair pulled into a knot and fixed with a chopstick saved from the last time they'd driven together to the mall in Coalsburg for a movie and Chinese. Two, three mornings a week she came home with some fucker she had found that night.

His daughter, a late-thirties woman whose gargantuan hams of shoulders hunched higher than his; his daughter, whose mere breathing was an epic, painstaking, sweat-producing task;

Caroline, whose short skirts showed knees like blue secrets beneath swollen flesh; his Blueberry, as he had called her since she was little, seemed to have no trouble finding men. He knew the places she went to get them—area bars, county fairs, stock-car races, roadside farm stands—and what they wanted; she had shouted at him once things he tried for a long time afterwards to scour from his mind. And still he had hoped that on this day, this one day, she might have come home to him alone.

Outside, a truck door banged. He heard her scold the slammer, ease her own door shut with a click. He smiled—good, considerate kid—then, focusing, eyes squeezed into a squint, he breathed louder to cover their footsteps, the whispering at the door behind his back. He could just make out her telling the man *Stay quiet* and *Meditation* and *Don't laugh, he's my dad.* He concentrated on the good, cold burn of the air in his nostrils. Behind him: footsteps up the outside stairs to the eight-foot-high landing at the door. The latch. A rush of cold air hit the back of his neck.

Stillman switched to "Wind in the Waist." Twisting at the hips, he flung one arm all the way behind him, his gaze following the fingertips: she caught his look on her and he tried to make his eyes appear too deep in meditation to notice the bloodshot in her's, her night-dried mascara, blue-black curls mussed by the fucker's pawing. Then back around the front, switching arms, the right one swinging behind him followed by his eyes: buckskin jacket; cigarette ash flecked across her mammoth chest; shorts showing blue-veined, goose-pricked barrel thighs. And back again, more rapidly now (the man, the *boy*, looked no more than high school) the effort pushing at his breath (his

crew-cut hair the color of Tang; his black mesh shirt showing
cold-hardened nipples; pierced eyebrow; even from that distance
it looked infected) and swung around, his breathing tight now
and all the chi gone wherever chi went and . . .

"Morning," the fucker said.

Stillman shut his eyes.

"Don't talk to him, Ted," Caroline said.

"Tad," the fucker said.

"Whichever," she said. "Give me your hand."

With his eyes shut "Wind in the Waist" made Stillman
dizzy. He opened them long enough to see the fucker looking
back as she led him for the stairs, and stopped in mid-back-twist,
one arm pointing straight at the fucker's face. He tried to put
in his look all he wanted to say: *How long have you been doing
this?* and *Do you keep it safe?* and *How do I know?* and *You give
her something nasty, I'll rip your throat out with my teeth.*

The boy pulled his look away and whispered something to
Caroline's broad back. She looked over her shoulder at her dad.
"Oh, shit, sugar," she said. "Trust me, he's fine." Then she
leaned in and said something into the fucker's ear that purpled
his neck and made him grin.

Stillman watched them head up the stairs. The boy was
forced to take them at her slow speed. She grunted with each
step, her breathing loud enough to fill the downstairs. The creak
of her heading for her room. The tap of the bedroom door tugged
shut. They were already thumping.

He was eating breakfast when she came down again. He
paused in the crumbling of his dried seaweed over his oatmeal
long enough to listen to her footfall on the stairs. Over all these
years he had learned to tell her moods from the way she came

down to him. When she was small—eight, nine, before she had gotten fat—the methodical thump, thump, thump of her sliding down the steps on the heels of her socks meant a tranquil mood; if she gave up after the first few and walked the rest, she was pensive; when she was depressed she came down so quietly the creaks seemed made less from her weight than a natural breathing of the stairs. And always there had been the rapid thudding drumroll of Caroline happy. Until she was a teen. Until she'd begun to heft up. Now, just shy of three hundred pounds, his Blueberry would have broken something—ankle or knee or just maple-wood step—if she didn't make it down slow and careful every time. But he had adjusted with her, learned to hear the subtleties. She sounded done in.

Through the kitchen opening, he watched her finish the stairs. She'd wrapped a nappy, cream-colored blanket around her. Sunlight bloomed in its bottom edge of fuzz. She gazed around the living room.

"In here," Stillman whispered. If the fucker was sleeping, let him sleep on. "Blueberry, I'm in here."

She turned to him, her hair groped into a wilderness of curls, makeup still on. He wished she wouldn't wear that stuff. No telling what chemicals seeped in through the pores, and, besides, she was plenty pretty without it.

"I'm gonna take a bath," she said, and he could hear she was lost in that after-sex dreamy fog, hormones leaving depression trails in the brain.

"You eat yet?" he said.

"At the bar."

"That's not eating." He lifted the bowl at her. "Here, I just made it."

To his surprise, and pleasure, she came.

"Watch your hands," he said.

She blew a noise at the heat, and put the bowl down on the counter, shaking out her fingers.

"Hot," he said, patting her fingers with his. On her hands, or the blanket, or from inside the blanket, he could smell something that he didn't like to think about. Each time it filed a corner of his heart a little more raw.

He gave his attention to preparing a second bowl for himself. Shaking glops of oatmeal off the wood spoon, he listened to the floor-groans of her crossing the room, then the suction pop and squeal of the fridge door. He turned. Her blanket-shrouded back was like a mattress stood on end and around it glowed the inside of the fridge, her shelves gaudy with plastic packages of processed foods, his all browns and greens and cardboard. The rustle and grunts of her stooping to take things out. Fake maple syrup. A stick of butter. Cool Whip. He watched her load the first two into the bowl, shove it into the microwave, and nuke it. Stillman gave her a good hard look. She knew he didn't like her to use that cancer box while he was in the room, but she stayed where she stood, right smack in front of it, as if she wanted her breasts zapped with tumors. He opened a cabinet door to shield his brain from the leaked rays. When the thing beeped, he shut the cabinet door and saw her loading in a scoop of Cool Whip. He tried not to stare as she added a second. He poured flaxseed onto his oatmeal, paused, then walked over to her and carefully shook the small, dark specks onto her pile of fake cream.

"Helps the heart disease," he said. "High blood pressure. Plus, it'll uncork your bowels better'n grease."

To avoid meeting her eyes he opened another cabinet, dug at pill bottles. Her bowl sat untouched on the counter. By the time he'd picked out six bottles, turning them around to read the labels, the dark seeds had sunk into her cream like road sand spread on ice. He peered around the cabinet door. She was almost out of the kitchen, hands empty, heading away from him towards her bathroom down the hall.

The six pill bottles in the palm of one hand and her bowl of oatmeal in the other, he stood outside her bathroom door, listening to her fill the tub. "Blueberry?"

"Shouldn't you be in the shop by now?" she said. "Diddling 'round with your secret?"

He could hear she thought that was funny, could picture her smile. It sprung a smile on him. "I don't diddle," he said. "Saps the body." Then, "I've got your bowl," and went in.

The metal rings scraped at the rod as she yanked the shower curtain closed. Ever since she was a little girl, her own cleverness had tickled her in a way that was, at least to him, more endearing than smug. Ginny had been like that. Sometimes it seemed the pleasure his daughter brought him was soft fruit grown around a pain so old it had lithified into a stone waiting to crack his teeth. Caroline was like her mother in so many ways. Except for size. And style. He'd rebuilt this bathroom for her—extra-wide tub, metal grip bars on the wall to help her get out, the raised toilet seat with personal cleansing cutouts, a pull cord attached to an alarm—but the ambience was all Caroline: a round black bathmat stamped with Dale Earnhardt's racing number, 3; gaudy, clashing beach towels bought solely for square footage; and the shower curtain with its western mountainscape and foot-long cigarette and oversize Marlboro Man squinting out at Stillman from beneath his hat.

"Hello, Dad," she chirped from behind the curtain in a voice he knew meant she was rolling her eyes.

He set her bowl on the corner of the bathtub.

She shut the faucet off and her hand pushed aside the curtain just enough that he could see her face, her head reclined against the wall. She looked sideways at him. He handed her the spoon. She took it in her wet fingers, but her eyes stayed on him and the pill bottles in his hand. Under her gaze, he popped off their tops, spilled one of each into his palm.

"What are those?" she said.

He looked at the tablets as if, to his surprise, some small creature had squatted in his palm and crapped them.

"Dad," she said. "I thought we agreed."

"Oh, just take them."

"I don't want them, Dad."

"For your daddy who loves you," he said, and dumped the pills onto her oatmeal.

He sat back on the toilet lid, cleared his throat. Her arm sloshed over the tub side, her hand searching the floor like a blind water creature scouring a lake bottom for food. Each time she found a bottle, she picked it up, read the label, and hunted for the next one. When she'd read all six, she lined them up on the tub sill with their warning labels facing him. Every one bore bright red cautions directed specifically at women in the pregnant state. The look on her face dared him to look back at her.

"What?" he said.

"If these things could keep me from getting pregnant, you think they'd sell a bottle of them for"—she checked the sticker—"four ninety-nine?"

"You worried about getting pregnant?"

She loosed a breath of disbelieving laugher. "You think I'd let Ted up there—"

"You don't even know his name."

"You think I'd get juiced in just to—"

"Caroline."

"—give you a grandkid?"

"I don't want one. I've got a daughter. If you don't mind, I'd rather keep this one around, rather keep—"

"Oh, Jesus."

"A," he said, holding up a thumb. "Each year over thirty-five a woman's chances of complications, serious complications, life-threatening . . ."

She had taken the spoon from her bowl and now she clanked its edge against the tub sill. A bird dropping of flaxseed and grayish Cool Whip sat where she'd tapped it.

"B," he said, "the breast cancer thing's only good if you have a kid *before* you're thirty five. D—"

"You're on C," she said, and tapped out another turd.

"D, pregnancy's tough on any woman, but there's complications when you're a big—"

"Fat," she said.

"When you're a big woman it can seriously . . . It can kill you. And E, I don't know, maybe you've forgot about diabetes and—"

"I don't have diabetes."

"Not yet." He felt the strain behind his eyes that hit him whenever he thought of her with anything worse than the burden her weight already gave her, and he went quiet to keep his voice from giving him away.

"Dad?" she said, with a brightness that let him know he'd better look at her and be sharp.

In an attempt to head her off, he pointed at her porridge bowl, told her it was going to get cold.

Covering her chest with one arm, she rose a little in the tub and showed him her other shoulder. "What do you think that is?"

Above the tattoo of the license number of the car she'd driven to victory in the '94 demolition derby were five welts, straight two-inch lines fanned out like the footprint of some strange bird.

"There are diseases," he said, "that they don't have immunizations for."

"It's birth control, Dad. Ninety-nine percent effective."

His mind worked through her numbers; at one in a hundred he figured she'd be pregnant within two years.

"It's more effective than a rubber," she went on.

He looked from the bird print to her face.

"It's like the pill, but it's time released. This'll last me—what?"

"You don't use a condom?"

In the silence he left, he listened for the sounds of the fucker upstairs, waited for him to creak or snore, as if that would prove a point he had not yet made. There was just the lapping of the tub water and the roar and honk of a truck going by outside. Finally, he pointed at her bird print and, in his I'm-your-father-and-I'm-older-and-I-*know* voice, said, "Caroline, you don't know what they might have."

"Not again," she said.

"Him," his eyes flicked upward. "*Any* of them."

"What do you want, Dad?"

"You don't *know*."

"You want me to take samples? You want me to save it in baggies and send it off to a lab?"

"What I want is for you to stop taking risks with your life every other night."

She had let her arm fall from her chest and now she covered herself again. "Risks?" she said. "What would you know about risks, Dad? You've never took a risk in your life."

Either she wasn't truly looking at him, or she was too mad to see the hurt that caused him, because otherwise he could not account for how she could go on saying, "If I lived my life like you . . ." and "Thirty-nine years . . ."; how his daughter, who could almost read his mind, could not know how deeply that had cut. Well, he told himself, she didn't know what was buried that far down. And never would.

"Sometimes," she said, "I swear I'm gonna move the fuck out."

He sat there as if his spine was a part of the commode, a pipe rising up out of the porcelain to attach at the back of his skull. There had been five times that she called moving out and he called running away: when she was seventeen, for two days; when she was twenty, for a month; then not again until twenty-nine, for three weeks in the summer; thirty-one, for most of January; and for two weeks last year. And, by whatever name, each time drove him ill with worry and grief.

Slowly, he stood, taking more time than he normally allowed his legs, didn't even block his face from wincing at the stab in his knee he still wouldn't admit had persisted long enough it might be permanent. She shut the curtain. The Marlboro Man, forehead deformed by a curtain fold, stared back with one hard eye. Outside, another truck honked. He opened the bathroom door and was about to step out when she said something.

"What?" he asked from the doorway.

Her hand jutted out from behind the curtain, holding the bowl. Except for what she'd done to the seeds, it was untouched. He took it.

"Dad," she said.

"Yeah?"

"It's not I don't appreciate it. It's just the seaweed kinda stinks."

"Yeah," he said, "but I hear it's good for the mood, helps improve the disposition."

Her eyes appeared at the curtain's edge. "You better have mine, too, then."

He tried to make his smile look like it couldn't come from a man who harbored hurt, and failed. He set the bowl on the tile, lowered himself to sit at the foot of the tub, and reached a hand under the curtain.

"Give me your foot," he said.

She had a normal-size foot. Looking at it sticking out from under the curtain, off the edge of the tub, you wouldn't have known she was anything special. He held it in his hands and rubbed at the arch, thinking *This is for her liver* and slid his thumbs along the inside ridges of each foot thinking *This is for her back pain,* and then *This is for her blood pressure,* and *This is for her heart.* Outside, a convoy of trucks passed, lobbing their horn blares into his yard the way someone did Michelob cans every Saturday night. It was the day before the Festival of the Hills. They'd be getting to Narrows early to stake out overnight spots in the high school field. He had read up on reflexology long enough to know his stuff and her voice was sleepy and soothed when she spoke again.

"You'd think," she said, "that you'd be happy I got laid as much as I do. It's supposed to prolong health, isn't it?"

"Other foot," he said.

"Well, I know I heard somewhere it's supposed to make you live longer."

"No," he said. "It's the feeling of closeness," and he worked his fingers gently over the soft, warm arch of her foot.

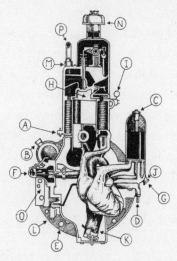

He enters that fall morning after breakfast through the small side door, like he has done all the past year, unlocking it and stepping in quickly, and relocking it behind. The Deutz sits where he left it last. There are days when the world outside his shop seems spinning too quickly for him to get his hands on it, and he comes in, and the Deutz is there like a bolt right through the axis of it all. Sometimes, gripping the chassis to help pull himself up from a crouch, or resting against a high wheel rim, he can feel it shake, just a little, as if everything spinning around has finally begun to rattle it loose. But when he comes again, it is always there, solid as ever.

He has split the chassis, the front wheels off in a corner, its bones tagged and shelved, the engine block resting alone in the center of the room like a heart on ice waiting for transplant. The thing is seized up. He's freed a hundred stuck engines, but always using the hydraulics at Pfersick's to press the pistons out. Pfersick's: if he cups his hands over his face and sucks in he can smell the years at that place in the creases of his skin. He crosses the room and plugs in the electric heater. The outside has darkened with soothsayer light, a morning storm coming. It will strip the trees of all the last leaves. In the window glass, he looks at himself: his hairline all wrong, the forehead too high, as if the top of some other man's head has screwed itself onto his skull. His breath clouds and disappears, clouds and disappears. He's heard Pfersick's son hired a woman to come in and look after the old man. He's heard Les can't go to the bathroom by himself anymore. He looks away from his reflection, from how it looked thinking about that.

The heater coils have filled with red. He extends his hands. His knee pads hang around his boots. He has to suppress an urge to rip them off and hurl them at the wall. Just for a month, he promises himself, till the first of the new year, to let the joints get back their strength, and then the goddamn old-lady pads go in the first-aid bin with the rest of the unnecessaries. But damn, the heat feels good on the bone. He has tracked in snow-sogged leaves and he squats down now and, plucking one from the floor, holds it to the red coils, smiling, until it is dried out and can keep its own shape again. He sets it down carefully, and stands. Tries to stand. Breathes once, sharp, and stands up right through the spike that pierces his femur to his hip. When he pulls the knee pads up they press his heated pants against his skin so it burns and he pounds on them, rapid fist hammerings, pounding.

He will have to soak the engine free, dissolve the rust until the thing unseizes. A long time—months maybe, maybe a year. He mixes the brake fluid with the penetrating oil, fills the cylinders through the spark plug holes till they brim, then screws the plugs back in. Long leaked rivulets dripping on the newspapered floor. Outside the windows, the snow is eye-hurt white.

He shuts his lids for a while, lets them soothe the dryness of his eyes. He is so tired of not sleeping. All night Caroline was up flushing the john, the thuds of her walking the hall back to her room, a few hours of quiet, and back to the john again. He is sure she has diabetes. He'd tried to explain to her, sat her down to lay out how his parents had both had the disease.

Well, that's not what killed them, was it? she'd said.

That's not the point.

Yes, it is.

It's a hereditary—

Dad, it's my point.

With the first warm hint of spring the carpenter wasps come out. They crawl the windows and buzz at the screens. When he was a boy he knew another boy who got stung and swelled up till his eyes closed and his throat shut off. What was her point anyway? Occasionally, he tries the hand crank on the engine to see if anything has penetrated deep enough into the rust. Nothing.

And why the hell does that pup have to sit beneath the spruce hedge and sing? For half the summer it seemed the Booe child wouldn't ever learn to speak, but then it just started singing. "Mary's Lamb" and "Twinkle Stars." Words and all. He opens the side door and peers out to see where it is. It's lying on its back in the pine needles, its mother's shape barely visible on the other side of the hedge. The boughs hang so low over the child's head they seem to squeeze it against the ground. Maybe it's trying to hide; maybe it's looking for a way out of the heat. Regardless, it's learned a new one. One he doesn't recognize, tune nor lyrics. Maybe it just made them up. "Hey," he says, sharp and throaty, the way you do to shoo a dog. It stops singing. It looks at him. He slips back inside, shuts the door before it can see in. And there's the damn tune again, right through the screens. It's too hot to shut the windows. He takes the plastic mallet and the brass rod and goes at the pistons through the spark plug holes—bang! bang!—as if to drown the child out.

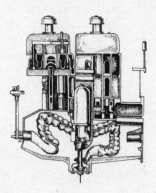

It was the rain that eventually did it, either sent the Booe child hauling for inside, or smothered its noise in the tumult that poured down. There was no other sound left in the valley. Just the hammering on the roof, the roaring through the last autumn leaves, the drops drilling at the surface of the Swain. He stood back from the engine block and wondered if Caroline would worry about him. They had fought that morning. He'd sat her down to talk about her drinking—bowel cancer and throat cancer and mouth cancer and liver collapse—and this time she'd gone so far as to snap the *Eads Eagle* open to rentals and start calling numbers. That was when he left, told her he was going to cool off with a long walk on the road. But once he was outside, the Deutz drew him again.

Now, the clock above the extinguisher read a sliver to noon, but it was almost like dusk inside. He'd left the lights off so she wouldn't know he was in there, so she'd think he was still walking in the downpour, so she'd feel the guilt. Through the window, the streaking rain, he could see her up above the flood stilts in the kitchen making the cake. Ever since she was a little girl, his Blueberry had felt guilty after their fights. He felt that old barb of shame and turned from the window, back to the Deutz. The engine block hunched in the rain roar, black and grease-smeared, like a prehistoric animal excavated from a swamp. He had been waiting to try the last thing; if it didn't work, there'd be nothing left he could do to unseize that tractor heart.

He dug out the wood baseball bat he'd bought for Caroline thirty years ago, hauled over the sledgehammer, lay them beside the engine, opened the thresher kit, took out the socket wrench, and stood there, breathing loud. He did not want to touch it. He tried to shake himself out of it, but the rain beat directly on his mind and his fingers squeezed the wrench so hard they felt like they'd snap apart at the knuckles. He tore his eyes from the engine block—*What the hell's wrong with you, Charlie?*—and, breathing his short, sharp, calming breaths, crouched by the engine and began to drain the petrol mix. He took off the head, hauled away the pan, disconnected the rods. There the pistons were. Bare as carcass bones picked clean. Carefully, he set the wood side of the bat on top of the first one. In his other hand he took up the sledge. And brought it down, gently, one light tap. Walking around the engine block, he did the same to the next, then the third, the fourth, and he was moving counterclockwise now, hammer on wood on each irreplaceable piston crown, the hits coming harder and harder until they were slams that shook the bones of his arms.

As he circled the engine, he could see Caroline in the kitchen through one window. And through the opposite window: the old orchard. In the sky above the autumn trees, the blinking light of an airplane bled through the rain. He was around another engine circle before it struck him: *What the hell was an airplane doing in this kind of weather, flying that kind of low?* And had gone around another when *What the hell was it still doing framed in his window?* It blinked on and off, on and off, a distant red spot in the shredded gray. Something in him iced over. He could feel it spread like frost dusting his bones. What kind of airplane hovered in this weather, or circled, or whatever it was goddamn doing, and why over him, and then he was slamming at the engine, over and over, the sledge on the bat on the pistons until he knew he was going to ruin it, going to kill it beyond repair, and his throat was tight and his eyes felt as if thumbs were pushing at their raw backs from inside his head, and the sledge clanged to the floor. The bat slipped from his fingers. For a long time there was just the sound of the wood rolling slowly along the concrete.

In the car, rain pummeled the windshield, streamed down so thick the old wipers couldn't clear it beyond a blur. But he had always felt safe in this car, from the day he'd bought all five thousand pounds of the low-set cruiser a quarter century ago; it was the first car with an air bag, and first with auxiliary brake lights, too, but he would have felt safe in it even without all that. Ever since he was a baby, cars had calmed him. Or maybe it was these back roads. His mother would pack him squalling in the car and drive them. They used to roam the swales and curves at rolling speed, the hills rising and falling beneath their wheels like a resting giant's chest, until, one morning, the undulations did too good a job on them both. She woke up at the bottom of a cattle pasture, the front wheels stuck in a creek, the road high above at the top of a hill they had apparently rolled down. The way she told it, she woke with a bloody forehead and a broken nose and saw him lying there on the dash where he'd been thrown, drooling out of his smile, still asleep. How she laughed at that. And how his daddy laughed with her. It had never seemed funny to him. But that was them. That was the way they were.

He drove on through the downpour, the road lined with hay bales hunkered together like horses trying to keep warm; stands of wild asparagus in roadside ditches, their brittle autumn seed sprays broken by the storm. He passed through Narrows with its banner stretched across Route 42 reminding all to come back next week for the Festival of the Hills, and he went on through Ripplemead out towards the far end of the valley until he passed the Breedloves' dairy farm, its big gray-board house

and windows lit like night, milling with all the water-brained
souls of that Breedlove woman's massive brood.

Or almost passed it. He found himself idling at the two-
track dirt path that cut between the silos and the rows of white
crates, their doorways dark with the movements of veal calves,
warm breath steaming through the bars into the rain. He told
himself he didn't know why he was there. And then he told himself that was a lie. And then he took the track. The car tires
splashed a wake. Behind the Breedlove home, halfway up the
hill, the fields of cut cornstalks gave way to a clearing.

He turned off the car. Without the engine noise, the rain
seemed twice as loud. Next to the track a low chain-link fence
surrounded a square of lawn as green and wet as pondweed. On
it stood the stones. There were maybe a half hundred graves,
maybe more, but the two he'd come for were planted smack next
to the track, just on the other side of the fence. The car windows
were fogging up. All he could see was the shapes of the slabs, cut
the same day out of the same chunk of stone. He reached over
and wiped at the inside of the passenger window, squinted at the
graves; he couldn't make the engraved letters go sharp. All that
streaking rain. Rubbing his face, he sat back. He didn't need to
read them, anyway. On one was cut the words: *Lyle Clemens
Wing, husband of Lynelle Opal Wing, father to Stillman Hershel
Wing, b. June 3, 1905, d. April 22, 1938.* The other read *Lynelle
Opal Wing, wife of Lyle Clemens Wing, mother to Stillman Hershel
Wing, b. October 12, 1908, d. April 22, 1938.*

He reached over again, rolled down the window, and
squinted hard at the stones until his eyes ached from the effort.
He sure wasn't going to get out into the goddamn rain to read

them. He didn't know why the hell he had come. He didn't care anymore. Had not cared for a long time.

Even years ago, when Caroline was old enough to hear it, he'd told it to her with his eyes dry as they were now. She'd been six. He'd had her two and a half years. A Saturday. Supper time. He was home, in the kitchen, trimming fat off pork chops. He looked up from the knife blade—just a whisper in his lungs that something was wrong—and through the window caught a movement in the orchard across the road. There stood his daughter among the trees. She was just near enough that he could see her uncombed head tilted back on her twig of a neck. One arm jerked upward as if throwing something at the sky. Then, quick, her whole body moved, lurched to a stop; she bent to the ground; her head tilted back; her arm jerked; she repeated the whole thing. He watched for nearly a minute before he realized what she was throwing: hard, unripe apples. She hurled them at the sky between the branches, high up as she could, and stood still, and then, at the last minute, dodged. . . . No, she was trying to move *into* them. She was trying to line up her face so they would hit her. His six-year-old fool daughter was trying to catch them in her mouth. By the time he got to the road, she was running through the trees to meet him, wailing, her open mouth a well of blood.

Inside, he made her swish some rubbing alcohol around, made sure she spat it back out. Then he sat her down and told it to her as a lesson:

"Blueberry, you ever thought why you don't have no Grandpa Wing? No Grandma Wing?"

"They dead."

"All right. But you ever thought why?"

"They old."

"No."

"They got sick."

"No."

"Somebody killed them?"

"No."

She whispered through the ball of Kleenex at her mouth: "They done a sudicide?"

"Might as well've," Stillman told her. "They were gamblers. They were fools. You know what barnstormers are?"

"Germans," she said.

"No."

"Yes," she told him. "In big boots."

He squinted at her. Sometimes her child mind confounded him in a way her mother's grown one once had, too. "No," he said. "Barnstormers were pilots, them who fly airplanes."

"I know what pilots is."

"But they were a special kind of pilots. A stupid kind. Daredevils. Hothead fools. They should've never been parents. Listen, your Grandma Wing and Grandpa Wing had a airplane. They owned it, understand? Old Curtis JN4. Was called a Jenny. Couldn't be bothered—"

"Why?"

"Why what?"

"Why was the airplane called Jenny?"

"Just was," he said. "Like you name your dolls, okay? What I'm getting at is—"

"I wouldn't pick Jenny."

"Okay."

"I'd call it Virginia."

He looked at her hard. Over the years since she'd arrived, he'd bought her dolls of every variety and she'd named them all Virginia, every one. He wondered what her child's brain remembered from its infant years. He had always known her mother as Ginny, but he didn't know her in the years his daughter had.

"Well," he said, "They called it a Jenny. It was just what it was called. And they couldn't be bothered to pay off the farm, but they owned that Jenny as if crop dusting or folks who paid for joyrides excused it, which it didn't. It was a toy. They put their lives into a toy. Saturday nights, just like tonight, they'd pack me in it with them, sit me on my—"

"Can I have one?"

"One what?"

"A toy airplane?"

"No. It wasn't a . . . It was a real airplane, Blueberry. Listen, your grandma'd put me on her lap—no seat belt or nothing, just hold me to her, like I was nothing but a purse—and your grandpa'd sit up front and we'd take off from the landing strip beside our house—which, by the way, if they were responsible adults they'd have put that land in crops instead—and we'd fly into Narrows and they'd come in low and buzz Main Street so the wheels almost hit the tops of the cars and everyone screaming—"

She screamed, like it was her job to do sound effects.

"Right," he said. "And Ma and Daddy was laughing it up—"

She did a Santa Claus laugh.

"This is serious," he said.

She made her face serious.

"Now, listen. They come whooping into town that way Saturday nights, pulled the plane around, landed it on Ripple-mead Road and taxied all the way down, waving at people on the sidewalk, letting people jump on for a ride, till they got to the dance hall and parked it in the big lot behind back."

"Where there's the painted people," she said.

"That's right," he told her. "It's called a mural."

"The heros of the valley." She grinned like the phrase was a trinket she'd filched from school.

"Behind that mural," he said, "in that back lot was where they'd leave me to watch over the plane. Like a dog. I know now that's 'cause they were keeping me from all the drinking and gambling and fights and stupidness inside, 'cause they were a big part of it—the fightingest, drunkest, stupidest of the bunch —but back then all I knew was they were some long hours wait-ing outside, sitting on the wing, hanging off the propeller, noth-ing for company but all the painted stares of those giant painted people, having to hear all the time the sounds of so much fun going on in there."

"Why didn't you go inside?" she asked.

"I had to watch the plane."

"I would've gone inside."

"Sounds like fun, doesn't it? Dancing around? Sound like fun? All them men and women and that music making every-one crazy? Hm? Sound like a good time? Getting drunk sound like a fun idea to you? I ever catch you drunk, Caroline, I'll—"

"Daddy—"

"What?" He was close to yelling. "You think you're gonna grow up and be a gambler? Big Gambler Caroline? Hm?"

"I don't know what a gambler is," she said, quiet.

"Your Grandpa and Grandma Wing, that's what it is. Thrill seekers. The kind of person who gets a kick out of taking stupid risks. Like throwing a damn apple up in the air and seeing where it might land on your damn face. Let me tell you what happens to people like that. One Saturday night—this is when I was ten, just a few years older than you are now—they wrapped up their stupidness sometime around two or three in the morning, came out the back door of the dance hall. I'd gone to sleep in the backseat hole, but they woke me up with their hooting and laughing and pawing at each other. Well, I just stayed curled up down there on the seat, waited for them to wrap up so we could go home. But that Saturday night they got it in their heads they wanted to do something else, try some new thrill—"

"What was they wrapping?" she said.

He looked at her. "All you got to know," he told her, "is it wasn't exciting enough for them on the ground, they wanted to . . . I'm talking about . . . Listen, all you got to know is they were up there for the plain and foolish fun of it. They'd left me in the dance hall lot. They were flying up there, without any lights, circling around and around. I couldn't see them, but I could hear their engine going. Not more than a few hundred feet up above my head. And then it sounded like they were gonna land back down. And then it sounded . . ."

He blinked beneath her stare. She was holding the Kleenex to her mouth with both hands and blood had dried on her fingers.

"They crashed in a tobacco field," he said. "They died right away." He cleared his throat. "Now what the hell did you think was gonna happen when you finally managed to catch one of them apples in your mouth? Hm?"

"That's how Grandma and Grandpa died?" she said.

"It is."

"What happened then?"

"That's how the story ends, Blueberry. Let me see your mouth."

She took the wad away and tried to speak while he looked in at her teeth.

"What's that?" he said.

"Weren't you sad?" she said, again.

"Yes, I was. Now you hold on to these two teeth. Put them—"

"Why aren't you sad now?"

"Put them under your pillow, Blueberry. See if some little fairy I know doesn't—"

"Why aren't you sad now, Daddy?"

"Who said I'm not sad?"

"You don't look sad."

"Well, it was a long time ago."

"You look angry."

"Tilt your head back," he told her. "Try not to swallow too much blood."

He took the tissue wad and balled it in his hand and went to the bathroom with the bloody thing. He dropped it in the toilet. The water went pink almost immediately. She was watching him from the living room, her head tilted back just like he'd said. He pulled tissue after tissue from the box and balled them in his hand and then took the box with him back to her. "Here," he said, handing her the mashed ball of fresh Kleenex. "Spit into this." When she was done he said, "Now, what if one of those teeth had got stuck in your throat? Or that apple had come down and squished one of your eyes?"

"I'm sorry," she said.

"That was kind of stupid, wasn't it?"

"I'm sorry, Daddy."

He hugged her to him. "That's all right," he said. "I don't want you to be sorry. I just want you to be smart. Smart and careful, okay?"

"What were they doing up there in the air?"

He spoke into the apple scent of her warm hair. "Just being careless," he said. "Careless and stupid."

The rain was coming in through the open car window. It stained the empty passenger seat with dark spots the size of children's fingerprints. He rolled the glass back up. The car had become cold and damp. His knees ached. In the places where his hair had died off, his scalp felt icy. He'd forgotten to take his knit hat. He hadn't even taken a coat. It had been stupid to come out here, stupid to take the drive, stupid to still be angry.

Unbuckling his seat belt, he reached around to dig at the junk in the backseat. The black plastic basin he used for changing oil was full of things he'd salvaged from the side of the road: bolts, washers, a plastic funnel, a hammer's head with the handle broken in jagged shards at the neck. He dumped it all out on the seat.

Turning the basin upside down, he held it over his head and got out. The rain beat above him. It was cold on his fingers. He splashed around the car, crouched beside the fence, scrunched his eyes at the chiseled stones. He tried to summon some kind of sadness. He thought how it had been to stand there listening to their engine circling above, to hear that sound change, how he had backed to the side of the lot to give them room to land. Thought about how it had been in the moment he'd known it was not sounding like he'd ever heard it before. Tried to recall the way his heart had shifted into something else, too, as if, in synchronicity with the Jenny's engine, it was struggling to pull the falling plane back up. Oh, he could remember it just fine. But he couldn't feel it. Didn't cloud his eyes. Didn't do anything, really.

Even the run through the woods behind the dance hall lot, the breaking out into the wide open field, the moon shining down on all the long rows, the wide-leafed plants. Soft-looking, the shadows in the lower reaches dark as anything in the deepest part of the sky. And all over their tops the nicotiana flowers glowing, white, luminous. In the middle of them all jutted one of the wings. The tobacco plants slapped at him, and there between two rows was part of the propeller; there was the tail; and, further on, the entire massive engine block mashed through the center of a row. He was a dozen yards away when he saw it, and a few steps closer when he heard it sizzling, and closer still when he saw them: they must have been sitting together. Now his mother was smashed atop his father, the engine block smashed atop them both, pinning them together, driving them into the ground.

Stillman stood up from the wet grass. *Wallowing,* he thought. *Keep your eyes on the road, Charlie,* he told himself, *not on the rearview.*

But, running towards them across the tobacco rows, he had seen one of them raise a head. When he was five rows away, he came upon legs. He could see, then, that one of them had been

STILLMAN WING   133

squeezed apart at the waist. The other—it was his mother—was looking at him. Three rows away, he saw her hand move. She was trying to wipe the blood from her eyes. And he was two rows away when the engine flamed, a sudden flare of heat that crackled at his skin, light so bright it burned him blind. He jerked back. Covered his face. Still he could hear her.

The rain-battered basin tremored atop his head. *God, he was angry. God, God, it was stupid to be so angry.* Thinking it, he was angrier. It made no sense, no sense at all: Ginny should have been the one to heat his blood; she had earned his fury. And yet, there he was, trying to dip into memory and bring back cupped hands of it dripping with sadness for his parents, and he couldn't do it, and couldn't do it, and then there was Ginny and it was simple.

The house smelled like warm cake. He thought Caroline would be in the kitchen, but she wasn't. Just a disastrous mess of cookware and slopped batter thrown about. The oven door gaped. He stood in its remaining heat, pried off his wet shoes, dropped his soggy support socks on top of them, peeled away his slacks and turtleneck. He found a damp dish towel and stood in his underwear, drying his hair.

She came in from the dining room, a butter knife in one hand, a cigarette lighter in the other.

"Smells good," he said.

"Eu de cake la choc-o-lat," she said. "You'll bitch about it, but you'll like it."

They worked at their respective kitchen tasks in easy silence, Caroline getting the last of the lunch together and Stillman

making his tea, four bags draped into a saucepan: ginger, cha-
momile, ginseng, and, finally, to shore up the health of his pros-
tate, a homemade bag of dried hydrangea, sarsaparilla, and
nettle. By the time his tea was steeped, she was done with all
the rest. He brought the saucepan into the dining room with a
hot pad and a mug. He had given up trying to get her to drink
tea after he'd paid over fifty bucks one year for a pound of
premixed burdock and chickweed and cleavers the mail-order
company swore would help with weightloss; she had thanked
him for it, drove down 684, and fed it all that very day to Don
Demastus's Lemosine bull.

The dining room was reserved for special occasions, which
meant they only used it two or three times a year. It had always
seemed a waste to him, but Caroline said it was the only thing
that fooled people into thinking a lady lived in the house. Clear
plastic covered the six chairs and an oval of more plastic, padded
and white, did it for the table. On the table pad she had laid out a
spread: two place settings, one at each far end, replete with their
own chopsticks, take-out salt and pepper packets, and beer steins
—his filled halfway with wine, hers to the top. The cake sat in
the center of the table, large enough for a dozen guests. She'd
sprinkled his granola on the white icing to spell out DAD and the
number 74. The dried strawberries leaked a border of pink. A tall
incense stick stood stabbed in the middle, trickling smoke.

He sat down. "Cake looks real good."

"Well, I sure hope it's better than dinner."

She had tried her best to cook his kind of food. On the
plates were bricks of tofu deep fried and smelling powerfully of
olive oil. She had doused them in soy sauce and shriveled scal-
lions. Brown rice sat in a wet heap next to a few soggy baby car-

rots. She'd tried to jazz it all up with a splattering of Mrs. Dash and a limp strand of parsley sagging off the side of the plate.

She said, "You want to skip it and just go for the cake, I'm game."

"It all looks real good," he said, unfolding the paper napkin. "Makes it feel like a restaurant."

"I stole them from the Bread Basket."

"It's all real sweet."

"Happy birthday, Dad."

They had moved on to the cake when the phone rang. She said she'd get it and he waved—a motion they both understood meant "answering machine." When it clicked on in the kitchen, a woman's voice intruded into the room. It said things like *Yes, it is still available* and *I could show it tonight* and *deposit* and *rent* and then it clicked off. They ate in silence. She refilled her stein. He couldn't look at her. He was trying to form the words *moving out* on his lips but he seemed less capable of making a sound than the machine.

Finally she said, "The thing is, I'm sick of having to get up those stairs."

He nodded at his forkful of cake.

"I take a bath and I'm all sweaty again by the time I get up to bed."

"I could . . ." he swallowed the cake in his throat. "I've seen these things you can get that'll hook on the rail, kind of like a chair, it's got a motor, just takes you up."

She started laughing.

"Well, it's expensive," he said. "But I could take out a—"

She was laughing so hard he couldn't go on. She pinched her nostrils as if wine was going to shoot out.

"What?" he demanded. "At least I'm—"

"Those are for little old ladies," she managed.

"So?"

"I was just picturing me getting on one of those things. I'd tear the banister right off. What I was thinking, Dad . . . I thought I could move down here."

He held his fork perfectly still. "You mean the dining room?"

"Well, I'd rather that than the kitchen."

"Well, hell," he said, and had to go quiet to keep his voice calm. His mind swept through an image of the two of them thirty years from now, eating another birthday dinner, this time in the kitchen, and he was already pushing back his chair to stand, already picturing those far-off years when they would begin to grow old together.

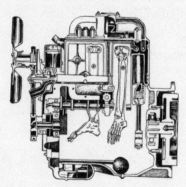

When he flicks on the lights, the rain-dark world outside disappears. Just the reflections of the workshop in the window glass and, against the heavy vise at the far wall, the baseball bat lying where it rolled. In the center of the room, the sledge on the floor next to his gloves. The engine. Standing over it, he reaches down to touch the pistons, one by one by one by one, his fingers grazing their smooth metal tops. The last one he pauses over, lets his fingers float, then grips it. Tugs. It slides free. In his surprise, he almost drops it. Laying it gently on the wooden work table, he tries the one next it. It comes, too, and the next, and the last. It is as if they had been jammed in between his ribs: as he extracts each one, he can feel his lungs expand, his breastbone relax back into place. The damn tears are trying to rise up his throat again. *Ridiculous,* he tells himself, but the feeling is seeping in through his spinal cord, along his back to his skull, as if it has been dammed until then. He can feel all the muscles of his face smiling. He walks back to the engine block and checks the bearings and pulls out the old piston sleeves, and it's when his hand is in the second cylinder, feeling the walls for cracks, that the tears come. He leans against it, muttering *Get a hold, Charlie,* and *fool,* and *old man,* and crying just the same.

Always, after his parents had been in the dance hall for an hour or two, his mother would come out to him. If it was summer, he would have stretched out on the Jenny's bottom wing, the top wing blotting out the stars above, his face turned to stare at the hall's back wall, its own giant faces painted there: bristly-bearded men in coon-tail hats, a bonneted woman with washboard and rifle, a black boy with hunted eyes bright as headlights. He made up stories about them to pass the time, loves and fistfights and all the ways they met their ends, until she came out: the hall's back door yawning open beneath the hooves of a leaping rider's horse, her shape in it, the glimpse of the rowdy crowd inside, the noise of their boot stomping and bellowing and bursts of laughter coming through the doorway and buffeting her dress like hot wind.

Always, there would be the tapping of her high heels on the wood steps, then the soft scuff on dirt, then her weight as she sat on the wing beside him. *Hey, Huckleberry,* she would say. Her wrist next to his face smelled like rose hips, her blouse sour with drying sweat; the combination made him dizzy with how much he wanted her to stay outside with him. She sat and smoked. Looking up at the stars, he watched the gray wisps of her breath drift across his sky.

Always, one of the tunes she liked would slip out of some crack in the dance hall walls and out to them. Then she would slide off the wing, pull him with her, and they would dance. "Begin the Beguine." "Sweet Leilani." "Don't Be That Way." Her neck and her hair. Rose hips and sweat. Tobacco on her breath and spilled whiskey on her clothes and how he shuffled around on that tire-marked back lot dirt, breathing her in. She taught him all the steps from Black Bottom to Varsity Drag. When she had finished her cigarette, she would inhale deep to make it crackle and, tossing the butt, plant a kiss on his cheek, a kiss that swam with the swirling smoke leaking out of her lips against his skin. And pull away. And smile. And go back inside.

To start the top end overhaul, he has to first remove the head. He stares at it, waiting for the energy to get to work. Mind-weary. He hasn't dreamed in weeks; how can he dream when he can't sleep? His mind seizes up at night, sweat prickling his skin. Cleaning the carbon from the valves, he leans in close to get his eyes focused, searching for any warps or cracks. He scrapes the head clean of carbon, too. Some nights, hunting for the cause of his sleeplessness keeps him up till dawn. There are nights when he walks out to the autumn orchard, and stands still in the windless air, and listens to the last hanging apples drop.

His eyes hurt from the strain of trying to make the lines of the world get sharp. He leans back, inhales. On sunny winter days like this, he keeps the windows open, despite the cold, so he can smell the sweet scent of the downed and rotting apples on the gusts. Squeezing the springs, he takes out the keepers, removes the washers and rotators, puts them aside. He refaces the valves. When he's done, he lies down on the concrete floor in his gray mechanic's suit and thinks of all the worries he has. He breathes them out into the world. And breathes in all the love he has for Caroline, holds that seven seconds in his lungs, and searching the cavities of his mind for tension, breathes out again. On his next breath he searches out his love for his one-time nearly wife. Seven seconds of holding that memory in his lungs. The anger, and fear, and regret boil to the surface like pot scum. He breathes them out into the world. Outside, the snow covers everything in quiet. He will sleep. He will rejuvenate and heal and sleep.

". . . cee, dee, ee, eff, gee . . ."

He forces his eyes open. Outside, the Booe child is learning his alphabet. He finishes up to *p* and then starts again. Over and over. Stillman thinks, *I'm gonna go tell that pup to shut up.* He thinks, *I'm just gonna sit up and . . .* But he can't. Every time he begins to lift his chest off the floor, the muscles of his back feel like they will drop clean away from his bones.

". . . el, em, en, oh . . ."

By the time he rolls onto his shoulder and elbow-jacks himself onto his knees, the kid is doing the whole thing straight

through and back, through and back. Did they let it just stay out
in the cold all day? Didn't it go to school?

After a while, Stillman is hearing the letters so much they
jumble in his brain; sometimes, saying them to himself, he
isn't sure if *s* comes after *t* or before *r*. He coats all the parts
with clean engine oil and puts them back in the exact reverse
order that he'd removed them. Tapping the end of the valve
stem with his mallet to be sure the keepers stay in place, he
thinks through the birthdays of his mother and father and
Caroline and Ginny. He does all the phone numbers he's ever
known, even Ginny's out in California, though he never called
it and she never called him from it. He does the exact color of
his first girlfriend's eyes, and moves on to old Les Pfersick's,
and Caroline's, and Ginny's—which he is startled to remember could look purple in the right light; could look deep, deep
blue in another kind of right light; they had thin silver flecks
in them in the light that came through her bedroom window
in the mornings when he would wake before her and lie there,
patient, watching the golden strip find the window, slip in it,
crawl the sheets gathered at her shins, and rise up her thighs
to her waist, her shoulder, her neck, her lips, and finally her
eyes; her lids lifted: those dark pupils looking at him, those
wondrous silver flecks in the blue. Reassembling the bottom
end, he forgets to replace the crankshaft oil seals and has to
start all over again. During the disassembly, he'd made careful marks on masking tape strips stuck to each rod bearing-
cap; he can hardly read them, now.

He lifts his eyes to give them a rest. Outside the window,
snow is streaking past the glass. *Snow?* he thinks, *in May?* and,
for a moment, feeling his body slip loose from time, he nearly

panics. His hands fumbling at his head, he flips the macro loupe off his eye and swings down the telephoto one. Not glasses— he doesn't need glasses—just headgear made of stiff plastic straps that circle his skull like a hatband. He'd ordered it from a catalog along with the two loupes, one for close-up work, the other for distance, both attached to the headgear at his forehead; he can swing the macro down to his left eye, the telephoto to his right, or leave them both up like a second set of eyes mounted on his brow. Squinting his left eye shut, he swings down the telephoto. It isn't snow at all. Framed in the window across the room, the white apple blossoms swirl on gusts. The sight lifts his heart. He hauls himself to his feet, walks stiff-kneed to the window. The orchard stretches away up the hill. Late blossoms alive with the wind. He stands perfectly still, watching them, so big and close in the telephoto, like a million white moths fluttering on the dark branches of the old trees.

By the time he gets the plunger unstuck, his hands are sweaty from the July heat and shaking too much for him to finish the job. He tries to pick up the copper gasket but his fingers flutter uselessly at it, devoid of muscle and bone as feathers on a wing. He washes the grease off his hands, the cold water already easing the throb in his knuckles, then puts on first one Air Massage Glove, Velcroing the strap around his wrist, then the other. Giant blue mittens with power packs that sit on the backs of his hands, they fill with air around his fingers, compress again, loosen, squeeze. Their air pumps whisper. He sets them to level two and sits on a stool in the open doorway trying to get what breeze the hot air will allow. The log house stands on its thin stick legs, high above the lawn, in all its emptiness.

It has been exactly two weeks since Caroline left.

At least she is not there to see him like this: his fingers thin as bones inside the clear blue plastic flesh. Here is the breeze. He shuts his eyes to feel it better, turns the air massage up as high as it will go. With his eyes shut, his other senses seem to sharpen. He can smell the deer in the woods, their feral stink. It comes to him on gusts. He can hear some vehicle coming in the distance: its engine murmur rises from a distant hum to a rumble to an oncoming rush of sound. Any moment it will show itself, burst around the corner of his road. He tears off the mitts and hurries outside, where he stands at the edge of his workshop, trying to peer as far as he can around the curve.

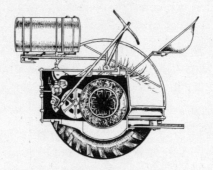

Surely, that was her truck, Caroline coming home. Surely she'd come home at least for this day. The chill window glass bit at his cheek above the cold-weather mask. She had been gone almost three months. Ever since the fall had come again, his lungs didn't seem able to get enough air down, or keep it in long enough to do its job, and, finally, he'd bought the mask—a flesh-colored thermal exchange module that covered his mouth and nose and prewarmed the air for his lungs. He listened to the sounds of the truck until he lost it in another gust of wind.

Through the pane, he could see the driveway, a rich glow of late afternoon light trying to give life back to the scattered brown leaves. And the sound was gone. No big black Power Ram rolling around the corner, scattering road leaves. He flipped the telephoto lens back up. In the middle of the room, the Deutz sat in its blur, its engine back in the chassis, the wheels reunited, but its governor disassembled; the thing wasn't correcting for changes in the load. He left it that way, unlocked the door, stepped out, locked it behind him again.

Months ago, way back in spring, the Swain had burst its banks, come boiling out of the wild woods of higher hills with flotsam on its back. And then receded, leaving its litter on the lawn: broken canning jars, pale piano keys, a hog-slaughtering post studded with handmade nails. Strange artifacts of a hill people he had never till then believed in. He had let their things lie. Now they were buried in leaves like land mines.

He slid his hands into the hip pockets of his winter-padded mechanic's suit and walked carefully across the yard towards the drive, eyes on the treacherous ground, feet shuffling carefully around the things the world had laid out to trip him. Inside the mailbox, a few white letters nested like eggs. He slid them out, slipped the macro loupe over his left eye: propane bill, coupon pack, some politician's pamphlet asking him to vote. A photocopied flyer listing all the times of all the events that weekend at the Festival of the Hills. He scanned it, skipping over the two-man saw contest, the antique tractor pull, until he found the demolition derby. Friday night at seven. Two days away. He'd find her there.

Something rattled the branches in the orchard. He looked up: an indistinguishable blur of rust color and sky, branches shaking in the second row of trees. Leaves fell. Apples dropped, drumming at the dirt. *What the hell's in there?* he thought, and switched to the telephoto loupe. The leaves shot into focus. Blue jeans. A tiny, dirty sneaker shoe. The Booe child. It rattled the branches again.

"I see you," he called at it. Either the kid didn't hear him through his face mask, or didn't care. The shaking went on. Another apple dropped. He shouted, a second time, "I see you!"

The branches quit shaking. The sneaker shot up into the camouflage of leaves. Through his distance loupe, Stillman could make out a hand, maybe a face. "You oughtn't shake down those apples!" he shouted. The child tried to scrunch itself further behind the leaves. Stillman moved along the roadside till he had the child in clear sight. It stared back at him, its face stiff with fright. He wondered what the hell was wrong with it. "Those apples are all rot," he called at it. "They aren't gonna do you no good. Why're you knocking them down? You let them fall in their own time. You—"

The pup jerked, a movement so fast and unexpected that Stillman jerked, too. Something tore through the leaves, hit the grass beside the mailbox, smacked his shin. Apples. The kid was throwing apples at him. Another hit the road and rolled. He flipped the lens back up to his forehead and, hunting the blurred brown balls, found two, grabbed them up, and hurled them back—one, two—hard. No apples came in return. The kid was a still blue blur. Stillman started to thumb the lens down to see again.

"No." The kid's voice was high and frightened and hit Stillman as unexpected as the apples. He lowered the lens the rest of the way but, before he could get it settled over his eyes, the kid was shouting. "No," it shouted, and, "No, please," and, "No."

Slowly, Stillman pushed the mask off his mouth. It hung at his neck. The kid went silent. Stillman reached up to the plastic band around his skull and slid the headgear off. "It's okay," he told it. He struggled to remember the kid's name. "It's just me. Mr. Wing. Your neighbor."

After a moment, the kid said, "The old man."

Without the loupe, Stillman couldn't make out the kid's face. "My name's Stillman," he said, squinting hard. "Stillman Wing. You know my daughter Caroline. She works at the Wades in—"

But the kid was already scrambling down from the tree. Stillman listened to it rushing through the underbrush at the side of the road. Then—there!—a blur of movement as the child darted across to the Booes' yard. He called after it, "I've been a mechanic for more than fifty years," but it had already disappeared.

Inside the house, he took off his shoes, pushed them against the hallway wall. The paint was scuffed in a gray line at toe level from all the years of his and Caroline's shoes side by side. He unzipped his mechanic's suit, put the headgear back on. Now that she was gone, he just wore it around the house: flip down the telephoto loupe if he wanted to see who was in a passing truck, flip down the macro to read the numbers on the phone or knobs on the stove. Whatever of hers she hadn't taken he'd left exactly the same. In the kitchen, her mermaid mug on the table, coffee dregs coagulating at the bottom, brown drips dried over the ceramic breasts and curve of green-tail handle. Her fast food coupons magneted to the fridge. Inside, all of his food still kept on the bottom racks. The top ones held only a used-up bottle of her hot sauce, an open can of Vienna sausage, and half a shriveled lime. The only thing he'd changed was her slippers. She had left them in the bathroom, but last night, in one of his sleepless hours, he had carried them out to the kitchen and arranged them under the table in front of the chair she sat at when they ate together. They were there now: giant, red, fuzzy racing cars with the *Dale Earnhardt #3* on the sides and *Eat My Dust* written across the toes.

Forty-one years ago, when Ginny left for California, he'd cleaned house as if that would help him to forget. It was only afterwards, when everything she had owned was in the dump, and the trailer they had lived in together smelled of glass cleaner and Murphy's oil instead of that vanilla lotion, hash smoke, sun-dried laundry smell of her, that he realized he didn't want to.

He shook that from his thoughts; it was only a matter of time before Caroline was back. So what if this time she'd moved in with a fucker instead of on her own? He didn't see why that should sit in the pit of his belly as leaden as it did. He opened the freezer, took out a catfish fillet, and was thawing it under a stream of warm water in the sink when he suddenly shut the faucet off. Leaving the fish over the drain, he got a pot of water boiling, measured out some brown rice. He took out a brick of tofu, filled a pan with olive oil. He didn't have any baby carrots, but he cut the carrots he had to just the right size. He had the entire meal prepared and was sitting across from her slippers when he remembered that she had put something on the rice. He got up, opened the cupboard, and went through the spices one by one, opening the tops and setting them on the counter, until the cupboard was bare. Whatever it was, she must have taken it with her.

He had refused to help her move. So she had asked the fucker from the commune to come over and help her. And the fucker had. She called him her lover. She said, *Dad, this is my lover, River*. The man held out his hand. *River, huh?* Stillman had said, pretending not to see the fucker's paw, thinking, *Lover my ass, you River fucker*. The River fucker had lent her a hay trailer. He didn't even have his own car. They hooked the trailer to the back of her Ram. She had known him for a month. For a week, they'd been staying together—trying it out, she'd said—at the commune on the onetime Demastus land. It was as bad as he could imagine. Not just the River fucker—the River fucker didn't even warrant describing. But the idea of that place with all its shared germs and spread diseases and communal pots of food and probably orgies going on every night—he'd heard, like everyone else, about the naked swimming parties—and shower stalls crawling with toe fungus and toilet seats still warm from the last whoever's freewheeling ass. They loaded up the hay cart and the bed of her truck and drove away. He had not talked to her since. Once, there had been a message on his answering machine that sounded like her breath and swallow, but that was it. When he sat back down to the table, the tofu was cold and the olive oil had rethickened to a gel. He ate the plain rice.

Halfway through the meal, a truck pulled into the drive. By the time the engine shut off, he was making a beeline for the door, flinging it open before she could even get out her key.

But it was Eric Pfersick, old Les's son, who stood on the stoop. He wore a camouflage sweatshirt with the hood up and a beard over his face, and he was standing just far enough away to be fuzzy, but Stillman recognized him. He forced his eyes not to glance the way of the garage and the Deutz taken so many years ago.

"Stillman," Pfersick's son said. "How's life treating you?"

"Good," Stillman said. "Yourself?"

"Been better." Pfersick's son shoved his hood back on his neck.

It was only then that he noticed how old the boy's eyes seemed to have gotten. He hoped his own eyes didn't look that tired. "You want to come in?" he said.

Pfersick's son shook his head. "Thanks."

Stillman waited.

"What's that on your head?" the boy asked.

"For my work."

The boy nodded, looked at his boots. "You still have that tractor?"

Stillman stared at him. "What tractor?"

"Dad's old Deutz diesel."

Stillman tried to make his eyes look lost in thought. "There was a lot of tractors back behind—"

"Stillman." Pfersick's son smiled in a way that turned the act sad. "The one you took."

"Did I take one?" Stillman asked. "To another shop sometime? Maybe I borrowed—"

"Took, borrowed, stole, whatever. Christ, Dad wanted you to have it anyway." He dug in his pocket. "He wrote this up. Just before he died."

Stillman's eyes kept losing themselves in the pattern on Les's son's camouflaged chest.

"I thought you knew," the boy said.

"No." Stillman cleared his throat, then said it again so it could be heard. "I thought you brought in a nurse to take care of him?"

"That was years ago."

"I thought he was all right except the stroke."

"Well, the stroke—"

"Listen, the way I understood it—"

"Now there's nothing to get mad at," the boy said. "He went as good as possible. I would've thought Caroline would've told you."

"My daughter?"

"She and him got real close."

"What are you talking about?"

"At the hospice."

"What hospice?"

"Over at what used to be the Demastus farm."

Stillman licked at the dry corners of his mouth. "You mean the commune?"

"Don't you talk to Caroline?"

"You put your dad out there?"

"They were good to him. Your daughter was good to him. They spent his last days together, every hour."

"How'd he go?"

"Easy," the son said.

"I didn't know," Stillman said and then, as if just realizing it, "I knew your dad since I was your age."

"Since a lot before that."

"Yeah," Stillman said.

"Well, he wrote this out for you."

He took the note. It bore old Les's near illegible scrawl. He tried to read it, but it was no good. The boy unzipped his sweatshirt a little, reached inside to a shirt pocket, and brought out a pair of glasses.

Stillman waved them away and flicked down the macro loupe. The dead man's writing jumped into focus: *Deutz pneumatic tires in B-26 = Stillman. Bring note Nov. 2.*

Dead Pfersick's son said, "You'll want those if you're gonna drive it on the road."

Stillman nodded.

"You get it running?"

Stillman shook his head.

"Well, if you want them, you can come get them. You want pretty much any of that old stuff, you come get it."

Stillman nodded again. "He write this just before he went?"

"He was trying to tie things up."

"He write anything else?"

"Lots. Him and your daughter went through pads."

"When was it?"

"Oh, back almost a month."

Stillman looked up from the note. "You know it's my birthday?"

"No," the boy said. "November second? No, I didn't know that."

When he was halfway back to the truck, Pfersick's son turned and said to Stillman, "Can I ask you something? How come you and he both never had no other friends and, I mean, you worked together all those years and, well, in these last few you didn't even—I mean, neither of you did—neither of you didn't even pay a visit?"

Stillman looked down from the high stoop, across the drive littered with the river's leavings, as if it had never occurred to him. "I guess we weren't the visiting kind."

Pfersick's son nodded, but his gaze stayed on Stillman in a way that made him picture how he must look to outside eyes. The overgrown hairs of his beard itched his sunken cheeks. "Take care of yourself," Pfersick's son told him before he got back in his truck and left.

The yard was spread with low sun. In it, the scattered pieces of Ball jars shone, the white piano keys like a dozen finger bones, and watching them he knew that bigger things must have lodged against the stilts beneath the house—rust-eaten tubs, the broken handles of old tools: artifacts of a long-forgotten world unearthed and hurled against the underpinnings of his home.

Inside again, Stillman picked up the phone. He stood listening to the last of the truck noise, the drone from the receiver that replaced it. Then he called the number Caroline had left. One of the hashheads came on the line. "Caroline Wing," he said.

There was some asking around on the other end and then the question *Who is it?*—as if it took a minute and a half, and a group of five hashheads, just to formulate the thought.

"It's her daddy," Stillman said.

"Oh, hi!" the hashhead said. "Welcome!"

He let his silence sit.

"Can you hold on?" the hashhead said.

"That's what I'm doing."

"Yeah, well, I don't know, Dad," the hashhead said, as if he was Stillman's son-in-law. "She might be down by the Spirit Pond. We're all pretty—"

"Is this River?" Stillman had to stop himself from adding *fucker* afterwards.

"No, this is Star. I was just saying we're all pretty caught up in the preparations for the ceremony tomorrow night and it might be a long time before someone can locate Blueberry—"

"What?"

"I'm just saying Blueberry—"

"What?"

"Dad," the hashhead said, "I'm just—"

"Don't use that."

"Man, I don't know what you're taking about." The hashhead started laughing. "I'm just saying Blueberry might be in the barn or down gathering firewood or—"

"You just go get her," Stillman said.

The hashhead must have put the receiver down on the counter, because Stillman could hear in the background someone singing and lots of talking. He tuned it out. It wasn't hard. He was thinking of how he had never called Les Pfersick, not after the stroke, not before. When Les's wife had got the cancer, Stillman had gone to work like always, just waited for the day when Les would come back in. When Les finally did, Stillman had said, "Sorry to hear about Addy" and Les grunted, and they went on with business. When Addy died, he'd gone to the funeral, stood as silent as Les. And in Stillman's own bad years, those hardest ones from '61 to '64, after Ginny had gone out west without him and before Caroline had been sent back, Les hadn't called him, either. He couldn't imagine what Les would have said. *Sorry she left you, Stillman.* Or maybe just, *I heard.* Even that seemed like more than would have come natural between them.

On the other end of the line, he could still hear a woman singing—some kind of black people music. He wondered if Les would have asked him, instead, *Why'd you leave her?* and could almost hear Ginny saying to him, *You're the one that's refusing to go with me.* Oh, he could remember all the details all right. But he wouldn't. Not why he had not gone with her, or how ludicrous it would have been: Ginny who lived her life with hair in the breeze, Stillman who lived his with it under a hat. They had been such a bad match. And he had loved her so much the worse for it.

He wished that woman on the other end would quit her singing. It was mashing up his mind.

The last time he saw his nearly-wife had been at the junction with 42. He had driven there faster than he had ever driven, and on roads that, back then, were still all dirt and twist, driven there with his nose bleeding from the hairbrush she'd used on him, taking the shortcut past the Demastus farm to head her off. He'd parked at the junction with his truck broadsided across the road, got out, leaned against the hood, and waited for her. When she came, she burst around the bend at a speed that made what he'd just done seem like a crawl. He watched her come. She didn't slow. Arms crossed, focusing all he had in him on not moving a muscle, he waited—until he saw her start to skid. He didn't remember deciding to run, but he did, bolted, hurled himself into a ditch. Crouched there, hand clapped over his mouth, he'd waited for the bang. But she pulled up in time, stopped a good dozen feet from his truck. *Man,* she said, *man, man. Stillman, that is just so, so like you. Couldn't even stand there. Couldn't even face it.* That was her all over, the way she turned a sensible reaction into

something to make him feel shame. She came out of the convert-
ible slamming her door and pushing her hair out of her eyes. In
the wind, her yellow sundress pressed against her belly. She was
already starting to show. *Did you come here to ask me to stay?* she
said. *Or to ask me to get rid of it?*

He took the phone receiver from his head, as if it was pushing the words into his ears, dropped it into its cradle. He stood
there with his hand on it, listening to the dead silence where
the life of the commune had been.

Sometime later, the phone rang. He picked it up, said,
"Stillman."

On the other end, the woman from the orphanage was
saying how glad she was to talk with him at last. She had meant
to call before, but things had been so busy. And was he sitting
down? And had he heard? And did she have any other family?
And did he know she had done drugs? And did he know she'd
had a little girl?

"No," he said.

"Her name is Caroline."

"Caroline," he said.

"Yes, Daddy," she said. "It's me. You there? You okay?"

"Come home," he said.

"I can't," she said.

"When will you, then?"

"I'm not."

"What did Les Pfersick tell you?" he said.

There was a long time of quiet in which he could hear some
chair creaking. The woman had stopped her singing.

"Nothing that surprised me," his daughter said, and
hung up.

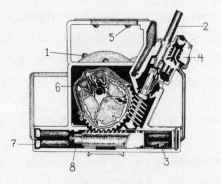

Through the westward window the evening sunlight slips in and paints its glow over the dismembered Deutz, over Stillman as he gives his knees one more minute by the electric heater, then, as stealthily, it slips back out into December's dusk. The heat brings out the stench in his clothes. For a moment, he cannot remember when he wore anything other than the dark blue work pants, the sweat-yellowed long underwear shirt, but when he zips up the mechanic's suit the smell goes away. Lowering his loupe, he starts the engine, again: it skips a beat, stutters. Slowly, feeling for the ground behind him, holding onto the Deutz, he lowers himself to a short stool on rollers. He goes from cylinder to cylinder, opening the bleed ports, listening. Sometimes, when he has been out in the workshop all day, he feels, upon entering the house, like his daughter has been in there. Sometimes he feels it so strongly that he goes from seat to seat—kitchen to living room to bathroom—touching them as if he could sense the memory of her weight.

The early January darkness makes him more tired than ever. All his limbs want to do is sleep. But he can't. He takes his dose of wine before bed, measuring it out like cough medicine, but it does nothing to ease his thoughts. Sometimes his groin aches so sharply that he is sure it is a harbinger of far worse to come. The voltometer tells him the power is getting only halfway into the circuit, but he can't seem to figure out exactly where it's blocked.

The tiny black-and-white TV sputters and flickers when he plugs it in, but it works well enough to show the video he feeds it: the Indian man on an Indian rooftop surrounded by a circle of Indian followers watching their rising sun. Stillman, in the new darkness after his setting one, stands just like they do. Arms loose as they will get, thighs relaxed, belly out. Abruptly, like tree leaves hit by a gust, all the rooftop Indian people start clapping. Caught off guard, Stillman joins late, his claps echoing in the empty workshop.

From the TV, a high male voice intones: *Hearty laugh. Forty-five seconds*. The Indian man opens his mouth wide and laughs a hearty laugh. The followers laugh hearty laughs. *One-meter laugh*, the voice intones. *Jumping laugh with mouth closed*. The Indian man jumps and laughs with his mouth closed. Stillman, standing beside the cot he has moved into the workshop, follows as best he can.

He has spent long hours contemplating the nature of the magneto ignition in the Deutz, but still—the hand crank driving the magnetron, the rotor leaping forward to ignite the charge, utterly self-sufficient, electricity made from nothing, a machine brought to life where it was dead just a moment before—it astounds him.

Cocktail laugh, the Indian voice says. *Spastic roar*. "Train Laughter" strengthens the muscles of the hands. "Bird Laughter," the entire body. On the promotional segment, people speak joyfully to Stillman of improved sleep, better breathing, joints miraculously healed. *Our son was hit by a truck,* a beaming couple says. *He was paralyzed from the neck down, a vegetable. Now look at him.* And he is there, laughing "Charlie Chaplin Laugh," walking around and around, his booming voice filling the workshop air. Dr. Kataria himself speaks to the neuroscience, shouts, *Lift your hands and say, Yes! I am the happiest person in this world!*

"Yes!" Stillman shouts. "I am the happiest person in this world!"

His hands are still raised, his face beaming, when he sees his blurred reflection in the window: young and healthy and beautiful as a boy's. Then it slips away and he realizes the Booe child has been looking in at him the whole time.

And the next red sunset the Booe child is in the window again, beaming, hands raised. And every evening after that, at exactly this time, watching, mimicking.

"Ayiye, ayiye, hasya darbar mein ayiye," Stillman chants with the others on the screen.

"Ayiye, ayiye, hasya darbar mein ayiye," he can hear the Booe child say.

And Stillman is circling the Deutz, arms and hands spread like wings, the muscles of his face strained with trying to get "Bird Laughter" right.

Sometimes, at the end of these spring-stretched days, he cannot remember what he has worked on on the Deutz. He stands in his insect-net hat, the hot breeze from the window fan stirring the mesh against his cheeks, and stares hard at the tractor, trying to recall each task of the past hour, of the one before that, as far back as he can. He spends all day splitting the Deutz at the bell housing, propping one half on blocks, sitting in the

last light with his loupe over his eye, smiling in wonder at how
well the throw-out bearing has lasted—no discoloration, or
looseness, or . . . Gradually it comes to him that he replaced it
the week before. Sometimes the redness of sunset comes upon
him through the window and he looks up, as surprised as if it
were a person who had crept in and touched him with a finger. Some days the sound of the mailman's truck is his only
company.

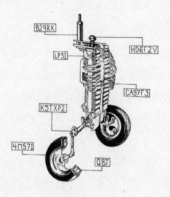

He had the front of the tractor lifted and was trying to figure
out whether it was the kingpin or the front wheel bearing at fault
for the looseness of free play, when he realized it was his birthday. He went to the calendar on the wall and flipped the month.
On the November picture, a loggerhead shrike stared back at
him: the butcher-bird, black streak across its eye, beak hooked
meanly. It was one of his least favorites. When he was younger
and walked more, he used to come upon shrike prey—a half-
gnawed mouse, a warbler with its yellow chest spilling bloody
meat—hooked on barbed wire where the bird had stored it for
a later feast. Pathetic beast, he always thought, the way it packed

as much viciousness as it could in its three short years, as if to stick a thumb in the eye of the God that had given it a lifespan shorter than almost any other. It was the fourth year of the decade. He was seventy-five.

Leaving the workshop for the first time that day—perhaps for the first time since yesterday or the day before; he couldn't be sure—he lifted the yellow, unscrewed mop handle off the wall where he had left it leaning whenever he'd last walked from the house to the shop, and, using it to take some of the weight off his bad knee, he made his way slowly down to the end of the drive.

The mailbox was stuffed full, as if he hadn't checked it in a month. He wondered if he hadn't. The dusk light was too poor for him to make out even the larger printed addresses without the loupe, so he put the lens over his eye and turned the pile of mail over to begin with the oldest. He was almost at today when he came across the photo. His daughter had mailed it like a postcard, but it was just a glossy four-by-six, too thin; it had been bent across the middle. On the plasticy back, she had written in smeared pen: *I am so happy! I hope your proud! Love, Blueberry*. He turned it over. It was a picture of the demolition derby site behind the elementary school in Narrows. The Festival of the Hills must have already passed, he thought. It must have gone by a couple days ago. In the picture: a plywood stage, Caroline standing on it, Russell Arbogast putting his hands around her neck. She looked different. No thinner, but something about her skin seemed to shine. Her shoulders weren't in their usual slump. For a moment, he wondered if she was finally wearing the support bra he'd gotten her years ago for her posture, the one with the magnets along the vertebrae to make the circulation flow, but, no, he could see it wasn't anything she had on; it was something in her that threw her shoulders back on its own. Her hair was in braids, draped down her chest with feathers tied to their ends. She held a motorcycle helmet in one arm. Behind her smoked the wrecks of demolished cars. The thing Russell Arbogast was holding at her neck looked like a medal. Through the macro loupe, Stillman peered at the giant close-up of her face. He had not talked to her in a year.

When he went back to the workshop, he was filled with a sudden, overpowering need to show her the tractor. It sat there on its iron hoops of wheels, nearly ready, but not for hardtop road, not without the tires Les had stored in the belly of his plane. In his mind, Stillman could see how it would be: him driving up to her on those new tires on the new hardtop they'd put down through town, the rumbling Deutz agleam with new paint, her eyes opening wide. He would say to her, *I am so proud of you.* And she would say, *Is that what you've been working on all these years?* He would beam. *It's beautiful,* she would say in the breathy way she did when she was shocked beyond the sarcasm she usually held in reserve. *It's yours,* he would tell her. He could almost feel the expansiveness of her arms.

Through the early dusk the Toronado rolled the gravel road, wending alongside the Swain, trailer rattling on its single axle behind, and Stillman at the wheel. Both loupes were shoved up on his brow and he was leaning forward, chest almost hitting the steering wheel, squinting to make out the blur of road just before it rushed under the nose of the heavy old car. Its headlights swept the roil of river below, then showed the spilled dirt spread out on the asphalt: the Jefferson Forest Road.

He took it alongside the old Damastus land up toward the
dark ridgetop woods, the pines peering down from their looming granite slabs. Halfway up, he stopped. The empty trailer sat
in the quiet wake of its rattle. His taillights painted it blood red
in the rearview, and behind that, the cattle guard, its wide ribs
red, the gaps between them dark as grave holes after a rain. In
front, the headlights showed briar snarls and black bodies of red
cedars grown big as steers a month from slaughter.

He got out. Left the engine running. The growth was thicker
than it had been years before, but he pushed his way through
to the chestnut fence until he could see the swale below. Only a
few pieces of the fence line still stood in place, a lone unrotted
post leaning towards collapse, a cross plank hanging on with
rusted nails, its other end slanting down to dirt. In the tangle of
ground briars and grass, the old hill-people-hewn boards lay
scattered like the skeleton of a creature long forgotten by the
world, the chestnut still solid, the wood black as wet nut husks,
enduring as bones, undone by the irresolution of nails, the craven-
ness of dirt.

He stood over where the fence had once stood, looking
down at where the Demastus farm used to be. A wide distance
of blurred dusk. He swung down the telephoto loupe and peered
at the scene below. The lens exaggerated every movement of his
head, the world shivering and shaking, but he could make out
dim shapes in the dim fields: the old two-story, double-porched
Damastus home had been engulfed in what the commune people
had done. They had attached structures to it, all kinds from plywood shacks to double-story brick. The additions crept outward
from all sides, wending their way along the land wherever they

found it flattest. Strings of colored flags ran roof to roof, flapping frantically at the wind like birds snagged in a tangle of net.
Down by the road there were tepees. The dark rectangles of
cultivated fields, the metallic glints of two dozen trucks, cars,
vans, even a bus. Three tractors stood too far away and dimly
seen for him to guess their make.

The sounds of all those people drifted up to him from the
lit windows, homey sounds that conjured scents of soup pots
and fresh bread, and he realized how little he'd seen people the
past year. A nod in a grocery store. Someone pushing conversation at him as he filled up with gas. Still, it seemed more
natural than this. These were a strange people who lived down
there, a people not of this land, not of this valley. This valley was
a place of homes scattered far from homes, and meant to be that
way, of lives built around cattle more than conversation, timed
to rhythms of the crops, not the need to keep pace with other
people's heartbeats. This was a place where people knew how
to keep apart. No wonder, Stillman thought, these commune
kinds could call a place both hospice and home and go on living there with all those incurables shuttled in to die. They must
just be used to it, the way they were used to knowing a half
hundred people's smells, to hearing night sounds of neighbors
through the walls.

He'd read the *Eads Eagle*, knew how the entire county was
whispering its concern. Not just about the old folks dying there
—though three had died in the last year—but about the kids.
Two infants had passed away. A toddler had been hospitalized
and might go, too. Even the adults suffered sicknesses in waves
of plague. And his daughter was among them. It made his insides squirm. But he could see how she'd gotten there. All her

life it had seemed she was trying to do the worst to herself that she could. Now she probably had. He wondered if she had ever peered in the windows of his workshop, ever seen the Deutz sitting there—how cared for it was, how nursed over—wondered if when he brought it to her now it would be enough.

Overhead, geese were coming in. He listened to their calls. It was a sound he loved: another year keeping the pulse of the ones that had passed before, promising the same for the next year to come. He liked to think they were the exact same geese— they could live for almost thirty years—liked to think maybe they knew him, too. Scanning with his telephoto loupe, he watched them land. One by one they broke the stillness of the pond, shook it to noisy life. Strange, though: he didn't remember a pond there. The commune people must have excavated it, but it showed no sign of recent digging. The saplings at the water edge looked older than the commune itself, four or five years at least. Some part of his memory sent the roar of a backhoe echoing in his skull. The thunder of rifle fire. The screams of the cows. It had been right there, where the water was now. Did they know about it, the communal people? Had he ever told Caroline? He watched the gray geese draw their glinting wakes across the gray canvas of the pond. Beneath the soles of his shoes he could feel one of the last old chestnut boards crumbling.

It was fully dusk when he pulled in behind the giant gray shapes of the Pfersick garages. Everything was the same. The tractors and the backhoes and the bulldozers. The hill behind rising black as ever. And against the darkening sky: the shapes of those old war machines.

He drove the rutted track through the field and up the rise, the grass scraping the car's belly, drove past the howitzer, the earthmover, until he was beside the rusted hulk of the B-26. He shut the engine off, exchanged his loupes for his head lamp, and got out. It was cold and nearly dark. The wind moaned around the fuselage of the plane. Beneath it, Stillman could just make out the crying of that wolfish dog. It must be twelve, thirteen years old, he thought. And yet listen to it! A howl to turn his marrow cold.

Gingerly, he walked towards the bomber's high flank. A huge wing sliced overhead. He ducked beneath the dark mass on an engine and, to steady his balance, took hold of a propeller blade. It was thick as the edge of his palm and wider than his thigh. He had forgotten how huge these machines were. Room inside for a group of men and all that cargo and the bombs. The tires came up to his waist. He gripped their cold rubber to take some weight off his thighs, forced his back to bend, got under the plane's belly. His legs were shaking by the time he stood up into the blackness of the hatch. He took hold of the metal and, with a grunt, hauled himself up.

Inside, it was so black the dusk behind cockpit glass seemed to glow blue from outside light. He switched on the head lamp. The beam was as unsteady as his breath. His lungs made a noise like he had torn something loose in them. It echoed. In the beam, he could just make out blurred shapes and he moved among them, remembering them by touch more than sight: the upholstery on the seats, crumbled to dust; the drooping wires that once carried the voices of the men; fire extinguisher; door to the bombing bay. He opened it. Inside, a world of old tractor parts: PTO shafts, radiators, fenders, and there, towards the back, the tires. For a half hour, he worked to free them. When he opened the cargo door, the metal fell away, his headlight beam showing a sudden swirl of wind-whipped grass. He rolled a tire out. It fell with a thud, smashed the grass flat. He had rolled out the second and was about to lower himself after them when a sound stopped him.

At first he thought it was the dog. But it was too high-pitched and steady for a howl. The longer he listened, the closer it sounded. He stood straight up: it was coming from the plane. The stored parts glinted in his head lamp light. It came from further forward. From the cockpit.

He made his way back through the bay, the transport room, and stooping into the cockpit stood beneath the arced ceiling of glass, his hands on the backs of the empty pilots' seats, listening. He couldn't hear anything but that ringing now. Maybe, he thought, it was whistling through the glass above his head. He crouched to get away from it. But it was only louder down there. Directly in front of him gaped the crawl space to the nose gun, dim blue glow leaking in through the half sphere of gunner's glass. There—it was coming from there. He got down and crawled. The dome opened up around him: a translucent bubble suspended in the air. On his knees, he swept his lamp beam over the ground below. The grass swirled, slapping at the barrel of the machine gun, almost reaching to the glass beneath his pressed flat palms, his knees. He imagined, for a moment, that this must be what it would look like if you could freeze the second before a plane touched down, if you could stop time right at the moment of the fastest rush before the wheels hit the ground. In his shaking beam, a crack in the dome caught the light and glared its streak across the world outside the glass. Through a missing pane Stillman could feel the wind; it stirred a strand of his hair; he could hear it moan. And on that moan was the dog's distant howl, still. And beneath that howl: the ringing of the bell. Ring ring. Ring ring. Over and over, from way down there in the dark brick block of Les Pfersick's old home. Listening to it, he suddenly felt watched. From outside the plane, his head lamp would make the half globe of glass at the nose glow like a firefly atop the hill, and show him in it, scrunched up like a child in a womb. He shut the head lamp off. But still, he could feel dead Pfersick out there in the night, watching him, knowing his fear. Crouched there in the tight glass bowl at the nose of the plane, steeping in the acrid smell of his own body, he hated them, then. Not for their reckless, wild ways, not for leaving him when he was so young, not for any of the simple things that were a part of who they had been. But for how all of it had shaped him—for how he had *let* it shape him—his shape that had driven the course of his life that had shaped his Caroline, too, he knew, in just as hurtful a way.

The Booe child found him. The Toronado, stopped in the middle of the bridge. The Swain gurgling below. It was night.

The kid seemed to come out of nowhere. One moment, Stillman was sitting behind the wheel, staring at the rain shredding the headlights. The next, the child was there in the brights. It was wearing a green plastic trash bag that reached all the way to its feet and yellow dishwashing gloves that came up to its elbows. In one glove it held a flashlight. In the other, a long black pipe. Its head, jutting from a hole in the top of the bag, was covered by a red plastic fireman's hat. The number on the front gleamed in the headlights.

The child stood there as if it was as surprised to see Stillman as Stillman was to see it. Then it walked around to the passenger door, opened it up, and got in. It slung a backpack onto the middle of the seat, put the long black pole between them. They sat in silence.

"You want to see what I got?" the child said.

"Where did you come from?" Stillman asked.

The child pointed at the river. "You want to see what I got in my bag?"

"How long have I been sitting here?" Stillman said.

The child shrugged.

Stillman peered at it. It was mostly blur. "What are you doing out? This late, in the rain."

The child unzipped its backpack and held it up to Stillman. The backpack smelled like river mud and giblets dug out of the cavities of chickens. Something in there let out a feeble, horrible croak. Peering close, lowering the loupe, Stillman could just make out the glint of frog eyes before he jerked back at the smell.

"Most of them are dead," the child said. It jiggled the long black pipe. "I got them with this. It's my dad's. He taught me how to use it." It slid something out of the pipe: a long silver dart. "I bet there's a hundred in there. If you take me home, I'll give you some."

They sat in silence.

"I don't know how," Stillman said. He could feel the child looking at him.

"You don't know how to drive?"

"Oh, come on," Stillman said. "This is my car. I bought it in 1976."

They sat in silence again. In the child's backpack, one of the speared frogs let out a noise like air being squeezed from a bag.

After a long while, Stillman asked, "Is it upriver or down-river?" After a while longer, he said, "Well?" And then he said, "Where. My . . . your home. I can't remember where it is."

The child pointed up the road. Stillman eased the car that way. For a minute, he rolled it forward. Then he stopped. He leaned close to the windshield, rolled the car forward again till he lost sight of the edges of the road and had to stop once more. The child was staring at him.

"You can get out and walk if you want," Stillman said.

"Are you blind?" the child asked.

"It's dark," Stillman said. "And it's raining."

"My dad wears glasses when he—"

"Your daddy's half my age."

Stillman crept the car forward again and the child said, "We're going in the ditch!" and Stillman slammed the breaks.

"Gotcha," the child said.

Stillman glared at it.

"Hey," it said, and then was pushing Stillman's arms aside, climbing on top of his thighs. The wet plastic bag smeared his chest and cheek. The brim of the fireman's hat cracked him across the forehead.

"Okay," the kid said. "Let's go."

"Can you see?" Stillman asked.

"I'm five," it said.

Slowly, watching the back of the child's head, Stillman gave the car a little gas. They rolled forward. It was a strange feeling to move all those tons and shut his eyes. "You know what you smell like?" the child said.

Stillman's teeth were clenched too hard to let him answer, even if he'd wanted to.

"My grandpa," the child told him. "Only older."

"No older than you," Stillman tells it.

The Deutz doesn't answer back.

While he was crossing the yard, returning from a bathroom trip, the wet breath in his beard froze; now, he feels it dripping down his neck. He has already sandblasted the cast iron. The Deutz's skeleton looks back at him like it wants its flesh retuned. He has all the sheet metal lined up and he puts on the breathing mask and goggles and loupes and heavy gloves and gets out the Mar-Hyde Tal-Strip II. It's a thing so strong they use it on aircraft metal and when he slathers it on he can almost hear the paint squeal.

No—he smiles at himself—that's the sound of the geese. He pauses in his scraping. Their calls come from the south, then are directly overhead, and he listens for long minutes until they have passed on north. Then he scrapes off all the paint, wipes it with lacquer thinner, searching for putty someone might have used years ago in an attempt to cover up the faults.

Outside, the small bright chirps of the peepers do to the summer night what the fireflies in the orchard do to the air. He can hardly hear them through the high constant tone that seems forever humming in his skull. He shakes his head, as if he could shake the tinnitus out; it would fall like a fly to the floor, buzzing on its back, legs paddling.

But all he can do is lay himself down on the cot, turn on his side. He slides the collecting plate above his ear. Slipping the linen and beeswax cone into the hole that leads to his ear canal, he lights the candlewick and—aroma of jojoba and honey—waits for the vacuum to drain his ear of pressure and pain, to sharpen his sense of smell, give him back his balance, clear his eyes, purify his blood, open the spiritual centers of the auric bodies, and all the other things the package claims to do along with get rid of the damn ringing in his ears.

He is lying there with his eyes shut when he hears a knock at the door. By the time he has opened them, the Booe child has come in.

"Go out," he commands.

"You forgot to lock," it says.

He flicks his eyes to the blurry Deutz. "Get out right now. And shut the door."

"What's in your ear?"

"You didn't see anything."

"What's that?" the Booe child says. It is looking at the Deutz.

He pulls the candle away and elbows himself up to a sit. There's nothing to do now but answer. Sitting there, the warm candle in his hands, he realizes that he doesn't know how. "What do you think it is?"

"A tractor."

Coming out of this small child who had not even been alive when he had brought the tractor here, the word seems like a slur.

"It's a Deutz," Stillman says.

"Oh," the child says. It points at the candle in Stillman's hands. "What's that?"

"It was made in 1928."

"Is that hot?"

"Do you know how old that is?"

"Can I have that?" The child is still pointing at the candle.

"No," Stillman says. "Listen, it's as old as me. We were made in the same year."

"My birthday's next week," it says. "I'm going to be six years old."

"That Deutz is seventy-six," Stillman tells it.

"So?" it says.

Stillman looks away. He sets the candle in a bowl of water at his feet. He watches all the pieces of dark things from inside his head drift out. Some fall to the bottom, some float to the surface. Pieces of skin and chunks of wax and oils that swirl in tiny eddies of their own.

"What is all that?" the child says.

"All the crap from my head."

The child comes forward and stands across the bowl from Stillman. The two of them look down for a while. The child is wearing oversize glasses pushed back onto the top of its head. They keep wanting to fall forward; it holds them in place with one hand.

"Where did the fat lady go?" the child asks.

"She's my daughter."

"I know that. I remember when she lived here."

Stillman nods.

"Did she get married?"

Stillman starts to shake his head, then stops himself. "I don't know."

"Dad said I should invite you and her to the—" The child pauses, as if trying to remember a word. "Recycle?" it says. "The dance. Next week is my birthday and also it's the dance recycle for the Festival of the Hills, both on the exact same day, and I'm in it, so you should come. It's in town. If I see the fat lady I'll tell her, too, okay? And if you see her—"

"You do that," Stillman says.

"Where does she live?"

"Do you know what a commune is?" Stillman asks.

The child looks up fast from the bowl of ear leavings. "My dad says the cops are gonna shut them down."

"What do you mean?"

"I don't know," the child says.

"What do you mean?" Stillman demands, again.

"It's something about the water. And the dead people. Dad says I'm not supposed to talk about police work." Then, as if in apology, it reaches up and takes the glasses off its head and puts them on the cot next to Stillman. "I stole these for you," it says. "They're my dad's." And then it's gone.

Stillman picks up the glasses and folds them and holds them in his hands, looking at them as if they're an animal and he's just broken its legs. The ringing is still there, but now he can hear something else, too: a distant drone. The engine of a car, maybe. Sometimes it seems to come closer. Then to fade

away. And then it just runs alongside the coordinates of his
home, as if it is not moving any more than he is, staying even
with him on parallel treadmills of time.

Roy Booe's glasses were too weak, but strong enough that, when
Stillman held the paper up to his face, he could just make out
the words. He had bought *The Eagle* days before, and had read
the article in between putting the last touches on the Deutz, read
it so many times between the remover and the primer, between
masking the tires and the spraying and the sanding between the
coats, that he had memorized most of the words. It was on
the front page, beside a list of all the events on this last day of
the Festival of the Hills: *Cops Say Pond Ritual Kills*. Beneath that,
an aerial picture of the pond, and, deeper still, the image that
had grown in his mind: all of them stripping down on the cold,
muddy shore, their nakedness flashing beneath the moon, the
priestess (as the paper called her) leading them by the hand, a
chain of naked men and women moving together into the pond
until they formed a floating mass gathered in the deep, leaning
back, looking at the sky as the priestess called her chants and,

from town, the first of the fireworks to end the fair lit up the
sky, and amid it all, floating in that toxic pool, Caroline.

He had not slept. Nor was he fully awake. All night he had
moved between body and parts, back and forth, uncoiling the
air pump's hose, dragging it until his legs gave out, and resting, and starting across the room in fresh air mask and latex
gloves, and it was into day again—how many times had the earth
rolled its hours beneath his shuffling feet?—before he was ready,
finally, to bring the Deutz at last into the world. Now, the crown-
ing grill, polished to such a silver it looked slick with gleam; now
the radiator cradled in his shaking palms; now the gentle, tender straightening and untwisting of belt pulleys. He fit the hood
on and tightened the instrument panel into place, attached the
steering wheel and the seat, and by the time he was done, dark
had again found the windows to the outside world. He pushed
the black rubber respirator off his mouth. It hung at his neck,
beneath his chin. He wiped his face. He checked his watch. Just
after seven. In three hours they would begin their suicidal wade
into the malignant waters of that carcass-strewn pond.

He made his way up the high steps to the front door, holding onto the rail, going as slowly and breathing as hard as she
used to. Inside the house that had been their home he found
the scrap of paper where he'd written down the commune's
number. His ribs squeezed; his breath struggled with his heart
for room. Two years since he'd seen her. He had the receiver in
his hand before he noticed the blinking light on the machine.

"Dad," the message said. "The Booes' kid called. Gonna
be in the dance tonight. Said maybe you'd come. I'd like that.
I've got news." There was a pause so long he thought the machine had just forgotten to beep. "It's a birthday gift," she said

and hung up. The house let go of the sound of her voice too quickly.

Through the windows he could see the grackles settling into the November trees. The house lights caught their small eyes. Glinting, they stared back at him through the glass. Outside, taking the steps down, he listened to the hushing ruffle of their thousand wings. Behind him, beneath the house's belly, the stilts fenced off an emptiness black as a mine shaft.

Leaning his weight on the mop handle, he made his way again to the workshop. The Deutz waited on its fresh-blacked tires. He set the stick against its flank, and rested his hands on the thing. Both palms. Not steadying it and not leaning on it, just touching it the way he could remember his father had once touched the plow horse—warm withers muscles—in the years after they'd replaced it with the tractor. He stood in the murmuring of the birds' wings, the sound like wind caged, unable to move on, passing over and over again.

He filled all the fluids. Then he climbed up. It took him time. The Deutz waited silently beneath his shaking. He eased down into the seat. His joints rattled from the effort, then calmed. He took hold of the starter and cranked the Deutz to life. Its roar ran his spine.

He rode it out onto 364 and turned it toward town. The Deutz rumbled beneath him, its tires crumbling their gravel through the dark. All along the road, the grackles woke to its sound, lifting in wild wing clatter through the trees. They rose and settled in his wake and rose further down and settled behind, a black rolling wave of them following the Deutz, rippling along the banks of the road. His head lamp shot its blue beam ahead of the tractor's grille. No other light at all, not even the moon. Occasionally, he passed a farmhouse up high off the road, a herd of cattle staring and silent behind their wire. On 42, head- lights slapped his back. The blare of a horn. They veered around. Hunched over the steering wheel, shaking with the rumble of the Deutz, he rolled on.

Till there below him was the town. Its four streetlamps made a line straight as a landing strip laid through the undu- lating darkness of the hills. On the road the cars were thick, taillights like blood drops beaded along a wire, all heading into Narrows. It was more traffic than the town saw on any other night of the year. The church barbecue would be over, but there was still to come the dance recital, and the fiddle action, and the fireworks—their booms ricocheting from ridge to ridge— that would bring the Festival of the Hills to its close.

In the rear lot behind the old dive joint, he shut off the Deutz's rumbling. Crowd applause came through the building's back wall, and he wondered if it was over, if she'd come already, seen he was not there, and left. But the clapping died and trick- led into the new sound of music starting up. The foot thuds of the dancers echoed from the second floor. On the brick, the mural seemed almost to shake. Something about it seemed wrong, and he sat, unsettled, trying to see what it was. The rifle- clenching woman, the black-faced boy, the Confederate rider in midleap: for one long moment he stared at them like he had not since he'd been a child.

When he finally climbed down and walked around to the front, the street was empty; everyone had already gone in for the show. Over the door, the bulb showed the flyers town people had thumbtacked to the corkboard. Inside, the shelves were all bare. The bar was a lonely plank. After the dive joint died, it had

been a dry goods store, and after that went under it was a meeting spot for the VFW and Elks, and, as they had passed away, it
dropped into emptiness and unuse. The only part that ever saw
people anymore was the old dance hall on the second floor: town
meetings, and the grade school pageant, and closing night of
the Festival of the Hills.

At the top of the stairs, he eased open the double doors.
The hall held most of the town. They sat on folding chairs, hill
folk and valley folk and new arrivers and those who'd come back,
and even a few hashheads in their eyeglasses and beards. Up
there on the stage, the children's feet battered the wood; he
didn't even throw them a glance. She was sitting right at the
aisle. A pink bandana on her head. Her hair hanging down her
back in one thick python braid. The mop handle thumped along
the aisle. People turned to look. He didn't care—his focus nailed
to her—till she turned, too.

Her eyes showed no surprise, just worry and sadness creeping in. For a moment, he wondered what caused that. Then he
remembered his cane: her dad was an old man thumping on a
stick. He mustered his breath, whispered, "It's just till my knee
gets better." Someone told him to hush. He leaned down to her
to speak, but she tilted her face away as if he reeked.

"You better sit," she said.

When he did, her thickness pressed at his shoulder, his
arm, all along his thigh; he could sit right there forever.

But the dance went on only another couple minutes. On
the stage, the children did ballet, or modern moving, or whatever kind of foolishness they'd been trained to do. They were
dressed as butterflies, boys and girls both, in tights and leotards
and small bright papier-mâché wings that rattled till they nearly

drowned the music out. The thudding of their feet finished the job. Over on one side, two butterflies from the edge, the Booe child did its part. Aside from stomping a little harder, it did no worse or better than the rest. Even if it had, Stillman wouldn't have noticed. Oh, he was looking at the stage. But his attention was on the stink of whatever his daughter had smeared on and his determination to sniff through it to the scent of her that he had known ever since she came into his life. Listening to the rhythm of her breath, he focused hard on matching it with his own.

The audience clapped. The children ran to get out of sight. Stillman's throat closed up. Around them, people rose. He stayed seated. She stayed seated. They looked at the empty stage.

"I'm sorry I missed it," he said.

"It's intermission," she said, and nodded at a table in a corner: squashed brownies and Rice Krispies treats and cookies smothered in plastic wrap. "You want something?"

"Sure."

"No, you don't."

"Yeah," he said. "That's true." They both gave up smiles as if their faces, at least, remembered how it was.

"Don't ask me to move back," she said.

"Okay."

"I mean it."

"I know."

She looked at him again, let her eyes hang on him a little longer. "Nice glasses."

"They're not mine."

She reached over and picked something out of his hair. "When was the last time you washed yourself?"

"You let it, a body'll keep itself oiled pretty good." He waited until she had finished her small laugh, then said, "I'm not gonna ask you to come home."

Her smile slipped. "You say that one more time—"

"I just don't want you to stay up there."

"At Whistler's Meadow?"

"At the commune."

"Well, that's where I am, Dad.

"There's people dying up there."

"It's a hospice. People come there to—"

"Other people."

"Oh," she said.

"Babies."

"This is about the cops."

"It's the pond," he said. "It's the water in the pond."

"You mean on the commune?"

"I mean the *water*," he said. "It's probably in the ground-water. It's probably got in the well. The whole thing's a graveyard."

"What are you talking about?"

"I saw it. A hundred head out there. In that hollow. Years ago. The Demastuses shot them and planted them under."

"No, no, Dad," she said. "It's where the spring comes out. There was a big sink spot there when the first brothers and sisters bought it. We just lined it to make it hold—"

"Promise me you won't go swimming there."

"We do it every year."

"Promise me."

"Dad," she said, "why do you think I moved out?"

"It was that River fucker."

"No."

"It was the way he—"

"It was you."

He could feel himself staring at her, but he couldn't seem to look away. He took off his glasses. Her face went soft. He didn't put them back on. The cookie eaters were throwing away their napkins and finding their way back to their seats. The lights dimmed.

He said, "Whatever I did, I did 'cause I love you."

"Oh, Dad," she said. "You think I don't know that?"

"You don't know how much," he said.

"You think Mom didn't know that?"

There was a long while of the crowd's noise sinking toward quiet.

Finally, he said, "I want to show you—"

She cut him off. "I was the one that asked you to come here, remember?"

There was a coldness running under her words. "Please," he said, and it sounded strange on his lips in this room crowded with people who could hear. "I just want to ask you to come outside with me."

"It's about to start," she said.

"Then after."

"Don't you even want to know why I—"

"I want you to go for a ride with me."

"No."

The lights dropped.

"We don't even have to ride, then," he said. The curtain opened. "I just want to show you what I've been working on all this time. I want to give—"

"Don't you even want to know what my news is?"

Then the clapping started and she joined in and he sat there, his glasses still off, waiting for them to be done.

When it died down, he told her, "I don't care if you're married."

"Thanks," she said.

"I mean it's okay." Someone called to him to hush. "You're still my Blueberry." The piano banged out its music. "They can call you that all they want. That River fucker can call you—"

"I'm not married," she whispered.

"You'll still be my little girl."

"I'm pregnant."

The children came on. They were doing some kind of dance that just looked like running to Stillman. He watched their blurred shapes go around in a circle with their arms spread like birds. The blurry movement made him dizzy. He put the glasses back on. But the clarity brought a sharpness with it that made his bowels hurt. He could feel them curling on themselves, his stomach rising up against his lungs. He tried to remember what year it was, and then from there to how old she was, and the answer cut off his breath.

"Are you okay?" she whispered.

"Fine," he said. Then, "I have to use the bathroom."

"Now?"

He rose noisily to his feet. Someone nearby took hold of his elbow and said, "Wing," and tried to pull him down, but Stillman said, again, louder, "I have to use the bathroom," and then he was pushing at his daughter, trying to get past her. Up on the stage he could see the Booe child in the center now, leaping and crouching, leaping and crouching, staring straight at Stillman and forgetting to shake its wings.

Outside the stage hall the double doors shut behind him. He leaned for a moment against the banister. His legs felt as if they were filling slowly, from the toes up, with sand. Behind him, he heard his daughter's heavy foot thuds coming up the aisle toward the doors and he forced himself down the stairs, moving his body as much with his hands on the rail as with his leaden feet. On the first floor, the old abandoned dive joint was quiet and empty as before. He stumbled his way through the space where tables had once been, into the bathroom in the back; shut the door; locked it. In one wall a broken window sucked at the cold night air. The sink and the toilet had been ripped out long ago; there was just the empty stall with its shut door and the torn gap in the tile where the urinal had been. The pipes to all the long-gone fixtures stuck out of walls like arteries missing their heart. The only time he'd ever been drunk had been in this bathroom, in this dive joint with Ginny and her friends, and after that he never drank again. He could still hear, now, Ginny's worried voice outside the door. No, that was his daughter, breathing hard as he was.

"Jesus, Dad," she said. "I go down those stairs any faster . . . Look, I know what you're gonna say. I'm forty-three. I got diabetes. I'm really fucking fat. Maybe that's the worst risk of them all. You're going to say risk, and risk, and risk, and I know it, Dad. You think we don't know there's bones down there in that pond? That's *why* we do it there. That's the whole reason for the ceremony. They say it's an old Indian burial site, and what the bones release makes you *stronger,* and I know that sounds crazy, but I don't care. And that I don't care is what makes it worth it. If I knew it was safe what the fuck would be the point? I don't know I can say it any clearer, Dad. And if you didn't want a daughter who likes the idea that it takes really wanting a baby enough to face some fucking risk, then you shouldn't've had me."

"I don't want to keep it," he said.

"It's not yours to keep or not."

"It's *half* mine."

He could hear her drumming her nails against the door. She was doing it out of sync with the music thumping from the bar and it was getting at his brain.

"Can you stop that?" he said.

"No," she said.

"Stop it."

"My fingers ain't yours to control."

"We're talking about a child," he said. "I'm not ready for a child."

"I am."

"Ginny," he said. "How can you possibly think—"

"I don't care," she said.

"I care," he shouted at the door. "It's *my* child."

"It's your *future*."

"Right."

"You don't care about *it*," she shouted at him. "You care about your future. About having your goddamn control over your goddamn . . . You just can't stand to have something thrown in your lap you can't fix to run regular as a truck."

"We're talking about the child!" he said.

"We're talking about *everything*. Smoking, dancing, driving, drinking. I mean look at you. You choose this one night to get drunk? We're talking about California."

"I don't want to talk about California."

"You don't always get to talk about what you want to talk

about. You don't get to make me. You don't get to control this, Stillman. This is a whole person in me whose gonna be a whole person you can't control. And if you ain't ready for that, then you're right: you ain't ready for a baby."

"If you'd just listen to me," he said, but she cut him off.

"If I listened to you, I'd be *like* you. I'd be a scared safe female version of you."

"If you'd just—"

"And if my *mom* had listened to you, I'd have never lived at all."

He stood tilted with his forehead against the old tile, holding himself up by the brass pipe that jutted from the wall. "Blueberry," he said.

"Don't," she said.

"Caroline—"

"Old Lester told me, Dad."

"I didn't *know* you yet."

"That's the whole point," she said. "You didn't know me when I was a year old, either. Or two, or three, or even when they shipped me back to you."

He tried to say *Blueberry* again, but his lips wouldn't seem to get past the first *B*.

"Did you sit there that first night I was home and look at me sleeping in your house and wish I was dead?"

He tried to answer, *No*, but it came out a dribble of a moan.

"I bet you did," she said. "I bet you couldn't stand not *knowing* how this kid was gonna change your life. Well, you know what, Dad? You don't know what tomorrow's gonna bring any more than you know my baby. And no matter how much ass-bark tea you drink and Chinese wing-bat shit you do, you don't know what's going to get you in the end. And I won't live with someone who can't love what they don't know, what they don't *control*. And *that's* why I moved out. So tell me, Dad, what is this thing you made for me that's going to show me all the big, big size of your love?"

He shut his eyes. A numbness was creeping down the left side of his face. In his ears there was the ringing, again: that half-dead man's warning bell. Somehow old Les Pfersick had rolled in here in his wheelchair and was scraping at Stillman's brain with that goddamn sound. It was coming from the stall behind him. He tried to turn his head to see, but he couldn't make his neck work. His daughter was saying something through the door that was drowned under the ringing and above him there was the drumming of all the children's feet. They danced over his head and he could feel each time they landed—*boom!*—and landed—*boom!*—on his heart.

He didn't know how much time went by before he could move again. His daughter was out there beyond the locked door saying, "Dad?" and "Dad?" and "Dad?" One half of his body was working well enough that he could shove himself off of the wall. "I've called the fire department," she said. He dragged himself toward the broken window. With his movable arm, he broke away the remaining glass, and hauled himself high enough to roll the rest of the way over. It cut him in places he could feel but not understand. Lying where he landed, he could hear the fire truck coming. There were no sirens, no flashers, just that sound of that engine coming near and near.

He got himself up enough to crawl. Then on two feet. And he discovered he could stumble and drag his way across the back lot. In the shadow beneath the elm waited the Deutz. All the long way to it, he could feel the painted eyes on him and when he reached the tractor, he clenched its side to keep from falling and turned to look: the mural *was* shaking, surely as if the figures, too, felt the dancers' footsteps thudding in their veins. But no paint flaked, no bits of brick crumbled off. And he knew then what was wrong with it: someone had retouched the thing, or scrubbed it clean, or somehow—impossible, awful—in all these years not one of the faces had changed.

It was hours later and the clouds had thinned enough to show the breath of the moon when he came within sight of the old Demastus farm. Bent over the steering wheel, he headed upland toward the lights of the buildings where his daughter had made her home. He could just make out the windows busy with the flitting shadows of commune life. They must be preparing, he thought, for the moment they would come down to here, to the pond, to perform their ceremony of bones and risk. The Deutz shook and murmured beneath him. Let it run, he thought, and slid himself off.

A dozen feet away, the pond spread black beneath the clouds. Its waters were so still the reeds at the shore might have been scratched into the rest of the night. He crawled through the cold grass, until he felt the mud, and then the water, and then was in. For a few feet, he splashed his way, limbs sliding along the slippery mud beneath, and then he let the water take him.

Slowly, he swam out to the very center. Over his splashing he could hear the people in the commune singing. Someone playing a guitar. Laughter. He turned on his back, filled his lungs as best he could, and, floating, listened to them. He could imagine those voices calling her Blueberry. He could imagine her liking it. He tried to make the word the way he thought one of them might, then loosened his throat and tried again, then just let the feeling of the sound leak out of his mouth on its own, drift across his lips, shape itself however it would.

For a while he looked up at the night sky: traces of cloud edges made by the moon, then disappeared again as they moved on. He wondered how deep the water was beneath him, how far down lay the bones. In his mind, he could see them: the white-picked rib cages, the tangled horns, huge teeth coming loose in the jaws, those black empty eye sockets staring up at him. His wet fingers found his face, lifted the glasses off. He let them sink. He leaned his chin forward over his floating chest until the water lapped at his mouth. He opened it and drank.

Now, either it would come or it would not. He could not see the ridges around, or hear the river, or recognize the lay of the stars, and he felt ready, unafraid, even eager to see at last what a new valley might look like. He drank again. The pond cooled his innards. Whether it came now, or later, didn't really matter; he could already feel the rest of time unspooling itself, rolling down a swale he did not know into a landscape more foreign than he could imagine. He shut his eyes. Each time the water lapped at his ears he went deaf. And each time it cleared again he could hear the commune's singing coming nearer.

When he opened his eyes again, he could see them. Over his floating chest, across the still water, beyond the reeds, the field was full of blurred shapes moving slowly down the slope towards the pond. His daughter's chosen family, his grandson's blood. They came on. Soon they would be all around him. Listening to their whispering passage through the dry grass, to their voices flooding the night, he waited. From the shore came the murmuring of the Deutz—that giant softness of dark blur— standing there, watching him, as if it was waiting, too.

SARVERVILLE
REMAINS

Friday of July

I want to say right here what I am sorry. I am sorry for where you is at and how you got there and I am sorry for calling you to the scene of the crime, as they say, and for the crime, and for if I hurt you something what's took too long to heal. Most off I am sorry about your wife.

You is most like thinking sorry ain't no excuse. Ma B says Excuse is just Use with a big X in front of it. So please do not think I do not know. It was just what your wife wasn't like any of the others at Eads High. I want you to know that cause that was why at first. Though why wasn't just what she was a full adult woman, or what she'd knowed so many jobs, or what she smelled like this or weared her hair like that or put her smoke behind her ear to free up her mouth. Please know at first she wasn't your wife. She wasn't even her. She was just the woman the guys knowed to do it.

If you is wondering why I'm writing to you it's just to explain so you'll know how it happened and won't hate her or hurt her when you get out. Which once I'm done showing you, you'll understand the fault ain't on her. It's on me. Sometimes I lie on my mattress in My Hall and listen to Jackie and the baby scream at each other on the house end, and on the glass end the big coon scratching to get in at Roy's Bahamas. Scratching and talking, scratching and talking. The rest of the street all quiet. I think about what you must think about. You and me, if Roy was here he'd say, You guys are like a pair of tits. Which is just the kind of mouth he's got and not my way of talking. But he's right. After all, you knowed her as your wife. I knowed her as your wife. It was only who was doing the knowing what made the difference. After all, it's because of her what you is there and I am here and everything.

Plus there's the fact what we's the only ones who knowed her through that kind of love. It's most like not okay for me to tell you how much I felt for her, so I will not disrespect you, though it was very very very strong. It's also most like not okay for me to use the word Love. You most like think it's a husband's word. But now what she's gone from you as much as me we's even more two of a kind, as they say, so I will just use it. I want you to know I never called her your Love words of Peach or Sugar Puss or your Hate words neither, not even Whore. The guys called her Whore, but to me she was just Linda. Linda I will guess is what you call her if she makes a visit. The guys say she don't even and Fuck off Geoffrey, but even if she don't visit Do you call her Linda in your head? In my head I call her Linda. But here out of respect to you I will call her Missus Podawalski.

Nobody is making me write this. Not Roy or Jackie or the cops or nobody. Do not even think for one iota what it's Linda. What it's Missus Podawalski I mean. Never erase is what Ma Wasco always said. Never cross out. She was a art teacher before her accident and she teached me what was sloppy and what was presentable to look at, so I am sorry also for any mistakes I'm due to make. But Missus Podawalski has nothing to do with this, rest assured. Truth be told, as they say, I ain't seen your wife since you ain't seen her. It is just one more way what we is like a pair of tits, you and me.

It's hard to put a handle on where to start. Jackie would say, Start at the beginning Nimwit. But it's hard to put a handle on what's the beginning. Get on with it Nimwit, is what Jackie would say. Well she may be older and have charge of me, as she says, but I've heard her style for telling stories and she don't got it down, believe me. Like Dad Kreager liked to say, she don't know her butt from her boobs. If you ain't seen her, she's so skinny there ain't no difference anyhow. Sides even a Nimwit knows what's got to be told. You don't got to be smart to see I'm the only one who can tell it. Me and Missus Podawalski. But she's gone.

Mister Podawalski, believe me I didn't even know Missus Podawalski till the night I met her. It was Russ made the hellos. This was weeks and weeks and weeks before you found out, but I just thought it was like any Monday done with work. Hanging out on the curb by the Sunoco. Waving at vehicles. Waiting for Vic and Russ to come by in the Party Van and pick me up. But that night, after supper and our practice time and near midnight when we was putting away the band tools, Russ said he had a surprise. Let's hustle, he said. Fifteen minutes later we was taking 502 for Crigger's Den at top speed. Top speed in the Party Van ain't much for highways, but on them curves how Russ takes it I was layed out in the back on the big bed hugged up with Mister Bean Bag.

What's the rush? Vic kept asking and Russ saying Who's rushing? and me from the back through Mister Bean Bag saying I gotta barf, and Russ saying, No you don't we'll be there in a sec you can barf then.

I don't do so good with vehicles.

Vic said, I don't like it.

Ho you will, Russ said. You gonna want to go back tomorrow and get more.

He wouldn't tell us more what, just pulled in out back behind Crigger's Den.

Why we going out back? I asked him.

I mean you have seen how Crigger's Den is Monday night midnight, just hardly no vehicles even on the road and the ones parked in the front lot under the beer signs pretty much just them's who work there, so seeing how we was going around back instead, Vic said, Geoff's got a point.

I got a point, I said.

I don't want to buy no shit off no fucker I don't know, Vic said.

I'm not talking about weed, Russ said.

Well what the fuck, Vic said.

This is better than weed, Russ told him and turned the engine off.

I opened the door and got out to puke.

Don't go nowhere, Russ told me, Or do nothing stupid.

When I was done I got back in and asked him, Like what?

Like fuck this up, he said.

I made the point, How can I futz it up if I don't know what it is?

You mean how can you *avoid* fucking it up, Vic said.

You'll know it when you see it, Russ said and put on the music. He put it on low. It was House of the Rising Sun. We sat there nodding to it.

I said, Is it gonna drive back here? Russ shook his head. I asked him how we was gonna know when it got there then.

It's gonna come through that door, he said.

I knowed he meant the screen door back the kitchen. For the next I don't know how long I tried to guess what it was, kept on till they was both laughing. Not atchya laughing, like Ma B says, but wichya laughing what's the only kind I oughta give my allowance to. Then the door opened and she come out.

She pushed the screen door open with her hip. That was the first nice thing. She was carrying the trash out in a bag near big as her. Her hair was come undone and stuck funny on her forehead. Her eyes looked punched. Russ turned the headlights on and off quick. She looked at the Party Van. She nodded, not like Hello but like Okay, and chucked the trash bag in the Dumpster and held up a hand with her fingers spread to five and gone back inside.

So? Vic said.

So we wait five minutes, Russ said.

And? Vic said.

And then I get to go first.

Who gets to go second? Vic said.

You want to go second, Geoff? Russ said.

Hey, Vic said.

Okay, I said.

You want to go third? Vic said.

Okay, I said.

That was how we got straight on the order. The radio was on ads. I listened to the Ripplemead Hardware one what they do that ch-ch-ch-chainsaws like David Bowie.

I don't know, Vic said. I don't want my first to be a whore.

She's not, Russ said. He asked me, She look like a whore to you?

I told him I thought she looked tired.

Well it's the end of her shift, Russ said.

How old is she? Vic asked.

I don't know, Russ said. Forty?

I'm not paying for no forty-year-old whore, Vic said.

Dipshit, Russ told him, She doesn't charge. She gives free blow.

Vic was quiet like he gets when he's trying to keep what he's thinking hid.

When was the last time you got some head? Russ said.

When was the last time you did? Vic said.

Last week, Russ said. Exactly about now. How about you, Geoff? When was the last time you got blowed? You know. Blowed. Like a blow job. Sucked off. You know what a blow job is don't you?

Yeah, I said.

He's never had one, Vic said.

You never did neither, I said.

Yeah, Vic said, but I just turned fifteen.

You really never had one? Russ said. Man the shit in your balls must be fucking fermented. Seriously fucking beer.

Fucking beer balls, Vic said.

Russ said, When it's your turn Geoff, tell her you got it on tap.

With good head, Vic said and they was laughing it up.

Sometimes when I don't get what's funny I just laugh along anyhow. Like Ma Wasco said, you fool them so they think you understand and how damn smart is their asses then hm? Mom Kreager used to swear up a storm, as they say. But I learned better from Ma B. Ma B always told to just stay quiet and let them laugh. Lying don't make no one look good in the Eyes of the Lord. The Eyes of the Lord is especially upon me since I'm one of them what needs extra care. Ma B says them Eyes of the Lord is the only eyes what matter and they's especial on all the diminished ones what's why I don't never lie.

I guess you're thinking that's a whopper right there. What Russ said. What Vic said. How I put it down exact. Just like a novel, I bet you think. Ma B said either a story's true or it's called a novel, what's just another word for fiction, what's another word for false, what's another word for pack of lies. She didn't allow it in the house. But when Jackie and me was small, before Mom Kreager took The Ride on High, Dad Kreager used to read us lies. He did it on the one about Narnia and the one about the boy and his coon dogs, and on My Side of the Mountain, what was my favorite.

Jackie liked it fine up till that one. It wasn't the story what was the problem. It's a good story about this boy Sam what runs off from home and makes hisself a life all alone up on a mountain.

It was how it was told, the whole thing from the first page like I did this or I did that, what was too much for Jackie.

Oh come on, she said, Like a lie can tell itself.

Well maybe it's true, Dad Kreager said. Maybe its writ down by Sam hisself. Bullshit Jackie said and Dad Kreager said, Watch it, and Jackie pointed out the name of who writ it right there on the cover. Jean Craighead George.

Well maybe Sam's growed up and changed his name, Dad Kreager said. You ever thought of that?

I told her, Maybe it's a fake name so's he can stay hid up there on that mountain and nobody come and bug him.

Whatever Einstein, she told me and showed the picture on the back. It was a woman.

You think you're so smart, Dad Kreager told her. You got no more brains than your brother. That's the editor, smarty pants. She's just the one who found all this how it was writ and put it in a book to make her some money. You think Sam even needs money? No sir. He got no taxes to take it, no woman to spend it. What's he need it for? Right? And he winked at me to let me know it was him and me what seen the truth.

That night Jackie said to me from the bottom bunk, Try not to be such a retard, Geoff. Even if it was Sam wrote it, how'd he remember all what this one said or that one said exact enough to put it down as truth. Hm? No one remembers that good. So even if some of it was true, which it ain't, the details is all lies.

When you think Jackie's wrong it's best to keep it to yourself. I just stared at the glow stars we'd stuck on the ceiling and thought out what she just said. Thought it out exact. Thought it out to what I said before. Thought that out to what she said before that. All the way back through story time, exact, and then supper and then school and what everyone said. All exact and I could hear all of it perfect.

Ma B says the Lord makes everyone good at something and it's up to you to make sure you use it the way He meant. After church, when she had the guests, she would sit me by her side and let me eat cookies and taste her coffee and when they was done talking she told me stand up and say back what was said and who said it. All them thought it was a blast. But Ma B never laughed at it. She just said quiet when it was done, Now there's a child who tells the truth like the Lord Himself was checking notes. She took me to a doctor once who named me a photo memory but he didn't know what he was talking about. I don't do so good with seeing the color of this or size of that or details like a picture. It's in my ears what I remember. I can play it back just like rewinding to that part of the tape.

Just to show you, how about this?

Someone's gonna get hurt. We've known that from the beginning.

Remember when you said that?

And she said, You're such a coward. And you said, Is that so? And she said, A pussy. And you said, Okay that's it.

Or the time you told me, Get off her.

See? This ain't a novel, Mister Podawalski. There ain't no editor like there was for what Sam writ from his mountain. There is just the Lord checking His notes. I am going to play it back just like it was a real tape and even if there is cuss words or ungodly acts to come I hope you will agree speaking the truth is what counts in the Eyes of the Lord. Everything I put down here is just what my ears remember. It is how it was.

Everyone else was gone that night by the time your wife come out again. She shut off the light inside and locked up.

She's going to her car, Vic said like he was worried. Shouldn't one of us go out and—

Hold your horses, Russ said.

Her car was right under the lamp pole. She opened a door and stood by it and took her apron off. It was a tiny little apron and she threw it inside the car, and got in after it, and shut the door.

We do it in there? Vic said.

Nope, Russ said.

She had the cab light on and the sun visor down and she was drawing on her face. When she come out again she was holding a towel. She gone behind the propane tank. That tank is so big once she squatted down you couldn't see her at all.

Now here's the rules, Russ said. You don't touch her. You don't talk to her.

Not even thank you? Vic said.

Not nothing. You do you'll fuck it up for everybody.

Who else does it? Vic said.

You just go back there and undo your pants.

Anyone from school?

Quit your fucking questions, Russ said. And don't try to make her take it deep and don't try to make her swallow. She does it how she likes and it's good. He opened the door. Be back soon, he said. Don't wait up.

When he come back Vic got out and met him. Russ slapped him back the head. You're it, he said.

While Vic was behind the propane tank, Russ lit up a joint. I climbed over the cooler into shotgun and he passed it to me. I buyed the beer and they buyed the weed is how it worked. Over at the propane tank you could see the top part of Vic with his back to us.

What about the end? I said.

He looked at me like What do you mean?

If I ain't allowed to say nothing to her—

Geoff, you don't say a word.

How am I gonna—

And don't touch her, Geoff. Put your fucking hands on your head if you have to.

Okay, I said. But how am I gonna—

How you gonna what?

How am I gonna warn her?

Oh, he said. That's what's got you worried. Man don't even. You don't got to do nothing but stand there. She knows what happens. You just give her a sign. Okay?

What kind of sign?

You know, he said.

How do you do it?

He laughed. Fuck, he said. I'm not showing you. Just make a noise. Wave your arms or something.

I tried to think how I did it in the men's room, but I always tried to be super quiet and not give away nothing in case there was a customer outside the door waiting to pee. Vic was coming back. I was hoping maybe if I waited long enough she would get up and go back to her car. Vic opened the side door. He was smiling.

I don't think I'm gonna, I said.

Fuck that, Russ said.

Fuck that, Vic said too, and took the last of the joint from Russ.

Get out Geoff, Russ said. This is your fucking chance.

She's actually kinda pretty, Vic said before he sucked in.

Do I got to? I said.

Fuck yes, Russ said. Friends don't let friends miss blow jobs.

Why? I said.

Because anyone old enough to be out of high school and hasn't had a blow job's got to be a fucking retard.

I'm not a retard, I said.

That's what I'm saying, he said and give me a shove.

Missus Podawalski was sitting on the towel with her knees under her. Come on, she said. I put my hands on my head like Russ said and she undone my button and zipper and had got my thing out by the time she said, You the last one? and looked up. Oh shit, she said. She leaned back a bit. I told him, she said. She said, Sorry pal. Put it away.

I stood there with my hands on my head looking at her.

Put it away, she said. I told him I only do kids.

Back in the Party Van Russ and Vic had turned the music up. I could tell even from that far it was Clapton doing Cocaine. They gave me thumbs up through the windshield. When I looked back, she was staring at me.

Hey, she said, You a mute? which I guess means your hands don't work because right after she said, Well your hands work don't they?

I tried to lean down a little.

Don't touch me, she said. Use your goddamn hands to zip up or keep them on your head, I don't care, but don't touch me.

Russ said don't touch anything, I told her. Even my own pants. I tried saying the words without making any noise.

What? she said.

I whispered it this time. She gave me the look people give me.

Then she told me, Well I say you can stop holding your hands like I'm gonna shoot you, and you can put your own dick back in your pants, and I'm old enough to be his mother so I should know.

I did it and stood there with my hands by my sides.

You with those boys? she said.

They's my buddies, I whispered.

She said, Huh. Well you better go back to them.

Missus? I said.

Yeah?

Can I please just stay here for just one nother minute?

She pulled her knees out from under her and leaned back. Her hands was on the gravel and I thought it must hurt but she was looking at me like she wasn't thinking about her hands. They make fun of you? she said.

No, I whispered. They's my buddies.

We spent the next minute with me standing there trying to look like Vic had looked from the van and her wiping at herself with a corner of the towel. Every now and again she'd spit on the gravel and make a face and spit again. Between spitting she looked at me.

Hey, she said. You work at the Sunoco don't you?

Yeah, I whispered. Then I said, Five bucks of regular please. And I said, Would you mind giving the back windshield a wash? It was what she'd said last time she come through and I'd been remembering it ever since she come out under the lamp post and I recognized her.

She laughed. That was the first time I heard her laugh and I didn't know what it meant yet, the way I would later when I had learned all the different laughs she got for all the different ways she feeled. But I remember thinking then it was a nice person's laugh.

You better go back, she said.

Okay, I said. Will you please don't tell I talked to you?

She pretended to zip her lips.

Sunday of July

I know in my deep deep part of my heart what this ain't a thing you gonna want to read. I can see the hardship of it for you. I wouldn't write it if I didn't know for sure it had to be writ. I've seen your anger up near, Mister Podawalski. I know come this time next year you is gonna be out. I've forgive you and I ask what you forgive her. She's a good good good woman, Mister Podawalski. She done a good thing. Thanks to her, I sit here tonight a new man looking at a new life. I ain't the same Geoffrey Sarver what met her that first night back in spring. Sometimes a person can't even know hisself till someone else figures him out, and then he got to look at her who's figured him and see in her what she knows before he can know it too. That's kinda how it was.

It's summer now and my jaw's just about good again. It still makes noises in the places where it was broke and they give me some new teeth what take getting used to, but my good eye is all cleared up. The other eye they said I ain't never gonna get back to see with. I expect once I can turn my neck all the way without it hurts I won't miss that one so bad anyhow. I been home from New Castle Memorial for weeks. Don't live in the Sunoco office no more neither. Got my own place. I guess it ain't much bigger than yours what you got now, but it's nice. Jackie said she woulda give me the spare room but the baby. It hollers all night anyhow. I'm better off here in My Hall.

Roy fixed it up for me while I was in New Castle Memorial. The long way I can lie down flat two whole times plus put the beagle between my head and the wall, and the short way I can do it one time plus one more time if I scrunch up in a ball, knees to my nose. Roy cleared off some of the metal shelves in the garage and put them in here for my clothes and there's the old rug what the beagle used to use before it got so old and bony and needed a fluff bed. I've got a bed what's not even on the ground. Jackie names it a cot and showed me how I can fold it up if I want. Give you some space in here, she said. She even put a picture on the wall for me. Not a old picture neither. I know it's a new one cause it's got the baby in it just after it was brung forth into the world, as they say, and the beagle looking near dead and Roy and Jackie sitting close like they never do. It ain't more bigger than a postcard, but My Hall's not big enough for a big picture anyhow. And plus she even writ cross the top in gold Merry Christmas from the Kreagers. They don't charge me but half rent. Since I'm Jackie's half brother she says which Roy says laughing I best be glad I'm not her full blood and how it worked out good for me.

We call my place My Hall or Geoffrey's Hall instead of My
Room or Geoffrey's Room because it used to be the hall before I
rented it out. Not a hallway, so much as kind of its own little house,
like Roy says, what just so happens to be the connection between
the real house and the room what Roy calls the Bahamas. One
end of My Hall's got a door to the office part of the house where
Roy does his numbers. The other end's got a door to Roy's Bahamas, what used to be a big glass greenhouse back in the olden
days, as they say, but what he's got filled up with sand now. I got
to go through His Office to use the bathroom but he got to go
through My Hall to get to His Bahamas so I figure we about even.

I have just looked at all I put down and it seems a lot about
me when I'm trying to tell you about Missus Podawalski. What
I mean is just I got a real place now and most off I mean what
it's due to her. Before, I was with the guys doing kid stuff living
in the Sunoco and now I'm living like any man with my own
bed and my own place and paying real rent. I don't got my own
mailbox. I wish I had my own number. But then there I go looking God in the mouth, as they say. After all, you most like got
your own number and your own mailbox and life ain't perfect
for neither one of us, nor no one.

I don't remember turning on the light but I must have. It's
got dark. Roy just come out the old greenhouse door and gone
through My Hall to His Office. He been back in His Bahamas
from after supper all the way till now, scraping and shoveling
and cussing. Weekends he's out there all day and I got to hear
him. He's got it pretty good already, but he says wait till her first
birthday. I said it was gonna be the best sandbox in Ripplemead,
but he said, Ripplemead my ass. It ain't a sandbox, boy. It's a
goddamn beach.

Once the baby's big enough to walk on her own she gonna be going in and out of My Hall to get to the Bahamas all the time and there's gonna be sand. He done lots of sand, and little banana trees what don't got bananas, and every time he goes to the Kroger and buys a coconut we got to save the shell for his pile. All his lizards is escaped, but he's got plans for frogs. Some kind of special warm weather frog what glows. He can't quit talking on them. Says they look like they's from another world what he's gonna make for hisself and for the baby too right here in Ripplemead. I don't know about that. Last time he tried turtles. They got out. The coons ate them. In the morning they was just two shells out there in the lawn. I'd like to see what'd happen with them frogs. I wonder if their bones glow too.

There goes Roy talking to hisself again. I can hear him walking back and forth in the Office on the house side of My Hall. He talks to hisself like a nut job is what Jackie says and she's right too. He's got his numbers on now. The radio's going through the door, Up .08 to 59.16, Up .45 to 73.92, Up .30 to 74.14. In a second I'm gonna shut the lights out and look for the coons. This time of night you can see them come out the woods. If you stand in the dark and look out the window you can see their eyes. They got shiny eyes and there's lots of them. Roy says they wanna get at the trash. If he sees one in the day he'll shoot it. I like them though. I wonder what them critters do all day in the woods. I bet they just sit there waiting for dark so's they can come into the yards and not get shot. Sometimes I can hear them right outside and it sounds just like they want in. Imagine them run loose in the house.

Up .39 to 62.52, Down .12 to 44.06, Down .07 to 53.17. There Roy goes talking to hisself again. I was gonna send you this bit by bit, but I think I best not. I think I best get it all down and make sure it's right, the whole entire thing, before the day what I will personal bring it to you in your cell.

Tuesday of July

The next time I seen Missus Podawalski I brung her a Coors.

Thanks, she said. I can use that.

It tastes bad, huh?

She shrugged while she swished the beer around in her mouth then spit. Next time tell the skinny one to go first so I can get him over with.

I said, His name's—

I don't want to know, she said and took a real swallow. She made that furry mmm noise down back in her throat like she does when she's glad on something. That's sweet of you, she said.

How come you do it if it tastes bad?

Honey, don't nobody do it for the taste.

Why you do it then?

Why would you do it?

I could feel Russ and Vic looking at me from the van. They had give me trouble about bringing the beer. I thought about what she said. I guessed maybe it felt good to her on the inside of her mouth. I put my guess out loud.

To me? she said. And then, Try sticking your fingers down your throat see how good that feels.

I tried it. The laugh she give was her one loud surprise laugh which was the first time I heard it. She shut her mouth around it to keep it quiet, like she does. When she'd got it done she said, You are funny. You sure you ain't a kid?

No ma'am, I'm full growed.

And still a virgin?

That was my turn to laugh. I may be stupid, I told her, but I'm not a girl.

She looked at me and said Huh in her quiet way like you must have heard her times when you talked close. Well, she said, there's some things that feel good but with a bj you give it cause you want to make the other person feel good okay?

I thought on that while she picked her rings off the towel at her side. She had a pile. When she was done putting them on the fingers of one hand, I said, Like I brung you the beer?

She gave me her Linda smile. Kinda. While she did the fingers of her other hand she said, How old are you anyway?

Least thirty.

You don't know for sure?

When she got me Ma B said we's just gonna call it fourteen and go on from there.

You still in school?

No ma'am. Like I told you, I ain't a kid.

Okay, she said.

I'm least thirty.

Too bad, she said and finished the beer.

When she was done I asked her, Can I have that back?

Don't you think they'll have seen the whole time that you wasn't drinking it?

I looked back at the Party Van. I told her, If I don't say nothing neither way it's not a lie.

Well, she said, next time how about you bring one and I'll bring one and we'll drink our own.

* * *

Next time I brung one and she brung one. We drank them together. I asked her if she liked Russ and Vic. She said she didn't
know them. Well then how come you want to make them feel
good? I said. She just drank her beer.

Do you think you'd like them if you knowed them?

Not particularly.

Do you like me?

She drank her beer.

I don't get it, I said. If you don't even like them why would
you—

What? She said. Have you been thinking about it all week?

Yes.

Well stop.

We drank our beers. When we was done she gave me her
empty can.

Now you got to take two back, she said. Explain that.

I was turning to go back to the van when she grabbed one
of the cans from my hand and threw it into the weeds behind
the lot. It didn't even make a sound where it landed in the grass.
You could just see it shiny in the dark.

Jesus, she said. You are stupid.

They figured it out anyhow. Next time, I shut my ears to the
words they give me and brung us two. She didn't even say thanks,
just wiped at herself and drank her beer and put on her rings and
threw the can into the weeds and waited for me to go back.

You know how she gets when she is real mad, like she pretends
not to be Linda no more or Missus Podawalski and to be someone who looks like Missus Podawalski instead but's got none

of her feelings, till she really ain't Missus Podawalski at all and don't even look like her because her face is so cold? You must have seen that in all your years together. You must know what I am talking about, so I will just say that is how she was the time after that.

Fuck, Vic said when he come back from his turn, She was really into it this time, huh?

I told you, Russ said. She must know summer vacation's coming up.

I might just stick around, Vic said. Fuck that counselor shit.

I don't know, Russ said. There's other mouths to try. Right Geoff?

I had got the two beers and was sliding open the van door.

The silent treatment, Russ said. I think Geoff's got a thing for her.

A beer and a blow job, Vic said.

Simultaneous, Russ said.

I just might try that next time, Vic said.

I told him, You better not.

Whoa, he said. Easy loverboy.

Don't even try it, I told him.

Russ laughed. You got it backwards, he said. Don't you know she's supposed to bring you the beer?

I'm not, I said. I left a can on the mattress and walked over carrying just one.

I had forgot to shut the van door and standing behind the tank I could hear them still laughing.

She was sitting Indian style rubbing at something on her shirt and she didn't even look up before she said, Why do you hang around with them?

One look at her I could tell she was gone cold how I said.
All it takes is seeing it once you know it.

They my buddies, I said.

They're in high school. You're thirty. Excuse me, at least
thirty.

You're mean tonight, I said.

What could you possibly do with them? She said.

We hang out. We got a band.

She laughed that laugh she does when she's being Not
Linda. Jesus they must be losers, she said.

I guess she figured on me bringing two beers again, cause
I didn't see none what she'd brung of her own. I opened the one
can, took a drink myself. I could tell she seen that, too.

Listen to them, she said. They're laughing at you.

At least they don't give blow jobs to people what they don't
even like.

Hey, she said. I'm just being kind here. I'm just letting you
know. She looked at me drinking the beer and worked up her
own spit in her mouth and spit it out on the gravel. And while
I'm at it, she said, here's another piece of advice. Standing out
on the curb waving like that makes you look like a retard.

Well you waved back, I said.

Everyone waves back, she said.

No they don't, I told her. There's all kinds of waves. You
can wave at someone so they barely know you doing it and you
can do it so they don't know whether to wave back or not or so
they think you waving at someone else or you can do it so they
know what you really telling them is futz off. I know them all. I
got them down. I stand out there every day and do them.

I know, she said. Your boss lets you?

I told her, Let me tell you something about the Sunoco. Its two cents higher than the 76 cross town. But you know what? We got more customers. We got more regulars. You think it's cause it's better gas? No ma'am. It's cause of the service attendant is what. Mister Gilkey says so hisself. He says I'm the best service attendant he ever had and I can stay in his office long as I want. Why do you think he keeps my sleeping bag in there? My wash stuff? My bag of clothes? Cause he knows I leave and he's sunk, is what. I bring in the customers.

That's why you do it?

No. I took another drink of the beer.

Why then?

I only stand out there when it's slow.

Hey, she said, I'm not too proud to ask for a sip of that.

I took my own sip. I told her, Sometimes they say, Good evening Mister Sarver.

What do you mean?

Sometimes it's How do you do Mister Sarver. Sometimes they turn around to the kids in the back and tell them, say hello to Mister Sarver, and the kids say it. Hi Mister Sarver. What's up Mister Sarver.

They don't really say that, she said.

Sometimes a guy shouts through the window at me.

What's he say?

See you at the game, Bud. Whyn't you come by for supper, Bud. Sometimes it's a woman and she says, I'll see you at home, Hon.

What do they really say?

Just going to do the shopping, Baby.

Hey, she said.

Be back by seven.

You could hear the yard dogs and a ATV somewhere and Russ turning on the engine of the van. Hey, he shouted, Hurry it up Superman.

It's not all you think it is, she said. I've been married eight years. My husband says all that. That everyday stuff. And says the other stuff too. The lover stuff you probably say to yourself, don't tell me you don't. He says plenty. You know the last time he actually touched me?

Hey, Russ shouted again.

Leave him be, she shouted back at him. Then she reached up and took the beer from my hand. I let her. She took a swig and washed it around in her mouth.

They my buddies, I said. They like to hang out with me.

She gave me the beer back and I drank and handed it back to her and she drank it and we finished it off that way.

Wednesday of July

I never had no one to write to before. It's strange, not like it was at first cause I didn't know you, but in a new way now because I begun to. Or least you begun to know me. Which ain't so different. Sometimes I expect I must be hurting you. I'm sorry for that too, atop of everything else. There's times I want to leave bits out or just pretend it wasn't never said like that. But it was. And you'd know good as God I was leaving bits out if I did. And then what'd be the good of it? The truth is, from here on out it's just gonna get harder and hurt you more. Ma B always said the more you fight it the more it's gonna sting, and Mom Kreager told how if you lie still it gets over quicker and less painful, and Dad Kreager said you touch me I'm gonna push ya, You push me I'm gonna slap ya, You slap me I'm gonna slug ya. So I figure you add up all three of them they most like right.

It was the weekend after we shared the beer what your wife stopped by the Sunoco to fill up.

Hi, I said.

Hi, she said.

We said how much gas for how much money exact the same way exact the same time. While it pumped I did the rear window. She looked at me in the mirror the whole time. When I give her her change she said, What's your name?

Geoffrey, I told her.

I'm Linda, she said.

I'm sorry, but she didn't say Missus Podawalski. She didn't mention Podawalski at all. I hope you got somebody to write to there in jail.

Saturday of July

I was wanting to go down to the river. Do some fishing. But it's raining the slow big kind what ain't gonna let up. Sides, I want to write to you. Truth is, now I begun it I want to write to you all the time. I want to put down everything. For instance, I got to tell you what I have decided not to call her Missus Podawalski. I have decided not to call her your wife neither. I'm gonna call her Linda from here on out. The reason being Jackie at supper last night, what she said.

She said, Geoffrey Sarver you got to leave off that woman, hear?

She was feeding the baby. Her and Roy's got two supper times. One for him and her. And one for me and the baby. They do the baby first so's it'll sleep sooner enough what they can eat them a late supper without dealing with its fuss. No you can't eat with us, Roy said. That's adult time, Sharpie, is what he said. If he don't call me Sharpie, he calls me Boy. I'm more years than him. I used to tell him, Don't call me Boy, and I got a name, Geoffrey Sarver. But he never pays heed. So I don't figure I got to pay heed to nothing he put a name on neither. I just say it like the baby this, and the beagle that, and it riles him. But not like when I call him Mailman which he hits me. Roy don't name his work the Mail like everyone else. He names it the Service. He says it's the United States Postal Service and people oughta give it more respect. There's a tattoo on his arm down after his elbow what shows USPS with a eagle chewing on the letters. If I name him Mailman he hits me and makes me look at it. He don't hit for play neither. So on that one I mostly use his name, Roy.

I was just asking, I told Jackie. Just wondered if you seen her.

The baby was spitting out food and Jackie was scooping it up and stuffing it back in. Till my jaw's full better I got to eat my supper out my own baby jar. The doctor said Jackie could blend up regular food and told her the name of a recipe book but soon's we got into the parking lot she told me what she wasn't gonna work extra to make me my own special supper and what no I couldn't futz up her kitchen stuff and baby food was good enough for hers it was good enough for me.

Anyhow, I was just asking if she seen Linda and she got all mad no account.

She's not who you think, Jackie said.

I know her pretty good, I told her.

Oh yeah?

I just ate my spoon.

He thinks he knows all about her, Jackie shouted to the TV room. Roy was in there watching a sitcom. He was still in his postal worker uniform, minus the shoes.

Who? He shouted back.

That Podawalski woman, Jackie told him.

I don't want to hear another word about it, he said. You understand? Both of you. The whole thing's a disgrace.

You know so much about her, Jackie said to me, why don't you tell me just why she did it?

I started to, but she said, Swallow that. I got enough of a mess to clean up. Let me tell you something, Nimwit. Few months from now she's not gonna have the same name, same address, same nothing. And you ain't gonna know her from Jack.

I asked her what she meant by that.

You don't even know, do you? Mister I Know Her Pretty Good. Whyn't you go down to the courthouse check who filed for divorce?

Who? I said.

Day after it happened. And her husband stuck in jail.

Bitch, Roy said from the TV room.

They divorced? I asked.

Separated, Jackie said.

Put something in that thing's mouth, Roy shouted. I can't hear my own head think.

What do you think I'm doing? Jackie said.

Well then give her a tit, Roy said.

She's hardly—

Give her a tit Jackie, he said. Shit. Something funny happened I didn't even hear it.

Why don't you give her a tit, Jackie told him.

Ha, he said. Then, Shit. They're still laughing and I don't know what the hell's going on. Everybody shut up till the commercial.

Jackie took it out and put it at the baby even though there was still baby food all over everywhere.

When she'd got it quiet enough I asked her, What's separated?

Same as divorced, she said.

Mister Podawalski, if this is the first you heard of it, I hate to be the bear of such bad news. It must be bad, there where you is, knowing this. It must give you a whole lot of hurt. I will not lie to you and say it's bad news to me, but I don't take pleasure in your pain, neither. After all, you and me is bounded by something what's most like even more thick than blood. You and me is both the only ones what know her in the deep places of our heart. Jackie says I should find another woman more my speed. She don't understand. You and me, we understand. We most like the only ones in the whole world what do.

Your exxed wife was not the first woman what I ever kissed. I have kissed them before. Two of them, in fact. I know that ain't no grand number to brag on. You most like kissed much more than that. But you stopped when you hit upon Linda, and I stopped when I hit upon her, and don't you miss her? I wish you was here so I could ask you what parts you missed and put them next to mine and see if they was the same. I'll make a list

and some day when you read this you can put ex-marks next to
the parts you don't and chex-marks next to the ones you do.

WHAT'S TO LOVE IN LINDA
Them tiny wrists
Them long long fingers
How her elbows come to them points what are so sharp
The skin between her chin and her neck
Dark spots on the skin between her chin and neck
What she's so shy about them and don't like them
talked on, but liked the way I talked on them. I could tell
by the way she tried to hide her smile.
I never knowed a person had so many kinds of smiles
and could make them mean so different.
Do you like the way she does her fingernail between her
teeth when she's listening to you talk? At first I wanted to
ask her to stop, but then it got so's the sound of it kept
rhythm to what I was saying like she was saying it too,
but just with her fingernail on her teeth instead of words.
Her french fry smell. Her sitting in quiet how I never
met a person could sit like that and make it loud just by
thinking together. She loves crickets. She's the first who
ever made me feel full growed. She's who growed me.
She's who fit me into my whole age. She put me in me
and said to look around and where did I fit now and told
me it was time to prove it.

Sometimes sitting here writing to you I don't even know
how quiet it's got till something makes a sound. A second ago

there was a boom what should've woke the whole house, but
they all still asleep, even the old beagle. One of the yard critters
must have knocked over the trash can. Most likely coon. I can
hear him working at the lid, but he ain't gonna get it off. Roy's
got them kind with latches.

Yup. I just gone to the window and brung the flashlight
and it's a big fat coon. He keeps on, he's gonna wake Roy, get
hisself shot. In that book what Dad Kreager read us there was a
coon. If someone tried and sneak up on Sam out there on his
mountain that coon gone and told him so he could hide. Them
critters is just about my best company out here. Hardly a night
goes by one of them don't come and try to get at something. I
wonder what they do in the day. I wonder if they head back to
the woods or just hole up in what yard scrub they can find and
wait it out till dark. They is strange critters. They ain't like woods
critters what know they's meant for the woods. You come on a
mess of turkey you can tell they's satisfied with life beneath the
trees. There is house critters too, such as dogs, what spend some
time in the yard but know they place is with the people what
live in the house. But them yard critters don't seem to know.
They don't seem never satisfied. It's like all the day they's in the
woods they got one eye on the yards, and all the night they's in
the yards they got one eye on the next step, what's the inside of
the houses shut off to them. Roy's got squirrels in his walls. You
can hear them chew at night. Week after I moved into My Hall,
Jackie found a possum in the basement sitting there hissing at
her so's she screamed to set the baby crying and Roy gone down
there with his shotgun saying, I don't want no bitching about
the mess. That possum shoulda just stayed in the yard. They all
oughta. But you can't blame them. They got them flashlight eyes

what look back at you with longing for the inside like they want so bad outta that yard, and why should they got to stick with it just cause God up and decided one day that was their spot.

I just come back from outside. I took off that lid. If Roy knowed, he'd shoot me and the coon both. But there ain't nothing coming from the house end except the old beagle breathing and snorting his old lungs out what keeps me awake so I wish he'd die. In Roy's Bahamas the lagoon is making its lap lap lap. He left the wave maker on. Outside, the coon's come back. I wish you could hear him get at it. What with all the tearing and ripping it sounds like Christmas out there.

Sunday of July

Weeknights, the Sunoco goes self serve after eight what meant when I was living there I'd got to hustle if I was gonna get supper before the Pine Top closed. If you ever tried to get such as a piece of cornbread from Noreen after 8:30 you know what I mean. So I'd wash my face and lock up the Men's Room and get on my bike. Ride cross town. Mister Gilkey didn't much like how I give my money to them at the 76 what's competition, but them's what had the hot food and he was too cheap to pay for a microwave, so I didn't see much choice. Sides I didn't so much do it for the food. Don't get me wrong, I like to eat at the Pine Top. I miss it now. You never knowed what was gonna be the special that day and it give me a surprise every time I come through the door. The whole time I lived at the Sunoco I never once ordered nothing but whatever was on that special board, and I wasn't never sad at it, neither. I'd come in and sit at the counter and no matter if Noreen was near or cross the room she'd shout over, What'll it be tonight, Hon? And I'd shout back Give me what's special, and she'd shout, Well, I can't give you yourself, now can I Hon? Sometimes she named me Hon but more times she named me Aqua Boy. Like, Now how's Aqua Boy like them chops? Or, I bet Aqua Boy wants some of that coconut cream, doesn't he? I told her it was Aqua Man what was in them comics, but she said how I'm giving her lips and she don't need them and has knowed me since I was just a little water head so I should eat quiet. She has been around a long time and gets lips from everybody, but she always brung me extra at the end to show I was a valued customer and I miss the excitedness what come from not knowing dessert.

But it was the ride back what I miss most. I'd take the back streets, just wind around them for a while. Rolling, rolling. Just give it one pedal and coast till I got to give a pedal again. Sometimes I'd stop. If it was a real good window with the curtains open and something good inside I'd sit a while and watch. Didn't have to be nothing special. Might just be someone doing dishes or running a brush on the dog. I had a game what was to make like I could feel the hot water on my hands and think on how I could figure from the plates what'd been for supper, and how many people'd ate, if I had a wife or any kids or maybe watched after my folks what's got old. If it was a dog being rubbed down, I'd give it a name and think on what kind of dog it was and all the years I'd had it. Sometimes, if I didn't feel like bed, I'd bike on over to the low house what's just off Main Street, where the home sellers do their work. It was closed and dark but if I come up near so's my flashlight was right to the glass I could see what house picture they had put up. They didn't change house pictures regular as the Pine Top did specials, but that just made it all the better to come up on it wondering if they'd got a new one put in the window. If it was one I ain't seen yet, nor wore out with my thinking on it, I could stand there for a hour, just looking.

But that Friday I'd already gone to the Pine Top to get the fixings for my plan, and I was too nervous to focus on no windows. I stayed home, watched the dinky TV what Mister Gilkey kept in the office, ate Slim Jims and chips and sunflower seeds till I thought it was late enough.

I don't like to ride on the big roads heading out of town what with the vehicles and the way Roy's so strong on legal rules. He spends his time in the mail car going slow piece by piece, so when he gets on the big road he wants to go full out and no futzing tractor or bike riding idgit getting in his way. But I know all the back ones what get you anywhere you want. That night where the Pembroke Road hits town I took it. You can get from the Pembroke Road to 502 on a bike, but I wouldn't try it with no vehicle. If you take good aim with your eyes when you come up even with the creek you can see way out there the lamppost back of Crigger's Den. I cut straight cross.

Her car was out there like it was on the Mondays. I leaned the bike against her driver door. There was music still coming from inside and the kind of noise what means a pile of people. I knowed she might work more late Friday. I come prepared to wait. I took off my bag and took everything out and got it all ready behind the propane tank. You ever tried to count all the stars there is? Dad Kreager said it was the best way to improve the mind. He said it was like push-ups for my brain.

Ain't nothing the matter with your brain, he said. It just ain't been trained right account of how you was brung into the world and passed on from owner to owner like Carter. He said,

I got Carter from the pound when he was a pup, but he'd already been fucked up by two other owners. You know what they said?

I said, What?

They said he was brain damaged. Look at him. Come here Carter. Come here Carter. There. Look at those eyes. You ever knowed a smarter dog?

I said, No.

That's right. There's not a thing wrong with his brain, is there Carter? They just didn't train it right is all. Once I got my hands on him I knowed what to do. Didn't I Carter? Look at him, Geoff. Look at that smarts in them eyes. You can see it. Paw, Carter. Good boy. Give me the other paw. Good boy. Find the ball. Ball Carter. Find the ball Carter. Look at him go, huh? You think you got that kind of smarts in your eyes? What do you think, Geoff? I tell you what, time I'm through with you you will.

From then on out, times Mom Kreager left for work Dad Kreager put me out in the backyard and told me not to come in till I'd got a number on the stars. I'd stand out there and do it. He'd get on the kitchen phone and start his love talking with who was on the other end. I could hear it through the windows. It didn't stop till I come in with my count.

Hold on baby, he'd say and look up and say, You getting better, Geoff. Try it again.

I'd go back out. You'd think it'd be easier on cloudy days, but it ain't. The open bits keep changing so's you got to start over all the time. I like clear nights better. Clear nights I'd be out there hours. Carter'd come and sit by me. One thousand twenty one. One thousand twenty two. I'd pat his head on each new count.

That Friday night back of the Den what with no Party Van and it not Monday but Friday, like I said, I walked out into the crap field to get away from the lamp. It was the time for peepers. They was loud. I moved a little bit more toward the creek till I thought their noise was exact as loud as the noise coming from Crigger's and I stood there, right smack between, looking up. It's not easy, but it does pass the time.

I'd done all the ones one thumb up from the top of things and was doing the last bit over the dead trees on the hill when the music shut off inside Crigger's. I could feel it gone from my left side. After that, I couldn't keep my place in the sky. I kept looking at the kitchen door. The customer noise was going. The last cars pulled out the front. I was so nervous, I quit trying to do nothing else but breathe. When she come out it took me a while to get even that working. She made it all the way to her car and was looking at my bike leaning on it by the time I called her name. She looked my way.

Who's that? she said.

I come out the scrub into the light.

She said, Geoffrey?

What? I said.

Jesus, if you didn't creep me out.

I come by to say hi.

This yours?

Yuhuh.

You ride all the way here from home?

Yuhuh. I brung you something, too.

Let me guess.

Okay.

Beer. She laughed at something. Look at your face, she said. What'd you think I was gonna guess?

It's only part beer, I said.

What's the other part?

Come on, I said. I'll show you.

She didn't move. Geoffrey? she said. You know what time it is?

Nuhuh.

It's past two.

You eat yet?

I'm bushed, Geoffrey. And yeah, since you ask, I've been picking all night.

Well you still hungry?

Not really.

For a sec she didn't say nothing and I didn't say nothing and then she laughed again. You oughta never talk, she said. You oughta just make those faces. Get me to do anything.

She followed me over toward the propane tank.

She said, You know there's all kinds of other places we could go to talk.

And then we was back there and she got quiet at what I'd done.

Even though I'd pinned them down with stones, one of the paper plates was flipped over by something. The one with her name on it was still good, though. I'd done it in ketchup. I could see her looking at all the little white packets I'd throwed in the weeds.

I did yours in seven, I told her. Took ten for mine, cause it's got more letters.

She took a step off where she'd stood on the tablecloth. You could see the print she'd left on the white lacey part.

It's my sister Jackie's, I said.

She know you have it?

No.

She gone down and picked up one of the dish rags. Cloth, she said.

Them is hers too.

Very nice, she said.

I tore open the six pack and opened hers for her. It's not cold, I said.

That's fine, she said.

I put one of the Styrofoam carryouts in front of her, told her, That's not hot no longer, neither.

They were gonna mix to medium inside us anyway, she said.

Some bugs had got themselves dead in her name and I told her Sorry and Excuse the reach, just like Ma B teached, and picked them out of the ketchup for her. I said, Don't worry, these got tape. The sound of me peeling it off the styrofoam made her scrunch. I told her, Sorry.

You gotta stop saying sorry so much.

I told her okay and how I didn't know what she wanted so I'd just got us both chicken suppers. I said, I got them lunchtime cause they's cheaper but they been in the fridge.

She sat there looking at them. Oh I wish I'd told you, she said. I'm a vegetarian.

You don't eat meat?

No.

Not even fried?

It's okay, she said. I'll just eat the crisp give you the rest.

I started to peel mine but she said, No, no.

I looked at her.

Oh hell, she said. Go ahead.

While I took the crust off and put it on her plate she dug in her purse for something what turned out to be a lighter. She kept digging and come out with one of them rubber bands what women put in their hair, and lit the lighter and put the rubber band around it and took her thumb away and it stayed lit.

Hey, I said.

Old trick from high school, she said.

She took her biscuit out the Styrofoam and put it on the ground and stuck the lighter in it.

We watched the flame while we ate. When she'd ate the crust off hers, she give me a piece of meat.

What's your mom like? she said.

Which one?

Your mom.

I got three of them. But I don't live at home. I got my own place.

In Ripplemead?

Yuhuh. In the office.

Your dad's office?

No. I told you. I don't live at home.

Right, she said.

I'm not a kid.

I know, she said. She stopped wiping at her fingers with the rag. Not the gas station office?

It's only for now, I said.

You live at Sunoco?

I make good money. I could afford another place.

Is that even legal?

I buyed that bike didn't I?

How long have you been there?

I got a sleeping bag and a duffel bag and my own key to the Men's Room round the side.

How long have you lived there, Geoffrey?

I don't know. Three four years.

She reached into her bag and tapped out a smoke and lit it in the lighter candle.

Well that's shameful, she said. I don't care how many mothers you have.

I got three.

Shame on all of them. And especially your real one.

You mean my—

I mean the one who gave birth to you. Shame on her.

That's what Ma B says.

Well shame on Ma B too. Letting you live in a gas station. Where's all the rest of your family?

I got Jackie who's called a foster.

I mean blood family.

You mean the Sarvers?

Sure. The Sarvers.

There ain't no Sarvers left.

What do you mean?

They all dead.

All of them?

All of them. They was all of them found dead. You never heard how it goes?

No. How's it go?

Goes like this. They was hill people. Used to live in town like anybody but they wasn't like nobody. So's nobody much cared for them. They was ugly what they had stupid faces and some walked funny and some did fits and some even howled and moaned at night till the whole town knowed they was wrong in the head. And the whole town gets together and thinks up how they wanted them out. They come to all the doors of all the Sarvers. Got fire in their hands and guns and whatnot. And they say, We don't want you near our daughters. And we don't want what's wrong on you to come off on us. And you don't belong, is what. And get or else. So's all them Sarvers was drived out, way out to the hills, drived far as the town people could push them, drived with everything what they got from dogs and mules to tables and chairs, drived away from Ripplemead, and Narrows, and Pembroke, any other town, what put them smack in the middle way out where the Swain comes down through the New Valley. You ever been out there?

Sure.

There ain't much.

No there isn't.

That's why they was put out there. They was told don't come back. Don't nobody know what them Sarvers lived on or how they done it. But they did. Dug roots. Killed what animals they got in their traps. There was some what said they lived in caves and some what said they builded houses and some what said they just sleeped out under the stars. It was a place all of their own what they called Sarverville. Only time they left it was to sell the trees what they cut down. Every now and again they come out the woods to the towns. They come on carts drug by mules, come sitting top them stacks of logs. You could smell them a mile away. They was crawling with critters. Gone on like that for fifty years. Except when they come to town to sell that wood, God was the only one what woulda knowed them Sarvers even lived in the valley at all. Which was why it took so long for the news to get out how they was all dead. Nobody knows why. Just the guy owned the beef farm up the valley found his dogs sick one night and thinks they ate too much groundhog what they ain't used to, but what they throwed up ain't groundhogs. It's pieces of people. Fingers and toes and ears. So he follows them the next day down to Sarverville and they every one of them dead. Some of them lying in beds made of bark. Some crawled out into the woods. Some holding to each other or curled on their own, but not a mark on one of them save what the dogs done. Out of the whole family of them there was only one little baby left.

And that was you, she said.

That was me. They found me pinned tight in my dead Mama's arms.

They did, she said.

They had to cut them off to get me out.

Who told you that? she said.

Dad Kreager.

Let me guess. He was the one who found you?

Nuhuh. The State give me to him.

Hill people, she said. I bet he told you lots of stories.

Yuhuh. He was good at them.

I bet he was, she said. I'll tell you something though, and I want you to listen to me. There are lots of good stories that aren't true. In fact most of them. Now listen Geoffrey. You've got family somewhere.

They's all dead.

Did you ever look?

For Sarverville?

No, for your mother. Your father.

Dad Kreager told me—

I mean even in the phone book.

They ain't no Sarvers in it, I told her. They didn't have phones out there.

Let me guess, that's from Mister Kreager too.

They's all dead, I tried to tell her.

Listen, she said. I know this much. If I had a little baby and everyone was dying around me I'd sure as hell find some way to get him out.

The lighter candle looked done and then did a little more and then was done.

You don't got a little baby, I said.

What makes you say that?

You's too pretty.

She laughed. It was a strange sound after all our quiet talk. What's that got to do with anything? she said.

The way you get upset. It ain't like the way a mom gets riled, what it makes you look more younger stead of more old.

It does, huh? she said. Well I could use a little of that. And no I don't have any kids.

Why not? I said.

She drank her beer till it was empty and then she shook it and said, This is empty.

I got her one and got me one and opened both.

When we was drinking again she said, I'm married you know.

You is? I said.

She held up her hand. Under the big lamp there was all her rings.

Which one is it? I said.

She pointed to it.

Oh, I said. How come you don't got kids?

She laughed. You don't let go, do you?

I put down my beer.

She said, Waker doesn't want any.

Is Waker your husband's name?

Waker Podawalski. I can't have kids, she said. After I got— after the operation it was hard to get him to even look at me. So when he said he wanted me to get my tubes tied—he liked to finish inside a woman and he didn't want to worry he said. And you know things were already bad enough by then that I went along with it. I thought maybe it would average things out, you know, make him overlook the—what they done to my breasts. You know even things out a little. It's not many women you can just finish inside and not worry.

She looked at me. You aren't getting any of this are you?

You had a operation? I said.

This time her laugh was one of her not really laughs and she said, Oh Honey. I'm sorry. I didn't mean to confuse you. There's nothing complicated about it, actually. I had what's called a tubal ligation.

What's that?

It's when you get your tubes tied.

I must have been staring at her because she said, Oh honey again.

You got tubes? I said.

Down here. She pointed toward her place. Then she said, Maybe we better pack up. She took her lighter and pulled off the band and threw it into the weeds with the ketchup packs. She took the band and started to put it in her hair.

Can I see them? I said.

When you hear her best good laugh it makes all her other laughs seem like they ain't worth the name.

No, she said. They're inside.

Which is why he can finish in you?

Could, she said. If he wanted to. You know what I mean by finish?

I wiped up the last of my name on the plate but then I felt strange about putting my finger in my mouth so I just held it there. I thought he said he wanted to, I told her.

I thought so too, she said. Not that it would make any difference. I mean, how the hell would I nurse anyway?

It's easy, I told her. Ma B just had a button on her shirt what she'd undo and—

Listen, she said. I don't want you to think what I do back here has any weird thing to do with the fact that I don't have kids or nothing, Okay? She picked up her plate and scraped the leftovers back into the Styrofoam. She said, I only do kids because it wouldn't be safe to do anybody else. Not for me, and not for them. A grown man—Waker'd kill him. Waker found me with a grown man, he'd beat the shit out of him, and then he'd beat the shit out of me, and then he'd divorce me, and I can't afford that. So that's why, she said. She stacked her

Styrofoam container on top of mine. It's not anything wrong with you. Okay?

It was quiet. Them crickets musta either gone to sleep or moved on to another part of the crap field.

Listen, she said. It's really pretty simple. Kids don't count. It may seem strange, but Waker's a strange man. He knows what I do back here and I know what he does. Paid women. Women who're still whole. We have a agreement. But if I was to do a kid all the way—you understand what I'm saying? Or do a full grown man? He doesn't even like me talking to men outside of work. Except for his brother. His brother's the only one he'll let me alone with, the only grown man Waker will allow me to talk to like a friend. The last time I had friends, I mean male friends, God it must have been high school. We were high school sweethearts. You have any idea how long ago that is?

Nuhuh, I said.

A long time.

I put my empty down and reached for the last two and opened them and she put a hand on my arm instead of taking the can.

I gotta go, she said.

Okay, I said. So you can't give me a blow job because I'm a full grown man?

Her hand stayed on my arm. I could feel her looking at me. I watched the cans. I could feel her looking at me more. What? I said.

She said, That's what I'm trying to figure out.

What's what you're trying to figure out?

Just exactly what you are.

I put the cans down. Her hand stayed on my arm the whole way.

I'm Geoffrey Sarver, I said. I'm not retarded.

I know, she said.

I'm not a kid.

I know, she said.

I'm just a little slow.

You're handsome, she said.

I looked at her hand on my arm and I told her, Mom Wasco used to say I looked like someone smacked my forehead flat with a clothes iron.

That was when she kissed me. She kissed me right under the ear. Then she kissed me on the forehead. Then she kissed me right on the mouth.

That, she said, was against all the rules.

Monday of July

I wonder does she come and visit you.

Tuesday of July

Last night was the night I decided to do it. My face is healed pretty good. I got the wires off but there's still them ugly red marks all over, and them bruises what make my neck look wrunged. Last night I got into Jackie's makeup and done my best, which wasn't much good. But I guess I never been a looker, as they say, and Linda never cared nohow, so I thought heck to it and lets get it done.

After I come back, I was too plain beat to write you. To-night too, but Roy and Jackie is shouting and yelling again behind the door to the house part and I can't sleep. So, I will put it down. I have missed her terrible horrible and deep. I wish I knowed how you did for yourself when you felt the same. How you get yourself shut of it. I know there must be a way but I am new to this life of the adult kind. There's got to be a way to get on. I know I ain't the first to miss somebody. Sometimes I look at everyone what comes to fill up their tank and I think, Who do you miss? And, Who do you miss? And, Who do you miss? Till it seems the whole of Eads County knows a secret to how to go on and don't want to clue me in. I'm fed up with it. I was fed up last night. Let's get it done, I said. Get on your bike, I said. Go over say hi.

Now what I'm living in My Hall, it was strange yesterday to get ready after work in the Sunoco Men's Room how I used to back in the spring. Felt like back in them times what was after she lay her kiss on me.

Back then I'd get washed every single day after work. Full body washed. Done my hair in the sink and brushed my teeth and shaved and combed like it was morning and the first customer rolling over the bell. But outside, the Sunoco sign was lighted up for nighttime and the lights over the pumps was turned dark to show we was closed. I'd lock it all up and get on my bike.

Them first weeks way back in spring before it all gone bad, I rode out of town to Crigger's every night. Took 502 all the way, didn't even mind being on the big roads with the vehicles what used to make me shaky. Them spring weeks all that looked to me like kid stuff what I'd kicked off and left. I just let them vehicles wait or go around. Even then, at the end of April, it was already late for redbuds, but a mile or two before Crigger's, where the creek cut through the pipe beneath the road, there was some hangers on. I'd stop, go down in a spread of crap land, pick off a branch. Redbud's pretty tough. First time I tore it up, had to use my teeth. After that I brung the wire snips.

I'd park my bike round back and knock on the kitchen door and wait outta sight. If she wasn't back there, one of them in the kitchen would tell her. Pretty soon, she'd come out and I'd give her the branch. She'd switch the old one out and put the new one in. With all its buds. After the first couple days, she'd come to the door ready with last night's branch what she could just toss and take the new one and put it in the jar top the dishwasher. I know that's where she kept it cause sometimes I'd sneak to the door and look through the screen and see it there. If the machine was working that branch would sit up and shake.

She didn't like me to look through the door but sometimes, if I'd been waiting there more than a hour between her visits, I'd do it anyhow. If she was real busy she wouldn't even notice. Sometimes though, she was just sitting there talking with one of the kitchen people. Or at the bar, talking with someone else. If she seen me then, she'd give me a look what sent me packing. I didn't mind. Cause it'd bring her out in a minute. She'd tell me what I wasn't supposed to be hanging out there and I'd better keep my face hid so she didn't get in trouble and I'd tell her, All right, and Can I have a kiss?

Three, four times during the night she'd come out for real. She'd light up and sit with me against the back of the Dumpster and we'd talk about everything could be talked about. End of her shift, she'd close down. I'd help with what I could, throw the bag up in the Dumpster for her and whatnot. Sometimes we'd share a beer after she locked up. Sometimes we'd just do some good-night talk and she'd get in her car. But either way I'd follow her out of the lot onto 502. Head back the way we'd come. And every time she'd start to pull away up front she'd hold her cigarette out the window so's the tip glowed and give it a little shake, just to say one last extra good night.

Mondays there'd be Russ and Vic in the Party Van waiting too. The first time they come they seen me sitting out there by the Dumpster and waved me over.

Russ had rolled down the window. Hey, he said. Long time no see.

Yuhuh, I said.

We went by the Sunoco but you wasn't there.

I was there.

You was?

I was in the office.

We honked, Vic said.

I know, I said.

Russ looked at Vic. They both shaked their heads and grinned. Good ol' Geoffrey, Russ said. Hey, get in the back. He patted the slide door with his hand.

It was the same in there, except it felt smaller. I hadn't been around that much smoke in a while and it made me cough.

Here, Russ said but I didn't want any. I could see through the screen door into the kitchen what they was closing up. After a while, Vic said, Our band practice has gone for shit. A while after that, Russ said, Where you been Geoff?

Nowhere.

I hope it was nowhere good, he said.

Vic laughed. Man, Geoff lives in nowhere. Right Geoff?

I don't know what you mean, I told him.

See, he said.

We's just joking with you, Russ said.

She come out and Russ flashed at her and she held up five. I seen her glance at the Dumpster.

I gotta go, I said.

You ain't gonna stick around? Russ said.

What the fuck, Vic said.

I said, Don't it ever get old? Don't you ever get tired of it?

Of blow jobs? Russ said.

There isn't a man on earth gets tired of blow jobs, Vic said. Anyone gets tired of blow jobs is either a homo or ain't hit puberty yet.

That's not true, I said. There's more than just blow jobs.

How would you know? Vic said.

You got something on the side? Russ said. Geoff? Geoffrey?

Just his hands, Vic said. Hanging left and right. Right Geoff? No, seriously though, you got a point. He's got a point.

I asked her last time, Russ said.

Maybe I oughta ask her, Vic said.

She won't do it, Russ told him.

You say please? Vic said.

She won't do it, Vic.

Do what? I said.

Open her cooch, Russ said. Like you was talking about. Then he said, Here she comes. I for one ain't complaining.

I watched him go behind the propane tank and I wanted to get out and drag him back so bad what when Vic said We oughta go over there too, I almost said okay.

Instead I said, She wouldn't like it.

How do you know so much? he said. A nympho like that gets bored with just one dick.

She's not a nympho, I told him. She's married.

He laughed.

Don't laugh, I told him. You don't even know her name.

She's Mister Podawalski's wife, he said.

I told him, You're almost done with high school and you still don't know what's more than just a blow job.

What's that supposed to mean? he said. I put open the door and got out. What's that supposed to mean? he said again, but I was already walking away to get my bike. That was the first time I rode back without her cigarette goodnight.

The next Monday I hid behind the Dumpster when I heard the van and stayed till they was gone and had a beer with her after. The next Monday after that Monday I did the same. Then, well, Mister Podawalski, it wasn't long after that what you showed up.

I wonder do you remember seeing me. Did you even know it? Did you even look? I know you could see right through the kitchen from where you sat at the bar, right through the kitchen to the screen door, because I could see you. It was the first time I'd got a picture of how you looked. For a while I'd been trying to think back on if I'd seen you come through the Sunoco but if I did I couldn't find it in my brain. You must have used the 76. I even asked Linda. I asked her how come I never seen you even anywhere in Ripplemead? She said you was always working on the highways over east. Or you was at the church out by Harts Run where you'd growed up. She said you didn't much care for any people who was between. Them was her words, but it is true I hadn't seen you till that night.

Even so, I knowed it was you. I knowed just from looking at her. She was leaning on the bar. You was talking. She
done the thing with her apron what I seen her do when she
was happy talking to me. But she done other things too what
I never seen. Like she picked at her earring till she took it
plumb off and then put it on again and she did it twice. I stood
in the screen door watching. Waiting for her to turn round and
give me one of her Oh Get Outta Sight Geoff looks. She never
looked my way once.

What was you talking with her? What did you do to make
her laugh that laugh what was entire new, I ain't yet heard. You
was in a suit jacket. You was the only man in there with a suit
jacket. I don't mind telling you you looked good in that suit
jacket. And, by the way, you looked better with a beard how you
had that night. I don't mind telling you how bad I wanted that
suit jacket for my own.

When she finally come out it was late. She stood there. Lit
up. I lit up too and tried to look at her without her knowing while
we smoked. By then I knowed her levels of tired. First time she'd
come out she'd be pretty good. Second time she'd be quiet and
just trying not to think about how long it was to go. Third time
she'd be a little mad at how long it'd been. Fourth, it was coming to a close and she'd got her wind again all full of zip. That
night it was her first time out, but she was looking like it was
the fourth. Full of zip. I will confess I'd thought she'd look something different if you come around. What with her talk of getting shut of you. But having seen you and her it made sense to
see her out there like that. After all, you two got married. You
two lived together in love. You two was husband and wife which
meaning I guess I'd simple forgot.

Sooner or later we got talking. Not good as usual, but I didn't mind. I was glad she'd chose to leave you there at the bar and come spend the time with me. I made the most of it. She give me the laughs she always give me and they was pretty good. When she gone back in I looked after her to see what you thought. You was gone from the bar. I didn't see you the rest of the night. I guess you done gone home.

It was on a few nights later what she come out with the old redbuds like usual and took her new ones like usual, but then was back for her first smoke more early than usual. She was full of good talk and didn't once complain about the coming night. She never did come for her second smoke. You know your end of how it gone from that. I won't go into it. There's no point, and I don't like to. I will say it hit me bad when she kissed you. I knowed you done more, but it was different to know it and to see it. The decent thing woulda been to take it somewhere else and do that stuff. Just so you know. I know you seen me sooner or later cause I caught your eye. Even though she didn't turn and look, I could tell you was talking about me.

Let me tell you from my side of Linda what you don't know. You don't know how that night at her car, once you was gone, I said to her, Why don't he stick around till you done?

Geoffrey, she said.

Why don't he drive back home with you?

I think you know that, she said.

He go to bed before you get there?

I'm not talking about it now, she said.

You liked to talk about it before he showed up.

I'm tired, she said.

Me too, I said. I been waiting out here all night.

I know, she said. She put her hand on my hand and moved it off the car door and shut the door and said through the open window, Come down here, Geoffrey.

I come down there.

You're a sweet boy, she said and give me a kiss the same side of the head she did you.

It was the first time she'd ever named me a boy.

You don't know neither about the night she forgot to bring the old redbuds out with her on her smoke break, and how she took the new ones back in with her and just left them on the counter next to the water jar, and how I watched them go bad slow over hours all night. You don't know how that night I followed her out the parking lot on my bike and how she reached out and did her cigarette wave and how that changed everything from bad to good in one shake of her hand.

You don't know how a night come what she didn't head out back at all. How I stood there with my fresh redbuds, looking at the old ones in the jar till I couldn't take it no more and gone in there on my own to swap them out. The kitchen people give me hell and made a noise so's she took me out back, and talked to me, and when I looked back through the kitchen I seen you standing by the bar watching on.

The next night there was no jar at all. When I looked in, them in the kitchen caught me at it and said to me stuff what nobody shouldn't got to hear and take it. She didn't come out once all night. Towards the end it was quiet enough I could stand there with my ear to the wall and listen to who was doing what and so I knowed when she gone out the front door to take her smoke break. She didn't talk to me at the car more than to say good night. I followed her fast as I could far as I could waiting

for her to shake her cigarette out the window, but you can't keep
a bike even with a car what don't want to be kept even with. I
never seen her hand reach out, just way up ahead in the dark
the sparks hitting the road. I looked for them when I got there,
but they'd gone black as the hardtop.

The next night I watched you through the window, and
when you left I watched her till she gone out front for her break,
and then I caught her at it.

Oh for God's sake Geoffrey, she said, I thought you'd gone
home.

No you didn't, I said.

Okay, she said. But you ought to.

We stood there for a while.

I'd like you to, she said. For me. Geoffrey. What do you
want to say? What's there to say?

I love you, I told her.

No you don't, she said.

I do, I told her.

That's puppy love, she said. Puppy love is something you
think is love, Geoffrey. It's something—

Well, do you got puppy love for me?

No, she said. I'm too old.

I don't care how old you is, I said. I'm gonna stand here
every night till you say—

Don't be childish, she said. You're acting like a—

I called her something I never called no one before.

I've gotta go back to work, she said.

I'm sorry, I told her.

You've gotta stop saying you're sorry, she said. Part of being
a adult is knowing when you mean what you say.

Did you mean it when you said you wanted to leave Mister Podawalski?

My husband? she said.

Did you mean it when you said he never touched you?

Yes I did, she said. Okay?

I don't understand, I said.

Sometimes I don't either, she said. That's how it goes.

What changed? I asked her.

I don't know, she said. I guess—I guess I started to realize I had feelings, that I had feelings I didn't think I was capable of having anymore. That sounds like it's from a soap. It probably is from a soap. Jesus Geoffrey I just—sometimes you don't know why you feel a certain way, you just do, and that's usually when you know it's—well, when you know it's not just puppy love.

I don't know why I got feelings for you, I said.

I don't know either, she said. After what you've seen and what you know I swear I don't know either.

That night she got out and into her car before I could get around the lot on my bike and by the time I hit the road she was gone.

She wasn't really gone.

You know that good as me. Or else you wouldn't be who you is where you is and I wouldn't be who I am where I just got out of. If she'd just gone then I guess our stories here would be pretty different. But she didn't. What you don't know is what I don't know how to say anyhow but this. She's gone now.

That is what I meant to tell you when I started to put all this down here tonight. Like I said, last night I rode out to Crigger's Den to see her. The redbuds what was in the creek was all done this late in summer and it was hard at first riding with just one eye. Plus it hurt on my face when my bike hit bumps. But it was sweet to see Crigger's with them lights on and the lot full. I rode on back and parked my bike by the Dumpster and knocked on the screen door. Them kitchen people looked out at me.

It's Linda's boy, one of them said.

They made jokes at me till I'd waited long enough and asked them straight out.

She quit, one said.

She don't work here no more? I said.

That's the usual result.

I gone around and in through the front door and right up to the bar. There was a woman who'd never even stopped at the Sunoco wearing Linda's apron. She told me the same. You someone to her? she said.

Once, after all this but before you all started your court-house fight, she come to my room at New Castle Memorial to talk. She brung me flowers in their own plastic wrap, said, They're not redbuds but. My jaw was wired up but I writ on a pad she brung me and it was near as good, just slow. We talked it out that way long and hard. She wanted to make sure I understood. There was some things she told me would hurt her real bad if the whole wide town got wind of them and how she couldn't live if I told her deepest things out loud.

You know I wouldn't, I writ her on the pad. It was a big pad of paper what she brung, long and yellow. The pen was chewed up by her. I liked the way it felt in my hand.

I writ for her to sit. There was a chair what everyone else sat on when they came. She put her bag on it and sat on the bed instead. Right by my hip. I could feel under me how the mattress

bent under her. The other side of the curtain was a old man what
peed his sheets. He was calling for someone to change them.

I guess she could see me up close better now cause she
was looking hard at my face when she said, What did he do
to you?

I started to writ her, but she put her hand on mine right
over the pen.

Shh, she said.

Her hand on top of mine was same as how if her lips was
on my lips.

Do you know how sweet you are? she said. I mean to me?
How sweet my feelings are for you? Anyone else would hate me.
She reached at me and touched the bandage what gone over my
eye and then down the wires on my face. Her fingers wasn't a
inch away. I could almost feel them. When she took them back
she said, Maybe you do.

I tried to write her No, but she made her Shh again and
pressed her hand more down on mine.

It doesn't matter, she said. You'll always be my sweet
Geoffrey. If he thought doing this would change that. I wish
you could be in court just so he'd have to see you.

I started to write again but she said, No it's better if you
put it down here, write it out the way, you know, the way we
discussed. She took her hand off mine. Before you do, she said,
is there anything else you need me to explain?

I was gonna write No but instead I writ Do. It just come
out. After that there wasn't nothing to do but write the rest. Do
you still go behind the tank?

She looked at me and said Whew and looked away again.

The nurse come and seen what the old man done and the whole time she was in the room Linda was quiet. When the nurse was gone to get new sheets Linda reached down and took my pad. She tore the piece off and crunched it into a ball of paper in her hands.

I hate for you to remember me that way, she said.

I tried to shake my head.

I don't know how to tell you. How to help you understand. I don't.

The nurse come back with the sheets. Linda looked at the curtain like she could see the noises they was making. Then she leaned down so close her breathing was more loud than the other sounds. I could feel it on my ear. Feel her sigh. Feel her breath gone when she sat back up.

Tell you what, she said. I'll write it out. It's easier for me that way. I'll write it while you write out for the lawyer the way it happened, how we discussed. Deal?

She tore out a page and another page. Then she give me back the pad. She got up and drug over a little table on wheels. She sat in the chair and writ and I lay with the pad on my chest and writ all what she'd told me how it would help her out. When I was done she was still working at hers. The nurse come round the curtain and asked on me and I told her fine. My ribs was hurting from sitting up to write but I wanted her gone so Linda would start writing again and finish up and come sit back on the bed. But Linda didn't start writing again. She just come and sit.

Push over, she said.

Then she lied next to me on the bed. The flowers was between us. I reached over and moved them to my other side. She moved in where they'd been. We swapped papers and read like that. What I'd put down. What she'd put down. Behind the curtain the old man lied there with nothing to do or talk to or nothing. All the carts in the hall what always gone by gone by.

When she was done she put the pad on her lap and leaned over and kissed me next to my one eye what I got left. I'd already read what she'd writ. I was reading it again.

I can't write it any clearer, she said. I'd have to burn it. She smiled like it was a joke but her voice showed how it wasn't. About all I understood of what she writ was how she didn't want me to tell it to no one. And I didn't.

She took what I'd done and got up and gone to put the pad in her bag but I reached for it till she give it back.

Come back? I writ.

She looked at me funny. She said, Maybe once this is all over I can explain it to you better, okay?

I tried to make the words with my mouth. Tried to say them at her. But the sound what come out of my wired jaw wasn't nothing like Come back and I could see on her what the sound I done was bad to listen to.

Of course I'll come back, she said.

Then she picked up her bag and gone around the curtain. There was her footsteps and the carts going by in the hall. Then just the carts.

I wonder, Can you get phone calls where you at? I'd guess so. I'd guess you can get letters too. I can get letters here, just in the box with everyone else's mail. I think I can get phone calls, too, but when I checked in the phone pages it was just Roy and Jackie by the number. I guess if someone tried, I'd find out.

Last night at Crigger's Den I writ out a note what told the phone number and Don't say who you is, just ask for me, and left it with the woman. I gone by Linda's house, which I guess is your house too, or was your house, or anyhow there's a For Sale sign out front and the place has been cleaned out. I gone by your home seller's office too, but they said, You mean Brian? And I said, No sir. I mean Waker Podawalski. And they said No, you looking for his brother. Which pissed me off, and I told them what I may not be smart but Look at my face. You think I'd forget who did that? They said they was sorry but what no Podawalskis period worked there no more. Which I guess makes sense since you's in jail. Today I stood out on the curb every chance I got between cars pulling in. I didn't even wave the smallest kind what people don't even know they see. I just stood there looking hard at windshields what passed. Sooner or later she got to drive by. When she does, I'll let you know.

Thursday of July

Two big things has happened. The first is they going to have what's named Open House for the home what was yours and Linda's. There's two homes being done. Your neighbor seems made up his mind to sell, too. Maybe he just don't like living next to the scene of the crime, as they say. There was a phone number on the Open House sign front of your and Linda's home. I writ it down. Last night Roy and Jackie gone out and left me to sit the baby till they come home. While they was out I called the sign number. It was a man. I asked if he knowed where I might find Linda Podawalski. He asked who it was wanted to know. When I told him he said, Oh well she don't live here. I asked

him where she did live and he said, Hell if I know, and hung
up. I want you to know I ain't give up hope. Soon as that house
opens up, I'm gonna go and wait there till she shows. And if
she don't, I'm gonna start asking. I'm gonna start asking anybody what might know anything about where's she gone.

The other big thing what happened is Roy got them frogs.

Friday of July

I am sure there's something of a sin in what I done tonight. If
there is I am sure Ma B will point it out and I will try to stop it
then. For now, I am not gonna stop it. I am gonna keep on. I
am sorry if this is hard to read. I just come in. My hand is still
shaky from the excitedness. I don't think there's no one else in
the world but Ma B what I'd tell about it, or maybe Linda, or I
guess since here I am, it would include you.

I been out to the neighbors' yards getting their trash. I got a
can and brung it over to our back yard and dumped it out right
along the edge of our house. Then I brung the can back and got
another from the next house and done the same. I got so I could
do a dozen cans in a half hour. You shoulda seen them critters
come. There musta been least two dozen. I gone out with my flashlight and just stood there for a while looking at all them eyes. They
was all kinds from possum to squirrel to coons, but mostly coons,
and them all coming down on all them leftovers from all them
families on Abe's Knob like something from the Bible. It made
me so happy to watch them go at it I had half a mind to open the
house door and just let them at all what they could ever want.

I'm glad I didn't though. It would have been a mess and
woke Roy up for certain. Even now, while I'm writing, I can hear

them going through what's left out there. Sometimes one will kick a can or turn over something glass and I'm sure Roy is gonna start shooting. But so far it's quiet. Except for the critter noises. And Roy's damn frogs. They make this peep peep peep peep noise all night like some jungle what's gonna creep under the door into My Hall. If I go over and put my mouth to the crack of the door and hiss like a snake they stop for a while. Then you can hear the scratching on the greenhouse glass. Scratch scratch scratch scratch. One of them yard critters trying to get in.

Saturday of July

It is late again. I am tired tired tired in my whole body, but my brain is up. My brain is thinking how sometimes things is done what makes other things done what I never seen coming. Sometimes I can't figure the why of something no matter how strict I am on my brain, no matter how I can feel everyone else around knows it. I've growed to know I just got to wait. I got to wait for what's to come and maybe it will show me the why of what come before.

Today when I come home from the Sunoco there wasn't even time to get off my bike before Roy was on me. He come down the drive with a gun in his hand. He told me things what if they was writ here would make the Eyes of the Lord mad on you and me both just for reading them. He said them the whole way round the house. In the back was the trash what I'd put out. It was in Jackie's flowers and in Roy's fishing boat and everywhere. Some was in the crap bush at the edge of the yard. Some was way in the woods looking shiny beneath the trees where them yard critters musta drug it. But some of them critters was still in the yard. You could tell by where the trash moved. Every time it did Roy shot it.

Go get that, he said.

He was using a gun what was too big. Sometimes I had to carry them critters in parts. He was still in his post office clothes and I guess he must have been out there shooting them since he got home from work cause there was already plenty dead ones spread in with the trash. He made me clean them all up. He said put them in big black trash bags. He shot new ones around me while I did it. When I'd brung all the dead ones and put them in the bags he gone back inside to get away from the stink. Cleaning up the rest of the trash was slow work. I tried to do it quiet so as to let what critters was still hanging on in the woods know it wasn't me who was shooting their coon babies and possum wives. If I seen one, I threw it a piece of something good so it could tell the others what side I was on.

When Roy come out again it was almost dark. Here, he said. He give me Jackie's yellow rubber gloves what she uses in the sink. I tried to get them on.

You learned your lesson? he said.

These is too small.

What the hell'd you do it for anyway?

For them critters.

He pointed at me with the gun. Boy, he said, Jackie's gonna be mad you stretch out those gloves.

I already done it, I told him.

He looked happy. Before he gone back inside he said, Don't forget there's the neighbors' yards too.

Jackie was done feeding the baby and they was on their own supper by the time I come in. Roy got up. Look at that boy's hands, he said.

I pulled at the gloves.

Jackie shaked her head. She said, Roy—

Like a duck, Roy said. Boy you look like a duck.

You owe me a pair, Jackie said to him.

He leaned down to the baby. He looks like a duck, Roy told it.

Roy took his gun in one hand and a flashlight in the other and said for me to follow. We gone back outside. He put the light on the yard.

Boy, he said, You're a pretty good worker.

I told him, Mister Gilkey says I'm the best service attendant what he ever hired.

I bet, Roy said. Then he said, Best you keep those gloves on. Jackie ain't—

Fuck Jackie. Roy done his neck so's to see back in the window what showed her at the table. She was scraping what was on his plate over to hers. He put the flashlight on her, shaked it around, done a circle with it. You could see she knowed he was out there, but she didn't even give him a look. You know what that is? he said.

Nuhuh.

Marriage. You want to take a ride to the dump?

While I brung the bags and put them in the truck, he hanged the gun on the hooks in the back window and started her up and sat there for me to get in. We drived. He put the radio on talk. There wasn't nobody on the road. They was all inside their homes. It was dark and windows gone by and dark again. I watched them lit up squares. Sometimes when the radio talked Roy talked back.

At the dump, Roy pulled up so his headlights showed all them squares of metal wire and the chain and the lock. Behind the gate was the dump hill.

How we gonna get in? I said.

Roy shut off the radio. You got a cigarette, he said?

Nuhuh.

He told me look in the glove box. While I done it he reached back and took the gun off the hooks. He stuck his hand in the glove box next to mine and took out a box of bullets. He slid the window down. When I found the pack he took a smoke. He give me one too. Lit them both with the plug in the dash. Then he leaned out and pointed the gun at the gate and shot it.

What you aiming for? I said.

The lock, he said.

I think you missed it.

I think you're a fucking genius.

He popped the old one out and put a new one in and shot again. He did the same twice more. But the next one brung so many sounds on my head so loud I don't know what come first. There was just the bangs and then the sound in my ears afterwards and we was both got all small down in our seats beneath our arms covering our heads. There was little bits of glass in Roy's hair. He was shaking. I thought he was scared and then I looked up and seen the windshield bust with a hole in it and I thought he was mad and maybe I oughta get out now but when I looked back at him he was laughing.

Holy shit, he said.

Yuhuh, I said.

He said, Holy shit we better get those bags.

But outside the truck he just run down to the road. He stood there looking back and forth like he was gonna cross it. The truck was off but the lights was on and it was making its beep. He still had the gun.

Throw them over the fence, he told me.

I was on the last one when he come up behind me. He stood there looking at the truck. How do you like that, he said.

I don't know, I said. I told him, I throwed them bags.

He turned around and looked at them. They was all five over there the other side of the fence. Well that's a good job, he said.

I started back to the truck.

Hey, he said. You just gonna leave them there?

Yuhuh, I said.

No, he said. No, I don't think we can do that.

I done it, I said.

Come on, where's your civic pride?

I don't got one.

He was already climbing the fence. He gone up it with the gun. At the top, he said, Turn off the truck lights. Then he gone over the other side.

I gone around to the cab and reached in and shut off the lights. The moon come through the windshield and showed how broke it was.

What you gonna tell Jackie? I said.

I couldn't see him anymore now what the lights was off. He didn't say nothing back. But soon as I shut the door, there come a shot. It hit the windshield. There come another and the windshield was hit again and then another just bust the glass right out.

Quit it, I told him. Quit it.

I ain't gonna hit you, he said.

You quit it, I told him.

Oh come on get over here.

You coulda hit me.

Get over here, he said, or I will.

I was at the top of the fence when I seen him standing there. He was pointing the gun at me.

Oh boy, he said. I got me a big one. Big old Sarver coon. I'm gonna make me a hat.

Futz off, I told him.

Big old coon tail hat, he said. Let me see your tail, Sharpie.

Futz off, Mailman, I told him.

He was laughing. Then he wasn't laughing. Get down here, he said.

Put down the futzing gun, I told him.

Get the fuck down here, he said. Now, Geoff. I'm not fucking kidding. Here come the cops.

I looked back at the road. Them trees around the bend was lit up colored.

We left the bags where they was and run for the dump hill. It was dirt put over top the trash and pipes what stuck out of the ground and it was hard running in the dark. I guess Roy was looking to get over the other side but we wasn't even at the top when the cop car pulled in behind his truck. Its lights come on. Roy gone down. I gone down with him. We lied there. There was two cops come out. They walked around the truck. They was talking to each other and looking at the windshield. One of them gone back to the car and done something in there. The other started talking out at the night how we should quit hiding if we was around.

Roy said something to me real quiet.

What? I said back.

This is great, he said. Right? Like being kids again. Fucking great. I haven't done something like this since I was—since I was a kid.

I looked at him. In the moonlight I could see his teeth smiling. He give me a punch in the arm.

Shit, he said. Shit, Geoff. Look at them. Look at those fucking cops.

I don't know what I ever seen him so happy.

I bet that's Jim Heatwole, he said. One of them sure as shit is. Fucking Jim Heatwole. Me and him were in the same grade. We used to go out to the overpass at night and fire bottle rockets at cars. I learned to call turkeys from his dad. Holy fucking shit Jim Heatwole.

He rose his hands to his mouth and done a turkey call. He had to quit when he started laughing. The cop come to the fence and shined his flashlight in. Roy rose the gun. He looked down it like he was gonna shoot the cop.

You're a bad influence, Geoff, he said. He give my boot a kick with his. You make me digress back to a kid.

I'm not a kid, I said.

Me neither, he said.

After a time the cops got back in the car. We watched them back down toward the road.

I haven't had this much fun since I got married, Roy said. Don't ever get married, Geoff, he said. He kept his gun on the cops till they was gone. Then he said, You ever been hunting?

Nuhuh. Jackie says I ought not be allowed near guns.

Jackie, Roy said. Jackie doesn't know everything.

What are the cops gonna do? I said.

I don't know. Maybe get the truck towed. Maybe call the house. You know, I haven't been hunting since I married Jackie. The house. The baby. All of it. What was the last good time you had, Geoff, I mean really, really good time?

I thought on how it was last night when I spread out the trash and watched them yard critters come out of the woods, but I didn't say nothing.

You know when it was for me? Roy said. It was hunting. Not the last time I went, but one of the last. I'd already met Jackie. We were already engaged. I was hunting with this other woman.

He was quiet for a time.

You want to go back to the truck? I said.

He just turned on his back and lied there looking up. He stuck the gun so the wood part was on his belly and the other part was at the sky. He said, She and me, we came to this place, this place that was—I don't know what hell it was, but it was— she'd got a buck, not a big one but her first of the season, you know, but she'd gut shot it and we were tracking it. Jesus, we'd tracked it I don't know an hour, two, way, way back up into the hills. It was getting dark. I wanted to turn around but she had a real thing about finishing it, you know, so it doesn't die that way, and we kept finding its blood till it was too dark to see it. I didn't know how we were gonna get back. I didn't know how we were gonna survive the night. And then she said, what's that over there? It was a house. I mean kind of. I mean one of those hillbilly houses, you know? No one there. Just left to rot. But there was a fireplace. We broke in the door and made a fire in there and it was—it was fucking magical, Geoff. You don't have a night like that twice in your life. Least I haven't. In the morn-

ing, we woke up and went out. It had snowed. It was so bright
it was hard to see but I could make out other houses. It must
have been an old hillybilly family's homestead or something.
There were three or four old houses and what looked like some
other stuff down by the river and—

What was down by the river? I said.

I don't know, he said. Me and her kinda went back again
in that one we'd slept in and. . . . He did a small laugh.

What was the name? I said.

Jen, he said. She was—

Of the river. What was the name of the river?

I don't know. Must have been the Swain. Jen wasn't as
pretty as Jackie, but she was. . . . We had a hell of a good time
together. We had a hell of a good time.

What was the road you was on? I said.

What road?

The one what crossed the Swain.

What's got into you?

What was the road you was on when you gone in after
that buck?

Hell, he said. I don't know. We came out on the—that one
that goes up to the national forest.

Off forty two?

Yeah. Why?

I didn't say nothing. We lied there looking up at the sky.

After a while, he give another laugh. There was this hip-
pie place, he said. At the corner. One of those wackos was out
there by the road trying to live in a tepee. I swear to God. Sticks
and tarps. A one-room tent and he was married, poor son of a
bitch. He came out with his wife. They gave us a ride to the truck.

Jen was embarrassed. She thought we stank like sex. Probably did, too.

Roy took the gun off his chest and poked the metal end at my knee.

Well, he said, you make your choices and you live with them. Then you marry women and live with them and they make the choices. He got up. He stared at me where I lied there. Look at you, he said. What are you thinking about?

Nothing, I said.

Something, he said. He stuck the gun end in my chest. Hey, you ain't gonna tell Jackie none of this are you?

Nuhuh, I said.

You tell her I'll shoot you like I did those coons.

I ain't, I said.

Good boy.

He stuck down his hand at me. I got up on my own.

When we got back to the house all the windows was dark. Roy looked at them while he picked at what glass he hadn't knocked clear of the windshield.

Guess she's already gone to sleep, he said. He looked at the windows like they made him mad. You know, he said, this winter we oughtta go hunting. You and me, Geoff. What do you think of that? Maybe I'll even get you your own rifle. I'd like to see her face then. He reached over and put his hand half on my neck half in my hair. His laugh come so quiet I felt it in his fingers more than heard it. He said, You ever hear the one about the guy that brings his retarded buddy on a hunting trip?

No, I told him.

Me neither, he said. I think I'm gonna make one up.

I know what you is thinking. You is thinking there's lots of them old hill folk places way back in the woods of them ridges. Most like you think there ain't no Sarverville at all. That's what Linda would say if she was here. She would say Roy was just telling me a story. How do I know he even ever been up there after some buck? She would say, Geoffrey, you got to learn what is stories and what is true. But she ain't here.

I wonder would you say the same? I bet folks tell all kinds of stories where you is at now. I wish I could ask you how you knowed which ones is true. Or maybe you don't. Maybe you is reading this right now and thinking the same about what I've writ. Do you wish you could get out of New Valley Regional even for one day so's you could hunt down something to let you know the truth? Sometimes I wish I could crack my head right open. Sometimes I near to hate all them who live outside my brain. Do you ever near to hate them in their houses with their windows and suppers and loved ones and lives going on like all them other lives going on?

It is late late late and I am tired in my brain now too. Them yard critters is back. Loud as they was before. Don't they smell the dead ones? Why don't they just go on to some other yard? Why don't they go wherever they go in the day? I have tried to find it. I gone back in them woods and stood there real quiet and looked all around and I ain't seen none. Must be they go to the way way back woods. Way way back where them true wild critters live. Them ones what don't want yards, what don't want towns, what don't want people or even people's trash. But if they do, why do they come back at night?

Here is what I think. When them yard critters go all the way to that way way back I expect they is turned away there, too. I expect they is beat back to the edge till they got to give the yards a try again. Well sooner or later they got to tire of it. Sooner or later they gonna come in the yards till them yards is full up and just stay. Either that or they gonna give up and disappear. Just be gone. Gone all the way to the way way back woods, and then to whatever is more back than that, gone so far they can't even see the yards no more, or smell the trash, too far for anything what might get in their brains and say to them come back come back you yard critters, come back and try again.

Monday of July

There's one more thing you oughta know about what happened last week, what I ain't told you the other night. While I was standing on the Sunoco curb watching for her, Russ and Vic drived by. That plastic they taped over the back window rattled more loud than the engine even, and the front end grille was still beat in. But they'd got new headlights, and the taillights was done up with colored plastic. They seen me and doubled back and come in for gas. Russ rolled down the window.

Hi, I said.

Regular, he said. Fill her up.

He didn't say nothing else till I told him how much. He give me a twenty.

Keep the change, he said.

Buy yourself a new face, Vic said.

They drived off.

I want you to know that was the first time I talked to them since the last time at Crigger's. I don't hang out with them no more. So don't go and dump together what happened with them with what happened with me. If you knowed how it started that night you wouldn't even try. If you knowed, you woulda come out of Crigger's a whole lot quicker than you did.

Even after that time Linda told me I oughta go home, I still rode over every night and I'd hunker down in the dark at the edge of the crap field beyond the lot and watch her come out for her smoke breaks, and sit there till I watched her leave. Once I seen you leave in your truck behind her. It gone on like that for three, four nights till Monday come again and Russ and Vic come again with it. From where I sat in the dark I watched them park. I watched her come out. She throwed the trash in the Dumpster and they flashed their lights at her and she looked their way and shook her head. The van flashed its light again. She shook her head again.

She said, Not tonight.

The music in the van got louder. Russ stuck his head out the window. What? he said.

I'm sorry, she said. I'm through.

After a second he said What? again.

I'm done with it.

I can't hear you, he said. Come here.

Why don't you turn off your music, she said.

He turned it off. It was back to just the music coming out of Crigger's.

Vic said, You want us to tell your husband?

Oh grow up, she said.

I know who he is, Vic told her.

Good for you, she said. Too bad he already knows.

You want us to tell everybody else? It was Russ. Come on, he said. Just come over here we'll talk it out.

She took a cigarette out her bag and lit it and stood there like she was thinking. Then she walked over. Once she was there they talked low. I couldn't hear what they was saying. I couldn't see her, neither. She was on the other side of the van and all I could see was Vic leaning in toward Russ, who must've been talking to her. Then Vic was gone from his seat, climbed in back, and I could see a bit of her then when Russ moved his head and I guess I must have been looking at that cause I don't remember hearing the slide door open.

What the hell do you think you're doing? she said, loud.

Then Russ was sudden out too and she said, Get your fucking—

I stood up from where I'd hid. The whole van was shaking. I could see pieces of them all moving like crazy and then they was inside and the door slammed shut.

Hey, I shouted. Must have shouted it a bunch more times before I started running. On my way I picked up a handful of gravel and chucked it at the van so's it hit all bangs. The door gone open. I heard someone else running other side of the van and figured it for Russ and Vic seen me coming, but when I got open the side door and jumped in, it was empty. Now what I was stopped running I could hear them. They sounded out toward the side of Crigger's like she'd been making for the front lot. I got out the van quick and seen them where they'd got her.

They was in the crap scrub, out of the light, halfway down a ditch, but I could tell it was Russ at her head sitting on her arms and bunching her shirt up to her neck where he'd stuffed it in her face and was pressing on it to keep her quiet. Vic was trying to get his pants off and keep her legs open same time.

I was on them so quick I hadn't thought what to do once I got there. I just grabbed Vic off and we was shouting, and then Russ was on her, and I left Vic to get Russ off, and Russ hit me in the face, and I could feel I was hitting something on him too, and then I heard her and seen Vic on her and Russ knocked me from the back. I almost falled on Vic. He was on her, going at her, and when I tried to grab him off he hit at me so's by the time I got him off Russ was on her with her legs kicking and her shirt over her head, and her top part of underwear come loose and took her things with it so they was slid off her into the grass and Vic shouting how she was a freak and how I was a freak, too, and I let go Vic and got Russ off and did all what I knowed to do. I laid down on her. Spread myself so she was covered up. Our chests lain flat to flat. It's me, I told her. It's okay. I got you. Then I couldn't talk for the kicking. I shut my eyes and put my hands over the back my head and tried to breathe through the beating what they give.

When it stopped, it stopped sudden. I ain't ashamed to say it, you was a better fighter than me. I don't know what you did to them, but when I rolled over enough to look up they was running off through the crap field and you was standing there with that skillet. I still remember the look on your face. You was so full of anger it come out like something pure and good. I could see in it while you shouted at them, could see how much you loved her. Even now, what with all you done to me, I remember that and I know you ain't a bad person. I know you and me, we is most like more of a kind than any other two men in all of Eads County.

Get off her, was what you said.

She told you it was me, Geoffrey, and what I didn't hurt her.

You said it again, Get off her.

I got up quick as I could but I guess it wasn't quick enough, which I understand why you done it. One more shove wasn't nothing anyhow. Don't think I didn't notice what you helped her up like a real gentleman, or what you give her your suit jacket and how you got down and picked up the parts of her body I confess I didn't know women could take off. Her underbra was sagged heavy with them. Funny how different she looked without the curves up front and how even when she strapped them on and pulled her shirt down over I couldn't see her woman shape the same way how I done before. I wanted to help her inside but I understand why you didn't let me. That's why I waited till she was gone in with the kitchen people what had come out to watch, so she couldn't hear, when I got up and said to you what I did.

You looked at me the way people look at me. Like somehow the fault what they's confused lies on me. I could tell you didn't believe me, neither. You asked me, What?

I repeat it now same as I did then: She wouldn't have never got to this if it wasn't what she married you.

I don't know what's so hard in that to understand. But I said it a third time and you looked like you finally got it. You may be a handsome man, Mister Podawalski, and I hold no grudge on you, but you got a ugly kind of smile. And it was double ugly then. Maybe once you read this you can write me back what you was smiling about, what with the boys who done it to your wife still out there in the crap field somewhere hid.

Are those your friends? you said.

They used to be, I said.

Is that their van? you said.

I said it was.

Then you gone to work with that skillet and the glass busting and smashing and all that metal making all that noise.

Wednesday of July

The strange thing is the more I write to you the more you take up my head alongside her. I wonder if you wake up same time I do what with the first trucks rolling down Abe's Knob Road and it still dark outside. Or if there's just lights what's in the ceiling and you get up whenever they turn them on. I wonder what they give you for breakfast, and if you think on what it was like to have breakfast with her. Sometimes I shut my ears to the baby crying upstairs and Jackie trying to fix it and Roy in the bathroom already cussing, and I draw your house in my head and the table what I sat at that one time, but I try and draw it how it would be in morning and I can almost make the sound of my chewing cereal into Linda chewing it cross the table. I wonder if you had just one Mom. I wonder if we drink the same kind of beer, and if Linda was the first and only, and if you use one of them electric buzzers for your beard. Once or twice when I been out on the Sunoco curb looking in the windshields for her, I thought I seen you. It couldn't been you, I know, but what's the strange thing is I wanted it to be.

After what you done to the Party Van I guess Russ and Vic quit going to Crigger's. I quit going too. I tried to just do as I'd done before, work the pumps, wave from the curb, ride over to the Pine Top, eat whatever they'd done up special, ride back, brush my teeth in the Men's Room, roll out my bag in the office. My clothes all smelled like Crigger's even after I washed them and I got so I couldn't stand to wear them. Maybe you been to that charity shop what's at the church on the Pembroke Road. I don't like to go. The old lady who runs it talks to me like I'm a kid plus maybe deaf and can't pick out my own clothes. She says how she knows I want a piece of candy till I want to hit her. It's better I just go at night, get the clothes direct from the trash bags what's left outside. All you got to do is tear one open and drag it under the lamp and you can dig through it till you find pretty much anything you need.

One night I seen something what I got to tell you. What I know you ain't gonna like. I know you don't know about it cause nobody knows about it but me and afterwards I was too shamed to tell nobody. So you's the first one to hear it. Which I guess is how it oughta be. I am saying up front here before the telling how I know the error of what I done. I am sorry for this, too.

But there is things what once you seen you can't stop looking. It was when I gone over to check the home seller's window. I could see soon's I turned on the street what there was a new one up. I parked the bike and put my flashlight to the glass. I don't remember what kind of house it was. Instead, for the first time I noticed the name next to it. Brian W. Podawalski. I never knowed Waker was your second name stead of your first, but there you was in a picture. You was in a suit jacket and looked good, never mind your smile. I moved the flashlight over your face. I tried to see what she seen.

After that I gone by the home seller's place every night. It was almost a week since I'd last been to Crigger's and I guess I was waiting to see if they was gonna take you down. Instead, I

seen a light on inside. I shut off my flashlight. I gone around
the side till I seen the window what was lit from the right room.
I said to myself what it wasn't no different from looking in windows like I always done, but I knowed it was. You was in there
with her. The window was open and the light come through the
screen so I had to stand back in the dark to keep it off me and
you was talking so quiet I had to listen hard to make it out. It
was all money talk what I didn't care about, so I give my mind
to just watching her. She was sitting down, busy at the knot of
her shoe. I watched her get it, and take it off, and then she gone
to work on the other. That was when you gone down on your
knees and took off her other shoe and she laughed. Then you
took off her sock. Then you started rubbing and squeezing at
her foot. I was watching her face show how good it felt when
she looked at you like she'd just got upset and I thought she said
my name. I put my mind back on listening again.

Well I don't know why, she said.

I'm just saying that's what he thought, you said.

She took her foot away from you.

He told me you wanted to leave, you said.

Don't act like that's news. She quit smiling. I've told you
that a hundred times.

What if he goes around telling it a hundred times? Telling
everybody he—

What if he does? she said.

You know what. And don't think it would be easy for you
either.

None of it's easy, she said.

Maybe it's better to leave it alone, not tell him anything
else, not—

So I'm not supposed to even talk to him?

I didn't say that.

I like him, he's sweet.

I'm not sweet? you said.

Look at you, she said. The only time you're ugly is when you're jealous.

You was laughing. She was right about the ugly. Maybe it's for the best, you said.

I don't want him to get hurt, she said.

You'd rather I got hurt?

You know that's not—

Someone's gonna get hurt, you said. We've known that from the beginning. I'm just saying think about it.

I don't want to.

Think about how much easier it could make things. Maybe this is a gift. Maybe this is a sign.

Oh bullshit, she said.

If we're really careful, if we talk it through with each other and—listen to me. I'm hearing you. I'm saying we respect how much and what the other person's willing to do and make sure nothing gets out of hand.

It's gonna get out of hand, she said.

Maybe not, you said. Maybe this is our best chance. Our one chance at a good life together.

What you mean is without you getting hurt, she said.

Or you getting hurt.

He's the only one that gets hurt, she said.

Well—

She said, You're such a coward, you know that?

I am, huh?

A wimp, she said.

Is that so?

A—

Say that again?

A pussy.

Okay, you said. That's it.

You grabbed her then. She was struggling and you got her by the wrists, but it wasn't like what Russ and Vic done. I could see that. She was laughing. Pussy, I heard her say. And then you was taking down her skirt and she was getting your pants off for you just as quick.

I'm not proud to say I watched the whole thing. Soon as you was done, I left. When I got on the bike I felt almost too sick to ride. But I did. I passed the Sunoco and kept on and circled back and did it more times than I can remember. The longer I rode the less of it made sense and the parts what did didn't seem so bad. After a while I was able to see it was good what she'd brung me up. And even her fighting with you about me was good. And what she said how she liked me and wouldn't back down, I was almost happy by the time I parked at the Sunoco. I was hopeful like I hadn't been in a week.

Friday of July

I would understand if you is mad at how I spied in at your most private doing. I will not try to change your mind. Like Ma B says, What we do on the outside is half up to us and half up to them what's got a stake in it, but what we do on the inside is ours alone. Even God, she says, can't make us feel what we don't want to feel. He just punish us if he don't like it. But I hope you will see it like I have come to see it. I guess by now you looked in at my most private thoughts and even doings what there was no way for you to know but what I told you. I guess we about even. What would you see if you looked in my window to My Hall?

Saturday of July

Not much.

Sunday of July

I have seen her. Today I seen her. I was standing out at the curb and she drived by just like what I'd been looking for and I seen her. She seen me too. She pretended not, but I know she did. Thing is. Thing is what I can't figure out. What I can't figure out is, in the seat next to her was you.

Wednesday of July

For a few days now I ain't knowed how I was gonna ever get all what I've writ to you. I asked Jackie if you was let go from New Valley Regional. Not what she knowed, was what she said. But I know what I seen. I'd ask Roy, too, but after the dump he has turned strange and quiet how he don't like to talk to no one. So I just got to figure it out on my own. Or I won't. Truth is, the only difference from before is now I don't know for sure how I'm gonna get this to you. And what you is to her, now. And what I am to her. But I guess I hadn't really knowed none of that anyhow. The one thing I know now is there's a good bet whenever I find her I'm gonna find you too.

Last time she come by the Sunoco was back in spring, not
but two days after I seen you and her in the home seller's place.
Her car pulled in just after lunch. It tripped the bell and I come
out the office. The whole walk over to the pump I made myself
not look at her.

Five worth of regular? I asked, like she was any customer.

Geoffrey, she said.

You want I should do the back window too?

I stood there and she sat there. A few cars gone by on the
road.

You okay? I said.

She shrugged.

Another car pulled in, tripped the ringer, parked cross the
other side.

I gotta get that, I said.

She nodded. While I done the other car's window I watched
her over the hood. She got a pack of smokes out her bag, put
one in her mouth. Her hand was shaking. She had on sunglasses
and her hair was down like I'd never seen and there was makeup
on her face more than what I'd seen before. The whole time I
watched her, right through to giving the change, she didn't look
at me once.

When the other car drived off I gone back to her.

You look different, I said.

Better?

Nuhuh.

She laughed at that and there was some of her real laugh
in it and some what wasn't.

You nervous? I said.

Her smile was the same parts as her laugh. I was leaning

down on her windowsill and she turned the other way to blow out the smoke. You aren't like anybody else, she said, still facing that way.

Neither is you, I said.

Sure I am, she said. Then she looked back at me. I wanted to talk to you, she said.

Okay.

I'm sorry about the last couple weeks.

It's okay.

No it's not.

I said, I stopped coming by like you asked.

I know, she said. I missed you.

The bell tripped again and a truck pulled in at the pump behind her.

I gotta get that, I said.

He wanted the oil checked so I done it, though the whole time I was under the hood my back was to her car and I could feel her looking at me. The driver honked what made me jump. He stuck his head out the window. How you doin' Linda? he said.

Good, she said. How's Patty?

Fine, the guy said. Kids is in summer camp for a week. And thank God. He talked to her like that and she talked back when she had to and I walked between them doing my job. When he drived off I gone back to her.

Maybe I should park somewhere else, she said.

Okay, I said.

You gonna have a minute?

Yuhuh, I told her. I'll put up a sign.

Good, she said. I'll wait for you.

Instead of parking at the office, she gone behind the garage outta sight. I heard her engine quit. On my way to the office I heard her door shut back there and she said so low I wasn't sure she said it, Shit. I got the Out Of Order signs and two Pepsis and put the signs on the pumps and gone back behind the garage with the cans.

She was standing by the front of the car smoking and looking nervous as before.

I held up a Pepsi. I said, We don't sell beer.

It was good to see her smile. She said, Just like old times. We should sit on the ground.

Okay, I said and was going to when she reached out and put her hand on my elbow. I'm joking, she said. That's what I wanted to come and tell you.

About the ground? I said.

About I don't want it to be like it was. I don't want it to be us sitting behind the tank like I did with them boys. You weren't never like one of them boys to me, Geoffrey. You ought to know that.

I know it, I said.

She sat on the hood of her car. Come sit by me, she said. I did. We drank our Pepsis.

You still with your husband? I said.

She breathed out smoke. Boy, she said, you get right to it, don't you? She was switching off between her smoke and her can and she took a drink and said, It's not as easy as all that. We haven't so far had much of a mature relationship, you know?

We wasn't doing the blow jobs, I said.

That's true, she said. But we never did have much of a chance to get to know each other in a normal way. You know, like dating. Like going out on a date even. It's hard for me to even think about up and leaving my husband when we haven't had a try at a adult relationship yet, you know?

You got another smoke? I said.

Here. She handed hers to me and I smoked it and handed it back.

You want to go on a date? I asked her.

I would love to, she said.

We sat there for a while drinking Pepsi and passing the cigarette back and forth till it was done. A few cars come in and tripped the bells and gone out again.

You know what I would like? she said.

What?

I'd like more than anything else to have a real homemade dinner with you.

Okay, I said. I ain't much of a cook.

She done something to the hair around my ear. She said, I can do okay when I want to.

I don't even got a microwave, I said.

Geoffrey, I don't mean here at the Sunoco.

Okay.

I mean at my house.

Okay.

God, she said, I would like to do it right, you know? Like we were starting over, you and me. At a actual table, sitting in actual chairs. We haven't even talked about music. I love music. I don't even know what kind of music you like.

I ain't particular, I said.

Well I am, she said. See you don't even know that. That's the point. I could play you some CDs. What do you think?

About the CDs?

About the whole thing.

I don't know, I said.

Huh, she said. I thought. I guess I thought it would be nice.

Me too, I said.

She watched me like she didn't know what to say.

I said, Is your husband gonna be there?

My husband?

Cause—

No, no, no. Geoffrey. No Geoffrey, that's the whole point. I'll make sure he's gone. I'll take care of it.

I wasn't worried, I said. It just seemed you was nervous about something and I thought maybe it was—

I'm not nervous, she said.

Okay, I said. You just seemed—

Well, I mean I'm a little. Aren't you?

She lit up another cigarette and I watched her smoke it and she watched me watch her.

Do you mean excited? I said.

She smiled. Yeah, she said. I guess I mean excited. She looked at me and then looked away and said, God I like you. God but this is gonna be hard.

What? I said.

Us. You and me.

Why's it gonna be hard?

Well, shit, Geoffrey, because I have a husband and you're— there's a lot of people who aren't gonna understand is all. I mean because you and I aren't exactly what most people would think— shit, I'm sorry. I'm being stupid, I'm sorry.

She took my face in her hands and kissed me.

I'm sorry, she said again.

You got to stop saying sorry so much, I said.

This time her laugh was like her old laugh. She said, You remember everything anyone says, don't you?

Yuhuh, I said.

She slid off the trunk of the car, said, Then I guess you can remember tomorrow night at seven.

She writ down the address on a Kleenex and give it to me. After she gone, I stood back there in the shade for a while. The customers come in and out tripping the bell and I let them.

There was hours after she gone what I couldn't even make the right change. I used the oil rag to wipe off the window scraper and the slick it smeared on the windshield made me want to grab my brain and slap it. It was when a customer ask for five bucks of Regular and I go with Super and fill it up what I knowed I was done for the day. I gone in the office and called Mister Gilkey and stayed there on my sleep roll behind the register till I made up my mind.

I think sometimes God looks down at the path you walking and shakes his head and reaches at you from on high and picks you by the shoulders and turns you just a little bit. Then he takes his big finger and give your back a flick. That evening, riding my bike out on the edge of 42, I could see, as each hour gone by, how much more different everything was gonna be. I took 42 all the way out over the ridge and into the next dip, and it was near five hours by the time I passed over Sinking Creek, round sunset, and there was still more than a hour to go. I kept on till I hit 329 what I took up into the hills. It was dark, but dirt's better than hardtop when there's a moon.

I will be truthful with you. I don't like going back to Ma B's. It'd been more than a year since I been to her, and I'd thought it would be a lot longer than that before I'd go back. I don't want you to think I'm ungrateful for all she done, or what I think I've growed past the time for my need of her, or what I don't love her none. I love her. I love her like I have never done anyone else, not even Linda. It ain't even what I don't like being there, or don't feel the deep deepness of her caring on me. Or what it ain't peaceful. Or none of that. I don't know what it is, in truth. I only know every time I think about going back something deep in me just wants to lie down and give up.

There was lights on in the house. I could see her truck was there and what she done all right with the veal calves. There was least a dozen more little white calf houses than there'd been last time I come home. I figured with one calf per calf house there got to be near fifty head she was growing. I rode down and parked my bike against the oak. The dogs come out and barked how they always do, gone crazy till I got to the door, and you can hear Ma B shout at them, and they shut up.

It's me, I told the door. Geoffrey.

It opened and she grabbed me. It was Ma B teached me how to give good hugs. At night she'd make us all practice. Line us up and warn us she wanted to feel it in every bone of her body before we was allowed to go up to bed. She's got a hug harder than any man what ever shook my hand.

Look at you, she said. Little Plum Head. I'm still taller than you.

I stopped growing a long time ago, I told her.

You know what I say, she said.

I know, I told her, but I think I stopped.

You think I can't see? she said. You've growed tall on the inside.

It's what she says every time I come to the door.

She took me in. Them dogs crowd your legs so bad you gotta move at half speed.

She said, ever since I got the Dish, it's like I lost all my children, the house is so quiet.

I could see them in the living room watching the TV. There was six or seven of them and one or two new. The older ones was holding the younger ones back from coming at us like the dogs.

You must be starving, Ma B said.

I told her I was.

What should I make you? she asked. What's your most favorite thing?

Whatever leftovers you got is fine.

Now Geoffrey, she said. What's your most favorite memory of all the things I make for you?

While I was thinking, one of the new kids bust free and come running out into the kitchen making a beeline for me. Ma B crouched down and made her noises how she does to the babies and says, You want your mama? You want a kiss from your mama, you Little Plum Butt? But the little plum butt kept going for me. Till Ma B reached out and sweeped him off his path and into one of her Ma B hugs.

Now what do you want super special? she said into the baby's belly. She looked up. I know, she said, just as one of the older ones come and took the baby from her arms and Ma B kissed her on the cheek and said, This is Joanne. The Lord brung her to me— what was it Joanne? Four years ago? Could it be four years?

Yes, ma'am, Joanne said.

Four years ago, Ma B told me. This is Geoffrey, Ma B told her.

Hi, she said.

He was one of my first little sugar plums. He's—he's—you must be more than thirty, she said.

Yuhuh, I said.

Well praise the Lord, she said. The girl was still standing there holding the baby. Joanne, Ma B said, Can't you just see how glad I am to see Geoffrey? Isn't it funny, what a silly old woman I am?

You not old, I said.

She said, still talking to the girl, When Geoffrey didn't come for my birthday I thought I was never gonna see him again. The baby made a noise and she said to it, Wasn't that silly? When she turned to me again she said, You just don't know how happy it makes me to see you again. And don't think I don't remember what your favorite is.

She gone off to make whatever it was. For a second the girl and me stood there looking at each other and then she said did I want to watch TV and I said no thank you and we split.

When Ma B was done she put the plate down front of me and sat cross the table with it empty in front of her. It was a veal steak, breaded and fried, with slaw and applesauce added for sides.

Now how's that? she said, giving me a fork. Wasn't no need for a knife what she'd already cut it up.

Looks good, I said. I ate a bite. Mm, I said.

I'm switching them from the starter feed to the grower a few weeks later, she said. Lose a little weight, but it's more tender right?

Yuhuh, I said.

Yes ma'am, she said.

Yes ma'am, I told her.

Now, she said. How're you doing out there?

Good, I said. Pretty good.

You know if it ever gets too hard you always welcome to—

I know, I said. Thank you.

You like the breading? she said.

Yes ma'am.

I can tell, she said. Now I know you didn't finally visit out here just to warm your Ma B's heart. She give me her look like Out with it.

I come to warm your heart, I said.

And?

Well I kinda got a question what I didn't know no one—

Kinda? Or you got a question?

I got a question.

Good, she said. She put her hands together on the table almost like she was gonna pray.

I asked her, Did you ever go on a date?

Sure, she said. A long time ago, but I been.

Was it for eating supper?

Well there was more than one, Geoffrey.

Was one of them for eating supper?

I believe so.

Was there—was there some kind of rules maybe what the man knowed what maybe I oughta know and didn't never learn?

Some kind of rules, she said. She lifted her thumbs from the fold of her hands a little and looked at them. Do you mind if I ask what kind of date this is?

I tried to think how to answer that.

Is it a first date? she said.

Nuhuh.

But it's the first time you're having supper with her?
Nuhuh.

No ma'am, she said. So you've been seeing her?

Yes ma'am, I said.

But it's gonna be formal, she said.

I guess.

Is it serious? she said. Are you serious about this girl?

Yes ma'am, I said.

She looked at me for a long time and I couldn't tell from her face what she was gonna do. Then whatever it was, she made up her mind on it.

Well first, she said, you got to pick the restaurant.

It's gonna be at her house, I said.

She let go of her hands and put them flat on the table. Do you think that's a good idea?

Yes ma'am.

You do?

Well it was her what thought it. She said we could—

What's the girl's name?

Linda.

Not a very pretty name, Ma B said.

Well Linda said we could have a nice supper together at her kitchen table what'd be almost like we was married.

How old is the girl? Ma B asked.

I don't know, I told her.

Well she sounds serious. It sounds more serious than you let on, Geoffrey. Is it really that serious?

Yes ma'am.

Then I suppose your Ma B better help you. You want another steak?

I'm okay.

She took my plate and brung it back full as before. You can't get veal like that nowhere else, she said while she cut it up.

No ma'am, I told her.

Now, she said, it's been a long time since I've been on a date, but the first thing you need to know is be respectful. Do you know what I mean?

I told her yes.

Respect is just Expect with a little more, she said. She's gonna Expect it. But the Re in front makes it twice as important. Next is, Watch your table manners. Do you have nice clothes? Okay. She pushed the plate to me. Take your fork with you. We're going upstairs and see what Daddy has.

She told me to sit on the bed and take off my shoes and my shirt and my pants down to my underwear. The plate was too hot to put in my lap but I remembered enough not to put it on the bedspread what had been in the family since Ma B's Daddy got married to Ma B's Ma. It was Ma B's Daddy's bed and Ma B's Daddy's bedroom what she'd took over when he died and God made him his new bed in the graveyard what's out back in them cornfields. I watched her open the closet what wasn't hers. All his things was in there. She gone through the hangers making a sound tough on the ears.

Reminds me of my prom, she said. You're gonna look just as handsome as the boy who took me.

There wasn't no suit jackets what fit me. Nor no pants. But she got a shirt what I could roll up the sleeves and a tie what pinched the collar shut. She talked to me while she done up the tie.

She said, Now when you take this off, just do it partway so it stays tied, okay? Then you can just slip it over your head and slip it back when you're ready and tighten it up. Don't get food on it.

No ma'am.

The boy, she said, is supposed to knock once at the door, let the girl know he's there. Don't knock again. Don't rush her. You gonna bring flowers?

I was gonna bring beer, I said.

Bring flowers, she said. You don't drink beer.

Sometimes.

Geoffrey, she said. You don't drink beer.

Okay, I said.

When she had the tie done, she stood back and looked at me. And when you leave, she said, it's up to the boy to leave early without her having to ask so's she's not made uncomfortable. She looked at my chest. That tie smells like Daddy, she said. Put on your pants.

She give me shoes, too. They was shaped inside like the bones of his dead feet. I moved my own feet around in them to try to get them unshaped.

Quit it, she said.

When she finished the second one, she stood up.

Let's see, she said. Is there anything else a boy should know?

Ma'am? I said. I don't mean to be ungrateful but is there anything different what a full growed man—

What do you mean? she said.

Nothing, I told her.

Geoffrey, she said. Have you thought about what you're really getting into? Are you sure this is something you want to do? Have you thought about whether you love her?

Yes ma'am, I said.

Yes ma'am what? You've thought about it?

I do, I said.

She leaned back from me a little. Do you even know what that means?

Yes ma'am.

I don't think you do. It's hard to know, Plum Head. The best way is to think of the person you think you love, and then think of another person already in your life who you already know for sure you love, and do you feel like that? Maybe you should do that?

I stood there doing it. When I was done I told her, I done it.

I kept waiting for her to ask me what I come to, but she just stood there looking me over like there was something about the clothes was making her mad.

We gone downstairs to the family room and she made the hellos all around. There was nine of hers. Most was girls, but there was a couple boys too. They was all diminished. That's how she names it. Some was just a little slow like me and some was a little slower and some you could see just by their faces what there was no way getting around calling them nothing but plain retards. Ma B said to them what I was Geoffrey who was one of her first babies, and brother to them all.

He has a date, she told them. He come to me for advice. Now doesn't he look handsome?

They some of them said yes.

Time for bed, Ma B said which don't mean sleep, and never did. It means All Together Time. They gone into the workroom. You wouldn't know it was the workroom less you knowed the work. What with no furniture but pillows and the sides piled with heaps of white cloths. They all sat in a circle on the pillows. Ma B took a cloth out a pile and spread it out between them all. She digged in the sewing box and passed the tools all around.

Well come in, she said to me. Take a seat.

That's all right, I said.

You don't think you're part of the family no more?

No, I just—

Kim move over and make room for Geoffrey.

I don't know how no more, I said.

Sure you do, she said. And if you don't it's time you relearned.

I sat down next to the one named Kim. They was working on a flower pattern like usual, but this one had little bluebirds on it too.

Where do you think the most important things in life is learned? Ma B said.

There was a couple wrong answers of School and the like before one of the older ones give Ma B what she was looking for.

That's right, Ma B said. In the heart. The only part of the human body that's capable of forgetting is the mind. The heart don't know how to forget. Once it's in the heart, it's there for life.

She turned to the one beside her. What was something you learned today? she said.

We gone around the circle one by one stitching the dai-
sies and bluebirds what she would sell once it was done and Ma
B asking each by name. What was something you learned today? Till it got to me.

Geoffrey? She said.

To leave early, I said, So's not to make no one uncomfortable.

That morning, I waked to the house all quiet but for the noise
of the birds and the Holsteins leaving the milk barn and the veal
calves calling after them. I got my stuff together and gone out.
A couple of Ma B's older ones come in past me, done with the
milking. Ma B herself was over in the rows of calves shoveling
out fresh cobs and hay for them to bed in. There wasn't no one
else about. I put the bag of clothes on back my bike and wheeled
it over her way. Them calves was making some noise.

Morning, she said when she seen me.

Morning ma'am, I said. We talked a bit about the calves.
Then she said, You got to work today?

Yuhuh.

You got a long ride to Ripplemead.

I know.

She got out the truck bed and drived the truck forward a
bit, and climbed back in the bed. I watched her shovel. Then I
climbed up with her.

Ma'am, I said.

She stopped her work.

Can I ask you something?

May you, she said.

May I?

Course you can.

You know the story about them Sarvers?

I told you it.

Is it true?

Sure it is.

The whole of it? I said. What nobody liked them and they was kicked out of town and go down that valley and wouldn't nobody talk to them till they—

That's not what I told you.

No, I said. I don't believe it was you what told me.

I told it to you, she said.

I believe it was Dad Kreager what told it before I come here.

Well Mister Kreager had it wrong.

There was a bull up the hill what was driving a dog nuts. The dog stood a couple yards from it barking its head off and the bull would turn and the dog would follow and the bull would look at it and the dog'd go nuts again.

That dog didn't never like a bull, Ma B said. Set down her shovel and sat on the tailgate and patted the metal and said, Come sit by me, Plum Head.

I did.

Here, she said and patted her leg. Lay your head down here and I'll tell you the story.

I stayed where I'd sat. I don't want no made up story, I said. I want the real one.

I know, she said.

I'm more than thirty, I said. I'm old enough for the real one.

That's what I'm gonna tell you, she said. Lay your head down here.

Give it to me straight, I said.

That's what I'm gonna, she said.

Ma B's got a lap what feels hard as wood.

First of all, she said, the Sarvers wasn't kicked out of nowhere. They chose to go. There was a big family of them lived in Pembroke and Narrows and some in Ripplemead and a few elsewhere around Eads County. It wasn't cause nobody liked them. They was popular as a pie. Now just cause they was popular don't mean they was the same as everyone. No sir. They wasn't much like anyone else at all. See, they was all of them diminished. Every one of them. Some in town called them slow or fools or whatever else the unenlightened ignorants still use for names. But they was diminished only in the narrow sight of them who was so alike they could be swapped from wife to husband or job to job and wouldn't nobody know the difference. Them was the bricklayers and millers and lawyers and doctors. But the Sarvers, they was the ones you knew was different soon's you come to town. They was veterinarians who could talk to animals, bookkeepers who could make sense of numbers no one else could. They was the ones writ the hymns and the ones who sung them best. You know the painting of all them history people done over the whole back side of that old dance hall in Narrows? It was a Sarver done it. You ever get to the library in Coalsburg, you ask them for The History of the New Valley. It was writ by a Sarver. They was the ones who all the others that was so normal wished in their hearts they could be.

So why'd they leave?

You want the movie version or the real one?

I want it all straight.

Well it was simple, she said. They just got bored. They got bored with the everyday hassle of living with all them who was everyday people. There was so many of them, lines of them at the bank, crowds of them at the markets. And the whole bunch of them, they was just so boring. Didn't take them Sarvers long to start to think, What would it be like to live among just Sarvers? A whole town of Sarvers. Well, once they got that idea it didn't take long before they was leaking out of the regular towns. The towns tried to hold them. Them who hired them upped the salaries. There was a whole lot a daughters offered up for temptation. Harts Run even elected a Sarver mayor. He refused it. Within the year, they was all but the last ones gone. Two three more years, you couldn't find a Sarver nowhere in the New Valley. Except for down in one hollow, where they all was.

They'd bought a mess of cheap land way up high on the Swain River. Wherever it was flat it was boggy. Wherever it was dry it was steep. Normal people wouldn't have lived on land that bad if you paid them. But they wasn't normal people. They turned it into what you would not believe. While everyone was selling off mules to buy up tractors, the Sarvers bought up all the mules they could get their hands on. There was timber on them steep slopes where no tractor could get and it was all chestnut. Practically the whole forest. Back then it was the most wanted wood, got tannins in it so it's near impossible to rot. Them Sarvers cut it careful, farmed them trees like corn. Under them, they run hogs. If you ever tasted hog raised on chestnut meat you best not get up hopes for the menu in heaven cause whatever they serve up there ain't gonna come close. Lower down, they planted orchards and that wet, sunny bottomland turned out perfect for berries. In the bogs they growed arrowroot and fields of rice and whole stretches of lilies. At its peak, it was gossiped there was a dance hall and three-story church and it was knowed there was a mill and must have been upwards of a hundred people living in twenty, thirty homes. Nobody knows for sure cause nobody but

Sarvers was allowed in. I see you looking at me, she said. You're thinking, If it was so good why'd they leave?

They got some kind of sickness, I said.

Who told you that? Mister Kreager?

Yuhuh. He said there was a farmer what found—

I'm sure Mister Kreager was a fine man, but it's clear he didn't know a nose from a knuckle. What they got was what the entire country got. Was what's known as the Blight. You ever seen a chestnut tree growing round here?

I don't know.

Well you haven't. They all dead. Was something come from overseas that wiped them out. All of them. When the chestnuts gone, about thirty years of careful plans gone with them. Without the trees the hogs gone. The slopes got washed out in the rains. The orchards was near buried. The Swain got dammed up. About the only thing that didn't go was the taxes. Well, you can start to see it now. The day the government come and tell them it was taking their land was the last day anyone seen a Sarver alive. That day the county sheriff come with his men and he seen too many Sarvers for his taste and decided he better come back again when there wasn't so many gun barrels that seemed to take a interest in his head, or at least when he had more guns of his own. It was two three months before he got up the nerve and gathered the men to come out and collect. Nobody knows exactly what happened in between. They found them in the dance hall, every one of them, dressed in their finest and laid out holding hands in a circle that wound itself toward the center like they'd been dancing in a long line and just expired midstep. It was suspected to be some drug. But the autopsies didn't show nothing unnatural in the blood. They must have done it right when they got word the sheriff was coming out, cause their bodies was fresh dead and there was a baby crying in—

I sat up. What about the buildings? I said.

What do you mean?

If there was so many houses and whatnot there must still be buildings there.

Well, it was a long time ago.

Couldn't be more than thirty years.

Well I imagine there's still something there.

You ever seen it?

No. It's way on up the valley other side of Narrows, you know. Over opposite way from Ripplemead.

Where? I said.

Well I don't know exact.

What's the nearest road?

I don't want you going out there, Geoffrey, she told me. Anything that was out there'd be all rotted and falling in, waiting to kill someone who stepped on it.

Well, I said.

I mean it, she said.

Forty two goes out that way, I said.

She give me her look what meant we was done.

Before I got down I said, So it's true what I don't got no family?

Plum Head, she said, You got all of us right here.

I'd just put a leg over my bike when she called to me. I asked her, What?

She jumped down and come over. Last night, she said, you was talking about a grown man.

Yes ma'am.

I just told you straight. Now I'm gonna ask you straight. Have you made love with this girl?

No ma'am.

Okay. Good. There's a lot of boys out there think what makes a man is having their way with a woman. You don't think that do you?

I didn't say nothing. Truth is, I wasn't sure.

I'm gonna tell you something. A while back I had two little plums what was sent to me. A little girl just twelve and a little boy who was eleven. It wasn't a month before I found the little boy was doing it to the little girl. Now the little boy was as sweet a little diminished plum as you ever seen, and a lot more slow than you, and he was only eleven years old when I had to send him away cause of what he done. This eleven year old little slow boy. You think what he done made him a man?

No ma'am.

No indeed. Now what does? That's the question you should have asked. Go on get back on your bike. You got a long ride ahead. While you're going I want you to think about that, okay? You love your Ma Blevins?

Yes ma'am.

Give me a hug, she said.

I braced myself for it.

Thursday of July

I am sure there is times you wondered about how it happened and why I done it. I am sure you thought on how I even knowed what you worked at the home seller's house in the first. About if I come by that morning or the night before, and why I would have slipped you that note. Why I put that note in the slot for the mail. But most off, you must've wondered why I writ you about me and

Linda. Why I writ you about our date. Why I wanted you to come and find us and see us and face it. Well, now you know.

I wonder if when you come into work that morning and found the note and read it, if you felt like I felt when I writ it. I thought on what Ma B asked for the whole ride back and I writ it all roadside before I come into town, sitting in the grass with the sun getting hot. Once I got back on my bike it was strange what I felt scared but at the same time easeful, like I had got a weight off my gut. Did you feel like that when you seen I told you the time and place? When you knowed we was gonna finally have it out? There is times I almost hope I find you with Linda just so's I can hear what you think. We could talk back and forth. Maybe you writ me something. I believe we could know each other pretty deep.

The truth is, even if you do not know it yet, we already do. I been thinking on how if you writ me a letter would I want you to keep some secret part hid? Now what you is out and Linda is riding with you in the truck again might be she already told you what was in the letter she writ me in New Castle Memorial. Might be she didn't. But if she writ something to you about me I believe I'd want to know. If you writ me something and kept her letter out I don't know I'd believe you was telling me the truth on all the rest. Mister Podawalski, I am telling you the truth.

What Linda Writ Me In New Castle Memorial

Geoffrey, I am going to be blunt. Because what you asked about is not just something I did but what happened to me in my life that brought me to do it and who I am that allowed me to when others probably would not have. And how do you explain all that?

Maybe if I told you before I was with Waker, when I was fifteen or so, I used to sit in the back of the bus and give blow jobs to the boys I liked. I was famous for it. It was high school, nobody questioned it. Once I did it with a teacher. He must have been fifty. Not a blow job. He went down on me. Funny, but I don't think I thought it strange that he wanted to. I don't think other people would think it strange either.

Other people are so often wrong. Like about what I just wrote. They would think aha when they read that. But I don't think you would. That's what I like about you, Geoffrey.

So I'll try to help you understand who I am, how I could have done what you met me doing. This is the best I can do. I think it's got more of all this in it than anything else. See, Waker loved cats but he hated dogs. So we all thought it strange, his brother, everybody, when he insisted on taking Dad Podawalski's. This was when Waker's dad died. Dad Podawalski hated dogs too. But he had a husky, or something, and he trained that dog from a pup to keep other dogs off his yard. If he saw a dog on the street, Dad Podawalski would carry the little thing out there and growl himself to show how it was done, until he got the pup going, too. After that he kept it in his yard without a chain or a fence or anything. Whenever it chased a dog off, he would bring it a treat. And all that time it never once bit a dog or even tried.

When Dad Podawalski died Waker took the dog and put it in a cage in the garage where it wouldn't be able to see other dogs and go crazy at them. Sometimes Waker would have a friend bring his dog around on a leash and they'd stand in the

garage watching Dad Podawalski's dog run itself in circles wanting to get out. He was untraining it, Waker said. And it was true,
after a year of that when Waker's buddies would come by with
their dogs the husky didn't do anything but stare.

All that time Waker wouldn't let anyone but him feed it
and he gave it better than he gave himself. I spied on him sometimes and saw him patting the dog through the bars and talking to it and I swear sometimes he cried to it and tried to hug
its head. But he wouldn't take it out. Ever. Not in the three years.
One night after he and I had fought I went out and opened the
garage door and opened the cage. That dog ran right out and
into the neighbor's yard and killed the first dog it found. It went
right down the street, yard by yard, going after dog after dog,
on chains and in doghouses and everything. By the time the cops
came and shot it there were six dogs torn to death and the whole
neighborhood was up in arms. Everyone thought the dog was
rabid. Until they cut it open and tested it and then the whole
neighborhood, and Waker too, just thought it was crazy. I never
thought so. It was after that that Waker started confiding in me
the way he did.

That is all what Linda writ. I ain't leaving out the end. She never
put it. Or writ her name at the botton neither. I guess most like
the nurse come in just then and she quit. I hope seeing this ain't
hurt you even more than what I hurt you already. But even if it
did it had to be. Now you know all what I know. We are on the
up and up. If you understand what she meant for me to understand I wish you'd tell me. Might be sometime after I brung this
to you we will sit together side by side and learn each other whole

and I bet we can talk it over then. I believe together we could figure it out, me and you.

Sunday of July

There ain't no doubt now. You is out. And you ain't hiding it. I'm gonna put this down here just so you can look at it later, when maybe you stepped back enough what you can see yourself and groan. I'm putting this down here to shame you. When I been all this time writing to you how I done, and looking hard at what is, and laying it out best I can to own up to what I got to own up to, and you go and act how you done today, I want to ask you Mister Podawalski Who is the child now? Who is acting unadult? Who? I want you to think on that while I give you back here every bit of your own.

It was just this morning what I brung my breakfast and got there early and I was there when you pulled up in your truck, even if you didn't see me. If Linda'd been with you I would have come up right then. After you opened the house door and gone inside I watched the truck to try to see if she was somewhere in the cab. It didn't look it. You gone about putting up the shades, turning on the lights. When I seen you come back out I almost got up and come over to stop you if you was getting back in the truck, but you just walked over to the neighbor's house and done the same there. Then you come out and get a magazine out your truck and lean on the hood and drink your coffee like it was anything normal. Well, it wasn't normal for me, Mister Podawalski. After all this time, there you was. In your suit jacket and your slacks and your leather shoes. You growed back your beard. I watched you shake your head at something what you read. If you seen me, you sure did a good job hiding it.

When the first ones drived up, you put your magazine away and met them with loud talk and smiles and shaking hands and I watched you take them in the house, in the same house where it had come down between you and me, the same one where it had happened between me and Linda, too. From then on out, there was cars pulling up and you meeting people in the door and taking them around and I could hear you said the same things to each one, and give them all your ugly smile. Didn't none of them act surprised to see you out of jail. It set me wondering as to how long you been out.

It was after I falled asleep what you come over. I don't mind saying it seems to me a coward way to do it. You musta woke me cause when I looked up you was standing there.

What are you doing here? you said.

I'm Geoffrey Sarver, I said. I been—

I asked you what you're doing here.

Waiting for Linda.

She's not coming. Get outta here.

You stood there with the magazine rolled up in your hand. I had not counted on the way seeing you again up close like that would put the scare in me. I tried to lean against the fence like I was just leaning.

You deaf? you said. You come out of it deaf too now?

I ain't deaf, I said.

Then get out of here. Do I have to say it simpler?

I been writing to you, I said. I had almost forgot that look what you had give me before and give me again now. I said, I been trying to explain. I figure we could—

Can't you leave it? you said. Can't you drop it?

I just thought—

Drop it. Drop it okay? For your own good drop it and let it be. Do you understand? For your own good.

I want to see Linda, I said.

You can't.

I—

She doesn't want to see you. Are you really that thick? How is it possible to be that goddamn thick? I'll tell you what, I don't think you are that thick. I think you're just being an asshole. Now get outta here. I got work to do.

But I didn't get outta there and now you knowed I was there watching. Every time you come out I'd try and catch your eyes, and usually did, too. She didn't come. I guess maybe you called her and told her something what wasn't true. That's what I was thinking when I seen you come out the final time, closing the lights and locking the door. That's what I was thinking when I got up and gone for your truck.

Don't you work? you said.

It's Sunday, I said.

You had a pile of papers under your arm and you said, Get outta my way Geoffrey.

You can name me Mister Sarver, I told you. I been all this while naming you polite, you can—

Geoffrey, you said, get the fuck out of my way.

I want to see Linda, I said.

We've been over that.

Nuhuh, Waker—

You gave me that look. I take it back, you said. You are that fucking thick.

That was when you reached out and shoved me.

I'm warning you, you said, and opened the truck door and got in.

You thought you was gonna drive off, didn't you? You thought I was just gonna back up and watch you go. Well, you know better now, don't you? I was in the truck bed by the time you turned the key. And boy you come out mad.

Oh for fuck's sake, you said. Get the fuck off of there. You reached in and tried to grab me and I jerked my arm away.

I said, I got a right to see her.

Oh for fuck, you said. Stop acting like a child. Don't you get it? Haven't you figured it out?

I'm more than thirty, I said.

Then act like it. You retard. Take it like a fucking man.

I told you, You got a ugly smile. She said so.

I don't know how you got up in the truck bed so quick or how you throwed me out so I couldn't land my feet. You musta climbed down while I was pushing up off the street cause you was already opening the driver's door when you pointed at me and said, Don't fucking move.

I got up.

You said, You better watch that jaw. Then you was in and shut the door. Before you drived off you said out the window, And my name's Brian, you retard. Try and get that in your tiny fucking brain, okay?

Dad Kreager used to say fighting is just another word for how we get along. Ma B thinks different. She says you don't realize how strong a rope is till you try to snap it. I will admit I was mad at you when I sat down to write this. But now I've finished telling about today I can see you don't got any idea how

I've writ to you. So, after all, how can I expect you to carry me in the same respect as I do you? You don't know what has rised between us. You just know your half of the story. And I know the same is true for me. There is parts what I don't know. Even me with my tiny brain, as you say, I can see that. I know your name is Brian cause of the home seller's sign. And I know your middle name is Waker cause of what Linda called you. So I ain't so stupid as you make me out. But I ain't prideful, neither. I ain't too proud to admit there's things what I don't understand. Like why you is out. And where Linda is. And why she ain't come to visit. But there is always been things I don't understand. This is where you estimate me too small. I have grown used to it. I know how to work around it. I will think on it and I will think on it and I will think on it, and you watch.

There's them coons again. They still coming to the house at night, more and more of them. It's like they can't get it in their heads what I ain't gonna put out the trash. I gone to the door and told them, Coons I can't do it. All you critters got to go back to the woods. Find some other yards. I can't let you in. They go quiet while I tell them, but then a minute later they's back to scratching at the walls.

Tuesday of July

Well I have thought it through how I said I would. And I ain't done it by myself, neither. I got help for it. I will tell you right off what I can't say I understand it any better. If there is any truth, I know it's what I understand it worse.

Yesterday when I come home from work there wasn't nobody in the house. Not Jackie or Roy or even the baby. There was just the beagle what come over like usual and try to make me pat him on the head. I got me a can of tomato soup and put in crackers and waited till they was soft enough what I could chew them, and the whole time there was no sign of no one, and I got done and gone through Roy's Office to My Hall. It was once I shut the door what I heard them. Heard the baby. Then Roy. They was in His Bahamas. I gone over, give the door a knock.

That you Geoffrey? Jackie said.

Yuhuh, I said.

Come on in, Roy said and, Shut the door, almost before I had it open.

Don't let out the frogs, Jackie said.

I looked for them but they don't glow in the day. It was late sun. Under all that glass it was hot. Roy was in his shorts sitting half in the Lagoon playing with the baby. It was in a floater. Jackie was laid out on one of them flat chairs in her swim trunks what's like two part of underwears. They was both drinking beers. I wished I brung one from the fridge.

We're celebrating, Roy said.

Okay, I said.

What do you think? he said.

Sounds nice, I said.

No, he said. What do you think about the Bahamas?

Looks good, I said.

It's done, he said.

All right.

One hundred percent, he said.

Well okay, I said. Maybe I oughta go get a beer.

You bet, he said.

Jackie said, Bring a couple.

When I come back I was careful to open and shut the door quick. I give Roy one and give Jackie one and sit down next to her in the sand where there was good sun. I took off my shirt and shoes and dug in my toes. We all drank. The baby was quiet.

After a while Jackie said, Roy? Come lotion up my back will you?

I'm busy, Hon, he said.

Bring the baby over here, Jackie told him.

Have the boy do it, he said.

Don't call him that, she said. You know he don't like it.

Then have your brother do it, he said.

He's not my brother, she said.

He give me a look like Jackie was crazy. Hey, he said to me, Make it easy on me will ya?

I'll put some on your back, I told Jackie.

What a husband, she said.

Hey, he told her. Look around you, huh?

You got sand on your hands? she asked me.

I wiped them off and looked them over. No, I said.

Let me see them. Once she was sure, she give me the lotion and leaned over her knees so I could put it on. I started.

You know, she said. I heard what you did.

What do you mean? I said.

Gone by that woman's house. Got in a fight. I heard you sat out there all day watching people go in and out like some kind of creep.

I was looking for Linda, I said.

You gonna get yourself beat up again, she said.

I didn't know he'd be there. I didn't even know for sure he was out of jail.

She turned around and looked at me.

I still got some on my hands, I said.

Geoffrey, she said. Who do you think that was?

Mister Podawalski.

Which one?

The man, I said.

No, which Mister Podawalski?

Waker.

No.

Brian Waker Podawalski.

Oh boy, Roy said. He sounded like he was getting ready for fun.

Sharpie, Jackie said. There ain't no Brian Waker Podawalski. There's Brian Podawalski. And there's Waker. They're brothers.

It got so quiet the frogs started making their noise.

They're two different people, Jackie said. Do you get that?

Okay, I said. Which one's Mister Podawalski?

You mean Waker? she said.

He what's married to Linda?

Was.

Which one beat me up?

You mean today or the real bad time?

The one what put me in New Castle Memorial.

Waker, she said.

Okay, I said.

Roy said, The one who beat you today—

I didn't get beat up today, I said.

That was Brian, he said. He's a couple years younger.

Brian never was in jail, Jackie said. It's Waker's in jail.

I know that, I said. You already told me that.

Don't get like that.

I'm not, I told her.

You are. Which is what you get. Now I told you to stay away from that woman.

I ain't seen her, I said.

And you ain't going to. You understand? You don't know what people say. You don't know. Drag me into it, no, no, no you ain't. You ain't gonna call her, you ain't gonna look for her, you ain't gonna see her. We clear?

I got to, I said.

She don't want you.

How do you know? I said. You don't even know.

I know what I hear.

Leave it alone, Roy said.

Why do you think Brian beat you up today? she said.

Let him be, Jackie, Roy said.

You stay out of it, she told him. Then she said to me, Why do you think? Hm?

Because he likes her, I said.

Very good, she said. But that's only half of it. What's the other half?

I could feel Roy looking at me in a way what he ain't looked at me before. He looked sad.

I don't know, I said.

Because she likes him, Jackie said. In fact, what I hear is that she's living with him, built themselves a home with all that money, gone out somewhere near Pembroke or maybe Harts Run, doesn't really matter does it? What matters is—

So her husband's still in jail? I said.

See, she said. See now this is what you get. I can see your brain twisting itself in knots in there. You already been hurt bad. You want to keep on getting hurt? Cause that's what's gonna happen you start messing around.

Why can't you just let him be, Roy said. He said it quiet to the fish in the lagoon but she talked to him just as loud.

Be what? she said.

Alive, he said.

In love? she said. She sounded like she was giving him one of her mean smiles, but there wasn't nothing on her face at all.

Go to hell, Roy said.

Nice, she said. In front of the baby.

He's not a kid, Roy said.

Might as well be, Jackie said. You know that. He knows that. You know that, Geoffrey. What did you think you was doing? There's girls out there. I'm not saying—what I'm saying is there's ones out there who're like you.

Roy was looking at my face again, but this time I didn't look back. Remember the hunting, he said. Remember she doesn't know shit about what matters.

What matters, Jackie said and turned so she give me her full face and Roy her full back, is that soon as they sell them houses they're gonna be way on the other side of the valley and outta our lives, including yours, and we can go back to how it was before we was the laughingstock. Don't look like that, Geoffrey.

You don't understand, I said.

Geoffrey don't. You remember how it was. Things was good. You got a good job. People like you. Like to watch you wave and wave back. You gonna make some new friends. It's the way it's meant to be.

No, I said.

Don't give me no.

I can't, I said

You got plenty, she said. What more do you want?

I want to talk to her.

Geoff, Roy said. Jackie and me both looked at him cause he don't never call me by my name. He said, Why don't you get out of here, Geoff. Go on and get the hell out of here leave me and Jackie alone. He stood up out of the water. It dripped all around him on the sand. He looked madder than I'd ever seen him. Go on, he said. And take the goddamn baby with you.

Even before I shut the door, he started yelling at her. He yelled, You have to kill it, don't you? You just have to kill it in everyone.

By time I gone through My Hall she was yelling back. I gone into the main house and shut the door on them. Inside, the beagle's tail thumped at the floor. Soon as I sat down at the kitchen table the baby begun to cry.

Wednesday of July

This is what I know. I met Linda Podawalski one night back in the beginning of spring what seems a long time ago now. She was your wife. Now she's not. You and she is split. You is in jail. She is with your brother, Brian. I guess there could be all kinds of reasons for that. Maybe he give her protection. Maybe she just need a roof. Maybe all along he was the one what she was with at Crigger's Den.

I ain't blind to that. I don't guess that changes nothing except I want to see her now with even more deep of a need than what was before. About what you is still in jail. I will be truthful. There is some of me what's glad on that, glad it wasn't you yesterday at the opening of the homes, glad you is still there where I thought you was from the first, you who I am writing to all this time. You. Waker. I hope you don't mind I call you that. Waker.

I am trying here to take each part of you what I know and think on do I know it or is it wrong? Most of them I think is maybe wrong. When it comes down to it, the last true thing I know about you is it was you who come that night and beat me and bust my jaw and done in my eye. I know this cause you is the one in jail. It is what I knowed when I first writ the first word of this to you. Everything after is unsure.

But the thing is, the thing what's got me, is this. You ain't the same Mister Podawalski what I begun to write to. You have stayed right where you was in jail, but I have growed to know you, Waker. Better than I know most anybody else. I have writ to you what no one else has ever seen. You have seen me as this new man what your wife made. The same way I have seen you as the man what your wife made. I know you, Waker Podawalski. Don't none of this change that, no more than it change the one thing even you can't deny is the truth between us. You is in jail for what you done that night. And so I will stick to that. I will tell what I know. If there is any two people in this world what deserve to have it straight, it is me and you.

That night I come to your home at seven just like Linda told me. And just like I writ you that same morning in the note I put through the door of the home seller's place. Her car was the only one in the drive. I looked for your truck on the street and I didn't see it, so I was already standing on the front door steps when there it was, your truck, is what I thought, in the neighbor's drive. It made me jump. But when the door swinged open it was her alone. In one hand I brung wine in a bottle and in the other the biggest candle I could find at the IGA. It was fat enough I thought it oughta last and it smelled good such as I thought she'd like.

Just like the movies, I told her.

I tried to see past her to inside and if you was there, and it seemed she was looking past me at the street for the same. We was both nervous, I guess. I wanted to get inside and outta sight so good thing she wanted me in there, too.

You had the nicest house I ever been in. I never seen it like that with all the windows having curtains and shades both. They was shut on the street side and shut on all the sides except one what showed the lawn and the neighbor's house. It wasn't yet full dark, but it was dark enough there woulda been lights on in the neighbor's windows if anyone was home. They was all dark as the rest of the house. It eased me a little. She seen me looking out that way and told how it was so much nicer to eat supper with a view and how the street windows was covered cause she didn't want people who drived by and looked in.

There was knobs instead of switches what could do the lights midways between off and on. I watched her do them while it got more dark inside than out.

How's that? she said.

Good, I told her.

She'd already done it up with knives and forks and glasses and everything.

I ought to do something, I said.

You just relax, she said.

She gone in her purse, come out with a lighter.

If I'd knowed you had that, I said, I woulda skipped the candle, just brung a rubber band.

She looked like she wanted to laugh, but all she got out was a smile. She'd put the candle on the table and she lit it.

That's nice, she said. That smells nice. What scent is that?

I don't know, I told her.

Well it's nice, she said. She told me about the last stuff she had to do in the kitchen and asked if I wanted to open the wine. Okay, I told her. She gone to that counter between your dining room and kitchen what's there instead of a wall and I seen she already had wine. Them bottles was laid on their side so I couldn't see if any was the same make as what I brung, but there was a whole three shelves of them so I figured yuhuh, chance was. She brung over the screw tool.

Oh that, she said when she seen me looking at all them bottles. That's all Waker's. Then she said, I'm sorry, does it make you feel awkward when I mention him?

No, I said.

Well it does me, she said. I'm not going to. That was the last mention.

Okay, I said. I looked at the screw tool she'd put by the bottle. I can tell, I said.

Hm? she said. She was doing stuff over in the kitchen. You can tell what, Hon?

It makes you nervous.

Oh, she said. Oh well no, she said.

Something in the kitchen took her thoughts to it. I tried to put mine on the bottle but she'd sat me with my back to the front door and I was having trouble. I got the foil peeled off the top but under they'd put a plug what I couldn't get out with my nails. The tool she'd give me had handles coming out all over it and I tried to turn it around where I could get the point to bite.

Oh, she said from the kitchen. That thing's ridiculous. And she come over with a hot pad in her hand.

It's just I ain't seen this exact style, I told her.

It was a gift, she said. He talked about wanting one every time we'd sit down to—shit, she said. See? Well, that was really the last time, I promise.

She got the bottle open and give it to us in glasses and I waited like Ma B said till she'd laid out all the food she'd done. She come around the table and kiss me on the side of my head.

When we was sitting, she said, I'm not nervous. I'm just excited.

She smiled till I knowed what she meant, how sitting on the hood of her car drinking Pepsis behind the Sunoco we had talked of excited and nervous. You remember pretty good yourself, I said.

To our memories, she said and we tapped our glasses. It sounded different from with cans. Just one thing different of a whole bunch more to come.

We talked while we ate, but we wasn't neither of us thinking with all our brains on what we spoke. I was thinking on when you was gonna show. A vehicle pulled up outside on the street. We both gone quiet. It was just the sounds of us finishing what was in our mouths. When the car door slammed we both of us jerked. Near knocked the plates off the table. She started laughing. She laughed harder than I ever seen her, and didn't seem like she was gonna stop, laughed herself out till she couldn't hardly breathe. I tried to listen through it, see if there was anyone coming up to the house door, but I couldn't help smiling at her going on and on. When she was done, she took her glass of wine and drunk it all down. She put it back on the table and breathed out, Whoooo.

God, she said. Look at us.

I guess we's nervous, I said.

I guess so, she said. Maybe this wasn't such a good idea.

It's nice, I said. The food is real good.

Maybe it's just crazy, she said. She said it like it wasn't meant for me to say yes or no. On top of what she wasn't looking at me. She was looking out the windows at the neighbor's house. It was still all dark. I tried to see in its windows and couldn't see nothing.

You think he's in there? I said.

Who?

Your husband.

No, she said. No, Geoffrey, I told you. It's okay. Really, I made sure he'd be gone. He won't be back till after midnight. Okay?

You is wondering how I coulda sat there and not told her how I'd writ the letter what would make you come after all, how I'd told you behind her back. You is thinking I am a liar for staying quiet just as bad as if I'd told her false. I ain't proud of it. But I knowed if I told her you was on your way she'd have made me go. And then what? You'd already know about her and me, and I'd have got sent out before I could show anything what I was made of, and then what on from there, is what I sat there thinking.

She poured herself another glass and give mine a top up and said, How about we finish up and go in the living room where we can just stretch out and be, huh?

Okay, I told her, but really I just wished you'd hurry up and come and we could get it done.

We didn't go to the living room anyhow, least not at first. First I did the dishes. She said she didn't want me to, but I said I wanted to, and she said, Not while you're a guest in my house, Mister.

Okay, I said. Just pretend I'm not. Pretend it's like I live here.

We both thought on that in quiet. Then she said, That'd be nice wouldn't it?

I didn't say nothing, just started stacking them in the sink. I like washing dishes and I'm good at it and it was nice with her taking the done ones from me and drying them and it going on like that, a good time together of no talking like we used to out back by the tank. It was nice but for the times when head-lights would come through the window screen and go cross the wall and we'd both try hard to show we didn't even notice. I figured I'd leave it alone. If she was worried what maybe you'd change your plans and be home early or other doubts, I figured that was maybe for the best, just make her more ready for it when you come.

When we was done, she opened one of them bottles you buyed and poured us more and said, A penny for your thoughts?

I didn't know what to say. I didn't want to lie. I just stood there drying my hands.

She said, You're supposed to say, It'll cost me more than that. Anyway, it's what I like about you. That you didn't. I'll tell you mine for free. I had a fantasy just then. I thought about how it would be for you and me to be married. I just kind of let my imagination go, you know? Did you think about that?

I never really thought that far, I said. I was just thinking about how good we was at washing dishes.

Yeah, she said. I guess that's pretty much what I meant. She took a drink. Hey, I have a idea. How about we go into the living room and pretend it was just our living room like on any night.

We lay out on the couch you got with its two parts like a L. She was on one part and I was on the other.

What do you like to watch? she said.

Anything, I said.

Come on, she said. You've got to help me with this or it won't be any fun.

I thought of what Roy watched this time of night. Survivor, I said.

She put it on. In the glass of the TV, I could see the picture of the light in the hallway entrance. I could see the front door. I watched that.

I'm just gonna do some chores, she said. I don't care so much for reality TV.

Well let's watch something else, I said.

She come up behind me and put her hands in my hair. Silly, she said. This is the whole point. You do what you would do and I do what I would do and we can feel what it would be like. Okay?

I lay there watching the TV's mirror picture of the front door while she gone around emptying the trash cans into a bag. I heard her doing it all over the house and then I heard her take it outside and then I could see her through the window putting the bag in the can out back. She was looking at the neighbor's house again and I looked at it too. It was night now and the moon was out and I could see the curtains wasn't closed on the windows in that house but I couldn't see enough more to look in. When she come back inside, I said, Where you think your neighbor is?

My neighbor?

You keep looking at the house.

Yeah, she said. I do, don't I. I don't know where he is. I just keep worrying he's gonna come back and see something and—you know. I guess we don't need the curtains open anymore, anyway. The view's all gone isn't it?

She shut them all along that side of the house. Then she put some more wine in her glass. She stood there behind me for a while. Then she said, Well I guess we know how this is going to be. About what you'd expect, right? How about we try what's it like in the bathroom.

In the bathroom? I said.

You know, like brushing our teeth before bed. It's got to be more intimate than watching the TV. She put her hands on the back of the couch next to my head. I could feel again how they'd been earlier in my hair and I wished them back there. But she just said, It'd be more close, don't you think? Sharing something like that together?

On the way down the hall to the bathroom I said, You share your toothbrush with your husband?

No, she said. You share the time.

Okay, I said.

The time before bed, she said. It's a intimate time. You don't know cause you've never had it. You've never done it, have you?

No, I said.

In the bathroom she give me your toothbrush.

I don't know, I said.

Oh come on, she said.

I mean it's his toothbrush, I said.

That's the point, she said. Like you're my husband. Why are you so resistant, Geoffrey?

I'm not, I said.

She looked at me till I took the brush. We scrubbed at our teeth. I wanted to get it done and spit it out fast. I didn't like the idea of you coming in and me having to talk to you with paste in my mouth. But she brushed long and careful and kept on doing it so I kept on and when she spit I spit.

Now my husband, she said. I know I said I was done talking about him, but I want to tell you that my husband brushes his teeth like a kid. Real fast and sloppy and hardly does anything. I know it sounds funny but I'm kind of glad, it kind of means something, that you and I both brush the same way, you know? That doesn't strike you?

I noticed it, I said.

Me too, she said. That's the kind of little thing. That's why I wanted to do this. Now, I want to do something else, okay? I've heard that men like to watch a woman put on her makeup, but I always thought if I was a man I'd much rather watch a woman take her makeup off. You ever seen that?

No, I told her.

What do you think? She said. Should I?

Yuhuh, I said.

You'd like that?

Yuhuh.

Okay, Hon. You just stand there then.

She took every bit of it off, including undid her hair, and when she was done her face was scrubbed red.

Come on, she said, and led me out of the bathroom toward the end of the hall. She'd dropped some trash from the bag what I had to step over. I was gonna say something or pick it up, but then I seen one of them things was a sex rubber like what I cleared up mornings when I washed the Men's Room at the Sunoco. So I let it alone. I just followed her through the door. It was your bedroom. She shut the door behind us. I noticed the window shade in there was still up and I told her, but she said, Oh to hell with it.

I'm not ashamed to say I was a little nervous standing there in your bedroom with her and not just because you was past due. In fact it was so long after the time I'd told you to come I was starting to think you never got my note after all. I'm not afraid to admit neither what it was a relief. Cause truth is, it was a good kind of nervous to have Linda alone in the room.

Hey, I told her.

What? she said.

I'm excited too.

She smiled at me and took my hand and put it to her chest right between her things. Can you feel that? She said.

Yuhuh, I told her. I took her hand and put it on the same place I had on me.

We stood there like that till she said, All right, but she didn't move till she said it again, All right. Then she said, I don't want to move too fast. Okay?

Okay, I told her. She walked cross the room and I watched to see if she was gonna move real slow, but she just gone at normal speed. When she'd turned on the bedside lamp she walked back, still at normal speed, and turned off the overhead.

Lets get undressed, she said.

You mean take off our clothes?

Just take them off, she said. Not do anything. We have plenty of time to do that.

You mean to make love? I said.

We'll save that, she said. Like a treat to look forward to.

You would—

I want to, she said. Just I want to do it right, in time, you know? I'm thinking we could just take off clothes and get in bed and—you must think I'm crazy.

No, I said. It's only I don't—

You must think I've got some serious problems. I understand. I understand perfectly.

I don't think you're crazy, I said.

It's just been such a long goddamn time since I've felt comfortable with someone, she said. I mean even at home, here, it's like him and me are sleeping in different beds. Now, don't, she said. I'm not talking about sex. I'm not. I'm talking about holding. Simple cuddling for God's sake for a fucking minute before sleep. I'm sorry, she said.

You want to cuddle? I said.

Don't you? she said.

Yuhuh, I said. I just don't want to be naked if he comes in.

He's not gonna come in, she said.

I don't want to have to talk to him naked.

Geoffrey, he's not gonna come.

What if he does?

Well what if? she said. I mean what if? So he comes in and sees us in the bed.

He's gonna think—

What if he does, Geoffrey? Then he knows, right? Then he really knows this isn't like the others.

The others?

The boys, she said. Behind the tank. So what if he sees us naked in the bed and thinks we're fucking, hm? That's right. Thinks we're fucking. Knows right then that I'm with a man who I'd sleep with and like it. So what if he knows you're that man? I hope he does.

I told her, I thought you said if he ever found you sleeping with a growed man he'd beat the stuff out of—

He's gonna go crazy no matter how he finds out, she said. That's the truth, Geoffrey. And it's something we're gonna have to deal with. But I'm willing to. Do you understand what I'm saying? If you are too, I'm okay with it. But we don't have to do it tonight, okay? We'll do it some other time, but not tonight.

Okay, I said. She started to take off her shirt. So, I said, do you still want to get in the bed?

She looked at me with her belly showing. Yes, she said.

We begun to get naked. Towards the end she said, I'm gonna leave my panties on, so I did too. But when I turned around she'd took hers off and was just in her underwears.

You sleep in your jeans? she said.

Sometimes, I said.

All right, she said. I usually sleep in this, and she put on a pullover dress like what Jackie wears to bed.

We got under the covers. She turned off the light. In the dark, I could feel all her backside parts push up against me. Put your arms around me, she said. We lay like that for a while and it was so late what I didn't even worry when a car gone by on the road.

Your heart's still going, I said.

I should hope so, she said.

I could feel it right through her into me and it was going fast.

A little while later, I said, When you said you'd like to sleep with me?

She still didn't say anything. Her heart was going and going.

I said, You didn't mean like a blow job what you do with boys, did you?

No, she said, I meant the real thing.

A second later, she said, I forgot something. She turned on the light and real quick picked up the phone and listened to it and moved it nearer to the bed and turned off the light again.

All right, she said. All right then.

It wasn't five minutes later what the front door opened and you come in.

I sat up. That's him, I said.

I heard you in the front of the house say, I don't see nothing, like you was talking to someone on a phone. Then you said, Fuck. I gotta go.

It's okay, she said to me.

That's him, I said again.

It's gonna be all right, she said.

You was cussing in the kitchen. There was bangs and things busting. You was shouting her name.

I'll go talk to him, I said.

No, she said. She was holding on to keep me in the bed.

I got to get on my shirt, I said.

No, she said. Stay here. Geoffrey stay here.

It's me what did it, I told her.

Then you was coming loud down the hall.

Get under the covers, she said.

No.

Get under.

He gonna see me.

Get under Geoffrey, she said, and then the covers was over me and she was holding me down. Don't do nothing stupid, she said just as you slammed in the room.

You fucking bitch, you said. You bitch. You fucking fucking bitch.

I couldn't see nothing with my face in the pillow and the covers over me and I started to shove her off to get free when something hit me in the back what shoved my whole middle down on the mattress. Something hit me there again and there was the weight on my back how it was gonna crack and something was banging at the back of my head. She was shouting and screaming and you was shouting and screaming but I couldn't hear what nobody was saying. My ears was full and I couldn't think of nothing but get myself turned around so the hurt at my head would stop and when I done it I seen you for one second, you staring down at me in the dark without your beard. Then you hit me in the face.

You could have stopped then, but you didn't. I guess I don't got to tell you what all you done. It's there in the records anyhow, both in the court and in my papers what's at New Castle Memorial. And, anyhow, I expect you remember better than me how it gone after that. Even when I shut my eyes, now, and try, I can't see much of it. There's the light going on what made everything bright red on top my eyes and there's Linda screaming at you and saying Brian, Brian come, come Brian, Brian, Brian, Brian over and over and then she's nearby cause I can feel more parts of bodies than is possible just me and you, and she must be trying to pull you off cause her voice is near and wild when she's saying, He's retarded Waker, he's retarded, God he's just a poor fucking retarded—and then she's crying. I guess you got off me. I guess from what was told later you must have gone at her, then. I don't got no memory of that more than what she's crying and saying, I already called the cops, I already called them, like she's talking to someone else in the room. And there is someone else in the room. Even through my blood and what I must be on the ground, I can see there's three of them. And hear one of them, might be you, might be the other, say Run, run Linda, Linda run.

Waker, I do not want to hear what you is sorry. That is not why I have writ this out. I know I brung it on myself. I know I brung it on Linda. I brung it on you. Ma B says its only a fool what cuts hisself and is surprised by his own blood. I ain't surprised. Of all of us, I am the one who come out of it most lucky. I know this. I know it beyond anything anybody can say to tell me elsewise. It is what Jackie don't understand. It is why I can't go back to what I was before. This is what I have been trying to

get at the whole time. It is what no one seen but Linda and me
and maybe you, also. It is why I know when she was shouting
to you how I was a retard it was only cause she knowed it was
the last thing what might save me. And it's why she left off trying, and begun to cry. She knowed it wasn't no longer true. It
maybe used to be I was more child than man, but it ain't no
more. I know what Linda was saying when she told me at the
first about sleeping with a man. And I know what Ma B was
saying when I left that morning how she told me about what
more was needed. I thought it through on the bike. When I writ
out that note to you I understood what I was doing. I knowed
for the first time I was beyond what no kid would do. I had
growed into doing what was right. And by doing what was right,
I have showed to the Eyes of the Lord what kind of man I have
become, and no one can call me elsewise anymore. And so here
is my half-healed jaw, and my insides what still don't work good
as they ought, and my seeing in the one eye gone from me and
ain't coming back. It ain't nothing. It ain't nothing to give for
what I got. I begun here saying I was sorry, but now what I am
here near the end I want to say instead what I am grateful. What
I want to say here, now what we both know how it come about,
what I want to say to you from me, is thank you.

It is more late than I thought. I have just got up and checked
the clock and it is almost two in the morning. A long time ago
Roy come downstairs and gone into His Office. For a while he
was listening to his numbers, but now it's stopped. The light is
off in there, but I think he is awake. I can hear him breathing
near the bottom of the door.

Geoff.

I just writ that cause it's what he just said.

Yes?

It's what I just told him.

He asked me am I awake and I said yes.

He's saying more now but I can't write it down fast as he talks. He asked me did I want to come in to the office. I don't really want to come in. I'll just stay quiet. Maybe he'll leave it be.

He has just told me he can hear me writing.

Come in and talk, he says.

I'm back. It's now after three. I ain't gonna sleep tonight. Roy is in the office still, but he's asleep now, I can tell. He dropped off right after I gone, like it was due him after all he just now told to me. When I come in there he was lain out on the carpet with the blanket from the TV couch on him and the Yosemite Sam pillow under his head.

He said, You write pretty much every night, huh?

I didn't say nothing. I didn't want him nor no one but you to know what I was putting down.

I know you do, he said. This isn't the first time I slept down here, you know.

I know, I told him.

That's one hell of a sister you got there, he said.

She ain't my real sister, I told him.

I hear you, he said. There's times I wish she wasn't my real wife.

It was a long time of us sitting there till I said, Can I go now?

He looked at me. I read it, he said.

He told me don't get mad. I was already mad. I didn't hardly pay attention to what he gone on about after that. He talked and talked. It was something about that woman he gone hunting with a long time ago and how he'd knowed her even after he and Jackie was new married and what he wished he'd done and where she was now and how he still thought about her and a lot else what I didn't truly care to hear. I don't care to write it all here, neither. I don't got time. It was at the end when I was thinking he was gonna talk all night what he said, Here, and give me his keys. He took a sticky pad off his desk and writ on it and give it to me. It said #72 Rt. 289.

It's off 33 out past Pembroke toward Harts Run, he said. It'll take about an hour and a half. You can use Jackie's car. Don't look at me like that, he said. It's not like it was hard. I'm the one's got to forward their mail.

Before I left the office I asked him how much he'd read.

Up to the part where you left Waker Podawalski that note, he said. It was all that you'd wrote yet.

When I'd shut the door, he said to me under the crack, Geoff. She's the worst kind. In the end she'll just about kill you. All the good ones do.

I wish you could have seen them critters' eyes. They musta been forty of them out there. I brung my flashlight and this pad and this pen and that's it and walked through them around the house down to Jackie's car. They didn't even move, not one of them. They just stared at me. No more scared than if I was one of they own.

Mellencamp
Springsteen
Eagles
Animals
Isaak
Dead

That's what's on the radio just before dawn.

There ain't no one up yet, but I can see in the sky what's over the ridge now it's about to come. I'm in the car looking at the house. It's big and made of logs and it's so new there ain't no plants around it yet. When I put this on the steering wheel to write I was worried I might press too hard and set off the horn. Now I don't care.

Someone is up.

I been here a hour and no one come out. I know they see me. I'm parked right down here at the bottom of they drive. Another half hour I'm gonna go up and knock.

Nobody. I knocked and I rung the bell and I knocked some more. I called to her. I could hear them moving around in there. Whenever I'd make a noise they'd go quiet and then I'd go quiet. It's sure now they know why I come.

* * *

As I write this I am leaning on the horn. It's hard on the ears after a minute. I been doing it for at least five. I'll keep doing it, too, till she

Thursday of August

This is the last time I will write to you. After I come back from her, I thought I might not, thought I'd just leave it alone where it was just quit trying. But there is something in me wants to put it down right to the end. Sides, it has turned out you, in the end, is the only one I want to tell good-bye.

When she come out the house I seen him what I once thought was you behind her in the door and her talking to him like she was trying to keep him inside. I didn't lean off the horn till she shut the door on him and begun down the path to me. I begun to get out.

Stay in there, she said. Then she was at the passenger side pulling open the door. She got in. Let's go, she said.

Linda, I said.

Just drive, she said.

Where?

Just go, Geoffrey. It doesn't really matter does it?

I drived on up the road. It was small enough it oughta been dirt but it was hardtop. She didn't say nothing and I didn't say nothing. I was scared to look at her. The only homes on that road was trailers or ones what didn't look lived in no more.

I didn't know you could drive, she said.

I musta never told you, I said.

Some dogs come to their chains and barked.

Can I ask you something? I said.

I figured you would.

When we done driving, we going back to that house?

She didn't answer for so long I looked at her.

Yes, she said.

I looked back at the road.

When we go back to that house, I said, We gonna pick up your stuff?

No, she said.

I drived on.

Geoffrey, she said. You can't come by that house no more. You got to stop looking for me.

I—

Hush, she said. Just hush and let me talk, okay? After I'm done you can ask me whatever you got to ask me and I'll tell you. Brian didn't want me to, but I told him I owe it to you. He said that you'd go to the—that you'd cause us trouble. I told him you wouldn't. I told him you were too sweet. Remember in the hospital when you said you wouldn't tell nobody what I'm going to tell you if you knew it would hurt me? Well, this would hurt me a lot. I know I don't have a right to ask you, but if you told it would ruin my life, Geoffrey. And my life is pretty good for the first time since almost ever. Can you understand what that means? What it means to have that?

I nodded.

And if I tell you what you want so that there's no more questions you won't come try and see me again?

How bad did he hurt you?

My ex? she said.

Waker, I said.

He broke my cheek. And my nose.

I looked at her. I said, You can't tell.

It's pretty much healed, she said. He wasn't supposed to hurt you so bad, Geoffrey. I want you to know that. That wasn't the plan.

I know, I told her. It was my fault.

No. No it wasn't your fault.

You don't know, but it was my fault he come.

No, she said. No it was Brian who called him. And it was me who let Brian know when to call. It was him and me who set it up, Geoffrey. You didn't do nothing wrong. Take that left, she said. It'll bring us around back to 33.

After a while I said, Was Brian in the room the whole time? In the bedroom?

Was he the other one in the room what told you to run?

He was across the yard, she said.

In the neighbor's house?

He was our neighbor. It used to be one big family plot. They split it up when their dad died. He could see everything that was going on, Geoffrey. That was supposed to make it safe, so he could see as soon as Waker came in. You were supposed to just get hit once or twice and then Waker would hit me once or twice and that's when Brian would come in and put a stop to it before it got too bad.

It took him a long time, I said.

I know, she said.

What held him up?

He said lots of things. They were a pack of lies. What held him up was that he knew about me and you and he was jealous. By the time he come, I had more of your blood on me than my own. He says that worked out fine, that it just looked extra good for the neighbors when I went out on the street and started yelling. It's true it helped us in court, but I want you to know I was mad at him about that for a long time. I still am. If I were you, I'd hate him.

Up ahead there was 33 going through the valley.

I told her, Roy says you's the worst kind of woman.

Do you believe that? she said.

I don't know.

You should.

I don't know what he means.

He's right, she said. You shouldn't just hate Brian. It was both of us who did the plan. That's what it was, Geoffrey. It was a trick. When it comes down to it, it was just an awful, awful trick. And it worked.

Because it got Waker in jail?

Because it got us this. She moved her hand at the car window and the road and the land what was all around us. When it comes down to it, she said, it's really that simple.

Us? I said.

Brian and me, she said.

I don't understand, I told her.

Who was going to believe that I was having an affair with a—you don't have to understand everything, Geoffrey. I told the judge, we told the judge, that me and you had become friends, that I was like a mother to you, that I took care of you and they put Waker in jail and gave us all we were asking and it worked.

The road hit 33. We stopped. To the right was back to Ripplemead. The left was back toward her log house. She looked at me like she was waiting. I looked straight at the bigger road what crossed in front.

I said, When you told me I was a man you'd want to sleep with was that true?

A car come along 33 and passed by and gone on. She was still looking at me. A truck come by. When it was gone, she said, Take a right.

That's back to Ripplemead, I said.

Just take a right. I want to show you something.

We drived in quiet and the sun heated up the car fast. I rolled my window down and she kept hers up and the wind come in and made a shaking sound between us.

At the big curve just before it goes down the hill to Harts Run she said, Let's go up there, okay? It was a brick building with big windows broke of their glass. I took the drive. It was gravel and loud till we parked. Come on, she said.

She got out and I followed her. There was a chain locked over the front doors but she walked past it and gone around down the hill to the side. There was a small door there come off its hinges and she asked me to help her move it and then we was inside. The stairs was wooden and some was busted but we gone up anyhow. We come out in a hall what looked like a school. It was in too bad shape for nobody to use. Her walking and me walking it was both real quiet and real loud like you only get in big places what's been empty a long time. She gone in a door and I gone in after her. It had the chairs what's attached to the desks and a blackboard and everything, but it was all covered in dust what hadn't been touched in a long time. She drug her arm cross the big desk at the front. Sit down next to me, would you? she said. We sat there.

When I was a girl, she said, I went to school here. It wasn't a good school, I don't think. Anyway, I wasn't a good student. I don't think my teachers cared one way or another about me and I didn't have many friends. Everyone I know now always says those are the hardest years, how tough it is to fit in, how mean kids can be. This was my homeroom in seventh grade. I've never been as happy again as I was right here. Do you see what I'm trying to say?

I thought you said life was pretty good now?

It is. I'm not really talking about me. I'm talking about you. I'm talking about how mean adults can be. What I'm saying is that's how it is, Geoffrey. Outside of here, out there, that's how it is. I am sorry for what I did, Geoffrey. I am sorry. But I also know I've had bad things done to me. And I've done other bad things. And there isn't no one I know who hasn't. Except maybe some kids somewhere. Except maybe you.

I done bad things, I said. I done things what hurt people. I writ a letter to your husband. I was the one what told him to come to your house that night.

Why do you keep on with that? She said. It wasn't your letter.

You didn't know about it, I said.

Of course I did, she said. You left it at Brian's work.

I left it for Waker, I said.

Waker never saw it, she said.

I wanted to do it right, I said. I wanted to have it out like growed men.

Grown men don't do it like that, Geoffrey.

I done it like—

They do it a lot worse.

No, I told her. No, I done it. I done it.

I stood off the desk and walked into the middle of the room but when I got there I didn't know where I was walking or what direction was out. I was still talking, but I can't now hear in the memory of my ears what I was saying. I can't hear it. Then I stopped and gone quiet. I sat down on the ground where I was.

She come over to me then and got down next to me. She tried to look at me but I wouldn't let her. She reached around and put her hand on my chest. Maybe she could feel my heartbeat. I tried to feel hers through her hand. I couldn't feel nothing under her fingers but the warmness and the weight.

All the whys there is. Or even one. Why in the end she told me how it was. Why for all I tried it was Brian who had in him the thing she wanted for her heart. Why the Eyes of the Lord didn't see that in her the first night we met. Or if they did, why didn't He let me know? Why did He let her break them rules and kiss me like I was a full adult? Why did He give her such elbows what come to such perfect points and let me love to hold them in my hands?

I do not understand a single one. The only thing I know is this. You most like do. You most like understand them all. I believe anybody but me would.

The whole drive back to Roy and Jackie's I wished it was you, Waker, who was out and going home. Wished I was where you is instead. You is the one who belongs here among them of your kind. Them all I passed on my way through Ripplemead, out at the end of their own drives getting their own mail from their own boxes, them talking streetside easy back and forth and no looks on their faces like what they would give me, them ones who drived by in their trucks sitting quiet beside their wives. Ma B says Hate is just Hell and Gate put together to get you through to the fires more quick. Well in the end she is only one of them too.

It was still before noon when I got home. The house was empty. In My Hall I got together all what I could think of and put it in my bag. It wasn't much. I gone into the kitchen and took as many cans of all kinds as the rest of my bag would hold. On the table by the baby's chair I left Jackie her keys. In Roy's Office I seen the gun. I looked till I found the bullets. I took them too.

I left the door from the kitchen to Roy's Office hanging open. Then I left the door open from Roy's Office to My Hall. I gone into Roy's Bahamas and jammed that door open, too. The sun was coming in almost straight down. It hit the fishes so they shined all kinds of colors. The frogs gone quiet at my sound. I walked over the sand to the door what gone from the Bahamas to the backyard. I opened it and stuck it open and left.

Tonight the yard critters will come. I can see in my brain how it will be. The first ones will sneak up slow to sniff it out. Then the rest will come. From the yard the Bahamas will be dark and all full of them hot weather plants and them frogs what glow blue hopping around. The moon, if there is one, is sure to shine on the water, and on the fishes sleeping in it, and on the eyes of all them critters coming on. It's gonna be a mess. If I'd time I would have done it all down the block. Done it all through the whole town. I'd have liked to see the hour them coons got into all them homes. All them living rooms and bedrooms and kitchens and lives of all them Ripplemead people what watched me eat my supper in the Pine Top and waved at me from behind the window of their cars and knowed me how they knowed me all them years.

Them years is done. When the coons come for the Bahamas, when they gone into My Hall, when they find their way into the house, I won't be there. Sometime back around noon I got on my bike and rode out. I gone out through Ripplemead, past the Sunoco where I was supposed to be at work, past Crigger's Den to 42 what I took all the way out to the national forest till I seen them big tents like Roy said all done of branches and tarps out by a dirt road what I gone up till I hit the Swain. I don't know how long it took. But the sun looked like it didn't have more than two three hours left by the time I hit the bridge. I thought about bringing my bike the rest of the way, but I didn't see how or what good it would even be to one like me where I was going. I left it roadside what some regular man or boy might find. I untied Roy's gun and took my bag and gone down through the brush to the creek bank and started up along the rocks. Sometimes the creek run straight so's I could see way up ahead how the woods was thick and the rocks come down straight off the ridges in walls what squeezed.

This is the story of all them Sarvers how I think it gone. I don't think Ma B was fully right nor Dad Kreager, neither. I think the truth of it lays somewhere in between. I think Ma B was right about them all was diminished. They wasn't regular men or boys or women or girls. I think they was like me. But I think she was wrong about why they gone. I expect they didn't choose what they wanted to go no more than what they got kicked out. I expect they just seen how towns wasn't made for ones like them. They spent their lives trying to fit into places

made for them who was natural, always trying to get back to the
last or onto the next, and always winding up between. I expect
they just got tired of trying. And so they all of them up and left
and come to the Swain. And I'll tell you what. Most like they
did okay. Most like they made them mills and had them hogs
and did the farming of the trees. Most like they come to fit a
place in this valley for them who's like us. I don't know why they
all disappeared. I believe maybe they didn't. I believe maybe they
just gone deeper in the hills. Maybe they got cabins up on the
ridges. Maybe they still come down here, bring their hogs to
water, gather what's left of them plants they once growed. Maybe
they come down at night and walk through here and go to the
old dance hall and have themselves a time.

I think it must be the dance hall what I'm in now. It's big
enough and there is a stage I think what has falled in and a piano
sitting in the middle of the room where it would be in everyone's way. Unless they danced around it in a big circle, which I
guess they might. There's a bench what runs around the edge
of the whole room. The floor is pretty good still, though there is
one corner of the place what has a tree growed up through it
and out the roof. The roof is pretty good too except one, two
spots. I can see the sky through them and it is getting late. I got
here two hours ago and I been writing since. Soon I'm gonna
have to leave my spot on the bench and get up and go see if there
is a better one of the other houses for me to sleep. When I come
up the creek I seen the orchards first. The trees was big as I ever
seen and twisted up and most of them dead. But on some of
them high branches I seen cherries. I think the fields of rice
must be gone, but just before I seen the first houses I come upon
the gardens. They was overgrowed with all kinds of plants gone

giant wild. I come on a old hog-slaughtering post what's mostly rotted. In between all the houses is trails worn down. I expect it's by the use of the deer what must come down here some big amount. Their droppings is everywhere.

One day when it goes cold and frosts and them first snow come I'll get one with Roy's rifle. I'll make a suit out of it like that boy Sam done way back on his mountain. I know the ways of it. I know all the traps what he done and all the ways he kept living on and I will even make a pair of gloves. Rabbit fur gloves. A hat. Might be I get me a woods critter what to scratch behind the ears and talk to and spill my heart, as they say. I believe I'll grow a beard. I believe that woods critter will warn me if ever anyone tries to come my way.

If one of them old time Sarvers does come down from some home what he made way up there on the ridge I guess I'll know it woods critter or not. I guess he'd know me too. I seen they done that church roof in pieces of wood and some up there the years ain't got to and what ain't lost their color and looked pretty new to me. I aim to sleep there. Let them come some night and find me in the church they made. Might be it's just one old boy coming through the trees holding a light. Might be a whole family of Sarvers. I wonder if they kept them mules. If I heard all them mule feet coming down through the leaves what's falled and all dry and noisy till they come out onto them deer trails of dirt and then towards me in my church I wonder how would that sound?

Through the roof, the sky is showing me to wrap it up. I don't guess there's any reason for me to write you no more. You and me have come together and gone our ways already without you having yet knowed. I will keep what I have writ safe in my bag till maybe someone come along who's going out to town. Maybe one of them like me what come here before will pass through with a load of wood they's taking down the river to sell. If I see anyone I'll give them this, and ask they get it to you somehow. I don't know if you and me will understand the other. I guess that is not my worry now. My brain was never fit for it anyhow. You is of a different kind. Of the normal world of towns. I have gone back where I should have never gone away from in the first. So long from Sarverville. I would think of something more better to end on, but I have a lot to do in the last light what remains.

ACKNOWLEDGMENTS

I owe deep thanks to the men and women of Sinking Creek, Virginia, who held out their hands to me and didn't shake too hard. Alan Lugar, who opened his truck door for me and taught me most of what I know about beef. Russell Lugar, who taught Alan, and who told me stories by the glow of his space heater. Lonnie Oliver, for letting me walk his land.

How blessed I've been to work with the team at Grove, especially Elisabeth Schmitz, whose thoughtful editing and care for this book helped lift these novellas another notch. PJ Mark, who brought me to her, is all a writer could ever wish for in an agent—and then some. And I'm grateful to Pia Ehrhardt for introducing me to him. She is part of a community of fellow writers and artists—Liz Gilbert, Porochista Khakpour, Margo Rabb, Suzanne Rivecca, Laura van den Berg, and Paul Yoon—whose support and friendship sustain me. Many of them I met at Bread Loaf Writers' Conference, Sewanee Writers' Conference, or Virginia Center for the Creative Arts, or in the MFA creative writing program at Columbia University, all of which helped in getting me to here.

I've been lucky to study under professors as talented and generous in the classroom as with the pen: John Casey, Robert Cohen, Jonathan Dee, David Gates, Maureen Howard, Binnie Kirshenbaum, Ben Marcus, Patty O'Toole, and Helen Schulman. I'm particularly indebted to Vincent Cardinal, who taught me my first rules; Christine Schutt, who helped me learn how to break them; and, most of all, my mentor and friend Mark Slouka.

With their wise and generous criticism, my dear friends Katherine Fausset, Michael George, Elizabeth Kadetsky, Robin Kirman, Johanna Lane, and Nazgol Shifteh each helped shape parts of this book; Mike Harvkey and Ben Weil did so with all of it. Ellen McKeown's mark is also on these pages, as much as it is on me; I am grateful for both.

Finally, none of this would be, or matter, without my family: my mother (my first editor) and my father—no boy who wanted to learn to write could have asked for a better place to do it than within their arms; my step-mother, a kindred spirit; my brother, whose mind and heart guided me from the beginning; and my grandparents, Shirley and Joseph Boscov, who gave me the freedom to pursue that most impractical and essential thing we call our dreams.

The New Valley

Josh Weil

ABOUT THIS GUIDE

We hope that these discussion questions
will enhance your reading group's exploration
of Josh Weil's *The New Valley*. They are meant
to stimulate discussion, offer new viewpoints,
and enrich your enjoyment of the book.

More reading group guides and additional information,
including summaries, author tours, and author sites for
other fine Grove Press titles, may be found on
our Web site, www.groveatlantic.com.

1. The trilogy of novellas creates a saga of the land and its people. How would you describe the world that Weil creates? Are there plot links or echoes of similar themes in the three stories?

2. What are the results of a hard life in near isolation in this unyielding country? Might a closer community have created easier warmth and better dinner-table conversation? Are there any people with these gifts in the stories?

3. Formal education has certainly not been available to the characters, yet some have remarkable competency in practical matters. Examples?

4. Are there moral imperatives in the trilogy? What behavior is criticized by a narrator or other character? What do we learn about tolerance? As we read about the stubborn aged, the morbidly obese, the mentally impaired, would we do a better job of living with these people than their families do?

5. Does the author provide different versions of the truth? Is reality something to be personally reconstructed by characters as well as by the reader? Did you find that your interpretations shifted as you proceeded in a novella? Can you give examples? In "Sarverville Remains," Geoffrey says to Brian/Waker, "You just know your half of the story. And I know the same is true for me" (p. 304).

6. What differentiates Osby from his father as recalled in these pages? For instance, "His father would have just

put a bullet in it" (p. 48). Are the two men alike in any ways?

7. "Osby wasn't considered the smartest man in Eads County" (p. 7). The kids on the school bus "looked at him the way they looked at adults. That still felt odd to him" (p. 20). What has kept Osby somehow frozen in time? Have there been any women in his life? Has he ever left home? Do you think his father's dying will liberate him? Might he begin to live in the present?

8. How does the outside world penetrate the story? Consider the "Save the Children" pamphlet. And the arrival of Jim and his dreams for the Asian crop kenaf. What is the effect of Whistler's Meadow, the hippy commune?

9. In a story largely about loss and loneliness, why does Osby reject Jim's friendship and nurturing? Could Jim evolve into a son figure for Osby?

10. How is Deb from the gas station brilliantly portrayed? What are some of the details that create this absolutely original woman with her sadness, generosity, and fantasies? In contrast, what are Osby's fantasies? What could he do to earn the declaration, "I don't know what I'd do without you" (p. 67)? Do we also think of Osby's imagined disasters for his cows, predicaments only he could help? In difficult calving, "the irrefutable fact that a living thing would not exist if it weren't for him" (p. 29).

11. When Osby retreats to the Old House in the snowstorm, what kind of sanctuary is he seeking? Is he given any revelation?

12. How does Osby resolve the problem of the dying steer? How are the fates of Osby, the steer, and his father intertwined? Are we looking at a shared miracle?

13. Do you see in "Ridge Weather" a hymn of praise for the land? Not only has it been home for multiple generations of Caudills, but how does it have an inestimable value of its own? Waste of land is sinful, as in the pasture land taken over by the government. The old hay bales once "had been large and round, but they'd sat there for almost three years now and had sunk in on themselves, decomposing, just mounds of rotten grass. . . . Now, what had been a smooth field of good grass was mostly scrub: junipers, cedars, broom sedge, briars that were getting worse all the time" (p. 30). Is there a note of hope at the end? What do you think Osby has learned?

"STILLMAN WING"

1. How are Stillman and the Deutz linked? What propels this "mountain-raised, long-working, hard-minded, fear-driven man" (p. 87) to steal and restore the tractor? A forced retirement and shaking his fist at fate? An offering—and proving something—to Caroline? "There are days when the world outside his shop seems spinning too quickly for him to get his hands on it, and he comes in, and the Deutz is there like a bolt right through the axis of it all" (p. 117).

2. Caroline accuses her father of iron control. How does his health obsession reveal his character? His diet and

exercise fetishes? Are his love and concern for his daughter heartfelt? To the point of sprinkling seaweed on her cereal and delivering it to her in the bath? Do you think it is old age and diminishing blood flow that accentuate his need to control?

3. In this land of elemental struggle, some events recall biblical catastrophes. One thinks of the mysterious slaughter of all the Demastus cattle (pp. 94–95). Recall the grackles smothering the trees "like some biblical plague" (p. 105). Does Caroline, bent on self-destruction, create her own Sodom and Gomorrah? Might she herself call it survival? And self-medication? Does her total lack of discipline reflect a perversion of Stillman's "carefulness"?

4. "Risks? . . . What would you know about risks, Dad? You've never took a risk in your life" (p. 115). (Can this still be said at the end of the story?) What might have made Stillman such a careful man? What does he recall of his parents? (Who besides them has abandoned him?) When told the story of her grandparents' death, Caroline, age six, said, "You don't look sad . . . you look angry" (p. 130). Even in old age, Stillman is haunted. The plane circling his workshop, real or hallucination? "Something in him iced over. He could feel it spread like frost dusting his bones" (p. 122). As he then tries to remember . . . and to feel . . . he goes to the cemetery. Are we reminded of several characters in *King Lear*? Of "unaccommodated man"? "Turning the basin upside down, he held it over his head and got out. The rain

beat above him. It was cold on his fingers. He splashed around the car, crouched beside the fence, scrunched his eyes at the chiseled stones. He tried to summon some kind of sadness" (p. 131). Later, thinking of his "one-time nearly wife . . . the anger, and fear, and regret boil to the surface like pot scum . . . Outside the snow covers everything in quiet. He will sleep. He will rejuvenate and heal and sleep" (p. 139). It is a stunning picture of old age and despair. In *King Lear*, how does Cordelia's standing up to her tyrannical father (and later reconciling) compare to Caroline's role? What other characters in novels or myth does Stillman make you think of, characters at the very verge of chasm or apocalypse?

5. How does the past become present in "Stillman Wing"? Think of the pond at the commune. And the "rusted hulk of a B-26" (p. 164). The ringing of Old Les Pfersick's bell. Other instances? Ginny's pregnancy?

6. What are some of the surprising acts of generosity in the story? Do you recall the surprise posthumous gifts of old Pfersick? And that of the Booe child?

7. How do you understand the end of the novella?" . . . he felt ready, unafraid, even eager to see at last what a new valley might look like . . ." (p. 187). After a heroic journey, has Stillman achieved his quest?

8. What do the time warps mean in the story? At one moment Stillman is waiting for Caroline to pick up the phone at the commune. The next ring he hears is from a California orphanage, an event of forty-one

years ago (p. 154). And there is the phantom plane. Other examples? Are these signs of deterioration and mental disorder? Or are they times when Stillman is trying to integrate disparate, jarring events in his life?

9. "These were a strange people who lived down there, a people not of this land, not of this valley. This valley was a place of homes scattered far from homes, and meant to be that way, of lives built around cattle more than conversation, timed to rhythms of the crops, not the need to keep pace with other people's heartbeats. This was a place where people knew how to keep apart" (p. 162). In vivid contrast, how does the commune serve as both refuge for the living and the dying? What are the ironic links between pollution and healing, or at least comforting?

"SARVERVILLE REMAINS"

1. What is Geoffrey's motive for writing? Is he seeking some unity with Linda's husband? Is it expiation he's after? Does the second-person narrative pull in the reader effectively? Is Waker the only (captive) audience Geoffrey could hope for?

2. Talk about Linda and Geoffrey's relationship. "You aren't like anybody else, she said" (p. 276). Does the man-boy give her some self-respect? And on Geoffrey's side, he says, "She's the first who ever made me feel full growed" (p. 219).

3. In the coon episode, what propels Geoffrey to commit this neighborhood chaos and carnage? At the

point of Roy's gun and rage, how does Geoffrey perform a Herculean labor, like cleaning out the Augean stables?

4. What do we learn about Roy at the dump? His nostalgic dreams of childhood? His capacity for "magical" moments (p. 260)? Comment on his question to Geoffrey: "You ever hear the one about the guy that brings his retarded buddy on a hunting trip?" (p. 262).

5. "Most like you think there ain't no Sarverville at all" (p. 263). Talk about the range of views of the Sarvers, before and after their fifty years out in the wilderness on their own. An Eden? Is it a deliberate rejection of conventional behavior that actually seems to work? Ma B says "all of them diminished . . . but they was diminished only in the narrow sight of them who was so alike they could be swapped from wife to husband or job to job and wouldn't nobody know the difference" (p. 292). What were the special gifts of the Sarvers?

6. "It was Ma B teached me how to give good hugs" (p. 281).What else has she given Geoffrey? Is it possible that living with her and her brood was the last time he felt normal? "They was all diminished" (p. 288). How does her insisting on "yes Ma'am" relate to her advice about how he should treat Linda?

7. If we read "Sarverville Remains" as a fable, does it make you think about other stories about "diminished people"? I.B. Singer's *Gimpel the Fool?* The film *King of Hearts?* Others? What truths of the heart are the writers trying to alert us to?

8. Is the story set up, with all its time shifts and misperceptions, to make the reader share Geoffrey's confusion about Brian and Waker? Do we begin to question individual perspectives and their limitations?

9. What is Jackie's idea of a good life for Geoffrey? "You remember how it was. Things was good. You got a good job. People like you. Like to watch you wave and wave back . . . It's the way it's meant to be" (p. 310). But Roy says ". . . just let him be . . . alive" (p. 310). What do these attitudes reveal about Jackie and Roy? And expectations for people who are different?

10. "I wanted to do it right," I said. "I wanted to have it out like growed men." But Linda says, "Grown men don't do it like that, Geoffrey" (p. 335). What is it to be a grown man in this story? Do we see any? "Why did He let her break them rules and kiss me like I was a full adult?" (p. 336)

11. Are the land and his heritage to be Geoffrey's salvation? Has he made the right decision? Do you think he will continue to write?

Suggestions for Further Reading:

Close Range, Heart Songs and Other Stories, and *The Shipping News* by Annie Proulx; *Returning to Earth* and *Legends of the Fall* by Jim Harrison; *Affliction* by Russell Banks; *Winesburgh, Ohio* by Sherwood Anderson; *Plainsong* by Kent Haruf; *The Memory of Old Jack* by Wendell Berry; *A Thousand Acres* by Jane Smiley; *Of Mice and Men* by John

Steinbeck; *The Ballad of the Sad Café* by Carson McCullers; *Bastard Out of Carolina* by Dorothy Allison; *Child of God* by Cormac McCarthy; *Wise Blood, Everything That Rises Must Converge,* and *The Violent Bear It Away* by Flannery O'Connor